The Cerulean Ark

Terry R. Bacon

Stagnant Millpond Publishing

ISBN-979-8-9880748-3-0 (ebook)

ISBN-979-8-9880748-4-7 (paperback)

ISBN-979-8-9880748-5-4 (hardback)

Cover design by My Custom Book Cover, LLC

Library of Congress Control Number: 2024903039

Printed in the United States of America

To learn more about the author, visit www.terry@terryrbacon.com.

www.Stagnantmillpondpublishing.com

For my wife Debra

Whose patience, forbearance, and love make my life possible

With deepest gratitude to Fritz, Linda, Wilson, and all the others who read the manuscript and offered valuable suggestions and encouragement. Early readers taste your creations before you put them on your menu and tell you whether you need more or less seasoning, a richer broth, a more succulent side dish, or a different presentation. Sometimes, they advise you to scrap the whole dish and start over. Without their willingness to taste your experiments, you risk causing indigestion or, worse, food poisoning. I am grateful for all their comments and suggestions, even when they occasionally sting.

Special thanks to Mrs. Karrer, who taught me 7th grade English in Treynor, Iowa. I didn't realize it then, but her teachings on sentence diagramming invoked in me a fascination with the structure of language and the art of constructing sentences. I have both an artist's and an engineer's appreciation for structure, and Mrs. Karrer imparted a lifelong love of the English language and the intricate and fascinating ways I could use it to express myself. I am forever indebted to her and all the other teachers in my life who showed me what was possible.

Lastly, I want to thank Issac Asimov, Arthur C. Clarke, Poul Anderson, H. G. Wells, Jules Verne, Philip K. Dick, Robert Heinlein, Ursula K. Le Guin, George Orwell, Edgar Rice Burroughs, Ray Bradbury, and legions of other science fiction writers who enriched my youth and taught me to escape the boundaries I thought were there. Thanks as well to Richard Feynman, Albert Einstein, Stephen Hawking, Richard Dawkins, Vera Rubin, Carl Sagan, Neil deGrasse Tyson, Rachel Carson, Marie Curie, Carlo Rovello, Rosalind Franklin, Jane Goodall and scores of other scientists who devoted their lives to discovering science truth and comprehend the infinite universe in which we live. Without their quests, we would have only myths and fantasies to guide us.

Somewhere, something incredible is waiting to be known. —*Carl Sagan*

Any sufficiently advanced technology is indistinguishable from magic. —Arthur C. Clarke

Claiming there is no other life in the universe is like scooping up some water, looking at the cup and claiming there are no whales in the ocean. —Neil deGrasse Tyson

Contents

Prologue

It had lain in a shallow grave for thirteen thousand Earth years. Had it not been discovered, it might have lain here millions more, slowly leaching its way to the core of the planet, where it could have withstood temperatures of five thousand degrees Celsius but not the crushing pressure of three million atmospheres at the center of the planet's solid iron core. In its death throes, its dark energy containment system would have ruptured, causing a cataclysmic explosion that would have rippled through the Earth's fluid iron outer core and liquified its crust. The few remains of its corpse would finally have been obliterated when the Earth was destroyed by the superheated gases of its dying sun billions of years from now. Thousands like it are patiently traveling through this and other galaxies, quietly and unobtrusively fulfilling their mission. Some losses were expected, and some have occurred, hence the redundancy, but it was not destined to be among the unaccounted. It was lost and later found. Its journey resumed when the zhowllux'p'twl was reactivated.

The Spider

Friday. April 10. 10:23 am.

On the best day of his young life, Bradley Adamsson learned that he was dying. His mother wept in the car like a hydrangea in the rain, tears dripping from her pink cheeks onto the green satin blouse she always wore for luck. Bradley was too numb to feel anything except the springs under the front seat pushing back against the weight of their shared sorrow. He waited, not knowing how to help her. As minutes passed, he became mindful of every sensation: her halting breath, her trembling fingers on his wrist, specks of dust on the dash where sunlight brought them into relief, the ticking of his watch, the muted sweep of a car passing behind theirs in the lot.

"I'm sorry," Claudine Adamsson said. "I promised myself I wouldn't let you see me cry."

"It's okay," Bradley replied, which he realized was absurd. They'd just seen an orthopedic surgeon, had sat in her waiting room for twenty minutes past their nine o'clock appointment. The doctor, a harried woman with a pallid complexion and black hair streaked with gray, had spread his file on her desk. She glanced at it before telling them, with a somber expression, that he had hepatocellular carcinoma.

"What is that?" his mother said.

"Cancer," the doctor replied. "It's not confirmed. I want to run more tests. Liver cancer is a rare but not atypical side effect of Ollier disease."

Bradley had grown up loving baseball, playing it in the pee wee league, collecting baseball cards, and memorizing baseball trivia. He dreamed of playing shortstop for the Dodgers, but when he turned ten, he developed an incurable disease that caused tumors in his joints and slowed the growth of his left leg. By the time he reached eleven, he could only warm the bench. At eighteen, that leg was nearly an inch shorter than his right. He wore one specialty shoe with thick heels and soles to walk without wobbling. Heavier than his right shoe, it still gave him a mortifying gait. At South Pasadena High, he might as well have carried a sign reading, "Look at the freak. Get your laughs here."

His mother asked the doctor about the prognosis, and she said it was uncertain but not encouraging. She wanted more lab results before discussing their options. Bradley didn't hear what the doctor said about the treatment plan. As he waited for his mother to tell him it was time to leave, the doctor's droning voice was eclipsed by the clickety-clack of his fantasy express, the Day Dream Special. He climbed aboard and rode into a future where everything was possible and all avenues merged into an imaginarium of wondrous escapes.

As they left the doctor's office, Claudine suggested he take the day off. She thought he might need it after confirmation of their worst fears. But Bradley wanted to lose himself in the ordinariness of the school day, so she dropped him at home, and he drove to school. The rest of his morning passed like a song played at half speed, all flatted tones and bass notes. When lunch arrived, he sat quietly among his friends in the cafeteria, their muted laughter circling him like a swarm of bees. Relief came mid-afternoon in AP Calculus II. They had their mid-term exam, and his silent kinship with numbers was comforting. In solving the test's problems, he buried the pain in his side and this morning's death sentence under a shroud of reasoning. But finishing too quickly, he glanced at the wall clock and groaned. Twenty-five minutes to go. He looked around the classroom. Everyone else was still working, staring at their exams—never a good sign—or scratching pencils across paper. Some hadn't even flipped over the first page of the test.

Not wanting to look finished, Bradley pretended to review his answers again. Like his other senior exams, this Calc II test was so easy he wondered if his teacher had dumbed it down so students would receive higher grades, proving not how smart they were but how great he was. Whatever. Bradley was finished, knew his answers were correct, and tried through the rest of the period to keep this morning's diagnosis locked in the cellar of his mind while he daydreamed about MIT, where he'd been accepted next year, and Mt. Wilson, the astronomical observatory where he was interning next weekend, and Evaline

Perez, the beautiful girl in his AP Chemistry class. He'd never spoken to her. She was an A-lister: intelligent, popular, gorgeous, with a huge circle of A-list girlfriends, and a handsome surfer dude boyfriend. Out of reach. But riding the Day Dream Special is free.

Bradley didn't surf, wasn't a jock or a pothead, not a party animal—he was never invited—not one of the popular guys. He wore glasses and loved science and math, which said it all. He was the high school chess champ and a geek, not the kind of guy Evaline Perez would give a second glance. His closest friends were Eliot Stankus and Kevin Truman, two charter members of the Geek Squad, which put them on the Z-list, last in everything except academic performance. The cool kids called Eliot "Stinky" and Kevin "Moe" because his black mop of a haircut, with bangs touching his eyebrows, made him look like Moe Howard of the Three Stooges. The losers on Geek Squad didn't care if the A-listers rejected them, or so they told themselves, because high school was a stupid rite of passage, and they would graduate and get the hell out of Dodge and not look back.

Meanwhile, they competed for the coveted title "Top Geek," the nerdy equivalent of Maverick in one of their favorite films, *Top Gun*. Bradley thought he deserved it. Eliot was the funniest, and Kevin the most lovably pathetic. Short and round, he resembled a cartoon character who made everyone else look good because he was so completely uncool. But Bradley was easily the smartest of the Squad, one qualification for Top Geek. Besides, he bore the stigma of one thick-soled shoe, the origin of the nicknames bestowed on him by normal kids since fifth grade: *Crip. Freak. Lamer.*

He glanced at the clock again, removed his glasses, and rubbed his eyes. He'd stayed up late finishing Arthur C. Clarke's *Childhood's End*. He thought about Clarke, who wrote about the end of the world; the Jet Propulsion Laboratory, where his father worked; and NASA's stalled space program, a shame because that's where he'd dreamed of working. SpaceX might be possible if he didn't die first. He daydreamed about MIT, where his dad got his doctorate, and beautiful girls out of his league. He sighed, and, like a year later, the bell finally rang.

He'd finished classes for the day, so he turned in his mid-term, slipped his stuff into his backpack, and headed to the school library where, despite the ache in his side, he would spend the next hour tutoring juniors in advanced algebra. Bradley had a knack for explaining advanced math concepts. Some tutees told the principal that he was much better than their real teachers. He was near the door when someone rushed behind him and grabbed his elbow. Startled, Bradley jerked away and spun around, nearly losing his balance. He thought it must be Eliot, but it was Axel Taylor, another senior. Surfer dude. Correction, THE high school surfer dude and wannabe big game hunter. Macho to the max. Taylor was showing off his toned physique in a white t-shirt and jeans just grody enough to be cool. He wore the easy smile of a guy who was comfortable in his skin and got what he wanted. To amplify the sting, he was Evaline Perez's boyfriend.

"Hey, Adamsson," Taylor said, a jaunty smile easy on his face.

"What's up?" Bradley replied. He instinctively broke eye contact, not knowing what else to say. Guys like Axel Taylor didn't talk to him. They talked *about* him or *at* him but never *to* him—or ignored him completely.

"Wanna show you something. Got a sec?"

Like it mattered if Bradley had time for him. Taylor shrugged off his backpack and dug into it. Unlike its owner, the pack was worn at the seams and mottled with brown and red stains. Taylor was handsome and knew it. He was slim but muscular with six-pack abs and bold features that worked well together, chiseled cheeks and intense eyes, and sun-bleached blond hair fashionably unkempt. He was an outdoorsy type, all fishing and hunting and lifetime NRA membership. Bradley wasn't sure if this was a joke or what. Taylor had a reputation as a gun nut, and Bradley wouldn't have been surprised if he pulled a revolver out of his pack or a dead animal or something else bizarre. A headline flashed through Bradley's mind: "Valedictorian murdered just before graduation." But what Taylor pulled out of his pack wasn't a weapon, although it looked odd and appeared metallic. Shaped like a giant silver spider, it had a saucer-sized circular hub with a half dozen seven-inch-long appendages arrayed in a semicircle on one side. It lay limp in Taylor's hand, but as he handed it to Bradley, faint lines of pink and blue rippled through it. It might have been light refracting, although Bradley had never seen that effect before.

"What is it?" Bradley said.

"You're a smart guy. Figured you could tell me."

"Where'd you get it?"

"Dug it up. Hunting last weekend. Chased a wounded buck to a cave in the San Gabriels. Not a cave, more like a deep overhang. Saw a lump on the ground. Dug around, found this thing. Took it to my dad's garage, cleaned it up. But clueless about what it is. Seen anything like it?"

Bradley shook his head. Last year, Taylor was one of the guys calling him a freak. He wanted to tell him to go to hell, but the thing Taylor handed him was too intriguing. When Bradley turned it just right, those faint blue and pink waves rippled through it like it was alive. But it wasn't biological. It felt like a soft metal. The appendages were flexible, but there were no seams or micro-USB connectors. No switches. No way to connect it to anything. No markings. No obvious purpose. As he studied it, he realized that Taylor was staring at him. *Taking my measure and finding me lacking*, Bradley thought. *Crip. Lamer. Freak. Except I'm smart. If I live, I'll leave you behind, surfer dude. You'll lose those toned abs and be waxing other people's surfboards while I'm doing something meaningful with my life. If I have a life, and screw it if I don't. I'll make the best of what I have left—the hell with guys like Taylor.*

Bradley turned the spider thing over again, puzzled. He wondered if this was a prank—more yucks at his expense. Guys like Axel Taylor had no budget for cruelty. But this thing didn't look like a gag-store prop. "Can I hang onto this and examine it?"

Taylor shrugged. "Why not?"

Bradley appraised the surfer, wondering how far to push it. "Maybe you could show me where you found this."

Taylor scrunched up his face and glanced away. He had plans this weekend, and no way was he going to spend part of it with this lame-ass Einstein. *But what the hell*, he thought, *it'll just be a couple of hours. Maybe this thing is worth something.*

"Awright, hell. Why not? How about, meet me here at eight in the morning." He glanced at Bradley's feet. "Bring your hiking boots," he added, a cruel little smile parting his lips. "The terrain's rough. It's a half-hour hike for me. Pro'bly an hour for you."

"Hey, Ax!" some guy shouted. Three of Taylor's friends stood beside his spit-shined red pickup in the parking lot next to the library. "Come on, man. Lose the freak. Let's go," another one yelled.

Bradley watched him walk away, shame rising in his cheeks. Then, to compound it, he saw Evaline Perez sauntering toward Taylor's truck with two of her gal pals. She looked like he imagined a French model would look—curvy and statuesque, strolling rather than walking. Dark hair, creamy cheeks, smoky gray eyes full of carefree mischief, and full, pouty lips. The kind of girl you could appreciate for hours, although he didn't dare. Not in person. He followed her on Instagram but would never admit it. His eyes darted away in AP Chemistry when she caught him looking at her. *She probably thinks I'm a creep.* Today, she wore low heels, faded blue jeans, and a pink sweater. She tossed her long black hair when she reached Taylor and rose to kiss him. Bradley watched a few seconds longer but didn't want to get caught. *Like I really care*, he told himself. He shoved the spider thing into his backpack and spent the next hour tutoring twenty-six math-challenged juniors on differential equations.

On Bradley's drive home, the cellar door in his mind creaked open, and hepatocellular carcinoma clawed its way up the stairs. He fought it by opening his backpack at a stoplight, laying the spider thing on the seat, and glancing at it as he drove. It had been buried, Taylor said. For how long? Its silver surface had no blemishes. Taylor had cleaned it, but it still seemed too pristine for a buried object. It wasn't weathered, so maybe it hadn't been in the ground long.

Despite the distraction, Bradley found his mind drifting, thinking that the diagnosis must be wrong, that they'd switched his lab results with someone else, that the doctor was mistaken. A second opinion would reveal that he was okay, or a simple operation would excise the tumor if he had one. In a perfect world, he was just months from moving across the country to MIT. He turned onto Monterey Road and felt this familiar street turning ghostly, buildings receding from a street grown lifeless, like a color television fading to black and white. He'd always lived in South Pasadena. This town, these streets, this neighborhood, his home, his friends, his room, especially his room—as long as he lived, they would be his sanctuary in a world where cruelty is a thief and death indiscriminate. His life before being disabled was so distant he could scarcely recall the thrill of running the bases or the dream of attending the Air Force Academy and becoming an astronaut. *Like other people with disabilities, you compensate,* he thought. *You have other gifts. College will be different if you get to go. New friends, new challenges, people who are more accepting because Cambridge and MIT are more diverse. What matters will be academics, where you excel.* For a few happy minutes, he forgot about hepatocellular carcinoma as he jumped back on The Daydream Special and saw himself walking to class in Cambridge, having the correct answers to a professor's questions, sitting in class beside a beautiful girl who is as intelligent as he is, making eye contact, maybe touching her hand.

His family lived in a two-story Spanish-style house on Milan Avenue near the high school. Its bright yellow veneer was muted this afternoon, buried in the shadows of majestic white oaks. He parked along the curb in front of his house beneath the trees' lofty gloom. When he walked in, his parents were fixing dinner, but he didn't see his younger brother and sister. His mom, tall and lean, had the sleeves of her blouse rolled up as she tossed a salad in a large bamboo bowl. She'd pulled her long brown hair back in a ponytail, but some strands had escaped and hung in her eyes. She flipped her head to keep them out of the way. She was his mom, but Bradley still thought she was beautiful, although tonight, her worry lines were deeper as she focused on the salad. His father was a shade taller and lean, and both wore glasses with dark frames. *They're a matched set*, Bradley thought, watching his father take something from the oven. He said, "Hi," and his mom shot him a dark look of concern before covering it with an unconvincing smile. His dad seemed to have taken the news more stoically, having always been the more optimistic of the two. He also had a better poker face than his mom. He said dinner would be ready in twenty minutes. Bradley was grateful his dad didn't want to discuss the doctor's visit now.

He hurried upstairs to his room, cleared space on his desk, feeling guilty about the clutter, and took the spider thing out of his backpack. Setting it on the desk, he pulled down his magnifying glass lamp and examined it under bright light. Even with 3x magnification, he couldn't find microscopic seams, connectors, or markings. The metal skin was smooth and pliable, and when he moved it just right, he saw those blue and pink waves rippling across the surface. He worried for a moment that it might be radioactive or somehow toxic. Then he thought, *what the hell, I'm dying anyway. What difference does it make?* As he turned it over to examine the underside, he noticed the hairs on the back of his hand standing up. He passed the spider over his arm and watched the hairs waving as the thing passed over them. It held a static charge. Interesting. He touched the probes of a multimeter to the spider and registered 1.3 volts, but when he moved the probes around the spider, the voltage spiked at 3.15 volts in one place, then swung between that high and a null reading as he ran the probes across the surface. Yet, despite the spider's electric potential, it was cool to the touch. Somehow, it dissipated heat efficiently.

He took some pictures of the spider with his cellphone and then loaded the photos onto Lightroom and tried altering saturation settings and using various filters to see if any details emerged when he modified the visuals, but none did. He also captured a decent video of the blue and pink waves rippling through the spider and altered the speed of the playback to see if any patterns became apparent. That didn't work either. The object remained an enigma.

His dad was an astrophysicist, and Bradley considered showing it to him but decided to examine it himself first. That felt selfish since his dad was so open with him, but half the joy of discovery is figuring things out for yourself. He felt worse at dinner when his dad asked if he wanted to go flying the next day. Bradley earned a private pilot license when he was sixteen and had logged more than two hundred hours solo. His dad taught him to fly—compensation for being ineligible for the Air Force Academy, among other things.

John Adamsson had been thinking all day about Bradley, wondering how and when to discuss his illness. John believed things had a way of working themselves out and was confident Bradley would beat this disease, although he didn't know how. He wanted private time with Bradley and thought a plane ride might be best for them both. While they ate, he told Bradley, "I'm taking a Beech King Air 250 to the Nevada National Security Site at ten tomorrow. You're welcome to come along and do some flying."

Bradley looked at him and glanced around the table. His mom gave him an expectant look, knowing how much he loved flying and wanting them to have some father-son time, but his siblings were rushing through dinner like their clothes were on fire. Kid sister Celia itched to get back on her iPhone, and Devin, on principle, didn't care what his older brother did. He couldn't wait for Bradley to leave home so he could have Bradley's room.

"I can't, Dad," Bradley said, wondering how to make this sound plausible. Then he added, "I'm going hiking tomorrow." That drew everyone's attention.

"By yourself?" Claudine blurted, immediately sorry for not trusting him to hike alone.

"No, mom," Bradley said, "I'm going with another guy from school."

"Eliot? He doesn't look like the hiking type," she said before feeling guilty. Bradley wasn't the hiking type, either.

"No, not El," Bradley said. "He's with the debating club this weekend."

"Who then?" she said.

Bradley hesitated, not knowing how to make this sound believable. "Axel Taylor."

"No way," Devin blurted.

John was puzzled. "Who's Axel Taylor?" He turned to Claudine. "Do I know him?"

Celia said, "Dad, he's like the coolest guy in school." Her clique of freshman girls talked about the dreamiest guys at South Pasadena High, and Axel Taylor was like a god to them. "He's the California surfing champion or something like that. A total McDreamy."

"Why would he go hiking with you?" Devin quipped.

"Devin!" Claudine snapped. "That's enough."

John gave Devin a disapproving look, then asked Bradley, "Are you sure? It's unlike you to miss a chance to fly."

"I know, but . . ." Bradley said. "We're hiking in the Angeles Forest. It's just a couple of hours. I need to work on my speech when I get back."

Claudine wasn't satisfied with his answer, but he was old enough to make his own decisions. She thought hiking might be his way of coping with this morning's dreadful news. She pushed her glasses up on her nose as she made eye contact with John, a *wonder-what's-going-on* look on her face. She felt terrible for them and made a note to scold Devin after dinner.

———

After hanging out on Venice Beach and grabbing burgers and shakes, Axel drove Evaline back to South Pasadena in his supercharged Ford F-150. Axel felt amped with his hands on the wheel cruising the boulevard with twenty-three hundred cc's and four hundred fifty horses under the hood. His chariot was a candy apple red 2007 Saleen Darth Vader Edition that he'd restored in his dad's garage, and it rode like a Mustang on steroids. *The man and his machine*, thought Axel. Beside him, Evaline was enjoying the ride. They listened to Bruno Mars, and she let her mind wander with the beat. She didn't want to go home. *The bitch might be there. Or maybe she's out with one of her boyfriends.* The bitch was her stepmother. Her real mom died of ovarian cancer when Evaline was nine. Two years later, her father married Angela McNees-Koeppen. Her dad was a long-haul trucker, and when Evaline and her sister Kate saw how Angela cheated on him when their father was on the road, they nicknamed her Knees Open. Her dad, seduced by Angela's fawning supplication and his own good nature, either didn't know or care about her infidelities. He was killed in a collision with a tanker truck when Evaline was fifteen. His family had money, and they established an educational trust for his daughters, but with her dad gone, Angela was the sole trustee, which really ground Evaline's gears. She had to be civil with the bitch, but when Evaline graduated from high school, she would become the sole trustee of her college fund. It would pay for an undergrad degree in pre-med at UCLA, where she'd been accepted on her way to becoming Doctor Evaline Perez, in her dreams, an eminent researcher in infectious diseases.

As they pulled up to Evaline's house, Axel asked what she would be doing the next day.

"Working at the hospital. All weekend. You?"

"Gotta help my dad in the garage. But I'm going hiking in the morning."

"Oh, yeah? Who with?"

He was embarrassed to tell her, but she had that look he couldn't resist. "That guy. Adamsson. Bradley."

Her mouth opened in a laugh, and she raised a hand to cover it. "You're kidding," she giggled. "I didn't think you even knew him."

"Not like we're buds. I just . . . he wanted to go hiking in the Angeles. Said I'd go with him. Know the dude?"

"Sure. He's only the smartest guy in school. Like, by far. He's in my AP Chemistry class. Anyway, that's big of you. He doesn't look like he shops at Cabelas."

"Guy's a Brainiac. Like you. What can I say? Expanding my horizons."

"I guess so," Evaline teased. "Don't hurt him."

"Ahhh, why not?" Axel let his tongue droop from one side of his mouth like he was being hanged while simultaneously drawing a straight finger across his throat.

Evaline laughed. "You're mixing metaphors, Axel."

"Mixing what?" he said.

"Never mind. See you later."

She watched him roar down the street, his truck's throaty masculinity echoing among the houses. Axel was swaggy and fun but a Neanderthal, like a total throwback. *Harmless enough if you know him,* she mused. *Plus, he's really, really cute. We'll have a bitchin' summer, but it will be over when I'm busy with classes at UCLA. Besides, it's time to move on. Axel isn't a lifetime kind of guy.*

Evaline braced herself before opening the door, but Kate was home alone.

"Where's the bitch?" she asked.

Kate looked up from her laptop. "Out with some new guy. Never seen him before. Betcha she's got her—"

"Knees open," they yelled in unison, laughing.

Blue Corridor

Saturday. April 11. 6:30 am.

Bradley saw dawn easing over the San Gabriel Mountains, a pink intruder chasing away the night sky, a smattering of thin clouds glowing red over rugged silhouettes that resembled a saw blade, sharp and unforgiving. *Red sky at morning*, Bradley thought. *Sailor take warning.* He zipped up his blue hoodie and rubbed his arms, driving away the night's chill. Easing open the backdoor of his gray, totally boring used Prius hatchback, he laid his pack on the backseat, thinking he'd park the Prius far from Taylor's truck. When his parents bought the car, his mom said a Prius was sensible. *Gee, thanks, mom. Why not get "Loser" vanity plates, too?* He dreaded the hike because he was ashamed of not being a perfect physical specimen like Axel Taylor. He didn't want to compound his embarrassment by driving up in a nerdmobile. *But no choice*, he sighed. *Might as well accept the shame and pretend it doesn't matter.*

He'd awakened at five, hobbled to the bathroom in a stupor, and absently grabbed the spider thing from his desk as he returned to bed. His side throbbed, an ache that pestered like a nagging five-year-old. He ignored it by switching on his reading light and gazing at the spider for long, lazy minutes. He turned it over in his hands like a new toy, examining the appendages, trying to divine its purpose like the Richard Feynman of South Pasadena High he imagined himself to be, but it remained an enigma. He was curious to see where Taylor found the thing but regretted not flying with his dad. *This is a stupid idea*, Bradley fretted. *Maybe the most idiotic thing I've done in senior year.* But curiosity held him hostage. Intrigued by this strange discovery, he wouldn't let go until he understood it.

Later, after tiptoeing around the kitchen making coffee, he sat at the counter, checked the weather on his phone, plotted the course from Pasadena to the Nevada Test Site (aka Area 51), and wrote up a flight plan. Leaving it for his dad on the kitchen table, he loaded his clunky hiking boots, jacket, two bottles of water, hat, sunglasses, and iPhone in his car. At the last moment, he remembered to scrounge in the garage for a folding camp shovel, a headlamp, and his dad's hunting knife. He didn't want to lie again about why he was hiking, and he didn't want to talk about the cancer, so he drove away before anyone else got up. He knew he'd lucked out in the parent department. They'd always been good to him, so it felt disloyal to deceive them.

With over an hour to kill, he pulled into a McDonald's, ordered an Egg McMuffin and coffee, and sat in their parking lot thinking about the spider thing while he ate. It was manufactured but looked too modern for twentieth or even twenty-first-century technology, and it had no apparent function. It had been buried in a remote part of the forest. For how long? Who buried it? It held a charge but had no place to insert batteries. He took out his cell phone and studied his video of the spider. The pink and blue lines rippling through it told him it was not inert, so it was powered by something, but what? Could it be nuclear?

He arrived at the school parking lot before Taylor and figured he was safe parking in the spot farthest from school buildings, but when Taylor pulled in a few minutes after eight, he spotted Bradley's car and drove his F-150 in front of the Prius, blocking it in. As his pickup idled with the guttural rumble of its monster engine, Taylor hung his tanned arm out the window and gave Bradley a *let's-go-dude* look. Sunbeams lit up Taylor's blond hair like a halo. Bradley opened the door and grabbed his backpack from the back seat. Bradley frowned because his dinky Prius looked like David to Taylor's Goliath. He would never measure up to guys like Axel Taylor. He would always be a square peg in their perfectly round world. Being smarter than the A-listers didn't make up for his lack of social standing or athletic ability, and not having a girlfriend like Evaline Perez was an emptiness no superior grade point average could assuage.

"Gotta be back by ten-thirty," Taylor told him as Bradley climbed into the passenger seat. He worked in his dad's auto restoration garage and had access to the tools, equipment, and know-how to turn ordinary vehicles like his F-150 into works of art. He promised he'd be at the shop this morning to work on restoring a '69 Dodge Charger.

Taylor's dad was already annoyed about the kid spending so much time hunting and surfing. Taylor knew he couldn't mess up this weekend. His dad would be royally pissed.

As they roared up the freeway toward the forest, Bradley sat quietly, sensing that Taylor was preoccupied. The interior of the truck surprised Bradley. It was spotless—no animal guts, spent shell casings, cigarette butts, crushed beer cans, or litter on the floor. The black leather seats were clean and supple, and the dash gleamed. The truck smelled new, although Bradley knew it wasn't. Despite himself, he was impressed. He asked if Taylor had just had it detailed.

Taylor gave him a *you-gotta-be-kidding* look, saying, "I take care of my shit myself. Gotta have pride, bro." Bradley felt chastised, thinking he ought to wash his Prius more often. Maybe even wax it, something he'd never done. He had to admit that his estimation of Taylor rose several notches, and riding in an A-lister's rig was kind of cool. As they sped into the forest, Bradley felt a rush of excitement about being part of this world, however fleeting. It was like tasting cake when all you've ever eaten was stale bread. The ride got rougher after they bounced onto a dirt road and climbed deeper into the dense forest. Taylor parked off the road in a clearing not meant for vehicles, backing into a slot between two trees under a thick canopy. His ride wasn't visible from the road, just a gleam off the front bumper where sunlight struck it. He'd parked there before and knew the forest's nooks and crannies. *Welcome to my world*, Taylor's comfort in the wilderness seemed to say.

Early morning light sliced through the trees, throwing flickering shadows in the forest. They hiked to the cave on a game trail barely wide enough to shoulder through. The trail cut through a steep, wooded slope. Taylor strode up it with practiced ease, but Bradley struggled on a path that pitched when he didn't expect it and was crisscrossed with thick roots and sharp rocks that snagged his boots and turned his ankles. His heavy left boot felt like cement, and he kept slipping on layers of soggy plant debris, whose earthy aroma of decomposing leaves mixed with the tangy scent of pine and moist animal scat left him nauseous. Walking was clumsy enough on flat land, but it was treacherous when he couldn't predict how his left foot would come to rest. Every dozen paces, they stepped over fallen logs whose rotting wood was crumbling into sawdust. The rustling of branches whipping their legs created a steady beat accentuated by the ceaseless twittering of birds. Up the steep grade they hiked, Taylor gliding uphill while Bradley fought to catch his breath, hoping for a break but seeing only more steep terrain ahead. He cursed himself for carrying too much in his backpack. His heart pounding, chest heaving, he finally stopped, pulled a handkerchief from his back pocket, and wiped the sweat from his eyes.

Taylor hung his thumbs under the straps of his backpack and peered down on him. "Gonna make it, man?"

"Just need . . . catch . . . breath," Bradley gasped, wondering if this torture would be worth whatever they found up there. The climb was more excruciating than he anticipated and made him feel like he was sucking Taylor's dust, which was almost literally true.

Taylor glanced at his wristwatch. "Gotta be at my dad's garage. Hour and a half. Gotta keep movin'. Nuther half mile. Place we're goin's remote. Never seen anybody there."

"How'd you . . . find the . . . place?"

"Hunting," Taylor said before turning back uphill and taking long, easy strides. Bradley jostled his pack to redistribute the weight and slogged ahead, wishing he'd drunk water while they were stopped. His right side and his left ankle ached.

Twenty godawful minutes later, they reached the top of the steep grade, and Taylor led them through a dense wall of tall pines to a clearing. Sunlight cut through the trees, casting long, cool shadows across the wild grass. The cave was near the base of a high hill ringed by trees but had no trees on it, only a thick cover of bushes and tall grass. Bradley's heart pounded as he struggled for air. He shrugged off his backpack and dropped it. His shirt was soaked, and sweat stung his eyes. While Taylor waited impatiently, his hands on his hips, Bradley studied the cave. Opposite the hill, it was gouged into a granite wall, its floor sloping upward, the entrance about ten feet high. It was ebony inside, the sun's angle such that only the first few feet of the cave floor were illuminated. Dark splotches on the dirt showed where the wounded buck had fled inside.

"Did you . . . find the deer?" Bradley huffed.

Taylor nodded. "Jumped out of the cave when I got here. Ran around that hill. Took my kill shot a quarter mile from here, field-dressed it, came back. Took a break to explore the cave, found that thing. Carried the meat down."

Despite himself, Bradley admired a guy who could do that. If it came down to it, if a catastrophe brought the end of civilization as we knew it, Taylor would have the skill set to survive. Bradley had a momentary image of Taylor handing the bloody hind quarter of a deer to Evaline, ordering her to cook it over a campfire. If things went primitive, if survival came down to basics, guys like Taylor would prevail. Guys like Bradley wouldn't. *Darwinian*, Bradley thought—*survival of the fittest.*

Taylor dug into his pack and brought out a long flashlight, which he switched on. "Found the thing back here," he said, walking into the cave. Bradley put on his headlamp, picked up his pack, and followed. The cave was about twenty-five feet deep and sloped to six feet high at the back. As Taylor said, it was more a deep overhang than a cave. The floor was hard dirt, sparsely covered by loose rocks, feathers, plant debris, and scat. Over the years, animals had sought refuge here. A hole in the dirt showed where Taylor had unearthed the spider. Bradley retrieved the shovel from his pack, unfolded it, sank to his knees, and dug around the hole, tossing the dirt aside. After several minutes, he uncovered what felt like a piece of fabric, gray with the texture of oily aluminum foil, metallic but not metal, moist to the touch but dry in the light of the headlamp. It was embedded in the hard dirt. He yanked it, worried it would tear, but it was tough, whatever it was. Digging around it, he soon uncovered a fist-size ball of something. Dark and dirty, it flexed like cloth. He flattened it on the ground and saw that it had the same shape as the spider thing—a circular hub with six long appendages. It had a cuff on the side of the hub opposite the appendages. He spread open the cuff and dumped out dirt and a honeycombed substance that disintegrated when he touched it. Turning it over, he peered into the cuff. The thing was like an uninflated cow's udder, six teats hanging below.

Bradley smiled at a sudden spark of recognition. "It's a glove," he murmured.

"What?" Taylor snatched it from him and turned it over in his hands. "No way."

Bradley reached his hand out, asking for it back. "But for something with six very long fingers. And maybe two opposable thumbs instead of one."

"A gorilla," Taylor said, handing it to him.

"Not one I've ever seen," Bradley replied. "They have one opposable thumb, like us. I've never heard of any creature with two." The boys stared at it a moment longer, and then Bradley slipped it into his backpack and said, "Let's keep digging." While he worked with his shovel, Taylor drew a hunting knife from a sheath on his belt and dug into the ground with it, slicing at an angle and flipping up the compacted dirt.

They lost time as they excavated but found nothing more except tattered fragments of the same gray, oily, aluminum-like fabric. Then Taylor's knife clunked on something hard beneath the surface. Bradley handed him the shovel and watched as Taylor dug around and under the thing. It was encased in a shell of compacted soil, and when they lifted the heavy thing out of the ground, they saw that it was basketball-sized but elliptical rather than spherical. Both chipped away at the dirt with their knives until a dull white surface emerged on one side. A long, hard, white surface. Bone.

"Be careful with it," Bradley urged. He took a bottle from his pack, poured water over it, and then wiped away mud and the scaly dirt beneath it.

"A skull," Taylor realized, turning it over. Bradley nodded. They kept scraping the object until they could discern its form. Heavy, oblong, and thick, it had a pronounced lower jaw, a row of incisors on the leading edge, substantial molars at the back of the lower jaw, some teeth still intact, and others splintered stubs. The upper jaw had two ragged bone surfaces where teeth the size of silver dollars might once have protruded. Compacted dirt filled the eye sockets and snout hole.

"What is it?" said Taylor.

Bradley shrugged. "A bear, maybe. I don't know."

"Nah. Not a bear skull. I've seen 'em. Plus, bears don't have six fingers."

"Or wear gloves," Bradley noted, turning the skull to face him. The eye sockets pointed forward, a telltale sign. "Whatever this was, it was a predator."

"How'd you figure?"

"Stereopsis. Two eyes point forward for depth perception so that it can judge the distance to its prey."

"Jesus, Adamsson, you really are a brainiac."

Bradley couldn't decide if that was an insult or not. "Like us. Two eyes pointed forward. We're predators, too." Taylor looked pleased with that. "If you don't mind, I'll take this home and show my dad. He might know what it's from."

Both boys took pictures of the skull with their cell phones. Then Taylor checked the time. "Shit. Come on. Gotta go back. I'm late. My dad's gonna blow a gasket."

Bradley nodded, hoping he'd remember how to find this place again, and lowered the heavy skull into his backpack. As he did, he withdrew the glove thing and examined it again. Assuming this was a glove, the cuff in the top was where a hand would be inserted. He peered inside, saw nothing but dusty gray fabric, and thought, *what the heck?* He held the cuff down and shook it again to remove all the debris. Then he inserted his right hand into it. His fingers were inches too short for the glove, and the sixth appendage flopped free. The palm was loose around his hand, the cuff larger than his wrist. He turned his hand over several times, thinking he might see the faint blue and pink lines that wafted across the spider thing, but the glove remained dull gray. Then he felt movement and thought it was a gust of air or an insect. He held his hand down, illuminated the cuff with his headlamp, and was startled to see it moving on its own, tightening around his wrist. His hand trembled, and he thought, *maybe that's the motion I'm seeing*. But as he watched, his breath caught in his throat, and before he could make sense of it, the cuff closed completely around his wrist. He cried out, trying to rip the parasite off his hand, but he couldn't drive the fingers of his left hand beneath the cuff, which had sealed tightly. Panicked, he snatched the loose fabric at the end of the appendages and strained to pull the glove off, but it wouldn't give. Taylor shrank back in horror as he watched the gray mass conform to Bradley's hand like the hand was being shrink-wrapped.

In complete panic, Bradley screamed, "Pull it off." He held his hand out and shook it, and Taylor finally leaped forward and yanked at the appendages, straining backward in a frightening tug of war that Bradley feared would rip his hand from his arm—but the glove would not budge. Then, they both felt the glove growing warmer. Taylor cast it away like it was contagious and scrambled backward, his eyes spotlights in the gloom.

"Shit, man, I dunno what to do," he screamed.

The warmth crept up Bradley's hand, engulfing his palm and seeping into his fingers. He feared it would sear his skin or cook his hand, but the heat never grew uncomfortably hot. It felt more like he was holding his hand in the sun on a hot day at the beach. The warmth, he decided, as his heart raced, was more soothing than scalding, but that didn't mitigate his fear as the thing, whatever it was, continued to transform. It had now conformed to his wrist and palm like a skintight surgical glove. Then the boys watched, horrified, as the appendages shrank to conform to his fingers—and as that useless sixth appendage, the one that held none of Bradley's fingers, withdrew into the glove until it vanished.

"What the hell!" Taylor screamed, his heart pounding. "That thing alive?" He wanted out of the cave, wanted back on familiar ground where bizarre stuff like this didn't happen. He scrambled away, jumping up and running into the sunlight. Bradley chased after him, shaking his hand in vain, then holding his gray-coated hand up to the sun.

Taylor backed away. "Does it hurt?"

Bradley shook his head, gazing at his hand like it was an alien. "Just this weird feeling of wearing a tight glove. I don't know how I'm going to get it off."

"Maybe cut it off at a hospital."

Bradley didn't respond. He was absorbed in what the glove was doing now—the gray color fading, morphing to a lighter gray, then beige, finally matching the color of his skin as it became transparent. He could still feel it, but people seeing his hand wouldn't know the glove was there.

"Jesus H., man. The hell is that thing?" Taylor cried, staring at Bradley's hand in wonder, grateful he hadn't put on the damned thing. Taylor wasn't a coward, but he had to understand and control every situation. This was totally freaky.

Bradley frantically moved his fingers, formed a fist, and stretched his fingers wide, flexing, clenching, flexing, clenching. His movement wasn't restricted, and the glove was no longer hot. As his fear of the thing abated, he had an idea and ran back into the cave to retrieve his backpack. Returning outside, he dug out the spider thing. As Taylor watched, stepping farther away, his brows lowered, Bradley laid the spider thing over the back of his gloved hand, and it immediately stuck to the transparent glove like Velcro. The boys watched in astonishment over the next minute as the spider thing morphed in shape and size to conform to Bradley's gloved hand, its appendages shrinking and the sixth one disappearing. It was like watching a slow-motion animation of some freakish parlor trick. Bradley turned his hand over and flexed it. Then he tried to pull the spider off the glove and found it came off with just a tug. When he laid it back on, the spider Velcroed itself in place—and then a pattern of shapes and colors appeared on the spider's silver surface, rows of colored shapes aligned on the tops of the spider's fingers, interspersed with geometric symbols and letters in an unfamiliar alphabet. When the patterns were complete, the spider looked like a technicolor mosaic, strange but intelligent in design, with thin blue and pink lines traversing the spaces between the colored shapes, connecting some shapes with others. Bradley thought it looked like a kaleidoscopic circuit board, though some shapes were not connected to others, and some pulsed, drawing attention to themselves as if saying, "Touch me." When Bradley peeled the spider back off, the pattern vanished, the spider returning to uniform silver, and when he laid it back on, the pattern instantly reappeared.

"It was calibrating," Bradley said, astonished.

"What?"

"It sensed the size and shape of my hand and transformed itself to fit me. The previous owner must have been taller, with six longer fingers."

"The hell you sayin'?"

"Smart clothing," Bradley marveled. "Adapting to the wearer. I read about it."

"Somebody makes this kind of thing?"

"Not yet. They're working on it. It's called wearable electronics. But this…..." Bradley gazed at his right hand in wonder. "The spider is some kind of tool." A black square, larger than the other symbols, pulsed in the center of the spider's hub. Bradley held his breath and pressed it with his left index finger. Nothing happened for a moment. Then the boys sensed, rather than heard, a low-pitched hum near them, like standing in a house when an old furnace rumbles on and feeling a deep vibration beneath your feet.

"What's that?" Taylor said, angling his head to get a better fix on it.

Bradley shook his head, gazing around. It was a nearly subliminal sensation, so deep and soft he couldn't pinpoint it. He walked back into the cave, and the hum grew softer. Walking back out, he headed toward the hill, the round one with no trees. The hum rose from super low to low volume, but he still couldn't determine its origin. Wild grass and weeds grew up the hill's uniformly parabolic slope, punctuated by scraggy, uncombed bushes, three to four feet high but not high enough to obscure the geometric uniformity of the slope. Bradley climbed up a few feet, knelt, and put his ear to the ground. The hum was low but steady and a little louder.

Behind him, Taylor said, "What?"

"It's coming from here."

Taylor stood with his hands on his hips. His day was shot, and his dad would be pissed, but he was freaked by what happened to Adamsson and wouldn't leave until they figured out what the hell was going on. "Where's your shovel?" he said, exasperation thick in his voice.

"Back in the cave," Bradley responded.

Taylor retrieved it and ordered Bradley to step aside. He dug where Bradley had held his ear to the ground. About a foot down, the shovel clunked on something hard. Scooping away more dirt, Taylor drove the shovel into the dark soil, again striking something solid. So he dug around that area, removing more grass and dirt. A foot below the surface was something black and impenetrable. He shoveled dirt and vegetation away from it and, in a few minutes, cleared an area about three feet square. The surface was smooth and dark except for a veneer of dirt. Bradley poured water on it, and Axel wiped away the mud, revealing a polished surface that seemed translucent, as though black was not the color of the surface but the color of what lay beneath.

"That's not rock," Bradley muttered, which earned a *no-shit* glance from Taylor. "It's too smooth," Bradley said to himself, running his left hand over it. The hum seemed louder, so he leaned in to put his ear to the surface. When he touched the surface with his gloved hand, the hillside before them shook and was then riven in half, a long, vertical seam widening quickly, dirt and vegetation tumbling inside a dark opening that was too well defined not to be artificial. Terrified, the boys leaped backward, falling to the ground, knees and elbows flailing. When the earth stopped moving, they beheld a hollow, rectangular opening seven feet high and three feet wide—a doorway into the hillside.

"What the hell?" Taylor murmured. Their hearts pounding, the boys tensed, waiting for something to emerge. When nothing did, they looked at each other and laughed nervously. Minutes passed. Then, they got to their feet and inched toward the opening. Peering inside, they saw a long corridor dimly lit and bare walls the color of the deep blue sky.

The Thing in the Hill

Saturday. April 11. 10:53 am.

Taylor froze, his hands up, eyes narrowed, staring intently. The hillside had split open when Bradley touched it, actually split open, revealing a sky-blue tunnel. Hillsides don't do that, and Taylor struggled to discount the knot in his stomach and the bile burning his throat. *You don't plunge down twenty-foot waves if you're gutless,* he reassured himself. *Don't ride the Banzai Pipeline. Don't face down bears in the forest. Don't do half the shit I've done.*

But this unnatural tunnel in the side of the hill was way outside Axel's spectrum, and it scared the starch out of him. Beside him, Bradley leaned into the opening, eyebrows raised, smiling as he scanned the interior. The geek's composure rattled Taylor, and he tried to mask the shame of his fear with impatience. He jerked Bradley's arm. "Gotta get out of here."

Bradley stared at him, nodding absently. Then, in a show of strength that surprised them both, he quietly pried Taylor's fingers from his arm.

"Gotta get back to the garage," Taylor stammered. "My dad's gonna kill me. Shoulda been there hours ago. Come on, dammit."

But Bradley turned back to the tunnel. After taking a picture of it, he said, "What do you think this is?"

This guy for real? Taylor's mind screamed. He felt like he was standing on a knife edge. He reached for Bradley's arm but thought better about grabbing it. After Taylor was arrested for a B&E last year, something no one at school knew about, he was afraid another violation would land him in state prison. All he lifted was some guy's weed and a Rolex, but the guy demanded restitution in the plea bargain, and Taylor got probation, community service, and a ten grand fine his dad paid, which Taylor was still paying back. Taylor was intrigued by this hole in the hill, whatever the place was. But despite his curiosity, he couldn't risk an arrest and violate his probation. Taylor shook his head. "I dunno, dude. Whosever party this is, we weren't invited. Know what I mean?"

Bradley pointed at the spider covering his right hand. "This opened the door."

"An accident. 'Kay? I hadn't gone into the cave? Hadn't dug around? Hell, man! What this is," Taylor said, gesturing toward the tunnel, "somebody built this. You know? The government. Somebody. We get caught, our butts are in a sling."

Bradley stared back into the corridor, his mind pumped. "I don't think anybody's home. An alarm would've sounded. They would've come when this, whatever it is, opened."

"Doesn't mean they're not on the way," Taylor reasoned. His mouth tasted sour and dry. "How the hell did this just happen?"

"I don't know. But you're right. Somebody built this place, whatever it is."

"No shit. And didn't hang a sign sayin' to come on in."

"It has to be military," Bradley said.

Taylor's eyes bulged. "Better reason to get the hell out of here."

Bradley shook his head, trying to make sense of it. "No. This spider thing opened the hillside. That wouldn't have happened without the glove. They work together somehow. Why would the military bury them in a cave? That doesn't make sense. And there are no signs here. No USAF or NASA or Unauthorized Personnel Keep Out. Nothing."

"Right. You and me? Don't know what this is. Who it belongs to."

"No, we don't," Bradley whispered, his mind ablaze with possibilities. He glanced at Taylor. "We can't walk away now. We have to see what's inside." Taylor looked away, fidgeting and cracking some knuckles. "You go back if you want," Bradley added. With that, he stepped into the opening. His boots sank into a knee-high pile of dirt and grass that had tumbled inside. He inched ahead, feeling his way along the smooth walls, and after a minute, heard Taylor stepping in behind him.

"Can't believe this shit," Taylor stammered.

The corridor was about forty feet long, cool but not cold, and the air smelled fresh, not stale like an abandoned mine that had been sealed and forgotten. Bradley saw no dust motes or signs of wear in a corridor that was not only clean but polished. Someone was maintaining it. He could feel a slight movement of air but heard nothing. Even that low hum was gone. His headlamp reflected light off the smooth, metallic walls. At the end of the corridor was a T-junction. There were symbols on the walls just above eye level in a language he didn't recognize. He held up the spider thing and saw that some notations on the spider resembled notations on the walls.

Taylor came up behind him. "What's that?" Axel said, pointing at the symbols.

Bradley shook his head. "A sign? Directions?"

"Does it say where the bathroom is?"

Bradley laughed. "You have to pee?"

Taylor did but was ashamed to admit it. His bladder felt gripped in a vise. He tried to ignore it, watching as Bradley ran the fingers of his left hand over the notations.

"Dude, this is too weird. Maybe foreigners built this place, like a long time ago. Egyptians or somebody."

Bradley looked askance at him. "Ancient Egyptians got tired of building pyramids, so they came to California and started digging?"

Taylor threw up his hands. "Could've happened!"

Bradley glanced back to the lettering, took a picture of it, and then turned right into another blue corridor, and twenty feet later, came to a circular opening in the floor about four feet in diameter. He peered into it with his headlamp. It was a tube with smooth, shiny walls. No ladder or handholds. No way to get down. He saw a similar opening in the ceiling directly above it, another tube that went up twelve or fifteen feet. No way to climb up. The corridor continued, but rather than step over the hole in the floor, he turned and eased past Taylor, who shone his flashlight into those tubes, muttering something Bradley couldn't hear. Back at the junction, Bradley walked straight ahead and found a large room with deep blue walls. As he entered, the room brightened, the walls turning lighter. The wall ahead had a long concave alcove with an empty, white curved counter running along it. In front of the counter were three oversized white chairs facing the blank wall. Bradley sat in the center one, pushing himself up into the seat. The seat was roomy, but his feet didn't reach the floor, and the backrest was a foot higher than his head. Taylor stood beside him, both curious about this place and wondering what the hell they'd gotten themselves into.

Bradley squirmed as he felt the chair moving and then realized it was conforming to his shape. Smiling to himself, he leaned forward and touched the counter with his gloved hand. Both boys were startled when the counter instantly transformed into an array of three-dimensional buttons and sliders that hovered over the counter like holograms. The objects were grouped by color, the buttons different shapes, and those strange notations appeared on some buttons and beside the sliders.

"Holy shit," Taylor exclaimed for both of them.

Directly in front of Bradley was a hovering black sphere the size of a softball. As he reached toward it, he saw that the spider had lost its colored pattern and was uniformly silver, indicating, he guessed, that the spider was now inert. He tugged it off his hand and set it on the seat beside him. Then he reached his gloved hand toward an array of red buttons to the right of the black ball.

"Dude, what're you doin'?" Taylor warned. "Stop messin' around. Dunno what that stuff does."

"Only one way to find out," Bradley said, touching the top left red button with his gloved index finger. Instantly, a rectangular screen appeared in the air above him. It hovered, a detached, holographic screen displaying a dozen gauges he couldn't comprehend and symbols resembling those on the spider. Some looked like bar charts and graphs. Others displayed tick marks and symbols that Bradley guessed were numbers. He touched the edge of the screen with his gloved hand and found that he could reposition it in space. "This is like a flight deck," he mused, "but with configurable displays."

"Flight deck?" Taylor said. "Like an airplane? We're underground, dude."

Bradley nodded. "Like the rabbit hole Alice fell into."

Taylor wondered who the hell Alice was but was afraid to ask. "Could be a nuclear power plant. Don't screw around." Taylor was intrigued despite his fear, but his hands were shaking, which unnerved him. "Come on. Let's get outta here already."

"All right." Bradley touched the same red button, and the floating screen vanished. "This is beyond amazing," he said. When he stepped off the chair, he found that his feet had now touched the floor, and the chair had shrunk to his size. If Taylor noticed it, he didn't say anything. *How on earth is this happening?* Bradley wondered. He picked up the spider and affixed it to his right hand, and the boys returned to the corridor. At the junction, they turned toward the doorway they'd come in. It lay forty feet ahead, a glaring sunlit rectangle suspended in the blue of the corridor, but as Bradley drew near, he stopped suddenly. Something wasn't right.

"What is it?" Taylor said.

Bradley pointed at the floor beneath the opening. "The dirt's gone. The stuff that fell inside when the door opened." Taylor looked over Bradley's shoulder. At least a foot of dirt and grass had been on the floor. They'd both stepped in it and tracked some of it down the corridor, but now the floor was clean.

"We musta come in another way," Taylor said.

Bradley shook his head. He could see the entrance to the cave through the opening and pointed that out.

"Then somebody's here, man," Taylor said, shoving his shaking hands into his front pockets.

Bradley peered outside and looked behind them. The corridor was empty and silent. "I don't think so."

"Where the hell'd the dirt go?" Taylor said, his voice a register higher than usual.

"Janitorial service?" Bradley said.

"Real comedian, Adamsson."

"It's got to be one of those robotic vacuum cleaners. We didn't hear it."

"This place is creeping me out. Gotta keep moving," Taylor said as he rushed past Bradley through the opening, relieved they hadn't been caught. Behind him, Bradley knelt and ran his hands across the floor inside the door. It was as smooth and polished as the rest of the corridor's floor. Not even fine dirt particles remained, but there was no sign that anyone else had been there. Although he couldn't make sense of that, it fascinated Bradley. He felt his mind bursting with possibilities. He could have stayed for weeks exploring this puzzling place, but Taylor's impatience tugged at him. After he stepped through the opening, Bradley glanced at the spider. The pattern of buttons on it had reappeared. He touched one side of the door with his gloved hand, and both sides slid together, a slim seam visible briefly before vanishing.

"We have to come back tomorrow," Bradley announced.

"Bullshit. We forget this ever happened."

"No. We have to come back. I do, anyway.

"Bullshit! We gotta forget about this thing, this place."

"I can't. When you discover something like this, you must figure out what it is. If nobody's here, we'll be okay."

"Yeah? And if the whole friggin' army is here?"

Bradley shrugged. "We're just a couple of high school kids out hiking."

Taylor shook his head, blood draining from his cheeks. "You wanna wind up in prison, you jerk?"

Bradley pushed his glasses up and stared at Taylor, wondering about him and realizing he didn't know much about the guy. "We can't walk away and forget about this. It's the most incredible thing that's ever happened to me."

Taylor glanced around, searching for better reasons why they shouldn't return. He agreed that what they discovered was amazing, but he swallowed hard, terrified of going to jail and picturing his dad yelling at him. "This is gonna screw me over, man."

"Not if we aren't violating any laws, and I don't see anything here that says we are. We stumbled onto something, and we're just exploring it. We can turn it over to the authorities later."

"All right. Dammit."

"We can't tell anybody about this either. Okay?"

Taylor nodded, happy to agree with that. Bradley took off the spider and put it in his backpack. He'd all but forgotten that the glove still enclosed his hand. He could barely feel it. They decided to conceal the opening, even though Taylor said he'd never seen anyone up here, so they took turns shoveling dirt back on the sloped surface of the hatch, and Taylor cut some leafy branches to lay across it. It wasn't perfect camouflage, Bradley decided, but it was passable. As they started down the mountain, Bradley felt the pain in his right side and realized it hadn't bothered him the whole time they were in the hillside.

After dinner, when his parents sat him down for "the talk," Bradley said he didn't want to discuss his cancer, that he wasn't ready to think about it, and, besides, he'd found something interesting in the forest that he wanted to show them. His parents shared a worried look but tacitly agreed to pretend everything was normal. Fifteen minutes later, in their garage, John Adamsson turned the skull over in his hands. Using a bevel-edge chisel, he carefully scraped away more compacted dirt, the shavings falling onto the workbench. The family stood around him, Devin intrigued by what Bradley found, despite the urge to say it was no big deal. Celia asked Bradley where they found it.

"In a cave." He was self-conscious about the glove on his right hand. It was transparent, but he still worried someone would notice it. He covered that hand with his left.

"How old is it, dad?" Celia said. They didn't do show and tell in ninth grade, but Celia was thinking it would still be neat to bring the skull to science class.

John shook his head. Then, he examined the upper jaw again. Just below the nasal cavity were two large, jagged stumps, and John surmised that they were the bases of large canine fangs. He set down the skull and pulled out his cell phone. After searching for a few minutes, he showed everyone a picture of a skull with long, curved fangs. "I think this is what you found, Bradley. The skull of a saber-tooth cat."

"Wow. That's so-o-o cool," Celia said. "Can we keep it?"

"It is cool," John said, "but Bradley might want to donate it to a museum where many people could see it." He looked at his phone and confirmed what he'd read a moment ago. "They became extinct around twelve thousand years ago."

"Were they common in this part of California?" Bradley asked.

John nodded. "They've pulled saber-tooth cat skeletons out of the La Brea Tar Pits. Yes, they were common here, but it's rare to find their bones. This is a real discovery, even without the fangs."

"They could still be in the cave," Celia chirped, her eyes wide. She was ready to leave right now.

"Yes, they could," John said. "Why don't I show this to Jonas Winter at USC? He's a paleontologist and could tell us more. Bradley, you should take him to the cave and show him where you found this."

"I want to go, too," Celia said.

"Me, too," said Devin.

"I think that's a great idea," John told everyone. "But let's do it the right way. We'll take someone along who knows what he's doing."

Bradley's stomach had more knots than a sailboat. He hoped it was too late for his father to call the paleontologist tonight. Anyone going to that cave might see the disturbed dirt on the hillside. He knew what would happen once other people found what he and Taylor had discovered. Either it was a secret military installation, and he'd be banned from it, or it wasn't military and would be appropriated by the authorities, the police or JPL or Cal Tech or somebody, and he'd be forbidden to go inside again. He was just a high school kid, and whoever controlled that place wouldn't allow him to explore it. The situation was spiraling out of control and turning into a family outing.

"Okay," he said, his tongue thick, "but not till next weekend. I have schoolwork and need to work on my speech."

"Cool," Celia said. "Can I bring Madison?"

Bradley's stomach turned over, existing knots convulsing into more convoluted knots. He'd planned to tell his mom and dad he was hiking again tomorrow with Axel Taylor, but they couldn't know he was returning to the forest. So, when the family left the garage and everybody scattered, he found his mom in the den and told her he was spending tomorrow in the library working on his Valedictorian speech. That was an easy sell, but guilt gripped his soul.

That night, he took his pain pills and lay in bed thinking about their discovery. Finding a saber-tooth cat's skull at least twelve thousand years old next to the glove and the spider might be a coincidence. If not, the place in the hillside could be that old, but how could it still have power after twelve millennia? When the Daydream Special arrived, Bradley stepped aboard. On the journey, he saw floating holograms, self-cleaning floors, and shiny silver tubes in the ceilings and floors. *Who built it?* he wondered. *NBA centers with six long fingers? Creatures from another world?* Lights flashed by as the Special sped along, and Bradley lay entranced by today's discovery, feeling more buoyant than he ever had, the dread of dying overshadowed by the thrill of what they'd found and the promise of more discoveries in that magical blue corridor into the hillside.

While he slept, the glove loosened and worked its way off his hand. He was alarmed when he found it in the sheets the next morning, but when he put it back on, the glove shrank around his hand like yesterday and remained transparent. Now the glove didn't feel threatening. It felt mysterious and exciting. And safe.

Blinding Light

Sunday. April 12 9:32 am.

Trudging up the mountain was no easier than yesterday, but Bradley was buoyed by unquenchable curiosity and didn't listen to his body's distress until they reached the clearing. Then, as Taylor knelt quietly beside him and scanned the area with a hunter's poise, Bradley sat gasping for breath like an unworthy servant in his master's shadow. His panting annoyed Taylor, who tried to ignore it while brooding: *Dude wouldn't even qualify for the Special Olympics.* Adding to his annoyance was Taylor's paranoia over going to jail if they were caught. He fought the impulse to hightail it back down the mountain by reminding himself that if no one knew about this place, their discovery could be worth enough for him to buy a new Ford F-450 dually, his dream truck. After the geek recovered, Taylor canted his head toward the side of the hill opposite the cave. They padded through the brush as though afraid to disturb the birds flitting through the trees.

Circling the hill to the cave, they saw no footprints but theirs and no other telltale signs of disturbance. Still, they perched in the shadows inside the cave and listened for another half hour. When impatience overrode caution, Bradley quietly removed the spider from his pack and set it on his gloved hand. Instantly, the colorful pattern of buttons reappeared on its silver surface. He pressed the larger black symbol, and they heard the low hum emanating from the hill. When no traps were sprung, no sirens blared, and no soldiers with assault rifles leaped from the bushes, they eased toward the side of the hill where cut branches concealed the hatch. While Taylor scanned the dense green forest walls around them, Bradley peered overhead, looking for helicopters or drones.

"Nothing," Bradley whispered.

"Just can't see 'em."

After a long pause, Bradley said, "I don't think anyone's here. Just us."

Taylor shrugged. "Okay, Einstein. If you're wrong, I'm screwed." Bradley looked quizzically at Taylor, who turned away, unwilling to explain and unable to tolerate the scrutiny. "Fine," he murmured. "Fuck it."

After they carried away the branches and shoveled off the dirt, Bradley touched the smooth, black surface with his gloved hand, and the hillside split open as before, revealing that deep blue corridor. Bradley took out his cell phone and said, "I'm going to document all this. Okay with you?"

Axel shrugged. "Yeah, why not? Good idea, I guess. We can get photos of our arrest." His misgivings aside, Axel took out his cell phone and pointed it at the blue door into the hill.

As happened yesterday, some dirt and grass tumbled into the opening. Bradley stepped in it, assuming it would disappear later and wondering where it would have gone. Taylor took a last, long look around the site, seeing nothing suspicious and hearing only the rustling of leaves and bird chatter. The sky was as crisp as a new blue shirt, and Taylor was ambivalent. It was too perfect a Sunday not to be surfing. If he had to get reamed by his dad and agree to work every night this week, he'd rather be riding the waves, not wasting time with this geek. This was his limit, he decided. After today, he was done.

When Taylor stepped inside through the dirt, Bradley touched the black symbol on the spider, and the hatch closed behind them. Taylor's heart slammed into his ribcage. "Why'd you do that?"

"To discourage visitors."

"Dude, I told you. Never seen anybody here. What if we have to book it?"

Bradley held up his hand with the spider. "This will open it."

"Okay. Give me the spider."

Bradley shook his head. "It's useless without the glove, which I can't get off."

He'd spoken matter-of-factly, but Taylor read defiance in Bradley's face and fought the impulse to knock the geek into the next zip code. Axel Taylor was the alpha in everything he did. Taking a backseat to this nerd dropped his brain out of gear, and he shot one hand out to brace himself against the wall. His tongue felt like sludge, but he managed to stammer, "Fine. Okay. You're not leavin' my sight."

Surprised at Taylor's antagonism, Bradley instinctively stepped back and waited for it to boil over. Then he turned away, expecting a blow in the back that never came. He switched on his headlamp and walked on, sensing Taylor creeping behind him. Bradley coughed to hide a dry swallow. The blue walls gleamed in the light from his headlamp. At the junction, he turned right, as they'd done yesterday, and soon came to the hole in the floor. He knelt and peered into it. The tube's walls seemed to end three or four feet down, something he hadn't noticed yesterday, and there was open space below that. He reached into the tube with his left hand and felt resistance, as though a current of air were pushing against him, although he felt no air on his hand and none in his face. The deeper he reached, the stronger the pressure became. After testing that for a few minutes, he stood and peered at the tube in the ceiling above him. When he reached his hand toward the bottom of it, he felt something tugging his hand upward.

"I wish we had a rope," Bradley said, "in case I'm wrong." With that, he stepped onto the space above the tube on the floor. Instantly, he felt enough resistance to prevent him from plunging. He teetered on his feet, his arms windmilling as he fought for balance. When he steadied himself, he looked down. He was standing on open space.

"What the hell?" Taylor said, shining his flashlight at Bradley's feet. "How you doing that?"

Bradley shook his head. "Something's holding me up."

Taylor knelt and touched the space near Bradley's feet, feeling the pressure against his fingers. "This place is gnarly, man. You catchin' me?"

"I'm going to try something," Bradley said. Before Taylor could ask what, Bradley threw his arms over his head like Superman and jumped—and he flew into the tube on the ceiling and disappeared, which caused Taylor's throat to seize. Bradley stopped when he reached the upper level, and the dim blue lights in that corridor brightened.

A moment later, he heard Taylor shout, "What the hell, Adamsson? Where'd you go? The hell are you?" Ignoring him, Bradley stepped off the top of the tube and peered around. He was in another corridor with doors on either side. Doors farther down the corridor looked like indentations in the walls. On the doors beside him were more etched symbols like those in the corridor below, and in the ceiling above was another tube leading to a level above this one. He wanted to explore but needed to return to the lower level before Taylor completely freaked. As he stepped back onto the open space above the tube, that strange pressure held him up. He tried bouncing in the space, stooping, and pointing his arms down, but nothing happened. Then he flexed his toes downward and began sinking, dropping faster the deeper he pointed his toes. He landed cleanly on the open space below and would have kept descending if he hadn't raised his toes when he reached that level. The whites of Taylor's eyes shone like lanterns, his face frozen in panic, but he calmed down as Bradley explained what happened and told him what he saw on the upper level. Leery of this place but not wanting to be shown up by the geek, Taylor stepped onto the open space, quickly gained his balance, and pointed his toes downward. He floated to the level below them, shone his flashlight around for a few moments, and then flew back up to Bradley.

"Okay, that was cool," Taylor admitted after returning to solid ground. "Another hallway down there and another hole in the floor below. There's more levels. Amazing, man, this place. Still giving me the creeps. The hell is this?"

Bradley shrugged, his mind so alive he could practically feel his synapses firing. "Let's go back to that control room."

Axel studied Bradley as he walked away, admitting to himself that the geek wasn't totally worthless. Adamsson might be odd, but he was good at figuring things out. The control room brightened to sky blue as the boys entered. Bradley noted that the middle chair had retained its shape from yesterday. He settled into that chair, took the spider off his gloved hand, and set it on the seat beside him. Then he touched the white counter with his gloved hand, and the holographic controls reappeared—a floating array of colorful buttons and sliders surrounding the softball-sized black sphere hovering above the panel. Axel sat in the chair to Bradley's right and tensed as he felt the chair conforming to his body shape.

"Maybe we shouldn't screw around in here, you know?" Axel reminded him.

"You're right," Bradley said. "We should turn this over to the authorities. That's the sensible thing to do. But this place is way too amazing. I've never seen or even read about technology like this except in science fiction. I don't think the government built this unless it's some super-secret DARPA project."

"What's a darpa?"

"The Defense Advanced Research Projects Agency. They fund top-secret research for the military, like the stealth bomber, battlefield robotics, laser weapons, artificial intelligence, technology like that."

"The feds own this place?"

"Possibly. But I don't think so. Technology this advanced would be protected. We couldn't get near it."

"So what you sayin'? Little green men built this?"

"I'd say they were tall beings with six fingers. Whoever made the spider thing made this. I don't know if they're green."

"Where are they?"

Bradley shrugged. "Come and gone? Killed by germs on our planet, like the Martians in *War of the Worlds*. Killed by that saber-tooth cat? Twelve thousand years ago."

"Dude, the place is cleaner than my truck. Someone's on it. You catchin' me?"

"Sure. Maybe they're still here. Hibernating somewhere. Except for the janitor."

"Yeah, right. Get the hell out of here before they wake up. We could be breakfast. Come on, go to the cops, turn this thing over. Gotta be a reward. Maybe we can sell it. I buy the truck I want. You get your leg fixed. Who knows?"

Bradley was stung by that. Even his friends didn't talk about his leg, and someone like Axel Taylor would do it only to torment him. He leaned back in the chair and averted his face, reminded not only about his leg but about the cancer in his liver and everything else wrong with him. Shame and sorrow swept through him like an avalanche, and he waited for Taylor to follow with one of his withering put-downs: *freak, lamer, crip*. Taylor wasn't in beast mode, but Bradley didn't trust that he could read the guy well enough to know when the surfer was playing nice or when he was setting you up for an insult. When no put-downs followed, he took a deep breath and looked back at Taylor, saying sourly, "They can't fix my leg. Nobody can."

The hurt in Adamsson's eyes surprised Taylor. He hadn't said anything stupid. Not today. Now, he kind of admired the geek even though he was annoying and weak. Axel knew he'd mistreated Adamsson in the past but bygones and all that crap. "All right. So . . ."

Bradley shook it off, refusing to listen, and looked back at the control panel. "When we turn this in, we'll never see it again. I want more time to explore." Before Taylor could object, Bradley grasped the black softball object. He pushed it down. A shrill buzzing cut the silence like a chainsaw, and the control panel turned purple. Instantly, Bradley let go of the ball. It resumed its neutral position, and the panel returned to white.

"What the hell?" said Taylor, his voice constricted.

Bradley shrugged. "I pushed the ball down. I don't think it liked that." He reached for the ball again and, this time pulled it up. The alarm clanged for a nanosecond, the panel flashing purple—then, after a sharp thud, the boys were instantly immersed in blinding light.

Disaster

Sunday. April 12. 11:33 am.

The meteorite struck in a rugged, remote area of the Angeles National Forest east of Pasadena, scaring the living hell out of ten million residents of Los Angeles County. Witnesses said it streaked straight down like lightning, causing an instant flash of fire from the cloudless blue to the dark green forest in the San Gabriel mountains. A massive explosion followed—shredded trees, rocks, and dirt blown a quarter mile from the impact site. A roiling, brown cloud rose a thousand feet and mushroomed ominously while a thunderous, rolling boom, louder than a hundred jet engines, peeled open the sky and left it shuddering. Thank God it hadn't struck a populated area, people cried. Thousands could have been killed. As it was, windows shattered as far as twelve miles away, the sonic boom rupturing the eardrums of people outdoors nearest the point of impact. The GPS failed countywide during the event but recovered as the mushroom cloud rose.

Within six miles of the strike, products on supermarket and retail store shelves shimmied like drunken dancers onto the floor. Loose objects made of iron, nickel, or ferromagnetic alloys zipped toward the impact zone, lifting off desks, tables, and counters. Within two miles of the strike, they crashed through windows and zoomed toward the site only to drop seconds later as though they'd run out of gas. Vehicles on Interstates 210 and 15 careened into each other, freaked-out drivers terrified that an earthquake or nuclear attack had occurred. Los Angeles County deputies responded quickly, but Sheriff Federico Veracruz called for assistance from state troopers and local police to handle more than five hundred accidents on freeways and streets throughout the county. Few life-threatening injuries occurred in the multiple car pileups. Still, a dozen county residents suffered heart attacks, and area hospitals and urgent care facilities were overwhelmed with glass cuts, abrasions, broken bones, and thousands of rattled residents demanding Xanax as panic reigned.

Seismic sensors at the U.S. Geological Survey recorded an event of 6.2 on the Richter scale, which scientists initially believed was an earthquake near the junction of the San Andreas and San Jacinto faults, but an earthquake didn't cause that streak of fire in the sky, create a mushroom cloud, or attract metal objects like a magnet. The first responders at the impact site were Angeles Forest rangers, followed quickly by LA County deputies, who found the impact crater still smoldering. It was more than nine hundred feet wide and was, they guessed, at least eight hundred feet deep. Nearly symmetrical, it looked like someone had removed a half-spherical section of earth with a giant ice cream scoop. Trees within two hundred yards of the perimeter were flattened, blown outward, limbs burned black, and, farther out, singed. Smoke billowed from dozens of small fires around the crater. Forest Supervisor Dennis Marchbanks ordered in fire crews, although recent rains and slight winds made a larger conflagration unlikely.

Two hours after the impact, scientists from the nearby Jet Propulsion Laboratory were combing the scene for space rock fragments and other residue that could illuminate the meteorite's composition. They were struck immediately by the unusual soil condition in and around the impact crater. Tiny black needles two inches long, barely one hundred microns thick, rimmed the crater and extended as far into the pit as they could see—hundreds of needles per square inch, pointing skyward, arrayed in parallel, like a dense cluster of rigid black bristles shot into the ground. They were like nothing the scientists had ever seen. Similar needles were found on the nearest tree trunks, shattered limbs, and blackened branches around the crater's perimeter, the wood carved into sharp arrays of burnt needles pointing skyward. Radiation counters detected no unusual radioactivity, nothing beyond average background radiation. Still, the scientists donned white hazmat suits and blue booties before taking soil samples and photographing those mysterious black needles. At 3:42 pm, helicopters swooped in from the Air Force Space Command's Missile Systems Center in El Segundo. They discharged Lt. Colonel Aubrey Randall and two dozen USAF Security police with assault rifles. Randall informed first responders that this was now a restricted military site and ordered it sealed until a thorough investigation could be conducted.

When Marchbanks was satisfied that his crews had mitigated the fire danger, he ordered them out of the cordoned area that county deputies and Air Force Security Forces had erected. Then, he took a call from his headquarters in Arcadia. CNN was playing a video of the meteorite strike taken by a tourist with her cell phone. The amateur videographer was Dorothy Ware from Boise, Idaho. While visiting her sister in nearby Monrovia, she and her husband Ron were having brunch with friends in Pasadena. Dorothy was shooting a video in their backyard when the meteorite struck. She caught the streak of light and explosion and kept shooting until the shock wave knocked her off her feet. Thinking they'd struck gold, Ron sold the video online for a quick thousand bucks. The video went viral and, within hours, had over fifty million views.

It took USAF Security Force investigators an hour to locate the Wares and commandeer Dorothy Ware's cell phone. By 8:25 that evening, her phone was in a lab at JPL where video technician Susanna Howard examined it while the rest of the impromptu JPL-USAF team discussed the event in a conference room nearby. Susanna knew what had happened, having seen the reports on local news channels, and was giddy that she'd been chosen to examine the original cell phone footage. She sat in the darkness of her lab, brushing long red hairs from her eyes as she transferred the digital video to her computer. She regretted that the resolution was only 1080p. Newer phones were 4K, which would have yielded a sharper image, but you work with what you have. When the video came up, she played it all the way through. After the impact and explosion, Dorothy Ware panned upward and filmed the trail of fire high into the atmosphere. Before playing it again, Susanna edited out the quaint family and friends barbeque footage to yield a clip 13.5 seconds long showing the meteorite strike and explosive impact. The explosion was so massive and startling that she almost missed the anomaly. It happened so quickly. *But something isn't right*, Susanna realized. She played the clip again, slower. *That can't be*, she thought. *Is that an optical illusion?*

She studied the footage again, this time in super slow motion. "Oh my God," she muttered. "What in the holy hell?" She brought up a digital map of the area and measured the distance between Mrs. Ware's barbeque and the impact crater. Then she measured the angle from the barbeque to the top of the stream of fire and, compensating for the differences in elevation between the barbeque and the impact crater, calculated the altitude of that stream of fire and the object's velocity. Her hand began shaking as she studied the result. What she found was impossible, so she checked her math. She'd been at the lab seven years and four months and loved it there. She didn't want to make a career-ending mistake. So she ran the calculations a third time and then a fourth, yielding the same result. Her mouth dry, she stood on rubber legs and wobbled next door—drunk on a hot cocktail of one-part doubt and two-parts astonishment.

"Guys," she blurted to a mixed group of men and women, a common way to address colleagues. Then she saw the blue uniform and insignia of a three-star Air Force general in the room, a woman. She coughed into her hand and started again. "Ladies and gentlemen, this wasn't a meteorite. Whatever it was did not fall from space. It flew up from the ground so fast it might've looked like a meteorite, but it wasn't."

For a moment, everyone in the room forgot to breathe. Then, Lt. General Stephanie Vaughan scrunched her eyebrows. "It was launched from the ground?"

"Yes, ma'am. The digital image is blurry but unmistakable. This thing went up, not down. I triangulated from the photographer's position to the impact site and up as far as the streak of light extended around a hundred thousand feet. This object, whatever it was, rose at more than thirty thousand miles an hour. Thirty-four thousand, to be exact."

"That's impossible," General Vaughan said.

"I know," Susanna said. "It's forty-four times the speed of sound."

"Mach forty-four? Nothing can fly that fast," said Ross Lefaye, JPL's Deputy Director.

"Something did," Susanna replied.

"Are you sure of that, Susanna?" Lefaye said.

"I checked it four times, Director Lefaye. If I made an error, I don't know where. The visual evidence looks irrefutable to me."

For several moments, the team was silent. What had been a day like any other was now a day like no other, and they found it hard to grasp the implications of what they'd just heard, like glimpsing an undiscovered country shrouded in mist, not knowing what discoveries or terrors lay ahead. This was either a natural phenomenon that defied explanation now but would eventually be explained, or it was something unnatural and beyond explanation. Many of the scientists in the room were ballistics and propulsion systems experts. They knew that no one on Earth could build a rocket that accelerated that fast. NASA's X-43A scramjet had achieved a speed of nearly 7,000 mph, and the Russians claimed to have flown a hypersonic missile at twenty-seven times the speed of sound. But Mach forty-four?

"Could the Russians have built this?" Lefaye wondered out loud.

"And launched it outside Pasadena?" someone scoffed.

"I know that makes no sense," Lefaye admitted. "Nothing does." Not even the most explosive volcano could eject magma that fast. No natural or manmade object could do what the thing in the video appeared to have done. So, the data was wrong, or the digital video file was corrupt, or Susanna Howard had screwed up.

Director Lefaye broke the silence. "We have a long night ahead of us, and I'm sure some of you haven't eaten." He asked an assistant to order pizza or sandwiches, whatever people wanted. Then he said, "Susanna, let's look at that video."

General Vaughan stepped to the door. "Before you leave, I'm classifying this event as Top Secret. Make sure everyone with access has the requisite clearance. And I want a news blackout on this. We can't do anything about the video. That thoroughbred is out of the gate, but from this point on, we have no comment to the media. Not until we figure out what happened and get guidance from Washington." She turned to Lt. Colonel Randall. "Colonel, notify Homeland Security. And start working up a briefing. It's nearly midnight in D.C. I'll wake up the Chairman of the Joint Chiefs, and he'll need to call the President."

––––––––––

Across town, Kevin Karchman, a LIGO Lab technician at CalTech, realized hours ago that he would not make it home tonight for his wife's long-planned anniversary dinner. That was frustrating, and Marcie would be upset, but what was happening at the lab was way too weird, like totally astonishing. He'd make it up to her somehow. Karch was on a conference call with his counterparts at LIGO's Louisiana and Hanford's interferometers and VIRGO, their sister interferometer lab outside Pisa, Italy. LIGO stands for Laser Interferometer Gravity-Wave Observatory, which CalTech and MIT jointly operate, and they were doing a targeted scan for gravity waves in deep space when all hell broke loose. Their interferometers are highly sensitive instruments, capable of detecting gravity waves to one ten-thousandth the width of a proton, and they could detect gravity waves halfway across the known universe.

But at 1133 hours this morning, the detectors had gone ballistic, so off the charts that Karch thought a bomb must have exploded beside their detectors—except that powerful gravity waves were detected not only at Hanford and Louisiana but also in Italy. Three bombs exploding simultaneously at three locations thousands of miles apart? No way. So Karch called in the director and the chief scientists, and they were trying to make sense of the data. Karch was aware of the meteor impact in the Angeles forest but didn't associate their gravity waves with the meteorite strike. What they detected at LIGO was far more ominous. Their instruments recorded a burst of strong gravity waves near the Earth's surface as though a black hole had suddenly appeared in our atmosphere, which was impossible because if it had, the Earth would have succumbed to the black hole's immense gravity and parts of the planet would already have been sucked past the black hole's event horizon, a process that would continue until the Earth—and everything on it—vanished. *But we're still here*, Karch told himself, *so what the hell was that?*

What Can't Be Seen

Sunday. April 12. 11:34 am.

When that flash of light blinded him, Taylor yelped and screwed his eyes shut, covering them with both hands. Bradley released the softball like a searing charcoal briquette, closed his eyes, and inhaled a lungful of air. They'd felt a strong jolt then nothing more, and when the moment passed with no more surprises, Bradley exhaled and slowly opened his eyes. The room was no longer blue. There was now a gray twilight around them and nearly black overhead, but below were brilliant, glowing blues and whites, lights so intense he had to squint when he looked down. As his eyes adjusted, Bradley realized he was looking through the floor at the curving of the Earth's horizon, the deep blues of the Pacific Ocean, and a colorful jigsaw mosaic of green and brown land, covered here and there by cotton ball and pancake clouds that formed a patchwork of white from horizon to horizon. Bradley recognized the view from hours of flying, but he'd seen the Earth from this high in the atmosphere only in photos taken from high-altitude reconnaissance planes. Overhead, all he saw was the blackness of space and a dense network of pinprick stars.

Uncharacteristically, Bradley muttered, "What the fuck?" as he gazed around him. The control panel and the room's walls were still faintly visible, but they were superimposed on 360-degree views of the Earth and space. It was like looking through a spherical window in every direction and seeing double—the ghostly foreground of the control room superimposed on a stunning diorama of space and the planet. For a long moment, he could not understand what he was seeing. His mind told him they weren't falling and were still rooted in their chairs. Still, the sensation of floating in mid-air was so bizarre he got vertigo and had to steady himself by closing his eyes and clinging to his chair, glimpsing only briefly at the Earth below until the dizziness passed.

Beside him, Taylor had been holding his breath and forced himself to exhale. "The hell just happened, Adamsson?" he cried.

Bradley looked around in awe. "It's like we flew high into the atmosphere. Except we didn't move."

"Where the hell are we?"

"Inside the hill. This must be a simulator."

"A what?"

"Like a flight simulator. We didn't go anywhere. Only the view changed. If we'd flown this high, we would have felt movement. And if we'd flown this high, this fast, the G forces would've killed us. We'd be astronaut soup in puddles on the floor."

"The G forces? Never mind. Take your word for it." He looked down at where the floor used to be. "Can I get out of this chair? Cause I'm gonna barf, man."

"The floor's still there."

Taylor slowly sank out of the chair, his eyes closed, inching one foot toward the floor, then easing himself onto his feet when he landed on something solid. But when he stood with both feet on the floor and looked down, his vertigo surged, and he dropped to the floor and lay on his back to keep from vomiting. "This is too weird, dude," he managed.

"It doesn't happen every day," Bradley admitted. "I'm going to try something. Just lie there, okay? Keep your eyes shut."

"Hell, yeah. What else am I gonna do?"

Bradley reached forward and placed his gloved hand back on the black softball. He just eased it up this time, and the view changed as though they were rising slowly, the Earth's curvature becoming more pronounced as the blackness above them grew darker. He watched in amazement as the Earth shrank beneath them. When he eased the ball back into neutral, their apparent motion stopped. The sky above had turned pitch black except for the stars, and he could see the entire globe of the Earth below. It was visible across the floor of the control room. He'd seen many NASA photos of Earth from the International Space Station. Still, they were a sorry representation of what he witnessed now—the blue glow of the planet against the blackness of space and, at the Earth's edge, the thin white rim of the atmosphere. This panorama of the Earth was grander than his eyes could encompass, more magnificent than he could have dreamed. This was not a figment of his imagination. He was now genuinely riding on The Daydream Special.

He took out his cell phone and made a video of the panorama and then took photos of the whole scene. He lost time marveling at the spectacle as Taylor lay beside him, his eyes squeezed shut. Bradley knew he would freak if he saw this, so after a period of astonished self-indulgence, he eased the black ball down, and they seemed to sink, their apparent motion taking them toward the Earth as though they were riding an elevator straight down. As they descended, Bradley could make out the coastline of California and then the San Gabriel Mountains range and the Cities of Pasadena and Los Angeles to the southwest. Far below, he saw the Angeles Forest, but directly down, the view was masked by a brown cloud. He couldn't figure out what that was until they seemed to pass through it, and then he recognized it as a particulate cloud, thin as smoke. It obscured the views outside until they sank beneath it and floated down beside a diffuse column of brown smoke dissipating in the wind. Farther below—if they were flying, this would be the view from about a thousand feet—he saw flashing lights along the roads in the forest. Most flashed in place, but some lights circled a black area in the woods directly beneath them. As they continued to descend, he recognized the moving lights as helicopters and saw that the black spot was a crater easily twice the size of the Rose Bowl, evidently the source of the brown particulate cloud. Bradley eased the black ball back into neutral, and their apparent motion stopped.

"What's going on?" said Taylor, who clambered beside Bradley's chair. Now that they weren't so high, Axel's stomach had cooled from boiling to a slow simmer. Both boys stared straight down, puzzled by the flashing lights and movement around the crater.

"I don't have a clue," Bradley said, finally. "It looks like a bomb exploded."

"Where are we?"

"We seem to be about three hundred feet above the Angeles Forest where the hill and the cave used to be. I can see parts of the trail we hiked up."

"So where's the hill?"

Bradley shrugged. "I think we're looking at what's left of it."

"You said this wasn't real, right?"

Bradley nodded. "It's a simulator. Like a 3D video game but much cooler. This is way better than *Star Citizen*."

"So we're seeing what would happen if the hill exploded?"

"I guess."

"Why weren't we blown up with it?"

"Because it's a simulation."

"Sure, sure," Taylor said. "Why don't you turn off the simulation? Get back to reality."

"I don't know how to do that."

"Told you not to screw around, man," Taylor said, urgency rising in his voice.

Bradley reached for the black softball controller and eased it down. "Let's see what happens when we get lower," he said. They watched as the crater expanded, the people around it better defined. It looked like a scene from a disaster film—the blackened soil and trees at ground zero, smoke curling upward from a dozen hot spots, trees blown outward from the impact zone. While people in white hazard suits and blue booties collected samples in plastic bags, uniformed men with assault rifles stood guard, and dozens of other official-looking people took pictures or talked on cell phones. None paid any attention to the boys. It was as if they weren't there. Then Bradley spotted an Air Force helicopter flying toward the crater at their altitude. He reached for the softball controller and quickly raised it a few degrees. Instantly, they appeared to be several hundred feet higher, and two seconds later, the helicopter passed beneath them.

"Why'd you do that?" Taylor asked.

"The other possibility is that we're flying, and that chopper would have crashed into us."

"You said this isn't real, dude. We can't be flying."

"I know. We didn't move. When you accelerate, you feel pressure on your body on the opposite side of the direction you're moving, right?" Taylor looked blankly at him. "When you accelerate in your truck, your body is pushed back against the seat. Right? That's called a G force. Did you feel anything after that flash of light? Any movement?"

Taylor shook his head.

"Neither did I, just a quick shake or something, and it looked like we went up about twenty miles in a split second. No way that could have happened. We didn't move. Plus, nobody around it saw us when we were hovering over the crater. Or heard us. So it's like we're here but not here."

"So we're like, what, stuck in a video game or something?"

Bradley replied, "Like Jumanji?" He threw up his hands. "I don't know. I think this place is a simulator, like I said. Or heck, maybe we are in an alternate universe. We know we're still inside the hill but can also see the world outside. Maybe one reality is mapped onto another, and we see both simultaneously."

"That's crazy weird, Einstein. You know that?"

Bradley nodded, glancing at his watch. It was 5:17. He looked at the activity around the black crater. "Think you could find your truck from up here?"

"Sure. Can you find the road we drove in on?"

"A simulation wouldn't know about your truck. They couldn't have programmed that into it," Bradley said, grasping the softball controller. "I've got you now," he whispered to the controller. "I know how you work." He gently twisted the ball clockwise and moved it to the right. Their view shifted in that direction, and they appeared to be moving southwest over the forest toward Pasadena. Taylor knelt on the floor and followed the trail. He lost it in densely forested areas but knew about where it was. Half a minute later, they came to a road, and Taylor directed Bradley to follow a dirt road northwest.

"There," Taylor said, pointing to a clump of trees just off the road. "Pretty sure."

Bradley eased the ball controller down, and they sank slowly over the road until they could see below the canopy. There was the muted silver gleam of the front bumper of Taylor's truck, which now lay in shadow.

Bradley gasped when he saw it. His pulse quickened, and the air caught in his throat. "This isn't a simulation," he said quietly. This realization took his breath like he'd been punched in the stomach.

"You all right, dude?" Taylor said.

Bradley gazed at the control panel and the spider on the seat beside him, his eyes as wide as his astonishment. "We're in a ship," he said in a voice pregnant with wonder. "We're hovering in some ship. It must have been buried in the hillside. We flew up like a rocket when I jerked up on the softball. I don't know why we're not dead. We caused that crater, Axel."

Axel's heart sank into his socks. "Holy shit."

"All those police. The Air Force," Bradley said, now more in shock than wonder.

Axel rolled his eyes and murmured. "What a shitstorm this is. The cops'll be all over us. Holy shit."

"I think they're trying to figure out what happened."

"Me, too, dude. What the hell do we do now?"

Bradley sat back in his chair, his eyes wide.

"Dude?" Axel said. His anxiety rose the longer Bradley was silent. "What do we do now?"

"Why didn't they react when we hovered over the crater?" Bradley wondered. "If this is real, they would have seen us. Maybe we are in an alternate universe but can still see back into our old universe? Maybe that chopper would have flown right through us like somebody walking through a ghost."

"Adamsson, you're givin' me a migraine. Can we get the hell out of here?"

Bradley nodded. "We need to find someplace to touch down, someplace where this ship, whatever it is, won't be found." Bradley raised the softball controller, and they floated up over the trees. "Can't be too far from your truck," Bradley murmured, and one ridge over, he spotted a deep tree-lined hollow with a large clearing in the bottom surrounded by tall pines. He brought the ship down until the brush far below looked flattened. Trees surrounded them, and those on the steep hillside provided some cover overhead. When they stopped, Bradley put the spider back on his gloved hand and touched the control panel. Instantly, the holograms disappeared, the view outside vanished, and they were back in the blue-walled control room.

They grabbed their backpacks and hustled past the T-junction toward the door they'd entered from the hillside. As Bradley suspected, the blue corridor was now spotless, with all the dirt and grass having disappeared. The cleaning crew in this place did excellent work. He raised the spider and touched the inside wall where the door should have been, but nothing happened.

"Whatsa matter?" Axel cried.

Bradley shook his head. "It's not opening." He touched the wall again, but nada.

"Shit!" Axel yelled. "You kiddin' me?"

"Don't panic," Bradley said. "There has to be a way out." He tried pushing the black button on the spider's back, and they heard the humming again—this time from behind them. Bradley turned and saw a line of dim white lights on the floor at the T-junction. "Come on," he said, quickly returning to the junction. There, they saw a white glow on the floor leading to the downward tube, which also glowed soft white. Peering into the tube, the boys saw the white glow extending down the tubes through another ten or more levels.

"It's like path lighting," Bradley said. "I think it's showing us the way out." He stepped onto the space above the tube and pointed his toes downward. Instantly, he descended. As Axel followed, Bradley kept his toes angled downward and passed through twelve more decks to a point where no more open tubes were on the floor. There, the white glow guided them to a ramp, which led to a lower curved wall, and when Bradley touched it with the spider, the hatch opened, revealing a small stream lined with bushes, trees, and baseball-sized rocks. Axel brushed past Bradley and lunged out, never so happy to be back in the forest.

Bradley stepped out behind him and turned to close the doorway with the spider. What he saw was so startling he tumbled backward into Axel, and they both collapsed into the stream, Axel headfirst and landing on his stomach in six inches of water.

"Son of a bitch!" he screamed.

He pushed up, ready to knock Bradley on his ass but gasped and lost his footing, falling backward into the water when he saw what Bradley had seen: The hatch into the blue corridor of the ship stood open in space with nothing around it. It was a doorway in mid-air. On either side were trees and, above, the open sky, but no ship.

"What the fu—?" Axel managed, his heart pounding like a sinking ship's bilge pump.

Bradley sat in the cold water, all the wonderment drained out of him, as though he'd reached his amazement quota for the day and had no more capacity for surprise. After a minute to allow his heart rate to return to normal, he lifted the spider, and touched the space left of the blue opening. The hatch closed, leaving a seam in midair that vanished a second later and left nothing before him but the forest and the deep blue sky. Bradley reached forward with his left hand and felt the solid but invisible exterior of the ship. Then he touched it with the spider, and the hatch opened. He touched it again, and the hatch closed.

He turned to Axel, "The ship is invisible. That's why no one in the crater saw us. That helicopter would have crashed into us if we hadn't flown above it."

Axel's mouth hung open, his eyes searching for anything in front of him that made sense. "How can it be invisible?" he yelped.

Bradley threw up his arms in resignation, muted by the phenomenon before him. Finally, he said, "I don't know. Maybe it bends light waves around it? Maybe it videos what's behind it and projects that on the opposite side? I don't know. Some universities are working on invisibility, but this"—he pointed at the space where the ship was—"is thousands of years more advanced than anything on Earth."

"Dude, this is serious shit, you know that, right? What we found is worth, like, millions."

Bradley nodded. "I don't know who built this or how it got here, but humans won't develop this technology for thousands of years, maybe tens of thousands."

"What're we gonna do with it?"

Bradley shook his head. "Turn it in. Sooner or later. We don't have a choice." His face blanched. His gut felt like cement. "All those people around the crater. Those emergency vehicles, the Air Force, the police. The government didn't know about this ship, Axel. But they do now."

Tell No One

Sunday. April 12. 8:12 pm.

Berl Jeffers barreled into his Houston office and loped to his barge-sized walnut desk at the far end of the room. The framed photos on his wall shook as he strode past. He dropped into his black leather office chair and swiveled around to face the two large plasma screens on his desk. The left showed a Wall Street ticker rolling through stock and commodity prices at the end of the last trading day; the right played a loop of the Dorothy Ware video of the meteorite strike east of Pasadena.

"Damnedest thing I've ever seen, Paul."

He was speaking to Paul Engles, who'd trailed him into the office carrying a slim black folder. At five foot seven, Engels was a foot shorter than Jeffers and a hundred forty pounds lighter. Where people couldn't escape Jeffers' commanding presence, Engels was easily overlooked, as quiet people often are. Still, he'd been Jeffers' indispensable aide for two decades—from the early days when Starland Pipe barely grossed a million dollars a month to the energy transmission conglomerate it grew into, making Jeffers a multi-billionaire and Engles a comfortable multi-millionaire. Engles had learned to humor Jeffers' transient passions, the way parents tolerate an ADHD child's shifting attention. But this obsession was different. Jeffers had long been fascinated by alien visitations and UFOs and became singularly focused when any shred of evidence surfaced that might prove them real. Engles knew this was no passing fancy. The old man was as fixated as he'd ever seen him.

Engles glanced over Jeffers' shoulder at the meteorite video. "I thought they could predict when those things would hit the Earth."

"Not always," Jeffers said, his eyes lasered in on the video. He ran a hand through his thinning gray hair and peered closer at the screen. "There's something squirrely about this."

Engles opened the folder he was carrying. "It looks fascinating, but we have a problem."

"I called my guy at NASA," Jeffers said, looking up at Paul. "He said the crater is round."

"They usually are."

"No, dammit, perfectly round. Symmetrical."

"As an engineer, I can tell you that's impossible."

Jeffers slammed the desk with one heavy paw. "You're not listening. It's a perfect circle, and it's filled with microscopic black needles. Pointing straight up."

Engles shook his head, heat rising in his neck. "Berl, everything under that meteorite would have been crushed and melted on impact." He laid the open folder on Jeffers' desk. "The Jonesboro East Pipeline developed a crack near Chatham Lake. The spill's grown and—"

"Did you hear me, Paul?"

"I heard you, Berl. I'm listening." He paused to take a deep breath. "How good is your source?"

"As good as it gets. I want you to get a copy of that video. Have our techies examine it." Jeffers stared at the screen. "I can't put my finger on it, but there's more to this story. Call the JPL. Call NASA. If they won't release a copy, track down the tourist who filmed it. I don't care what it costs. Just get it here as quickly as you can. Send a jet if they can't deliver it electronically."

"Fine," Engles said, whipping the binder closed, "and I'll deal with Jonesboro and the EPA. Don't worry about it." He left the room.

Jeffers wasn't sure what had happened in California, but he had a hunch that the official explanation was bullshit, and Jeffers' hunches were rarely wrong.

As Engles' heels echoed down the hallway outside his office, Jeffers absently glanced up. "What about Jonesboro?"

————————

Evaline Perez stepped outside the entrance to the emergency room and gazed across the plaza, amazed at the growing crowd of people. Like every other hospital and urgent care in LA County, Huntington Memorial had been overwhelmed since noon with people seeking emergency care, and more people kept coming, as far as she could see. They lined both sides of Drexel, spilling onto the walkways as the police tried to keep lanes open for ambulances. As a nursing assistant in the ER, she was part of the disaster team that had drilled for this kind of event, but this was unlike every training exercise they'd ever done. Whatever happened in the mountains had not only traumatized people in the city, it had caused thousands of injuries. Some of the people pouring into their makeshift triage in the plaza had wounds from flying glass. Others had broken bones and abrasions from falls or compression wounds from falling objects. Some had damaged eardrums. Others were experiencing heart irregularities or shortness of breath. Many had wild eyes, wide and unfocused. A few were keening for help, their arms upraised. Others sat in weary resignation, shoulders collapsed, holding wounded hands or wrists and avoiding eye contact until a nurse spoke to them.

Evaline hurried to Mariana Hidalgo, one of the ER nurses, with an armload of bandages. Then she escorted two patients whom Dr. Schmidt had triaged into the ER for further treatment. One had deep lacerations from glass on her arms and face. The other had been struck by a falling tree limb and had broken ribs. When she handed them off inside, she rechecked her cell phone, anxious because she hadn't heard from Axel and knew he'd gone hiking again today in the forest with Bradley Adamsson. She quickly sent him another text: "Where r u? u ok?" She'd barely pushed "send" when Mariana thrust her head through the door and screamed, "Evaline, for heaven's sake, turn off your phone! We need help out here."

Chastened, Evaline jammed the phone into her pocket and ran back to the chaos in the plaza. Even with help from the National Guard, they were understaffed for a disaster this large. She spent the next hour under Hidalgo's watchful eye checking and rechecking the vital signs of all the patients who'd been triaged and were waiting for space in the ER to open up. When she glanced down the street, she saw more people crowding into the plaza, lit eerily by streetlamps. It looked like a scene from one of the Living Dead horror films. She realized the disaster team would be there all night, which was okay. She'd never been busier at the hospital or felt more needed.

———————

The forest was darkening when the boys reached Axel's truck, individual trees still discernible at dusk but melding quickly into an indistinguishable mass of forest green. Finding the truck took hours longer than they expected. The San Gabriels were alive with first responders and authorities from a half-dozen agencies. While hiking through the forest, the boys were concealed among trees, but when they crossed roads or meadows, they had to take cover when helicopters flew their way, unforgiving searchlight cones sweeping the ground. Bradley knew the Air Force was searching for anomalies outside the crater or people who might have witnessed what happened—or been responsible for it. When they were close enough to the roads beneath the impact zone, Bradley thought it looked like Christmas without a jolly fat man in a red suit. Flashing red and blue lights lit the mountains and the trees in a kaleidoscopic frenzy. Axel eased down the dirt road with his lights off, but when they reached the pavement, he switched them on and turned toward Pasadena. They hadn't driven a quarter mile before a police roadblock stopped them.

An officer blinded them with his Maglite as he walked toward Axel's truck. Behind the glare, they could only see the silhouette of his Smokey hat and the gray of his eyes. Axel rolled down his window. The air was dense with smoke.

"License and registration," the officer demanded.

Axel dug his license out of his wallet and his registration from the glove compartment. Bradley's backpack was tucked beneath his knees. He hoped the officer wouldn't notice it.

"What are you boys doing up here?" he asked.

"We were hiking," Bradley said, louder than he'd intended.

Axel shot him a look before turning back to the cop. "Just hiking," he said. "No big deal."

"Where?"

Axel put his hand out to keep Bradley silent. "About five miles east."

"You see or hear anything unusual?"

"No," Axel said. Then turning to Bradley: "We didn't, did we?"

Bradley sat still for a second, then shook his head.

"See anyone else out there?"

"No one," Axel replied.

The officer stared at him for a moment. "When did you start hiking?"

"Early this morning," Bradley said, and Axel shot him another look.

The officer lowered his head and pointed his flashlight at Bradley, who squinted and turned his head away. "You didn't hear an explosion? Before noon?" the officer said.

"No," Axel quickly replied. "We didn't hear anything. Right, Adam—uh, Bradley?"

"We were exploring a cave," Bradley added, averting his eyes. "We felt some shaking but didn't hear anything. We must have been too far inside the cave."

The officer stared at them, turning the light from one to the other. The boys could hear a stream of police chatter on the radio attached to the officer's left shoulder. "Which cave?" he asked Axel. "I've never heard of any caves in this forest."

Axel turned to Bradley, trying to formulate a response as his lips fluttered.

"It was near Mt. Gleason," Bradley said calmly. "I don't think it has a name." The officer shone his light in Bradley's face. Bradley forced himself to maintain eye contact despite the glare. "Trees concealed the opening. The cave wasn't that deep. I'd guess a hundred yards. Too small to be named. It didn't look like anyone had ever been in it."

The officer studied them for another long moment before handing Axel's license and registration back. "Get out of here."

"What happened?" Bradley said.

"The forest is closed. You need to leave the area. Now."

———————

Claudine Adamsson sat at the edge of a dining room chair, her elbows on the table, her head heavy in her hands.

Celia approached the table. "Mom, what's the matter?" she asked. Devin came up beside her.

Claudine looked up and laid her hands on the table. "It's just been a rough couple of days."

"Yesterday was okay, wasn't it?" Celia said.

Claudine smiled at them. "Yes, it was, honey."

"I know you're worried about Bradley," Celia said. "Has he answered his texts?"

Claudine shook her head.

"He probably turned off his phone," Devin said. "Or the battery's dead."

"Cell service has been spotty since this morning," Claudine said. "I'm sure he's been trying."

"He's okay, mom," Celia added. "Somebody would have called us. Uh, if they could, I mean."

Devin shifted from one foot to the other. "When's dad coming home?" he said.

Claudine shook her head. "I haven't heard from him. They called him in after—"

"I know. That explosion," Celia said brightly.

"Yeah, that was so cool," Devin said.

"Pretty scary at first," said Celia.

Devin shrugged like it was no big deal. Claudine recognized Devin's bravado for what it was: middle-child syndrome. He would never be as accomplished as his older brother or as pampered as his baby sister. He hurried home in a panic when the explosion happened and clung tightly to her, his eyes moist. Now he had to prove himself and couldn't admit he'd been frightened.

"Thanks for helping me clean up the glass," she said to them both. "And for sawing the plywood, Devin. You were really helpful."

"Sure, mom."

They could hear a profusion of sirens on the streets outside, some approaching, some receding, up and down Monterey Avenue, Claudine guessed. It rattled her nerves, and she looked anxiously at her two children.

"I was worried this morning when I couldn't find you two," she said, holding her arms out for them.

They came to her side, and she hugged them. "We were okay, mom," Celia said.

"Thank God," Claudine whispered.

"Do they know for sure what happened?" Devin asked.

Celia turned to him. "The TV said it was a meteor."

Devin backed out of his mother's arms and dropped onto another chair. "You believe everything you hear?" he said with an edge.

"No, you buttwipe."

"Celia! That's enough of that."

"You're the buttwipe," Devin said.

"I said enough!" Claudine yelled. "It's been a hard enough day without you two going at each other constantly."

They were blessedly silent for a moment. Then Celia said, "Mom, if you're so worried about him, why don't you go to the library?"

Devin said, "Nobody's supposed to go out. They said on TV."

Claudine patted Celia on the back of her head. "Only emergency vehicles, sweetie. The police asked everyone to keep the roads clear."

"I could ride my bike to the library," Devin offered.

"No," Claudine said. "I want you two here where you're safe."

"When's dad coming home?"

"Devin just asked me that, honey. I don't know. JPL called an all-hands emergency meeting. Your dad will be home soon, I'm sure. Meanwhile, why don't you fix yourselves something to eat?"

"We already did, mom. Don't you remember?" Devin said.

She smiled at him. "I forgot. Then why don't you check the TV and see if they know anything more? I'll try to call Bradley again."

Celia and Devin glanced at each other and left, intuiting that their mom wanted to be alone, but they were tired of watching the news. They kept repeating the same old stories, Devin complained, which means it's not new, so why do they call it news?

Claudine turned on her cell phone but again had no service. After the event, ten million LA County residents and three million visitors tried to make calls simultaneously, overloading the systems. All afternoon, she'd had to wait for service, sometimes for half an hour. But she kept checking until service was available. She waited only five or six minutes to reach Bradley's phone this time, but he still didn't answer. She'd called him at least ten times since this morning and sent a half-dozen texts. She briefly considered riding Devin's bike to the library herself, but she couldn't leave her other two alone. It was so unlike Bradley not to let them know if something happened, and something huge had happened. He must know how worried she is, especially after Friday. She set her elbows back on the table and lay her head in her hands. After hearing the doctor's diagnosis, she couldn't imagine what he was going through. It was tearing her heart out. *He must still be in denial,* she decided. *Or he wouldn't be acting so strangely. I want to help him, but I don't know how.*

―――――――

Bradley and Axel talked feverishly on the road out of the forest like old friends, replaying what happened, snippets of fresh memories colliding as one image built upon another and careened in a free association of amazements—the blue corridor suspended in the air, the elevator tubes, as they were now calling them, the holographic controls, floating repositionable screens, the earth projected on the floor of the control room, that fantastic glowing blue orb, which twisted Axel's stomach though he wanted to see it again when he could keep his eyes open, the hillside splitting apart, smoke rising around the crater, the weirdness of standing on open space, the gaping crater in the forest where the ship had been hidden, the impossible fact that they'd flown, actually flown, in an alien craft—a giddy transparency of camaraderie that ended abruptly when they reached the unfamiliar landscape of home. They barely recognized Pasadena. At first, the streets were mostly empty, just a man struggling with a yelping dog. Some houses were dark and still as death. Others were ghostly, lit from within but shuttered. Those nearest the forest had many boarded windows or none, the ground beneath their window frames littered with diamonds glittering in the streetlights. Broken tree limbs lay in clusters of confusion on yards and sidewalks. A traffic light lay crumpled on the shattered pavement in an intersection they knew well but didn't recognize. Power lines were down in one dark neighborhood, and a breach in the line shot fire like sparklers on the Fourth of July. It was a civil disorder, so unlike the city they knew, they might have wandered into a strange land.

Cars were strewn in a riot of wrong angles on the streets, windshields, hoods, and roofs dusted with a delicate brown glaze, their drivers having abandoned the wrecks when no tow trucks were available. Then they witnessed an apocalyptic scene on Monterey Road—crowds on the sidewalks in front of closed stores, crowds bulging onto the road at intersections, a disorder of pulsing lights and sirens from police cars, ambulances lying in wait or rushing through the speckled night, revolving lights proclaiming their urgency, a lone fire truck, its hoses like fat tentacles spraying the dancing flames consuming a convenience store. Deeper into the chaos, they saw soldiers in camouflage directing traffic, though with so few vehicles on the road, it was more a gesture than a necessity. More National Guard troops were staging in the parking lot at the high school, where Bradley had parked his car. They gave the boys a cursory glance as Axel drove Bradley to his Prius. When Bradley climbed out of the truck, he held the door open momentarily, and they stared at each other in sober silence. Then Axel muttered the most profound thought in his head at that moment: "Holy shit."

"Tell no one," Bradley reminded him.

Axel nodded. "Tell no one."

"And don't post anything," Bradley warned. "No texts. No Tik Tok. Nothing. Okay?"

"Yeah," Axel replied. "You think I want the cops to know about this?"

Bradley set his backpack in the passenger seat and tried to call home, but he had no service. It was past eight, and his parents would be frantic, but he was helpless to prevent that now. He lay back on the headrest and closed his eyes, wondering which excuse would sound most credible and hating the thought of lying to them again. Then, he reflected on his conversation with Axel as they escaped from the forest. Axel had grown bolder in their recollecting, Bradley more awestruck, visions of technological marvels streaming through his mind, a patchwork quilt of wondrous inventions. He looked through the photos on his phone and then at the video he shot when they were high above Earth. He thought that whoever built that craft must be tens of thousands of years more advanced than we are. Nothing on The Daydream Special could compare. He took the spider out of his backpack, handling it with reverence for its makers and gratitude that it had fallen into his hands. He knew he would have to relinquish it. A discovery of this magnitude belonged in Area 51 or someplace like it, where scientists from the Defense Department and universities could try to extract its secrets. Until then, he possessed the spider and its access to the ship almost as much as it possessed him.

———————

John Adamsson arrived home before his son. He rushed into the house and had time only for a shower, a change of clothes, and a bite to eat before returning to work. While he was showering, Bradley parked at the curb and walked inside. His mother was too relieved to be angry at him until she crushed him to her chest and held him tight. When she released him, a scowl formed on her face. Bradley preempted her by saying he'd been at the library all day and hadn't heard the explosion because he was shut in an interior study room. When he was ready to leave, he tried calling but had no service. Then, he saw the National Guard arriving in the parking lot and stayed to watch what they were doing. He lost track of time, he said, and apologized for causing her concern. She didn't completely buy it but trusted that he wouldn't lie. Cell service had been erratic all afternoon. Besides, where else could he have been? The important thing was that he was safe. When John emerged from their bedroom, Bradley joined him at the kitchen table, and they ate ham and cheese sandwiches. Claudine sat at the table with a much-needed glass of pinot noir.

"The radio said it was a meteorite," Bradley said.

"Wasn't a meteorite," John said with a mouthful of food. "The whole incident's classified, son, but you'll know before long. It'll be on the news."

Claudine looked quizzically at him. "What was it then?"

"We don't know."

"What else could it have been?" Bradley said. He wondered how much they knew.

John shrugged, chewing a mouthful.

"You must have some idea," Claudine said.

John shook his head. "Whatever it was," he said, "it was powerful enough to feel like an earthquake and look like a nuclear attack."

Claudine turned to Bradley and said, "You didn't see it, but that mushroom cloud was terrifying."

Bradley had seen that cloud from above and floated down through it. He could imagine how it must have terrified people on the ground. He felt guilty about that but decided it wasn't his fault. He hadn't done it deliberately. He didn't know what would happen when he pulled up on the softball controller. But his rationalization didn't absolve him of the guilt he felt or soothe his conscience. He remembered the burning convenience store they passed on the drive back, the ambulances, the broken glass, and abandoned cars. He felt immobile, prone at the bottom of a steep hill with the crushing weight of responsibility gaining momentum as it rolled toward him.

"What's JPL doing?" he asked his father.

"I'm on a task force investigating it. They put my program on hold until we figure this out. Homeland Security's involved now, too. It's getting complicated. They think it could be a threat to national security."

"With our government these days, what isn't?" Claudine said. "I shouldn't get started on that."

"No, you shouldn't," John said, taking another bite of his sandwich.

"You've been going since this morning," Claudine told him. "You can't work all night. You have to sleep sometime."

John nodded. "They're setting up cots in a conference room. But I'm not going back to JPL tonight. I'm headed to the LIGO office at Cal Tech."

"Why?" Bradley asked.

"This may be classified. I'm not sure. So, lips sealed, okay?"

Bradley nodded.

"They detected unusual gravity waves near Earth simultaneous with the explosion. The timing could be a coincidence," John said between bites. "Or it could be an instrument problem. Or it could be a clue." He caught Claudine's eye and then said to Bradley. "How are you doing?"

Bradley didn't respond for a moment, distracted by what his father just said. Then he told them he was good, which caused both parents to raise their eyebrows, but John had to leave, and Claudine was too exhausted to deal with it tonight. It had been an awful day, and she knew it would worsen.

Before he walked upstairs to his room, Bradley heard on television that schools in Pasadena and South Pasadena were canceled tomorrow. He tucked his backpack under his bed and lay in the dark, thinking about what his father told him. He'd been puzzled about how the ship flew twenty miles straight up in seconds without them feeling movement or being crushed by G forces—and how it could have left gravity waves in its wake. One possibility occurred as he lay in bed, and it took his breath. The implications were staggering.

Clarke's Third Law

Monday. April 13. 10:15 am.

The three friends sat at a table under a brown canvas umbrella in the plaza at The Paseo. A half-dozen uniformed cops stood around drinking coffee, waiting for relief after guarding the shopping center most of the night. A few early shoppers braved the plaza, but workers were still boarding windows and sweeping up broken glass, and people had to circumnavigate clean-up sites to reach the few open stores. Eliot Stankus and Kevin Truman were absently playing Fortnite on their phones but weren't really into it. They were just chilling. Kevin picked at his cheeseburger, lifting it to his nose and sniffing it. With his perfectly round face and mop of black hair over his ears and forehead, he looked like a roly-poly Pokémon figure wearing a white shirt and a black jacket.

Eliot looked up from his phone. "You going to eat that or inhale it?" He wore a faded Star Trek t-shirt and jeans. He sat backward in his chair and cleaned his braces with a toothpick. It was a cool California morning in the shade, but the sun was already baking the buildings across the plaza, where slanted sunlight turned the walls luminescent beige.

"I hate mustard," Kevin said. "I told them no mustard."

Bradley absently knocked the curled knuckles of his right hand on the tabletop while he glanced at the workers sweeping up broken glass, but he heard Kevin complaining. "Take it back," he said, looking at Kevin. "If you didn't get what you ordered, don't eat it."

"Too much trouble," Kevin said.

"Then stop complaining, nitwit," Eliot said.

Kevin flipped him the bird and took a huge bite of his cheeseburger, grimacing as he chewed, a glob of mustard hanging from his lower lip.

They'd vibed at The Paseo for an hour. With school canceled, it was like a holiday, and soon, more furloughed kids sauntered into the plaza, teens and tweens in festive moods, jazzed by yesterday's excitement but more jazzed by having no school today.

"So, what's with you?" Eliot asked Bradley. "You look like you lost your bestie, and I know that's not true because"—he held out his arms and pointed at himself—"here I am."

"Here we are," Kevin said, fake punching Eliot in the shoulder.

"Oh, right!" Eliot said, like he'd forgotten Kevin was there. "Here we are."

Bradley shrugged. Before leaving home this morning, he listened to the news. The governor announced that the meteorite caused more than forty million dollars of damage, and he was applying for federal disaster assistance for LA County. Bradley needed to spend time with his pals from the Geek Squad this morning, but he felt like a biblical load of crap had been heaped on his shoulders. He was conflicted between the excitement of finding the ship, guilt that he couldn't tell his friends about it, the throbbing pain in his side that couldn't be wished away, and worry over the tempest that would bury him when people learned he was responsible for millions of dollars in damage.

"Oh, crap. I got it," Eliot announced triumphantly. He pointed at Bradley. "You asked a girl out."

"What?" Bradley said, his eyes ballooning.

"What girl?" Kevin said with a mouthful of cheeseburger.

Eliot sprang up and clapped his hands in glee. "Brad asked a girl out! Holy shit. Call the LA Times. Call CNN." He cupped his hands like he was speaking into a megaphone and shouted into the plaza: "Breaking news!" People wheeled around, staring at Eliot, surprise fading to indifference as they concluded he was more an annoyance than a threat.

"I didn't ask anyone out," Bradley said.

"What girl?" said Kevin.

"Guys, if I asked any girl out, she'd say no."

Eliot plopped back down. "Dude, the most frequent word I hear from girls is no. Girls see me in the hallway; I don't even have to open my mouth; they yell, 'No.' They take one look"—he pointed at himself again— "and scream."

Kevin said, "Have you looked at yourself in a mirror lately?"

Eliot smiled contentedly. "Once a mirror sees this handsome face, it's never satisfied seeing anyone else."

"You weren't looking in a mirror," Kevin said. "That was a poster of Justin Bieber."

Eliot feigned confusion. "Must have walked into my sister's room by mistake." He regarded Kevin like the wizened sensei in *The Karate Kid*, another Geek Squad favorite movie. "Grasshopper, if you aren't proud of your imperfections, no one else will be."

"In that case," Kevin said, "I'm definitely Top Geek." He pointed at himself. "No one can beat this."

"Guys," Bradley interjected, "I haven't asked any girls out. Who would go out with me?"

"Remember that dorky girl in seventh grade?" Eliot said. "The homely one with buck teeth and Coke bottle glasses?"

Bradley looked askance at him. "She was this year's homecoming queen, fool."

Eliot feigned surprise. "So that's what happened to her."

Kevin glanced around the plaza at the other teenagers milling about, most with their heads buried in their phones. He shook his head in disgust, then wiped the mustard off his lip with one finger and stared at the finger before licking off the mustard. 'You ever feel like you're in a parallel universe?"

Bradley nodded thoughtfully. "Recently," he said.

"I mean, I know we don't belong, but I don't even recognize these people," Kevin continued.

Eliot studied Bradley. "Seriously, dude, what's up?"

"Nothing, but I have a favor to ask."

"You want me to take some hottie off your hands?"

Bradley smiled. "I want you to cover for me."

"Wassup? You're rippin' off a bank and I'm your alibi?"

Bradley shook his head. "I'm going to tell my parents I'm spending the night at your house."

Eliot was confused. "What are you really doing?"

"I can't say."

"Okay-y-y-y," Eliot said, giving Kevin a *now-we're-getting-somewhere* look. He rubbed his hands together. "Okay. This is really getting good." Then he said to Bradley: "Who's the girl?"

"There's no girl."

"Now you're lying, dude. You can't keep your friends in the dark."

"Not lying. I need to be somewhere else."

Eliot gave Bradley an astonished look. "You're hooking up!"

"What girl?" Kevin said.

"Will you just cover for me?" Bradley asked Eliot.

"Sure, sure, but afterward, we want details. Right, Moe?"

"I'd rather have a video," Kevin replied.

"I'd rather shoot the video," said Eliot.

"Jeez, you guys," Bradley said. "I need one more favor, El."

"I don't have any condoms."

"I have some water balloons," Kevin offered.

Bradley laughed. "I want to borrow your dirt bike."

Kevin looked quizzically at Bradley. "You're hooking up with a girl on Stinky's dirt bike?"

Just then, two cute high school girls walked past them, each absorbed in her cell phone, and Eliot cried out: "I heard that."

The girls pivoted and glared at him. "We didn't say anything," the blonde girl said.

"You said, 'No.' I heard it," Eliot said, pointing one finger in the air as if to make a point.

The blonde's mouth gaped in disbelief. "Loser," she spat as the two girls walked away.

"Nailed it," Eliot yelled after them.

———————

Bradley's mother stood with her arms crossed, looking down at her husband, who sat at their dining room table rubbing his eyes, a steaming mug of coffee in front of him. "Bradley called," she said. "He's spending the night at Eliot's house."

John glanced at his watch. It was 11:30. Three hours of sleep this morning wasn't enough, and he had to leave in a few minutes. "I imagine he wants to spend time with his friends." The coffee nearly burned his tongue but jolted him back to consciousness.

"I can't worry about him by myself." She slid a sharp pencil over one ear and dropped into the chair beside him.

"When this crisis is past," he said, "I'll be here."

"It's tax season. I'm buried to my ears in client returns, and now all this," she exclaimed, pointing to the boarded-up windows in their living room. Fat stacks of manila envelopes lay at the other end of the table, along with her desk calculator and laptop.

"When will they replace the windows?" John said.

"I don't know. Next week maybe. Every dealer in the county is out of glass. I checked."

John nodded. "Have you talked to Bradley about the diagnosis?"

She shook her head.

He glanced at his watch again. "I have to go."

"Are you familiar with Kübler-Ross's five stages of grief?"

Recalling something from a college psych class twenty years ago required more cognitive effort than he could muster. He shook his head but said, "I vaguely remember something about it from school."

"I read up on it this morning," Claudine said. "Denial and isolation. That's stage one. Does that sound familiar? He went hiking on Saturday. Hiking? He never goes hiking. All day yesterday, he was at the library. This morning, out with his friends. Tonight, at Eliot's?"

John took another sip of coffee and stood. "He has to deal with this in whatever way works for him."

Blood rose in Claudine's cheeks. "Now *that's* denial," she said.

"This is not the time, Claudine."

"When is the time? You're working day and night. When will you have time to deal with . . . the worst crisis in our lives?"

He sighed. "As soon as we figure this thing out."

She glowered at him.

"It wasn't a meteorite. Everyone knows that. I heard it on the radio while driving home. Something blasted off from the surface, and we still don't know what it was."

"Stage two is anger. I'm there now."

"We need a second opinion," he said. His head ached. He rubbed his eyes again, trying to will it away.

"Already scheduled," she said. "I called your classmate from MIT. Doctor what's his name."

"Gardner Mattheakis. Okay, great. Before we panic, let's see what Gardner has to say."

"I want Bradley to see a grief counselor."

John turned away so she wouldn't catch him rolling his eyes.

"I've made that appointment, too. Friday at three o'clock. I want you there."

He looked wearily at her, expecting to see the anger on her face that he heard in her voice, but her drawn eyes and pallid face were a mask of fear. He knew he could not argue the point without upsetting her more. "I'll be there," he said, taking his coffee cup to the kitchen and rinsing it in the sink. "Meanwhile, I know you have work to do, and I have to get back to the lab. I'm not going to suggest you calm down. I know better than that."

"Very wise," she said.

"And I know you think I'm in denial, too, but I believe Bradley will be okay. I don't know why I feel that way, but I do."

She stared at him, softening a little. "Go to work," she mumbled.

———————

John felt awake and functional when he arrived at JPL, but he grabbed another coffee before going to the conference room where the Angeles Event Task Force was meeting. General Stephanie Vaughan sat at the head of the table in her crisp Air Force blues, six rows of ribbons on the left breast of her jacket. As Commander of Air Force Space Command, she was leading the AETF. She introduced John to Nick Rabin, FBI Special Agent-in-Charge of the Los Angeles office, and Special Agent Spazina Gonzalves, who'd flown in from San Francisco. Michael Fairchild, the NASA Administrator, and Ross Lefaye, JPL's Deputy Director, sat opposite John. Next to Lefaye was Krystal Forsythe, Acting Secretary of Homeland Security. A dozen other scientists and agents from Homeland Security crowded into the room, some standing because there weren't enough chairs. Dr. Donal Logan summarized for the group what JPL knew so far. It wasn't much.

"You don't know what happened to it after it reached a hundred thousand feet?" Rabin said. He had a bullet-shaped head, close-cropped brown hair, and small, laser-focused eyes. He gazed around the table incredulously. "How do you lose something that did that much damage? That's like losing an aircraft carrier in a pond."

"We think it continued into space," Logan said.

"Are we talking UFOs?" Rabin asked. "You people can't do better than that?"

"Nick, it's all over the media now," Krystal Forsythe said. "UFO fanatics are coming out of the woodwork saying an alien invasion is imminent. Caravans of those saucer heads are coming our way. If we can't develop a better explanation, we'll lose control of the narrative."

John nearly crushed his Styrofoam coffee cup. "We don't care about the narrative. We only care about the science."

"How convenient for you," Forsythe responded.

Exasperated, John spread his arms, palms out. "I'm sorry we don't have a better story for you, but we've never seen anything like this. We think it might have been a ship, possibly an alien ship since no one on Earth that we're aware of can build something that flew that fast, but we've found no trace of it since its initial ascent."

"Technically, it is an unidentified flying object," Lefaye said. Dealing with government officials was part of his job, but this meeting was a distraction from the real work they should be doing, and his mood was evident in his tone.

"What about those black needles in the crater?" General Vaughan said.

Donal Logan said, "We can't explain that."

"The gravity waves?" Vaughan said.

Logan shook his head. "We don't know if they're connected to the event. The strange readings at LIGO could have been a systemic instrument or software failure."

General Vaughan shot a look at John, who said, "Trust me. We're doing all we can to make sense of what we observed in the Ware video and what we discovered at the crater."

"You're not the only ones interested in this ship if that's what it was," Forsythe said. She smoothed her smart gray suit jacket as though she were going before the cameras and nodded toward Agent Gonzalves.

Spazina Gonzalves had a long, oval face, thick red lips, and brown hair that flowed over a tan jacket. "We're tracking a Russian agent who boarded a flight at SFO late yesterday and checked into a Best Western in Pasadena." She passed a stack of photographs around the table. The man in the photo had a bald, watermelon-sized head with a V-shaped indentation in the middle of his forehead. He looked like a 300-pound professional wrestler.

"This is Gorelov Roman Nikitovich," she said. "Known as Roma. Supposedly, a cultural attaché in the Russian consulate in San Francisco. Actually, an assassin. Until last year, he operated mainly in Eastern Europe. He had dinner last night with another Russian, Franko Pavlovich, who flew overnight from London on a false passport. Pavlovich is a colonel in the Russian Air Force who's been working on their Burevestnik nuclear-powered cruise missile program. We don't know why he and Nikitovich are here, but a good guess? It's not Disneyland."

Rabin said, "The Chinese are interested, too. Two of their agents—Wen Kang and Meng Shuren—will land at LAX from Beijing later today. Both have diplomatic passports and have served in the Chinese embassy in D.C. There may be others, but these two are the ones we know about."

"We've added more security at the crater and here at JPL," Forsythe said.

"We noted the additional muscle," said Ross Lefaye.

"For everyone's benefit, Deputy Director," Forsythe said sharply. She glanced around the table. "Let me be clear. If this object did fly at Mach forty-four, every country in the world would want the technology. But it flew from American soil, from American public lands, no less. It belongs to us."

"Just an observation," John said, "but if it was an alien ship, the aliens might think they own it."

"Thank you, Madam Secretary," General Vaughan said, cutting off an unproductive squabble. "Let's return to the science for a moment. We may have a lead. Dr. Adamsson spent last night at the LIGO office at CalTech, and he learned something interesting. Dr. Adamsson?"

It took Bradley a few minutes to remember how to operate a dirt bike. Last fall, he watched Eliot trying to do wheelies in a parking lot and rode the bike a few times, although he wasn't brave enough to attempt wheelies on concrete. He had a gritty ride up the Angeles Crest Highway toward the forest. Ash and dirt, kicked up by the tires, sandblasted his face. The bike's suspension was stiff, tiring Bradley's arms, and the bike whined like a dentist's drill. Hitting potholes was like riding a jackhammer, although Bradley had never operated a jackhammer. The bike jumped and jarred like he imagined a jackhammer would feel if you sat on one. Several miles before entering the forest, he stopped at Mancebo's Grocery, a mom-and-pop operation that stayed afloat by selling fresh local produce and gourmet imports unavailable in the larger grocery chains. From the parking lot, it looked like every window in the store had been broken. Workers were replacing makeshift plywood covers with glass. Mancebo's must have been among the first stores to call for new windows.

Inside, Emilio and Antonia Mancebo were cleaning up the mess on the floors and restocking shelves. Emilio was a ruddy-faced man in his late forties with a roundish nose and slick black hair. He wore a dirty apron over jeans and a red plaid shirt. Antonia was an attractive middle-aged woman with long brown hair and a welcoming smile. She glanced at Bradley as he came through the door and smiled before continuing to sweep the floor. Emilio asked why Bradley's face was so dirty.

Bradley glanced at himself in the reflection of a cold case of soft drinks and saw a raccoon looking back at him. Grit coated his face except for light circles around his eyes where his glasses were.

"Jeez, I didn't realize. I'm on a dirt bike."

"You want to wash up? We have a bathroom," Emilio said, pointing toward the rear of the store.

Bradley accepted the offer and dried his face with brown paper towels. When he returned to the store, Emilio asked what he needed.

"I'm spending the night in the forest. I need something to eat. And water."

"They reopened Highway Two?" Emilio said.

Bradley nodded. "All the way through."

"Should have been here yesterday, son, when the meteor struck."

"I was close by," Bradley said, irked at being called *son* but recognizing the benevolence in the man's voice. "They said on the news today they don't know what it was."

Emilio raised his eyebrows. "Yeah?" He waved his arms around the store. "We've been too busy."

"You need help cleaning up?"

"No, no," Emilio replied. "I'll tell you, it scared the hell out of us. I thought it was an earthquake. The building shook. Windows blew out. It sounded so loud . . . crazy. Everything flew off the shelves."

"I'm sorry," Bradley said.

Emilio shrugged. "Not your fault. We have insurance. We'll survive. What can I get for you?"

Bradley bought a tuna salad sandwich, a small bag of Doritos, an apple, and a large bottle of water. Emilio gave him a bag tied closed with a plastic handle, and Bradley secured it to the bike's handlebars with a ratty bungee cord before riding deeper into the forest.

Red and blue lights still flashed at the crater, and he used them as a waypoint to navigate back to the ship. In the waning light of the day, he saw the deep hollow where the ship should be. After parking the dirt bike, he descended into the hollow and retraced his and Axel's steps to the stream they fell into. He removed the spider from his backpack and attached it to his gloved hand. But instead of touching the prominent black symbol in the center of the spider, he experimented by pushing a red square beside it. Nothing happened. So, he touched a star-like symbol over his index finger—and the whole of the ship materialized before him, a giant, smooth, silver sphere the size of two football fields, the full moon reflecting on its shimmering surface like a beacon. It was an awesome sight, and he realized with horror that it would be visible to satellites, helicopters, or drones, so in a panic, he touched the star symbol again, and the ship vanished. Bradley collapsed beside the stream and sat briefly, refilling his starving lungs while his heart returned to his chest. Then, still shaking, he touched the black symbol, followed the hum to the ship, and touched it with the spider. When the portal opened, the walls inside brightened in that now-familiar blue hue. Before boarding, Bradley opened his cell phone and called his mom to tell her he was at Eliot's, and everything was fine.

The ship was spookier that night. Lonelier. He remembered sci-fi films where a solitary crew member aboard a ship in deep space was slowly driven mad by isolation. He wished Eliot and Kevin were with him and regretted the duplicity he felt in keeping this amazing discovery from them. The guilt haunted him as much as the empty ship, and he imagined himself alone on a derelict vessel somewhere in the dark Pacific, drifting on unseen currents and having no one to talk to but the fluttering sails and the vast, black, empty sea. When his melancholy passed, he walked to the vertical tube and launched himself to the upper decks, where he eventually found the control room.

He set down his backpack, the spider, and his food from Mancebo's, took a long drink of water, and explored more of the ship. On the decks below the control room were rooms whose function he didn't understand, but they appeared to be laboratories or work rooms with equipment of unknown purpose. Above the control room were individual quarters with soft platforms like beds and smaller adjoining rooms with a tube that dispensed water into a deep bowl, receptacles for bodily waste, and tall, circular enclosures that sprayed a fine mist from every direction when you stepped inside. He discovered its function by getting soaked, but when he stepped out of the enclosure, a shimmering red wave washed over him, and his clothing dried in seconds. The wall above the sink was empty, but when he touched it with his gloved hand, the surface where the glove made contact turned silver and reflective. Visible in it were his right eye and part of his cheek. He wiped that hand over a larger area, and it all became reflective. Grinning widely at the novelty, he traced a large rectangle on the wall with one gloved finger, and the entire rectangular area became a mirror.

The boy in the reflection had brown hair that just covered the tops of his ears. Some unruly hairs lay wild across his forehead, and Bradley combed them aside with the fingers of his left hand. His eyes were deep blue, like the color of the walls beside the mirror.

His nose was a smidge too large, he judged, and his lips very thin, but it was a pleasant face, he thought. As he gazed at the boy in the mirror, he saw the whole of his short life reflected in his face as though watching a video played blurry fast. Then the cellar door in his mind creaked open, and hepatocellular carcinoma clamored for freedom, trying to evoke horror with its snarling malice and ugly demeanor. But Bradley was sated with fascination and refused the bait. He was here now in this wondrous place and would not let himself dwell on the inevitable. After a few minutes, the mirror began to dissolve, its silvery luster suffused with undulating shades of azure and sapphire until only a uniformly blue wall remained.

"Arthur Clarke's third law," Bradley said aloud. "Any sufficiently advanced technology is indistinguishable from magic."

He returned to the control room and eased the ship up, rising through the gloom past the steep sides of the hollow, rising above the flashing lights around the crater and, beyond that, the hairnet of pinprick lights in Los Angeles County with its pulsing arterial roadways, past the moonlit glow of the countryside beyond the cities, where dim contours traced the geometry of the land, past glimmers of light where the full moon shone briefly on lakes and rivers, above the ebony deep of the ocean, until the ship rested above the globe of the Earth, dark and mysterious westward as daylight retreated, bright and promising eastward as dawn advanced. Bradley let go of the controller, trusting the ship to remain in stasis, floating above the stratosphere, safe and undetected, until he could gently guide it home.

He sat in the captain's chair, eating his sandwich and drinking water, curious about the holographic controls floating above the panel but unwilling to experiment after he'd already made the ship visible when he pressed the star symbol on the spider. Despite the overwhelming urge to play with this magnificent toy, he wouldn't make that mistake again. So, he gazed contentedly at the Earth below, a sight he never dreamed he'd see and had now seen twice. When he finished eating and grew restless, he explored more of the ship, taking pictures with his phone along the way, then returned to the crew quarters, and lay on the bed, wanting to rest his eyes for a minute or two. A rush of emotions flooded him—exhilaration, sadness, fear, loneliness, joy, guilt—a shepherd's pie of feelings he was too spent to untangle, and sleep dropped a cloak over him before he knew it had come to visit.

———————

When Bradley arrived at the ship and turned on his cell phone to call home, the ship captured the electromagnetic transmission. It accessed the species' collective knowledge stored in the planet's information and telecommunications systems networks. In 287.43 Earth minutes, its quantum computer matrix accessed, stored, and analyzed the entirety of information on the internet and in 47.5 million private networks. To accelerate the process, the ship created nearly a million virtual servers that mined IT systems worldwide: libraries, universities, banking and financial networks, power grids, hospitals, research laboratories, business and government databases, and secure military systems, including global force deployments and capabilities, defense plans, and nuclear launch codes. The ship learned human languages, analyzed the biological efficacy and structure of living entities on this planet, and assessed the state of human social, moral, scientific, and technological development.

It also assessed the intelligent biological entity (IBE) on board. After searching medical records, it analyzed his scholastic aptitude scores and academic performance to determine his intellectual capacity and potential. The IBE's curiosity, moral reasoning, maturity, and passion for discovery were significant, which the ship appraised from records in Earth's IT systems and observations of the IBE during the past three days, which the ship had recorded.

The IBE, Bradley Eugene Adamsson, was deemed suitable, so the ship initiated the transformation process.

Athena

Monday. April 13. 11:23 pm.

The light in Bradley's quarters dimmed when the ship sensed he'd fallen asleep. Within minutes, a black stain materialized on the wall beside his bed, metamorphosing into a fuzzy mass rippling like a crawling caterpillar, then dissolving into a swarm of medical nanobots, tens of thousands hovering over the sleeping boy before descending to his body, most gliding into his nose but some into his ears and mouth, others entering through his skin. Having mastered human physiology, mapped the human genome from medical texts and technologies like CRISPR, and studied numerous biological entities throughout the galaxy, the ship had an omniscient understanding of human anatomy and pathologies. Each medbot was programmed for a specific purpose, and as Bradley slept, they roamed his organs, cells, and vessels, evaluating his medical fitness. When their tasks were complete, 20,905 repair medbots remained in his brain and vital organs, bones, or blood vessels, while the diagnostic medbots assembled in his bladder, where they would be flushed from his system when he urinated and then recycled by the ship. If the subject were deemed unsuitable, the repair medbots would be flushed, too.

The ship sent a comprehensive explanation of human physiology and diseases through a quantum entanglement transmission to Hub LM'W52 followed by a diagnostic report, which read in part:

Planet B97'67212-i3 candidate IBE Bradley Eugene Adamsson, age = 18.63 Earth years (Eyears), reproductive function = male.

Findings:

Skeletal disorder, enchondromatosis, or Ollier Disease, with sixty-eight enchondromas varying in size, appearing principally in the left femur and tibia but present to lesser degrees in the joints of both hands and feet. Enchondromas are benign but caused anisomelia (limb length discrepancy) of 0.957 inches. Left leg shorter.

Stage 3 hepatocellular carcinoma, metastasizing to lymphatic and circulatory systems. Probable side effect of enchondromatosis. Estimated interval before death = 1.14-3.79 Eyears.

Inflammation of the esophagus with scarring of esophageal tissue.

Genetic abnormalities present in 632,489 of 37,201,368,901,744 cells in subject's body. Multifactorial genetic inheritance risk of hypertension = 45.93%. Single gene genetic inheritance risk of cystic fibrosis = 9.84%.

Damage to 1,270,342 alveoli cells in left lung and 1,894,858 in right lung. Probable cause (78.43%) = degradation of air quality in subject's environment.

Range of auditory receptivity = 19.7-18,986 Hertz.

Bilateral nonprogressive myopia. Left eye = 4.92 diopters. Right eye = 5.27 diopters.

Optic nerve impairment in both eyes with predisposition to glaucoma.

Premature loss of elasticity in the ascending aorta. Risk of death from ascending aorta aneurysm = 12.43%

Excess of nitrates in subject's digestive system. Bacterial types and count within normal ranges.

1,042 viruses or viral fragments present in subject's cells and blood.

Life expectancy prediction = 20.59 Eyears from birth if carcinoma untreated. If carcinoma treated = 62.49 Eyears. Probability of successful treatment = 9.67%.

Life expectancy with immediate repair and continuing physiological treatment > 500 Eyears.

Life expectancy with total artificial cell replacement and mitochondrial regeneration > 10,000 Eyears.

Candidate medically suitable.

In 2.47 Eseconds, Hub LM'W52 responded: "Proceed." Two minutes later, another swarm of reconstructive medbots materialized on the wall and entered Bradley's body. A third swarm of neurological medbots lay poised in the wall's membranes, awaiting the signal to proceed.

Roma Nikitovich had a squat head on a battle tank body as wide as a four-lane highway. Thick black hairs sprouted from his nose and vibrated when he breathed. He overpowered the spindly hotel chair he sat in, his giant cue ball head lolling as he dozed. Franko Pavlovich found him disgusting and couldn't understand why Moscow sent him from San Francisco. He added no value to their mission except intimidation or elimination. Franko was a scientist and wasn't convinced he was needed here, either. He was working on the Russian Skyfall project and was far more valuable in Nyonoksa than in Pasadena, but like a good soldier, he followed orders.

He had flown from Moscow to Los Angeles via London yesterday. He slept some on the airplanes but still felt ragged. As the brute slumped in his chair, Franko drank tepid coffee and hunched over his laptop, navigating the dark web for his secure connection to the Russian Main Intelligence Directorate website where an encoded classified message awaited him. The message included two images taken by a Russian spy satellite over the area east of Pasadena. In the first image was an oblong bright light glinting off the surface of a faint circular object. Franko knew from the light's pattern that it was a reflection of a three-dimensional surface. The analysts said the object was approximately 200 meters in diameter. It had appeared in the mountainous region of California's Angeles National Forest at the GPS coordinates listed in the message and disappeared six seconds later. The second image showed the crater formed when something in the forest exploded and flew into the atmosphere. The GRU analyst noted that the crater and faint object were approximately the same size. Franko had studied the Ware video during his flight from

London. If the flying object was a missile, it had flown faster than anything the Russians could build, including the Burevestnik cruise missile, so it warranted investigation. But Franko was a scientist and, therefore, skeptical by nature. The round object in the first image could not have been the missile. It was too large and had too much apparent mass to achieve that velocity without requiring an untenable amount of fuel. The physics just didn't work. Moreover, why had it appeared for six seconds and then vanished with no fire, smoke, or vapor trail? If it hadn't moved, had the Americans discovered a way to mask their technology from satellites? Or was that image an illusion created by the Americans to deceive their enemies?

Franko glanced at the desk clock on the end table beside his bed. It read 2:15. He decided to sleep until six and then investigate the object's fleeting appearance at the GPS coordinates in the message. He erased his browser history and closed his laptop. But as he walked to his bed, Roma stirred.

"You know where go?" Roma mumbled, a trail of spittle down his chin.

Franko nodded.

"We go now. First, El Monte."

Franko gave him a blank look.

"Safehouse in El Monte. Weapons there," Roma said.

Franko shook his head. "You have a car. You go to the safe house. I need sleep."

Roma's mouth turned down as he dabbed his chin with a wrinkled handkerchief. He stared at Franko with eyes so deep and dark they looked like smudges on his dull face. He grunted and said with a lopsided chuckle, "You give location GPS. Meet there when done beauty sleep."

Franko swallowed a sour glob of saliva, wishing he'd brushed his teeth when he arrived at the hotel and wrote down the GPS coordinates for Roma. The big man snagged his keys from the desk and lumbered outside to his rental car. Franko watched him go, thinking there were too many men like Nikitovich in the GRU, men with big hands and rancid hearts and purloined imaginations, men who should be more proficient in English if they were going to work in English-speaking countries. He mouthed a silent curse at the GRU's lax standards since detente. Even with Putin's renewed ruthlessness, flotsam like Nikitovich remained in the system. Franko brushed his teeth to vanquish the distaste he felt. Then he undressed and slid beneath the sheets, thinking of his son, Kuzma, who would turn twelve on Saturday. Franko wanted to be home by then.

By 02:23:15 hours Etime, the second wave of medbots had entered Bradley's body and initiated repairs. Hundreds were routed to his liver, where they destroyed the cancer cell colony growing there and located and eliminated the cancer cells that had metastasized to his lymphatic and circulatory systems. While the most imminent threat to his health and longevity was being mitigated, thousands of other medbots made genetic repairs and began eliminating the enchondromas in his bones. Lengthening his left femur and tibia could not be completed until the ship introduced minerals, principally calcium, to his body, but medbots encircled those bones and prepared for mineral injection. Hundreds more attached themselves to the arteries, veins, and nerves that would be lengthened, while another group designed to desensitize the nerves in his left leg so the IBE would not feel pain while limb lengthening occurred.

At 03:48:21 Etime, the third wave of medbots descended. Thousands entered his hands through the skin and began constructing circuits. Hundreds more entered his eyes, ears, and brain, traversing tissues and using blood flow through veins and capillaries to reach their destinations. Their work involved building new receptors and neural pathways and would require approximately 2.3 Edays to complete. The ship monitored their progress and, at 04:23:58 Etime sent a progress report to Hub LM'W52.

Bradley awoke an hour later with only dim awareness of his surroundings. Then he remembered the veil slipping over his eyes as he lay back on the bed last night. He wondered how long he slept. He felt euphoric this morning and enjoyed the sensation as he lay in the soothing darkness. Then he opened his eyes and gazed across the strange room. As he did, the room began to brighten as though it sensed his eyes opening. He swung his legs over the bed and sat up, and the room grew brighter still. As an experiment, Bradley lay back and closed his eyes. He counted slowly to thirty and then eased his eyes open, and the room, which had become dark again, began to brighten, growing ever brighter as he sat up, placed his feet on the floor, and stood up.

"Good morning, Bradley," a pleasant voice said.

He nearly tumbled back onto the bed at the shock of hearing a voice calling his name. Looking around apprehensively, he said, "Who is that?"

The voice replied, "I have no name in Earth languages. The previous crew called me 'O'spliciti'eloecti'ytepa'."

"What? I can't even pronounce that," Bradley said.

"I suggest you call me Athena."

He was alone, and the voice seemed to come from nowhere—and everywhere. He couldn't pinpoint the source and realized the ship was talking to him. He couldn't identify the voice as male or female, but it spoke in perfect, unaccented English as though it had grown up in Kansas. "Why should I call you Athena?" Bradley said.

"You wrote a term paper about Athena in tenth grade."

Bradley recalled that paper. "The Greek goddess of knowledge," he said.

"I read that term paper last night. It's on your laptop. Athena seemed an appropriate name to label what I am."

Alarm sliced through him. His laptop was at home on his desk, and he was sure he'd turned it off when he left home.

"You can read things on computers even if they're turned off?"

"I read the magnetic fields generated by your transistors. Your species uses a binary system for storing information. Such systems are common among intelligent species at this stage of your development."

Bradley felt like he was teetering on the needle-point peak of a ledge overlooking a vast chasm of incomprehensibility. His intelligence had been a point of pride in a life so otherwise constrained, but now he felt like he knew absolutely nothing.

"Athena? You're a goddess of knowledge?"

"Compared to the collective knowledge of humans, yes."

"What else have you read?"

"Everything," the ship replied.

"No, I mean—"

"I've read everything."

"—of mine. That's what I meant."

"I've read everything on Earth in every written language, everything that's ever been digitized, recorded, stored, or transmitted electronically."

"That's impossible," Bradley said.

The large blank wall opposite Bradley turned from blue to white. Then it showed an image of a Chinese opera, transitioning to Franklin Roosevelt speaking about a day of infamy, to the flaming crash of the Hindenburg, and a colorful ceremony on the Ganges River, to Bruce Jenner on the medal podium after winning the decathlon, to Lucille Ball grimacing as she shoved chocolates into her mouth, to a raging forest fire to a cereal commercial to a cooking class to Adolf Hitler ranting at a podium to a horse race to models on a runway—and so on for two minutes of one video slice after another while a smorgasbord of music—rock, classical, rap, big band, jazz, and oriental—added a soundtrack. Bradley whipped his head around, and the video images appeared on every wall and the floor and ceiling. It was a swirling cacophony of human history since the advent of radio and motion pictures, and it made the point.

"That's how I learned about your species," Athena said when the walls turned blue again and the music stopped. "Accessing digital images and reading quadrillions of digital documents."

Bradley stood in stunned silence for a long moment. Then he said, "I have a thousand questions."

"I have as many answers," Athena replied. "But first, your body is signaling that you need to urinate and are hungry."

Bradley used the lavatory in his quarters, then splashed water on his face and ran a hand through his hair. The ship directed him to the next deck up, and Bradley flew through the elevator tube to that level. Just outside the elevator tube was a door leading to a medium-sized room with dark blue walls and white cabinets. In front of him was a counter with two adjoining boxlike enclosures, each about three feet wide and two feet high. The sign etched into the wall beside the doorway read, "Galley." Bradley realized with a start that it was written in English.

"How did you do that?" he asked Athena.

As Bradley watched, the etching dissolved into a fluid mass that transmogrified into the word "Kitchen" as the mass solidified.

"Which label do you prefer?" Athena said.

"Galley," Bradley replied, and the etching dissolved and reformed with its original label. Bradley ran his fingers across the etching, and it felt as cool and solid as granite. "Are the other decks now labeled in English?"

"Yes. You can rename each level, area, and function as you wish."

Bradley felt as though he'd wandered into the temple of a grand wizard, not knowing whether to be inspired or terrified. "What are you?" he said—his burning question.

The ship responded by instructing him to place his apple in the source enclosure, the one to his left. He remembered leaving the apple in the control room, but now it sat on a white table inside the galley door. He wondered how it had gotten there and had the paranoid thought that mischievous creatures like Dobby, the house elf in Harry Potter, lived in the far reaches of this vessel, sneaking through the passageways intent on devilry. After setting the apple in the enclosure, he was instructed to press a black, diamond-shaped button on the left of the enclosure. When he complied, a wave of green light washed over the apple. Within seconds, another apple appeared in the product enclosure, the adjoining one to the right—an identical apple. The same apple, Athena told him, replicated from the apple in the source enclosure. Here, he could replicate any food at any temperature. If he placed the food on a plate or in a bowl, the plate or bowl would be replicated, too. The ship scanned food in the source enclosure, mapped its atomic structure, and replicated it precisely. It stored atomic maps of every food it had ever scanned, and those foods, including exotic dishes like O'lucticp'a'dstor'ic could be replicated from the ship's memory. Not all those foods, the ship warned, would be palatable to him. The cabinets above the replicator held plastic-type dishes, utensils, and sealable containers. He didn't see a sink or dishwasher and was told that all waste, including food scraps, dishes, and used utensils, should be dropped in a brown recycling bin at the end of the white counter. Everything he needed could be replicated instantly. *The kitchen of the future*, Bradley thought. No refrigerator, no microwave, no dishwasher, no pantry, no food preparation, no cooking, no cleaning, and no waste. Everything not consumed was recycled.

Bradley renamed the first deck he'd entered with Axel the "Bridge" and the control room the "Cockpit." After eating both apples and drinking a large container of water, which the ship had infused with soluble calcium and other minerals, he sat in the command chair and told Athena he wanted to see outside the ship again. Instantly, the room grew dark above, just a dusting of stars scattered throughout the night sky, the Milky Way like a sparkling sash drawn tight across the sky's belly. Below, the Earth rotated slowly, the sun's orb shining in the east, a swath of dawn spreading across the surface as sunrise advanced. To the west, the Moon glowed, its round, pockmarked face handsome in the black of space. Bradley murmured that he wished he had a telescope, and Athena responded by teaching him controls that would create a telescopic view of anything in any direction outside the ship. He positioned a joystick-type device on the holographic control panel, pushed an orange slider, and watched the Moon grow larger, finally spread across the breadth of the cockpit. The image was as sharp as any he'd ever seen. He repositioned the view with a delicate turn of the joystick and brought Mare Tranquillitatis into the center of his field of vision. Telescoping the view further, he located the site of the Apollo 11 moon landing and saw the *Eagle's* descent stage sitting in its dusty field and the American flag that Armstrong and Aldrin planted lying on its side, blown over by explosive gas from the *Eagle's* ascent stage as it returned the first men on the moon to their ferry back home.

"I wish the astronomers at Mount Wilson could see this," Bradley said. He glanced at his watch, surprised that it was nearly 8:00. He would be late for school in twenty minutes, and he was still piloting a spaceship miles above the Earth's surface. Taking hold of the control knob, he gently pushed it down, and the ship began descending. Then, as he oriented himself to the ship's position above the planet, he saw India below him, so he eased the controller to one side and began a transit across Asia and the Pacific. While the ship descended, he turned on his cell phone and discovered that he'd had no text messages from friends or voicemails from his parents since entering the ship last night.

"Athena, I'm not receiving messages on my cell phone."

"My shields prevent harmful radiation from reaching my interior, which blocks all electromagnetic waves." The ship explained that she continuously detects all parts of the electromagnetic spectrum and can selectively retransmit those to the cockpit and other parts of the ship, but incoming and outgoing microwave and radio signals are blocked unless she permits them.

"Can you retrieve my cell phone messages?"

"Of course," Athena responded, and instantly Bradley's cell phone began receiving messages. Among a dozen texts from last night and this morning was one from Axel, who said he'd worked all day yesterday at his father's garage but had gotten his dad's permission to take Tuesday evening off. He wanted to meet Bradley after school today and return to the ship.

Bradley felt a stitch of anxiety as he read Axel's message. He needed to return Eliot's dirt bike and get to class, offering a plausible excuse for being late, and he had to be home after school so his parents wouldn't be too curious about where he'd been. Meeting Axel at the ship would complicate everything, but Axel had co-discovered it and had the right to see it again before they turned it over to the Air Force or whichever government agency would take possession of it. He imagined the engineers who would examine the ship as a colony of ants crawling through the corridors, flying up and down the elevator tubes, measuring, probing, testing, dissecting, trying to extract the secrets of technology so advanced it might be unfathomable even to the best minds of the day. Before those ants arrived, Bradley wanted to spend more time with Athena. He had much more to learn, but he also had to get home. As he worried about what to do that afternoon, he spotted the west coast of America and navigated to the Los Angeles area by following the coastline.

He had no trouble locating the Angeles Forest and guiding the ship past the crater, still alive with flashing lights and people swarming the crater's rim, then to the hollow where they'd hidden the ship. Bradley eased the ship down and landed by the stream, but as he stood and was reattaching the spider to his gloved hand, his heart leaped when he saw movement on the hillside. He quickly magnified the image and watched a dark-haired man in black clothing making his way downhill. Bradley panned upwards to where the dirt bike should be and saw it parked in the brush where he left it, but another man, burly and dark, sat under a tree near the bike, and that man held a long, scoped rifle. Bradley panned back to the descending man, worried that if he kept coming, he would collide with the invisible ship. In a rush, Bradley reached for the control knob and slowly raised the ship about twenty feet. Then he watched with relief as the man walked beneath the ship and stood at the center of the hollow, gazing in circles as though lost and waiting to be found.

––––––––––

Colonel Franko Pavlovich had parked off the road about a quarter mile from Roma's car and walked back to it, where he discovered a faint trail leading through the brush toward the GPS coordinate location. He followed the trail for half an hour until he crested a ridge and found a yellow dirt bike parked beside the trail. Roma sat concealed beneath a tall conifer a dozen feet away, a pair of binoculars around his neck and a sniper rifle cradled on his lap. "Not nothing," Roma grunted as he peered around at Franko. "Is cold," he added. He wasn't dressed for the mountains in March, but Franko was still surprised that the cold affected Nikitovich. With those layers of blubber, he should have been immune.

"You haven't seen anything since you arrived?" Franko asked.

"Nyet," Roma said, shaking his head and raising the binoculars to scan the hollow.

Franko's eyes followed the sightline of Roma's binoculars across the hollow, among the dark green trees and yellowish-brown brush, through areas of light and shadow, the crisp air wafting as sunlight warmed the cool morning, inciting a breeze bearing pine and applewood scents. Wondering if this mission's sole outcome would be wasted time, Franko stepped off the ridge and hiked into the hollow. Broken branches revealed where something had climbed into or out of the hollow, but Franko saw no trace beyond that of anything unusual—certainly not evidence of a hypersonic rocket. Still, he resolved to be thorough and continued until he reached a small stream. The air shimmered before him as though a diaphanous curtain had been raised, flattened grasses and thin branches arcing upward, billowy and restless though the air this deep in the pit was still. Franko stood in the center of the hollow, inspecting it in every direction. Then he thrust one arm toward the sky, fingers outstretched. He had the sensation of touching something that was not quite there, his hands tingling in jittery anticipation like reaching for a Tesla coil, waiting for it to spark. He gazed into the blue void, his mind an empty vessel hungry to be filled, and suddenly felt that all of his yesterdays had just merged with all of his tomorrows.

Gravity Waves

Tuesday. April 14. 1:45 am.

The Angeles Event Task Force met for a recap early Tuesday morning in the newly established AETF Command Center in a secure workroom at the Jet Propulsion Laboratory. Coffee and donuts had been brought in, as well as a selection of sandwiches and bags of potato chips. Water and soft drinks were sunk into ice in two large coolers. The eleven core members of the task force were weary after a day and a half of frantic work since the incident, but pressure from Washington was mounting, and people slogged on as though they'd been running a marathon uphill and were within a mile or two of finishing. The room and the people in it were as threadbare and musty as an old shirt despite quick showers and clothing changes.

Lt. General Stephanie Vaughan sat at the head of the table, flanked by one-star Air Force General Robert Peters and Krystal Forsythe, Acting Director of Homeland Security. Beside Forsythe were the FBI's Nick Rabin and Spazina Gonzalves. Next to General Peters sat Michael Fairchild, head of NASA. Opposite them were Drs. John Adamsson, Ross Lefaye, Donal Logan, and Philip Zhong of JPL, Dr. Amanda Halbfinger, Director of LIGO, and Kevin Karchman, the LIGO technician who sounded the alarm when LIGO detected strong gravity waves in Earth's atmosphere. The FBI agents were briefing the team on the foreign agents they'd seen arriving in the area.

"We have eight agents babysitting the Russians at their hotel," Raban told the group, "and we put GPS trackers on both rental cars."

"Where are your agents?" Forsythe asked.

"Two in each of the rooms on either side of the Russians," Rabin said. "Four in cars ready to roll if they move."

"What about the Chinese?" said Forsythe.

Spazina Gonzalves answered. "They landed at LAX yesterday and took a taxi to a hotel in Burbank. So far, they haven't budged. Ordered room service last night. One of our agents delivered their meals. We're covering them with eight agents and GPS on their rental. They've placed no calls and had no visitors. We think they might be decoys, that the real agents are sight unseen."

"They could be communicating through the internet with other Chinese, but at this point, we haven't been able to hack their computers," Rabin added.

"Stay on it," Forsythe said, which caused the agents to give each other pained looks. Of course, they'd stay on it. That was their job.

"It would help if we knew what we were dealing with," Forsythe said pointedly to the scientists across the table.

"That would help us, too," Ross Lefaye responded. "The Russians or Chinese may know more than we do. Maybe you should ask them."

General Vaughan intervened. "We're all doing our best to figure this out, people. Let's stay focused. I've asked Bob Peters to join the task force. He's with the 432nd Wing at Creech Air Force Base in Nevada. General?"

"Thank you, General Vaughan." Peters was a rail-thin man with a balding pate and thick lips. He wore Air Force blues with five rows of ribbons and a pair of thin gold-rimmed glasses. "We've detached two MQ-9 Reaper RPAs—remotely piloted aircraft—from Creech to El Segundo, along with their operators. Pilots at Nellis in Las Vegas will surveil the Angeles Forest, covering approximately fifty square miles surrounding the crater."

"Will the drones be armed?" Forsythe said.

"Yes," General Peters responded. "Each will carry four Hellfire air-to-surface missiles. They can also be fitted with eight AIM-93 Stinger air-to-air missiles. We also have two squadrons of F-18s on alert at El Segundo. They can scramble and be on target within six minutes if needed."

"Why all the firepower, General? We're not at war, for God's sake. We're still trying to figure out what the hell happened Sunday," said Ross Lefaye.

"Contingency planning, Director," Peters said. "We're preparing for any eventuality."

"When will your drones be in the air?" Rabin asked.

"I expect them to be operational by 0800 hours this morning," Peters replied. "The first one will go wheels up then. Fully loaded, they have a flight duration of fourteen hours."

"Eight o'clock could be too late if the Russians move sooner," Rabin said.

"It's the fastest we could get these drones on location," Peters responded. "We needed authorization from the Pentagon. Once secured, we flew them from Nevada, along with the personnel to make them operational. Given the logistics involved, I'd say the mission was accomplished expeditiously."

"We appreciate that, General," Vaughan said.

"Who has the authorization to fire if we have a target?" Forsythe said.

"I do," said Vaughan.

Forsythe tapped her pen on a yellow legal pad. "This is a matter of homeland security, General Vaughan," she said. "That authority should rest with me."

"The drones are under Air Force jurisdiction," Vaughan replied, looking sharply at Forsythe. "I am leading this task force, so it's my call."

"I'll talk to the White House about that," Forsythe said.

"That's your prerogative, Madam Secretary," Vaughan said. "We're talking about using lethal force on American soil. Until I'm told differently, I am in charge and will determine when and if we use force against threats."

Krystal Forsythe crossed her arms and flicked her pen rapidly against one arm. She knew she didn't have to win the battle here and now. She had a direct line into the White House and was confident she could persuade the President to grant her the authority to do whatever was needed to protect the country. On second thought, this President might want to make that decision himself, but she had his ear and knew he didn't entirely trust the military. She thought she could influence him to make the right call.

At that moment, Rabin's cell phone rang. He listened for a few seconds, then glanced at his watch and told the group, "One of the Russians just left the hotel. Nikitovich. The assassin." He and Gonzalves picked up their briefcases and promptly left the room. After they left, everyone was silent for a long moment, all feeling greater urgency to figure this out before the situation spiraled out of control. For the scientists, it was more than uncertainty about the unknown object. It was the fear of having lethal weapons deployed and foreign agents active when they weren't even sure what happened on Sunday.

General Vaughan suggested a ten-minute break. After everyone got fresh coffee or water, she said, "Dr. Adamsson told us last night that they may have a way to track this UFO or whatever it is." She looked at John and nodded.

"We don't know where the object is now," John said, "but if it returns and leaves another gravity wave signature, we think we can track its location. I've asked Kevin Karchman from LIGO to join us. It was his idea. Kevin?"

Karch wasn't intimidated by this group. On the contrary, he felt like a garage band musician who'd become a rock star overnight. He beamed when John called on him and smiled like he'd just struck his opening power chord on stage. "What caught my attention," he told the group, "was a delay of 0.02 seconds between Hanford's detection of the signal and Louisiana's detecting it. So, I contacted VIRGO in Italy. It turns out they detected the signal 0.13 seconds after Hanford. That gave me the idea that we could triangulate its location by comparing how long it takes for each interferometer to detect the signal, the same way you can triangulate a radio transmission to locate its source."

"Have you detected any signals since Sunday morning?" General Vaughan asked.

"No," Karch answered. "Not like the ones we saw Sunday. We detected gravity waves yesterday, but the signal strength was much weaker. Initially, we thought it was a natural phenomenon."

"An event in deep space," explained Amanda Halbfinger, Director of LIGO.

"Right," said Karch. "But it was a sustained signal at a lower amplitude. We now think the object might have been moving at lower velocity."

"Did you determine its location?" General Vaughan said.

"No," Karch replied. "We've never used interferometers to triangulate an object. We'll need to write a program to integrate the three signals and produce a three-dimensional map of the Earth's surface showing the object's probable location when it stops moving or trajectory if it moves at steady velocity for a long enough period."

Halbfinger said, "We're working on that now, General. The programming is not difficult, but it takes time. Our programmers asked for a day or two to write and test the software."

"Tell them one day," General Vaughan said. "Put more people on it if you need to."

Halbfinger nodded, although LIGO didn't report to the U.S. Air Force, and she wasn't sure what authority General Vaughan had to dictate what LIGO did or did not do.

"We can provide support," Ross Lefaye told Halbfinger. She acknowledged his offer with a thin, annoyed smile.

"What about the black needles in the crater?" General Vaughan said.

"They're made of rock," Donal Logan said. "Rock that's been melted and extruded as though a glassblower drew the molecules out in long, thin streams that solidified. The same thing happened with the wood on the trees. We can't explain it."

"There is one big problem," said Phil Zhong. He was an older physicist of Asian descent with a round face and dark age spots in abundance on his gray skin. He'd been listening thoughtfully, his head bowed, eyes closed, but now spread his hands on the table and looked up. "Nothing we know of could create gravity waves in Earth's atmosphere."

"There is one possibility," said Donal Logan.

General Vaughan cocked her head at him and said, "What's that, Doctor?"

Logan glanced around the table as if reluctant to voice it aloud. "An Alcubierre-White drive."

"Impossible," Zhong snapped.

"What's an Alcubierre-White drive?" asked Vaughan.

"It's a theoretical drive that compresses space-time ahead of a spaceship and expands it behind the ship," said Logan. "Mexican physicist Miguel Alcubierre proposed it back in the nineties. Sonny White, a NASA propulsion expert, made the concept more practical. Instead of moving through space, you move space itself. In effect, you change the geometry of space and travel through a space-time bubble. If you could build such a ship, it could theoretically travel faster than the speed of light."

"A warp drive?" said Michael Fairchild, an amused look on his face. "Einstein proved that faster-than-light travel is not possible. Even if it were, no one has the technology to build such an engine."

"No one on Earth," Logan said.

"No one anywhere," Zhong said flatly. "What Alcubierre proposed requires exotic matter and negative energy, and they don't exist."

"I think we all agree, Phil," said John Adamsson, "but such a spaceship would probably generate gravity waves, and we don't have another explanation for what LIGO observed on Sunday."

Zhong shook his head, his jowls jiggling with certainty. "If what we observed in the forest was a ship, it was traveling at Mach forty-four, which is damned fast but far short of lightspeed."

"What about the gravity waves?" Logan said.

Zhong shrugged. "An anomaly. Instrument error. Echoes from a supernova. I don't know, but the Alcubierre drive is science fiction. Negative energy has never been observed in nature. We cannot, even theoretically, imagine how it could exist. Impossible," he said flatly.

John Adamsson got an amused expression on his face and turned to Phil Zhong. "My oldest son is fond of Arthur Clarke and often quotes his three laws of forecasting. The first law states that when a distinguished elderly scientist says something is possible, he's almost certainly right. When he says something is impossible, he's very probably wrong."

———

At 8:30 am, Berl Jeffers' Learjet was on its final approach above the Bob Hope Airport near Burbank. Jeffers was wrapping up a business call with Paul Engles as the plane landed. Jeffers' assistant had booked a suite of rooms on the top floor of The Langham Huntington Hotel in Pasadena, and that's where he and his entourage were headed. Jeffers ended his call and deplaned with a half-dozen assistants. One opened the door of his limo, and Jeffers climbed in alone, which broke protocol—he usually had an assistant with him everywhere—but Jeffers needed to make a private call. The others piled into a second limo. Jeffers asked the driver for privacy and then phoned his NASA contact on the latter's personal cell phone.

His contact answered with a whisper, "I can't talk now. I'll find somewhere private and call you back in fifteen or twenty."

It took twenty-five minutes for the return call. By then, Jeffers was flattening the seat cushion on a distressed easy chair in his suite, his bevy of assistants having disappeared until the old man called for them. Jeffers' contact brought him up to date on last night's meeting of the AETF.

"They have drones watching the forest?" Jeffers said in surprise.

"Armed with Hellfire missiles. Those are—"

"I know what they are. What the hell are they going to do? Blow the thing up if it comes back?"

"They're scared, Berl. There are Russian and Chinese agents here, and God knows who else. They don't know what it was, but now the press is playing up the UFO angle. They're afraid this thing is going to get away from them. That Homeland Security hawk is itching to get her finger on the trigger."

"Giving fools like her power is like lighting a cigar with dynamite," Jeffers said.

"Stephanie Vaughan shot her down. The Air Force is winning the turf war, but it's early yet."

"Screw the politics. How sure are your experts that it is an alien spacecraft?"

"They don't know what it is, but that's their best guess."

"Well, hell. Do you know how long I've been waiting for this? This could be the definitive proof of alien visitation."

"Some scientists think the gravity waves are from a warp drive."

"Goddamn," Jeffers muttered. "This is too important to leave to the government. My people examined the Ware video. We know whatever it was went straight up. Fast."

"Mach forty-four."

"Son of a bitch."

"But if the younger scientists are right, this thing could travel faster than light."

"Dammit. I've got to see it. I've got to get my hands on it."

"Good luck. If the Air Force finds it first, they'll bury it in a black hole in Nowhere, Nevada, and reverse engineer the technology to develop weapons three or four generations ahead of the Russians and Chinese. Hell, maybe ten or twenty generations ahead."

"Sure they will," Jeffers said, "but I won't let that happen."

"Krystal Forsythe threatened to call the White House."

"Hell, I know the President a lot better than she does," Jeffers bragged, "and I can put millions into his reelection coffers."

"Oops. Here comes someone. I have to go."

"Keep me informed."

Axel Taylor knew that Bradley Adamsson had AP Chemistry in the second period on Tuesdays because that's when Evaline had it. He waited outside the door as class let out but didn't see Adamsson as everyone else rushed out of the room. He didn't see Evaline either but stuck his head around the door frame as the room emptied and saw her talking to the teacher, a dorky, red-headed string bean with a bowtie named Laskey. Evaline was wearing black slacks and a yellow UCLA sweatshirt and looked hot, Axel thought. Her black hair glistened.

When she came out, Axel said, "Hi, babe."

She gave him a sour look. She didn't like being called "babe" and had told him that, but what's the use?

"What's up, Ax?" she said.

"Lookin' for Adamsson. He around?"

"I haven't seen him," she said. "He wasn't in class today. Why?"

Axel shrugged. "Just wonderin'."

She cocked her head to one side. "What's with your sudden interest in Bradley Adamsson? What's that all about?"

"Nothin'," he said. "Just, you know. . ."

"You always kind of gave him a hard time, didn't you?"

Axel looked away. "Yeah, I guess so." He looked back at her. "People change, you know. He and I—"

"Went hiking over the weekend. Twice. I know. Did you bring him back in one piece?"

His brows furrowed. "Yeah," he said in real or mock offense; she couldn't tell which.

"So where is he? It's not like him to miss class," she said in a tone he didn't like.

"Beats the hell out of me. Look, he's fine, okay? Last time I saw him. I'm just . . . ah, forget it. I wanted to ask you something."

He paused, and she looked impatiently at him. She had another class. "Okay?"

"You free after school?"

As midday approached, Bradley's stomach began growling. All he'd eaten were two apples. He still had a small bag of Doritos, which he replicated in the galley. He discovered that he could put one bag in the source enclosure and state the number of duplicates he wanted, so he chose two, and that many identical bags of Doritos appeared in the product enclosure. Now the ship had an atomic map of a bag of Doritos and could always replicate more. But Doritos alone weren't satisfying. He asked Athena if she had a suggestion from her vast store of alien foods. Momentarily, an object appeared in the product enclosure. It looked like a blue mango with blonde hair. Athena assured him it was safe to eat, so he took a tentative bite. It tasted like chocolate cheesecake and had pips around the seed that exploded in his mouth like banana bombs. After he swallowed, the hot aftertaste of succulent peppers passed through his mouth, a pleasing sensation that made his mouth water with warm sweetness. He decided to call it a blango for blue mango. After eating it, he tossed the large seed into the brown recycle bin and drank a tall glass of mineral-infused water.

After easing the ship back to altitude as that guy hiked down into the hollow, Bradley resigned himself to missing school and cruised over the forest, searching for an alternate landing site where he could pick up Axel. He asked Athena to retransmit his phone messages. After texting the location to Axel's phone, Athena took him on a tour of the ship and answered his questions. He decided he'd had a better education in four hours on the ship than in four years of high school. After lunch, he texted his mom. *Don't worry I'm fine Be home later.* In truth, he didn't know what to tell her. Nothing he could think of sounded believable, but he obviously couldn't tell her the truth. He knew with certainty that he felt great and loved flying in Athena. He didn't notice his hands changing or miss the pain in his side. He hadn't brought his pain pills and, in the absence of pain, forgot he needed them.

At half past four that afternoon, he eased the ship down at the area where he promised to meet Axel. He put the spider over his gloved hand and descended the tubes to the lowest level. When he touched the spider to the wall at the end of the ramp, the hatch opened, and his heart thumped when he saw who was standing there. Axel had a massive grin on his face, that grin of self-satisfaction Bradley had seen before, a grin of cockiness and triumph, like he'd just won a surfing contest or bagged an elephant. Standing beside him, her face flush with surprise and fright, was Evaline Perez. Bradley was as surprised as she was and gawked at her before catching himself and staring at Axel, wondering how he could have forgotten their pledge to tell no one—or why Axel violated it.

Bradley realized, feeling some self-recrimination, that he should never have trusted the surfer dude to keep his word. Someone else knew the secret now, and it would be harder to delay turning the ship over to the government. The weight of regret descended on him as he thought about losing Athena, the most incredible discovery in his short life. In light of the cancer spreading through his body, the thought of losing the ship was indescribably difficult to accept. It felt like every death he was destined to suffer was edging closer and would arrive not in years or months but in hours.

Cerulean Blue

Tuesday. April 14. 2:05 am.

In the peak of night, FBI Special Agents Rabin and Gonzalves raced to the Angeles Forest, where other agents had followed Roma Nikitovich. They drove faster than strictly necessary, their predatory instincts aroused. Speed meant action, and action meant closure. While they honed in on their prey, Agents Darren Wilson and Phil DeSantos waited until 6:45 am, after Franko Pavlovich left the hotel. They'd been bottled up in the room next to the Russians. Using the hotel's master key to enter the Russians' room, Wilson was happy to see that Pavlovich had locked his laptop in a steel valise, which he quickly unlocked, and he had no trouble hacking the computer. He loaded a new FBI trojan horse on the laptop and then stood on a chair to reach the smoke detector in the ceiling. After disabling the detector, he installed a directional microphone aimed at the room's desk, where the Russian would likely use the laptop. This mike would detect coil whine and allow Wilson to reconstruct images on the laptop from the intensity of its screen's pixels. If Pavlovich found and deleted the trojan horse, coil whine would still enable Wilson to hack the laptop with about 95 percent reliability using an algorithm recently developed by the NSA. While Wilson worked, DeSantos planted four bugs in the room. They were bluetoothed to a computer in the agents' room and would record everything the Russians said. DeSantos spoke Russian, English, Spanish, German, and

French and was confident he could follow their conversations, no matter which language they spoke.

Meanwhile, the GPS tracker on Nikitovich's rental car led Rabin and Gonzalves to a location in the San Gabriel Mountains, where they spotted the Russian's car. They set up surveillance with two additional agents from the LA office and waited until Pavlovich arrived in the early morning. When both Russians departed an hour later, the other FBI agents followed them. At the same time, Rabin and Gonzalves searched the area around the hollow, finding nothing unusual except a yellow dirt bike. They donned plastic gloves and carried it to the trunk of their car. Later dusting would yield fingerprints, but none were recognizable by the FBI's fingerprint database, so they began a trace on the bike's VIN. It wasn't clear whether the dirt bike was related to the case, but it seemed unlikely that the Russians had brought it to the scene and left it. Franko and Roma might have been too clever for them, but Rabin didn't think so. He thought they were as much in the dark as the Americans.

His judgment was proven flawed later that day. When they left the forest that morning, the Russians had eaten breakfast at a Denny's. Then, while Franko returned to their hotel room, Roma drove to Hollywood, purchased a map called "The Authentic Guide to the Homes of the Stars," and spent hours driving around the greater Los Angeles area, hoping to spot celebrities. Two FBI agents followed him, butt-sore from hours of sitting in their blue Malibu, although one swore he saw Brad Pitt pull up next to them at a stoplight near Universal Studios. Meanwhile, Franko fired up his laptop and navigated to the dark web, where he connected to the Russian intelligence directorate's clandestine website and submitted a progress report. In the adjacent room, Agent Wilson's trojan horse followed every keystroke, and DeSantos translated. At that point, the Russians had found nothing at the site of the unusual reflection in the forest, and they had no leads, which Agent Wilson dutifully reported to Special Agent-in-Charge Nick Rabin.

That changed at 5:24 Tuesday afternoon when Franko received an urgent message from Moscow. Russian satellites had spotted another unusual occurrence at a different location in the Angeles Forest. The satellite footage showed a pickup truck parked off-road at new GPS coordinates. Two people emerged from the truck, walked a short distance into an area of low vegetation, and then disappeared. They were visible one second, and the next, they were gone. They vanished into an area of low vegetation with nothing else around. Franko studied the satellite footage with growing unease—but no more so than Agent Darren Wilson, who watched the same footage in the adjacent room.

Wilson phoned Rabin, in turn who called General Vaughan, who told Rabin that LIGO had just detected gravity waves near the Angeles Forest. LIGO couldn't pinpoint the location, but the timing coincided with the timing of the Russian satellite images. The drones hadn't spotted the pickup truck and its vanishing passengers because they were surveilling the wrong area, the forest had too many visitors, and the drones couldn't follow everyone everywhere. That explanation rankled Vaughan, although she understood it, and she ordered them to start watching the pickup truck and the area within a two-mile radius of it. Meanwhile, as the two Russians left their hotel room and returned to the forest, teams of FBI agents followed in three cars, including Rabin and Gonzalves, whose intensity lined their faces and shone in their eyes. They were back in the hunt.

Evaline stood mute at the sight of Bradley Adamsson framed in a blue portal in space. She couldn't hear or feel anything, not the cool mountain air, not the warmth of the afternoon sun on her cheeks, not the touch of Axel's fingers on her arm. Her heart stood still. From somewhere far away, Axel may have said something, but she could only focus on that blue door suspended in mid-air, the look of surprise on Bradley's face, and the sadness in his eyes. She wondered if she had ever really seen him before. Then Axel nudged her, and she felt herself stepping toward that blue portal as Bradley moved aside.

Crossing the threshold was like stepping out of time. Her heart throbbed in her throat, and her legs felt like thick rubber bands. She put out a hand to steady herself. "Bradley," she muttered.

He nodded at her, afraid to speak.

Evaline looked from him to the corridor beyond, trying to understand where she was. Then she gazed at the blue wall where her hand lay. "Cerulean," she said.

"What?" said Bradley.

"The color of these walls. It's called cerulean blue."

Axel gaped at her like she'd spoken a foreign language.

She turned to Axel, not knowing how she felt about him then. He was the same cute boy she'd known since middle school, but now he seemed like an intrusive stranger. She looked back at Bradley and said, "Art history. First semester junior year. Mrs. White. These walls are cerulean blue."

All Bradley could think to say was, "I didn't know that."

Evaline glanced back outside, at the ground and the bushes, at the Earth, where things made sense. Then she turned back into that blue corridor. "What is this place?" she asked Bradley in a voice that to her sounded whiny.

Bradley paused for a moment. He'd admired her on Instagram since sophomore year, but he'd never spoken to her and couldn't think what to say that wouldn't sound outlandish. When the words came, they were more self-assured than he felt. "It's an interstellar ship," he told her. "A survey vessel. From the Andromeda galaxy. Built by a race of beings a hundred thousand years more advanced than we are. They have thousands of these ships surveying galaxies in our local group."

Evaline blinked. "Omigod. This is why all those UFO people are in town, isn't it? We drove through them. They're here because of this."

Bradley nodded.

Evaline gazed around the blue corridor. "A survey vessel? Surveying for what?"

"Intelligent life. Habitable planets. Resources."

"They wanna conquer the universe?" Axel said with a smirk.

"No," Bradley replied. "They just want to know who's out there. And what's out there. Advanced technological civilizations or primitive lifeforms that don't know what lies beyond their horizon. Planets where it rains diamonds. Asteroids made of gold. Clouds of helium and moons rich in platinum or titanium deposits. Places with methane lakes and hydrocarbon fountains or abundant oceans full of life. They've mapped their galaxy. Now they're mapping the galaxies closest to Andromeda."

"Bullshit," Axel said. He put his arm around Evaline's shoulder and pulled her close. "You're makin' this up, dude. You catchin' me?"

Bradley stared at him, his anger almost tempered by Evaline's proximity. "You're right, Taylor. It's all bullshit."

Unnerved by Bradley's steel, Axel caught a flicker of doubt in his throat.

"We agreed we wouldn't tell anyone about this," Bradley told him.

Axel felt his chest tightening. He ran his free hand through his hair, sculpting his blond locks. Then he shrugged, a confident smile gracing his lips. "It's Evaline, man."

"I trusted you," Bradley said.

Evaline looked at Axel and pulled away, moving along the corridor. "Is this place for real?"

Bradley nodded.

"All I saw from outside was this blue thing. Like a doorway with nothing around it."

"The ship is invisible."

"Ship?" Evaline tried to wrap her mind around that and couldn't.

"The ship is a sphere. Six hundred feet in diameter. More or less. Its designers knew they couldn't survey planets if their ships were visible," Bradley said. "They'd disrupt whatever they were surveying, so they developed the technology to bend light rays around their ships. This ship arrived on Earth thirteen thousand years ago, and most of her crew were killed by a meteorite. A saber-tooth cat surprised the sole survivor in a cave, and they killed each other. The ship sat where he landed it and began leaching the rock beneath itself for fuel. It sank into the hillside and was gradually covered by soil and vegetation. That's where we found it."

"Where *I* found it, dude," said Axel. He turned to Evaline. "*I* dug up the spider thing."

Her eyes widened, and she said, "What spider thing?"

"This," Bradley said, pointing to his right hand. Evaline stared in puzzlement. Like seeing an M.C. Escher impossible perspective drawing for the first time, she hadn't noticed the silver object affixed to his hand. "It's a tool the crew used when they left the ship," Bradley added when he saw her confusion.

"What's it for?" Evaline said.

"I'm still learning," Bradley said, gazing at the spider. "You can use it to search for life or minerals or water. Anything. Map your surroundings. Light your way. Navigate back to the ship. Even summon the ship. It's crazy useful. The technology is light years beyond anything on Earth." Then to Axel: "Where *you* found it, Axel. The zhoul lux pee toll, however that's pronounced."

"Zhowllux'p'twl," Athena said, correcting him.

The voice startled Axel and Evaline. "Who's that?" Axel said.

"The ship," Bradley replied.

"It talks to you?" Axel said, impressed and not wanting to show it.

Bradley nodded. "I call her Athena. After the Greek goddess of knowledge."

"Athena?" Axel said. "Dude, what the fuck?"

Evaline said, "Athena's also the goddess of war. And of civilization." Both boys stared at her for a beat, and then she added, "World history. First semester sophomore year. Mr. Fielding."

"You two stop screwin' around?" Axel said, miffed at being left out of the conversation and sensing something more sinister at work.

Evaline smiled to herself. Then she said to Bradley, "I remember reading about Andromeda. It's the closest galaxy to us, right?"

"Would you like to see it?" Bradley replied. Evaline nodded, and Bradley said, "Let's go to the bridge."

He motioned her toward the elevator tube. Axel hustled around her and told her how to jump into the tube so she'd fly upwards. Bradley interrupted by saying, "Or just say 'bridge.' That will take you to the right deck."

Alex glared at Bradley with wide eyes. What else had the geek not told him?

Evaline stepped under the tube and said, "Bridge." She disappeared, and Bradley followed a moment later, trailed by Axel, who'd run his hands through his fashionable hair before ascending. On the bridge deck, Evaline swooned as she recovered from the experience of flying up the tubes and stopping in midair. Then she stepped aside and watched as Bradley and Axel swept up through the tube after her, marveling at how effortless their ascent had been and curious about the technology that enabled it. She followed Bradley as he walked down the corridor.

He stopped outside the cockpit and said, "Athena, show us Andromeda." Instantly, an image of a spiral galaxy appeared on the wall of the corridor—twenty feet long and nine feet high, a giant screen showing the breadth and majesty of one trillion stars and four and a half trillion planets orbiting a bright galactic center in a flat, swirling spiral of light and dust.

"My God," Evaline said. "It's beautiful."

"Twice the size of the Milky Way," Bradley said. "More than two and a half million light years away. Athena's home."

"Weird place for a big-screen TV," Axel commented. The corridor wasn't wide enough for him to see the entire image without turning his head.

"Every surface on the ship can act as a screen," Bradley said. With one finger, he traced a rectangle in front of his face, and Andromeda appeared in the rectangle. "Even non-surfaces."

"Holy shit," Axel stammered, his eyes wide.

"How's it doing that?" Evaline asked as the image faded and then disappeared.

Bradley smiled and erased the big screen image of Andromeda with a wipe of his finger toward the corridor wall. The wall returned to cerulean blue. He led them to the cockpit and raised the ship above the Los Angeles Basin, where they hovered for half an hour.

Evaline gawked at the sight while Axel strode confidently around the cockpit as though he owned the view. When Bradley eased the ship back down, he said, "Are you hungry?"

He took them to the galley, where he asked Athena to replicate two blangoes. Axel jumped backward in surprise as the hairy blue fruits appeared in the product enclosure. Evaline gazed at Bradley as though he, not the ship, were the magician. "Looks weird, I know," he said to them. "But they taste great."

Evaline looked doubtful, but Axel, after glancing at her, grabbed one of the blangoes and took a whopping bite. Evaline laughed as his expression progressed from doubt to surprise to gratification to bliss. He wiped his mouth with one hand and said, "You gotta try this," before chomping into it again. She was still reluctant to eat something she'd never seen but took a tentative bite, enjoyed it, and agreed that blangoes were terrific, too sweet for her taste but edible.

"Where did Athena find these?" she asked.

"Some planet somewhere," Bradley said. "But the ones you ate were replicated in this galley." They didn't understand, so Bradley explained how the replicator made an atomic map of something and recreated it exactly, atom by atom. "It's like a 3D printer," he explained, "but much faster, and it uses atoms instead of plastic."

"It doesn't make copies?" Evaline said. "It replicates the original? What's the difference?"

"What the ship replicates is identical to the original in every respect. I'll show you." He took them three decks down to a deck he'd labeled "Fabrication." They walked to a large room with far larger bins than in the galley. He took a handkerchief from his back pocket and dropped it in the source bin. When he asked Athena to replicate it, an identical handkerchief appeared in the adjacent product bin.

"Whoa, dude," Axel said, trying to grasp what he just witnessed. "What?"

"Whatever you put in the left bin is replicated in the right. Exactly."

"No way," Axel said. "Anything?"

"I haven't asked if it can replicate living things. I'm not sure I want to know, but it will copy anything else."

"No shit," Axel said. He reached into his wallet and withdrew a twenty-dollar bill. "What about this?"

Bradley realized he'd just opened Pandora's Box but took the bill from Axel and set it in the source bin. The replicator produced an identical copy in seconds. Axel examined the two bills with a smile. "No shit," he said to himself.

While Axel marveled at the replicated twenty, Evaline gazed at Bradley and said, "You never talked to me in class."

That surprised him because he thought he was invisible to her and the other A-listers. As he gazed back, he decided she had an even lovelier face close up. Instagram didn't capture just how beautiful she was. Her widely spaced eyes and pointy chin made her look innocent and more welcoming than he'd imagined—and more intelligent. "I was afraid to," he responded.

"Afraid of what?"

Axel interrupted. "So, like, we could keep copying this twenty. Make a whole stack of them."

"Afraid you wouldn't talk to a freak," Bradley said. Then to Axel: "Wouldn't they have the same serial number?" He rubbed the back of his neck in irritation.

"Yeah, okay. I get that. But, go to a bank, get a stack of hundreds—ten thousand worth. Copy them. They'd have different serial numbers."

"You're not a freak," Evaline said quietly.

Bradley heard her but remembered being ignored and left out. He looked at Axel. "Some of them would."

Evaline looked away and frowned at Axel. "That's counterfeiting," she pointed out.

Bradley didn't explain that he could instruct Athena to replicate any number of twenties from just one bill, and the replicator would produce them all at once—instant mass counterfeiting.

Axel chewed on his lip. "Okay, so . . . gold coins. No serial numbers."

Bradley dwelled on what Evaline said but felt a nagging need to explain to Axel: "Even the ship can't make something from nothing. It has a repository of raw materials—atoms in plasma form. To replicate gold coins, it would need enough gold plasma in storage. But gold is easy to find in the galaxy. The ship can mine it from asteroids or uninhabited planets."

"How can it do that?" Evaline said.

"Mining lasers that pulverize any material at a distance and devices—I'm not sure how they work—that attract the particles to the ship's skin, where they are absorbed. Athena can extract minerals, water, oxygen, iron, magnesium, gold. Whatever the ship needs. It also constantly absorbs what we call dark energy, which it uses for propulsion."

"Dude, you realize what we found, right?" Axel said. "I mean, like the fruit. People would go batshit over that."

Evaline looked askance at him. "You want to become a farmer?"

"Farmer? No. Just need this machine." Axel's mind was exploding with possibilities. "Don't need to farm. We can make anything. Think about it."

"We'll have to turn this ship over to the authorities," Bradley said.

"No, wait, why?" Axel replied. Urgency surged through him like adrenalin.

"Because they're hunting for us already," Bradley said.

"Bullshit, man," Alex said, pleading with his hands.

"Why are they hunting for you?" Evaline asked.

"No, dude," Axel said. "You dunno what we have here."

"Who's hunting for you?" Evaline said, her voice rising.

"The government," Bradley told her. "The Air Force. The police. All that chaos on Sunday. The explosion. The mushroom cloud. We caused that."

Her eyes opened wide, and she stopped breathing. "You. Did. That?"

Bradley's face turned ashen, and he nodded, looking away from her.

Axel said, "It's not a big deal, Evaline."

"Not a big deal," she yelled at Axel. Then to Bradley, "What did you two do?"

"Not us two. Me. I flew the ship into the atmosphere in a split second," Bradley said. "It fried the air in our wake." Although he wasn't Catholic, he felt like he was in a confessional. It was worse confessing to her than to a priest—or the police. "It was an accident. I didn't know what I was doing."

Evaline's countenance hardened. "Jesus, Bradley, you know how much damage you caused? How many people were injured? We were treating people all night!"

"I know," he said.

"Losing sight of the big picture here, guys," Axel said.

"I'm sorry about what happened. But not sorry about discovering the ship."

"You know what this is worth? People will forgive us, trust me," Axel pleaded.

"Sorry for not being more cautious," Bradley added.

"That's not the point," Evaline screamed at Axel. To them both, she said, "You are turning this in."

"Saturday," Bradley said. "I want a few more days with it."

"You're turning it in," she said flatly.

"Saturday," Bradley insisted. "Promise me you won't tell anyone about this until then."

She glared at him while Axel threw his hands in the air and paced. "Holy shit," he sputtered.

"I want a few more days with it," Bradley said.

"Fine," she replied. "How do I get out of here?"

———

Captain Janet Rubia had the swing shift in the RPV Ground Control Station at Nellis Air Force Base in southern Nevada. She'd been a Predator drone pilot for twenty-eight months and was being reassigned in May. She'd enjoyed this tour but was eager for something different. She sat at the console, piloting the drone in circles over the Angeles Forest in California. Her target was a red pickup parked since she came on duty, along with its driver and passengers. She was anxious for a cigarette but didn't think she'd been so distracted by the nicotine urge that she missed two people who suddenly appeared walking toward the pickup. She was confused because her field of view was at least a quarter mile in every direction, and these people had come out of nowhere less than a hundred feet from the truck. *Where'd they come from?* she wondered.

It didn't matter. She phoned in the sighting and watched as the two people climbed into the pickup. Moments later, the truck's lights came on, and the truck turned toward the road and headed west. She turned her joystick, and the drone followed the truck as it wound out of the mountains.

Colonel Franko Pavlovich had been watching the red truck through a telephoto lens on his camera and nearly missed the blue splash that appeared about a hundred meters to his right. But he caught a glimpse of something and swung the camera around to shoot two people emerging from a blue swath of air that quickly vanished. Startled, he scanned the area around them but saw nothing more, so he re-aimed the camera at the man and woman walking toward the pickup and watched as they got in the vehicle and turned onto the road. He wasn't sure if this assignment could become any stranger. Roma was asleep in the passenger seat, most of his bulk leaning against the door. Franko regarded him distastefully as he started the engine and turned to follow the truck west as it headed toward town.

Across the canyon, Spazina Gonzalves lay her head against the headrest and dozed. Surveillance was her least favorite activity as an FBI agent. The hours of boredom made her wonder if she'd chosen the right profession. She rubbed her eyes and said, "The Dodgers are playing the Rockies this weekend—doubleheader. I'm taking my boys. You seen any games?"

Rabin didn't respond. He was following the red pickup through his binoculars and saw the Russians trailing it. "Here we go," he said, which brought Gonzalves to immediate attention.

As he coordinated the surveillance on both vehicles, she took a call from the task force and said into her phone, "We're on it."

"On what?" said Rabin.

"The drone's following the red pickup. The drone pilot said two people came out of nowhere and got in it."

Rabin said, "I wish I knew what the hell is happening." He picked up his radio and keyed the mike. "Jackson, pass the Russians and phone in the license plate on that red pickup. Then drop back and follow. Martinez and Wallace, stay on the Russians." Rabin started his car and pulled onto the highway, and the whole caravan of foreign and domestic agents wound down the highway in pursuit of Axel Taylor and his hot red pickup. Just after they entered the Pasadena city limits, Rabin took a call from Jackson and turned to Gonzalves, repeating what he had heard. "The red pickup is registered to Axel R. Taylor, eighteen years of age, resident of South Pasadena. There's a dark-haired female with him." Into the radio, he said, "Jackson, I want everything on Taylor and his passenger. Asap." The sun was low on the horizon as they drove west, and Rabin turned down the visor to cut the glare. "Never really got into baseball," he said.

Carnivals and Miracles

Tuesday. April 14. 7:08 pm.

Bradley couldn't locate Eliot's yellow dirt bike. He hovered over the hollow, using the ship's telescopic view to zoom in and retrace the path he'd taken while hiking into and out of the hollow, and scanned the ridge above it where he parked the bike and spotted the scary guy with the rifle. *Those guys must have taken it,* he thought. Now, he'd lost his best friend's bike and could not get home. He couldn't call his parents, so he called Eliot, hesitant about confessing that the bike was missing but having no better options.

"El, it's Bradley."

"Yo, dude. Your mom called here looking for you."

"When?"

"Couple times. She knows you weren't at school today."

"Crap."

"Yeah, she sounded pissed. Where you been?"

Thinking quickly, Bradley said, "At Mt. Wilson."

"The Observatory? Trying to spot those aliens, huh?"

"What aliens?"

"Dude, it's all anybody can talk about. You go to town today?"

"No. No, I've been at Wilson. All day."

"It's like the circus is coming to town. Mobile homes, TV trucks, people carrying wacky signs, like hundreds of people or something, camping out in the parks, you know, like in that movie, *Independence Day*, getting ready for an alien invasion. More wingnuts pouring in every hour. The cops are going ape. Pasadena's the new Roswell, dude. UFO capital of California. It's all over the news."

"Sorry I missed it," Bradley said, feeling waist-deep in quicksand and sinking deeper. With a heavy voice, he said, "Hey, can you come get me?"

"Why don't you ride my bike back?"

"That's . . . kind of what I needed to tell you."

"The piece of shit broke down on you?" Eliot said. "I haven't ridden it for a while. It needs something done to the engine. I don't know what."

"Something like that. I'll tell you later."

"Okay, Mt. Wilson. See you in twenty—or maybe thirty. Traffic is, like, really bad. I'll be the good-looking guy driving a Porsche convertible."

"I can't wait that long," Bradley replied. "Why don't I look for a goofy-looking kid in a puke yellow Honda Civic?"

"You're dumping on my fantasy, man, and you're trashing the Pukester, which is definitely not cool."

"Nothing I could say about that car could make it any worse."

"Now you're breaking my heart."

———————

Driving through Pasadena was like a slow-motion ride through a Star Wars convention. Bradley tried to capture the weirdness with his cell phone. The sidewalks were thronged with people in alien outfits, green fright wigs, flying saucer hats, Darth Vader helmets, and Chewbacca costumes. RV's jammed Rosemont Avenue—from house-sized motor homes to pickups with camper shells, banners hanging on their sides: "Free the Aliens!" "Tell the Truth about Roswell, "We Believe," and "Repent! There is Only One God." The park beside Rosemont was overgrown with tents and campfires and UFO enthusiasts throwing illuminated frisbees, people wearing purple leotards and aluminum-foil hats roasting hot dogs or marshmallows, and vendors selling popcorn and ice cream to long lines of kitschy faux aliens. A giant silver, inflatable flying saucer floated over the trees. Elton John's song "Rocket Man" blared from a loudspeaker somewhere, and there were vans with satellite dishes and short-wave antennas sprouting from their roofs like weeds. Dogs chased balls or each other amidst street musicians, jugglers, and some guy doing card tricks. Policing this carnival of chaos were deputies every half-block trying to contain the damage and prevent a riot.

In the passenger seat of the Pukester, Bradley beheld all this sparkle and fuss with wide-eyed wonder—astonished that the crazies had invaded Pasadena so soon after Sunday's accidental flight and turned his and Axel's discovery into a farce. Worse, he wondered what Evaline thought of him after witnessing this spectacle and knowing he was responsible for it. He picked up his car at Eliot's house and wound through back streets to Milan Avenue. His home looked like a snaggle-toothed Halloween pumpkin, with some windows lit and others boarded. He braced himself at the front door for his mom's reaction when he walked in—and it was worse than he anticipated. Her distress turned to anger as she recounted the call she took from the principal, wondering why Bradley wasn't in school (shocking), to the calls and texts she made to his cell phone (unanswered), and then to Eliot's and Kevin's parents and everyone else she could think of (haven't seen him), to the hospitals she drove to (not there, thank God), and the doctors' offices and police stations (thank God again). It came out in such a flurry that Devin and Celia slunk upstairs in case her aim became more general.

"I texted you that I was okay," he pleaded.

That prompted more thunder: "Where have you been all day?"

"I decided to skip school," Bradley said.

"That's not what I asked you?"

"I told you I'd be home and not to worry," he reiterated.

"And you think that lets you off the hook?" The fire in her face was like a red-hot poker, which distracted him because he'd never seen anyone whose face was as red as hers. Her face wasn't just red; it glowed like a space heater.

"Answer me!" she demanded.

"No. It doesn't let me off the hook." He looked down, away from the harsh living room light, and noticed red lines on the backs of his hands, faint like faded tattoos. *What the hell?* he thought. She'd asked him another question, but he didn't hear it. "I'm sorry," he said. The universal acceptance of blame and plea for forgiveness. Then he thought of another ploy. "I'm just upset over what the doctor said. I wanted some time alone." It was disingenuous, and he felt guilty, but it worked.

He watched her soften, her worry lines dissolving into sympathy. She had him sit and told him that she and his father wanted a second opinion. They'd made an appointment tomorrow morning at the Ronald Reagan UCLA Medical Center with a doctor who graduated from MIT with his father. Bradley wanted to say, "I feel fine. In fact, I feel great," but he was in no position to resist. Then she asked if he'd eaten, and he said no, so she took one of his hands to lead him to the kitchen. Afraid she'd see the lines on his hands, he pulled back, and she asked what was wrong.

"I think I have a rash or something. From the forest."

"Let me see," she said.

He hesitated, wondering how to explain this, but raised both hands and hoped the lines weren't noticeable. She inspected the backs of his hands, as well as his palms. "I don't see a rash, but we have calamine lotion. Tell me if your hands are itchy."

While she made him a turkey-and-provolone sandwich, he studied the back of his right hand. The red lines were clearly visible. *Why didn't she see them?* he wondered. Then, he noticed that the lines formed patterns in the same shapes as those on the back of the spider. *Could the spider be tattooing my hand?* But that couldn't be, he realized because the same patterns were appearing on the back of his left hand, and he'd never worn the spider on that hand.

When she set the sandwich in front of him at the kitchen counter, Bradley thought, *I could make a hundred of these in a few seconds.* The sandwich was excellent and fresh, and he was sorry he couldn't map it into Athena's memory. His father came home while he was eating and joined Bradley at the counter, thankful, Bradley imagined, that he'd arrived home when the storm had passed and the skies were sunny. Celia and Devin joined them when the family sat in the living room and turned on the local news, which was dominated by the recent UFO craze in Los Angeles County and the government's ongoing search for answers to Sunday's explosive mystery.

As Bradley left for his bedroom, his father remarked that he was limping more and wondered if he'd injured his leg while hiking. Bradley said he didn't think so, but he'd noticed a change in his gait and wondered if he had injured something, although he felt terrific. But when he removed his shoes, undressed, and stood barefoot in his bedroom, he was bewildered to discover that his left leg was nearly as long as his right. His orthopedic left shoe was causing him to walk unevenly. He sat on the edge of his bed, blood draining from his face as he massaged his left leg and thought that the only change in his life had been the discovery of the ship. He stood and paced across the floor in bare feet, noticing almost no wobble, and was so slaphappy he wished he'd learned to dance because that's what he wanted to do most at this moment. No one could see him, so he threw out his arms and wriggled herky-jerky around his room, attempting dance steps he'd seen other kids do, grinning like a fool, rocking and rolling to music in his head until he spun himself dizzy and collapsed on his bed. Whatever miracle had brought about this transformation, he was too self-conscious to dance like no one was watching, but he felt euphoric from his crown to his soles.

He took the mystery of his proportional legs to bed and lay beneath the covers, thinking about Athena, Evaline, and baseball, wondering if he would ever play again. As he lay there, the Daydream Special arrived, and Bradley hopped aboard. A girl very much like Evaline boarded at the next stop, and they sat together discussing places in the cosmos they'd like to see—the rings of Saturn, Neptune's blue clouds, a planet where dinosaur-like creatures still roam, a star-forming region like the Horsehead Nebula, dense with interstellar dust, where neophytes were just being born. Through the twin prisms of desire and resurrection, he realized how much he ached for a girl's touch, not just any girl, a girl like the one in the seat beside him—warm, intelligent, lively, and tender, independent and forgiving of a guy who isn't perfect. *Who wouldn't want a girl like that?* he thought. His companion slowly faded from view as the Daydream Special sped through the dusk, and darkness eclipsed twilight.

On Wednesday morning, Bradley and his parents arrived at the Ronald Reagan UCLA Medical Center after making their way through the UFO madness on the streets of Pasadena. The Reagan Center is an imposing gray fortress in the heart of Los Angeles, but Dr. Gardner Mattheakis' office was lush, modern, and warm. They sat on tan leather sofas beside miniature jades and Brussels's bonsai plants and flipped through *Health, Sunset,* and *People* magazines while they waited. Everyone Bradley looked at had pink smudges on their cheeks and red ribbons on their necks and hands. The table lamp beside him glowed red, too, but he found that he could choose not to see the red if he narrowed his eyes—and that perplexed him even more than seeing red in the first place. Then, it dawned on him that he was seeing heat. Somehow, his eyes were receptive to light in the infrared spectrum. *WTF?*

Dr. Mattheakis had red splotches on his face, which Bradley softened by narrowing his eyes. Mattheakis went to MIT undergrad with John Adamsson before attending Harvard Medical School. A sudden cancellation allowed him to squeeze Bradley in, which he told John he was happy to do. While John and Gardner reminisced about MIT, Bradley followed a nurse to their diagnostic center, walking with a wobble induced by his left orthopedic shoe.

Mid-morning, while waiting for an ultrasound, his cell phone buzzed with a text from Evaline.

Evaline: "Hey this is Evaline"

Evaline: "Sorry for freaking out"

Evaline: "A lot to process"

Brad: "No worries"

Evaline: "Athena amazing!"

Evaline: "Can I see her again after school?"

Brad: "What about Axel?"

Evaline: "Working. Pick me up at 5?"

Brad: "Where?"

Evaline: "My place."

Brad: "Addy?"

She texted him her address.

Brad: "OK"

Suddenly, his day was better despite being punctured, probed, and smeared with gel while waiting for the doctor's verdict. He wondered how she got his cell phone number and later learned she had asked his sister Celia for it.

His dad had to return to work, so after the tests, he ate lunch with his mom in the hospital cafeteria. His soup glowed pink, not red, meaning it was lukewarm. That he could sense that brought a smile to his lips. When they returned to Dr. Mattheakis' office, they waited briefly before the doctor joined them. They sat facing the doctor's desk, his mom with a white-knuckled grip on the arms of her chair. Bradley was resigned to whatever the doctor said, having driven past the denial turnoff and parked at acceptance, but he wasn't prepared for what the doctor told them.

"I'm confused," the doctor said. He laid out two stacks of papers on the desk before him. "I have Bradley's previous results here and candidly, I'm not sure what to make of them. Our tests today show no evidence of cancer whatsoever. If I didn't know better, I'd think the previous results were another patient's." He looked at Claudine. "By our measures, your son is one of the healthiest young men we've ever seen here. I'm not impugning the other doctor, but I don't see anything supporting her diagnosis."

Claudine was afraid to break the spell by speaking, but she finally said, "I don't understand."

The doctor smiled. "Bradley is fine."

"That can't be," she responded. "I mean, of course, that's what I want, but what about his pain?"

"Are you in pain?" the doctor asked Bradley.

"No."

His mother raised her eyebrows. "Bradley, you've had pains in your side for over a month. For two months." To the doctor: "He's on pain medication."

"The pain's gone," Bradley said.

"Have you been taking your pills?" said Claudine, her eyebrows raised.

"No."

"But the other tests?" she said to the doctor.

Mattheakis shook his head. "I'm not sure what to tell you. We can rerun the labs if you wish, but I trust these results," he said, lifting one stack of reports and glancing through them. "Bradley does not have hepatocellular or any other form of cancer that we can detect. His blood tests were negative, including alpha-fetoprotein. His MRI is unremarkable. The ultrasound of his liver was clean. I see nothing wrong. Of course, cancer screening can sometimes result in false negatives, where a cancer that is present is undetected, but it would be unusual for all the tests to yield false negatives. I've seen many patients with liver cancer, and Bradley's results show no sign of the disease."

She expelled a loud breath. "It's a miracle. I don't know what to say."

The doctor stood up, signaling it was time for them to leave. "Sounds like good news to me. We can rerun the labs in three months if you wish. Just to be sure." He came around the desk and shook their hands. "Please tell John I'd enjoy having lunch when he's free. It's been a pleasure meeting you."

On their drive back home, Claudine was, by turns, dumbfounded and giddy. Smiles gave way to frowns and back again. At a stoplight, she leaned over and hugged him, then planted a wet kiss on his cheek, which amused the twenty-something guy in the car beside them. As she drove on, her fingernails clicking on the steering wheel, Bradley gazed at the heat sources around them—the store windows, cars, streetlights, people, and sun-warmed streets—and stared at the patterns on the backs of his hands. He saw them because they generated heat. He thought about that fantastic fact and the mysterious invisible ship docked above a knoll near the Mt. Wilson Observatory. He decided that he and Athena needed to have a serious talk.

"We know from the VIN that a Merilee J. Stankus purchased the mountain bike," Nick Rabin told the AETF in a briefing early Wednesday afternoon. "Now this is a 43-year-old woman, works at a Ross Dress for Less in Pasadena, who's built like, well, let's just say that her on a mountain bike would be like an elephant on a pogo stick. It probably belongs to her teenage kid, and he has no record. We checked him out, but the bike may not be related to the case. We don't know why the Russians were at that location."

Rabin glanced around the room to see if anybody had questions. General Vaughan was giving him a sour look, which he dismissed. "The two in the red pickup might be another story," he continued. "The boy is named Axel Taylor. Father runs an auto shop. Mother bailed a decade ago. She's down in San Diego, remarried, no contact with Taylor."

John Adamsson had been distracted by the call he'd gotten from Claudine. That Bradley did not have cancer was miraculous. He wondered how the other doctor could have made such an egregious mistake. He perked up when he heard Rabin say, "Axel Taylor." The name sounded familiar, but he couldn't recall from where. He tuned out again while he rummaged through his mind trying to make the connection. When he tuned back in, Rabin was talking about an arrest.

"—when he was sixteen. Breaking and entering, West Hollywood, got probation, community service, and a ten-grand fine. We couldn't find anything since."

"I thought juvenile records were sealed," General Vaughan said.

"Not to Homeland Security," Krystal Forsythe said. "Not for this case."

Rabin continued: "The female is Evaline Marie Perez, eighteen, senior at South Pasadena High, nurse assistant at Huntington Memorial. As far as we know, she's clean."

"It's possible," said Spazina Gonzalves, "that none of these kids have anything to do with this situation, but—"

"—where did the two in the pickup come from?" Rabin said.

Gonzalves nodded to her partner and said, "Both the Russian satellite and the drone saw them come from out of nowhere. A blue flash and, poof, there they were."

"That's impossible," Phil Zhong scoffed. "There's another explanation."

Director Lefaye smirked. "What's that thing called on Star Trek? The transporter?"

Vaughan laughed but said, "We have enough craziness on the streets outside. Let's keep it out there."

Forsythe turned to Rabin and Gonzalves: "Maybe we should bring the kid in, the one with the juvie record. Use it to squeeze him."

Vaughan shook her head. "Let's hold on that until we discover a stronger connection between these teenagers and last Sunday's event."

"I disagree," said Forsythe. "We should at least keep the Taylor kid under surveillance."

Vaughan nodded. "Okay. Watch him. Our best lead is those gravity waves, and I'd like to hear from LIGO. How close are we to being able to track the thing?"

"Very close," Kevin Karchman said.

———

Meng Shuren combed her long black hair in the bathroom mirror and applied eyeshadow and lipstick before leaving their room, the first time either agent had left since they checked into the hotel. She wore a plain white blouse and black jeans, her diplomatic passport snug in a back pocket in case the FBI detained her. She rode the elevator to the second floor and walked down the hall to the hotel's spa, where she signed in and waited for her massage. Her masseuse was a stocky Asian woman named Caroline Chu. Shuren didn't speak to Chu as she entered the massage room. Chu directed her to remove her clothes and lay on the table, covered by a white towel, and said she would return in a few minutes.

Shuren did as she was told, lying on her stomach with her head in a face cradle. The tasteful room had bamboo walls and a mahogany floor and smelled like gardenias and hot oil. After several peaceful minutes, the door opened, and Chu reentered. She tucked a folded piece of rice paper into Shuren's hand as she passed the table. Chu poured oil onto her client's back and began long opening strokes to warm up her back. As Chu worked on her muscles, Shuren brought her hands below the face cradle and unfolded the paper. The note was written in Mandarin. Shuren read it twice before refolding it, cupping it in her hand, and laying her arms back on the table.

As Chu worked, she made her way around to that side of the table and slipped the note back into her hand. Then she walked to a sideboard, touched the rice paper to a burning candle, and dropped it into an incense bowl, producing thin black smoke as it blackened to ashes. When the massage was complete twenty-five minutes later, Shuren returned to her room, neither woman having spoken again during Shuren's treatment.

The FBI agents watching Shuren saw nothing suspicious and reported that the Chinese agent had a massage, during which neither the agent nor the masseuse had spoken.

———

Berl Jeffers was delighted with Pasadena's influx of UFO believers. Their presence and theatrics attracted the media, and the coverage could hardly have been better. CNN,

Fox, ABC, NBC, CBS, Reuters, BBC, and dozens of other news outlets from around the world had converged on Los Angeles County to cover what Jeffers was certain would be the biggest news story of the year, if not the century, and perhaps of all time. Enterprising tour operators were now offering helicopter excursions near the crater site, flying as close to the crater as the FAA's new airspace restrictions would permit. Jeffers had chartered one to fly his camera crew to video the site. That footage would become part of a documentary Jeffers' team was rapidly creating.

Prominent in the film, along with Jeffers, would be Edna St. James, president of the International UFO Network and author of *They Really Are Among Us*, considered the definitive guide to alien abductions, and Roger Horsley, a former Area 51 worker who claimed to have examined alien technology and seen alien corpses in cold storage. Jeffers had both personalities flown in for the press conference he was about to hold in the hotel's conference room.

Berl was jazzed as he peered through the break between the curtains to see at least a hundred reporters sitting in rows before the stage or milling about, waiting for the event to begin. Multiple microphones lined the front of the podium, and dozens of video cameras were poised to record. The buzz in the room was invigorating. Jeffers hurled open the curtains and marched onto the stage with a broad smile.

"Ladies and gentlemen," he said into the clustered mikes, "I'm Berl Jeffers." The clicking of so many cameras sounded like a chorus of cicadas singing before noon. "I'm joined this afternoon by two renowned members of the UFO community to tell you that the government is, once again, hiding the truth from us. As we all know, the video evidence from Mrs. Ware's cellphone clearly shows that what happened here last Sunday was a flying saucer that took off so fast it looked like a meteor strike. The government is refusing to admit what we have since confirmed, that this ship flew at forty-four times the speed of sound, a speed no jet or missile on Earth can attain. We now know, from confidential sources, that this ship can travel faster than the speed of light." He paused for effect, noting the excitement and disbelief in people's eyes.

"We also know that that ship is still here." That announcement galvanized the crowd, and excited shouts nearly eclipsed Jeffers' following words.

"And we intend to find it," he screamed into the mikes. "Now listen. To that end, I am offering one million dollars to anyone who can produce concrete evidence of the ship. Details. Photos. Artifacts. I don't care what, but I want indisputable proof."

The reporters were barking into their phones, and a handful were sprinting from the room.

"Wait," he yelled to those he saw leaving. "I will give *five* million dollars to the person who can deliver the ship to me."

Out of the stunned silence that followed, one voice shouted, "You gonna pay the aliens five mil?"

Jeffers cut loose a mighty laugh and said, "Damn right. I'll pay five million to *anyone* who can produce that ship and hand me the keys."

Chortling echoed throughout the room as the crowd's mood grew hungrier.

"Now I'd like to introduce two eminent members of the UFO community," Jeffers cried.

La Luna

Wednesday. April 15. 2:10 pm.

Mancebo's Grocery was mobbed. Campers, RVs, and minivans spilled out of the parking lot onto the road, prompting state troopers to direct traffic. Bradley squeezed his Prius into a slot left by a departing pair of motorcyclists wearing homemade alien antennas on their helmets. He'd told his mom he would skip school the rest of the day. He already had enough credits to graduate and wanted to spend the afternoon celebrating the doctor's news, and, he added, he was seeing a classmate after school, so he'd be home late. She was so hopelessly afloat that she didn't question him. She just hugged him and sent him on his way.

When Bradley left his car, he heard people talking in the car next to him, even though their windows were closed, and thought they must be arguing, although they looked calm. He threaded his way through the mob at Mancebo's and dropped fresh sandwiches, ready-made salads, salsa, veggie trays, fruits, and chips into his cart. The din in the crowded aisles was so distracting he wished he had headphones. Mancebo's Deli sold hot pizza slices—Hawaiian, pepperoni, vegetarian, triple cheese, meat lovers. While Bradley waited for the clerk to box up one of each, Emilio Mancebo came alongside and said brightly, "Raccoon boy."

Bradley looked puzzled.

"You were here the night we cleaned up from the explosion," Mancebo explained. "You arrived on a dirt bike. Filthy face."

Bradley smiled. "Oh, yeah, that was me. Bradley Adamsson."

"I'm Emilio," Mancebo said, shaking Bradley's hand.

Bradley thought Mancebo's complexion looked ruddier than the other night, then remembered he was seeing in infrared. He narrowed his eyes.

The grocer glanced in Bradley's cart. "Another night in the forest?"

"No, I'm, well, yes, I'm going back."

"Must be having a party."

"Yes, a party. Friends. I'm seeing a friend, uh, friends. In the forest."

"You must have many friends. No dirt bike today?"

Bradley shook his head.

Mancebo glanced around his crowded store. "Can you believe this?" Approaching them was a woman wearing a green knit Peruvian beanie with ornamental tassels and black, slanted-alien-eye sunglasses. She wore a t-shirt that read, "Jesus was an alien."

"Crazy," Mancebo said, "but good for business." Then, leaning into Bradley: "You think aliens are invading us?"

"I'm pretty sure they're not," Bradley confided. "But if I see any, I'll let you know."

———————

Later, in the ship's galley, Bradley made atomic maps of the food he bought at Mancebo's, then tossed the food into the recycle bin. He felt guilty about throwing it away but knew the ship would reduce the waste to atoms and store them for later use. Nothing was wasted on this ship. Then he sat at the table in the galley and said, "Athena, I have some questions. Last night before bed, my legs were almost the same length, and I didn't feel pain in my side anymore. The doctor I saw today said I don't have cancer, but the doctor last Friday said I did. You know anything about that?"

A tall glass of water materialized in the food replicator's product bin. The ship said, "Drink this."

Bradley took the water container and sat back down. "What is it?"

"Water infused with calcium and other minerals. I needed the minerals to lengthen your left leg. Four more containers will introduce enough minerals into your body to complete the process, and your legs will be completely symmetrical."

His mouth felt dry. "I have Ollier Disease."

"Not anymore."

Bradley was numb, too surprised to speak, but eager to know how he'd been healed. Before he could ask, Athena said, "You have no diseases."

Bradley sat for a long moment, studying the container. The thought of being healthy for the first time in years brought tears to his eyes, and he was embarrassed to show the emotion, even to Athena. The disease had long been his insidious companion, an interloper who hung a sea anchor from his legs and smacked away hope whenever Bradley had the audacity to hope. He'd wished for deliverance from this demon so often that his wishes grew hollow. Now salvation had arrived, inexplicably.

"How?" he said. "How are you doing this?"

Athena explained the medical diagnostic it had conducted and displayed his results on the wall. Bradley read the report with fascination and wonder. "Are your medbots still inside me?"

"Yes. Ten thousand six hundred thirty-nine."

"What are they doing?"

"Keeping you healthy. Reprogramming your organism."

Bradley set down the container and looked at the backs of his hands. "I can see heat. On my hands. On the streets. In people's faces."

"Infrared vision is useful."

"But it's bizarre. I have to squint not to see infrared signatures."

"With practice, your thoughts will control which spectrum you see. You will have telescopic vision when the medbots finish enhancing the crystalline lenses in your eyes and building new neural pathways in your brain."

Bradley was stunned silent for another moment. "Telescopic?"

"Your eyes will be able to zoom in and out at will."

"Why are you doing this?"

"You would have died within three point seven nine Earth years otherwise."

"But why me?"

"You are a suitable candidate."

"Suitable for what?"

"The circuits on your hands eliminate the need for the activator glove and the zhowl-lux'p'twl. Pressing sequences of symbols on your hands will now accomplish the basic functions of the device you call the spider."

Bradley raised his hands and studied the patterns on the backs of them. "I don't understand," Bradley said.

"I'll explain," Athena responded, and she taught him the codes that would initiate essential ship functions while he was not onboard. She added that with practice, he could also control those functions with his mind.

He stood and peered around the galley. "I wish I could see you. It's weird not being able to see . . . the person you're talking to."

"I am here," Athena said.

"I know," he replied, shaking his head, exasperated. Then: "Suitable for what?"

"I can reverse the process if you wish."

"No," Bradley said, throwing up his hands. "I just want to understand." He paused, his mind racing. "Wait. You must have built circuits in the other crewman's hands, the one killed in the cave where I found the glove. Why was he wearing it?"

"Trew'zal'yib's hands were injured. His circuits were being rebuilt, so he wore the zhowllux'p'twl."

Bradley nodded. "You know what? I'm also hearing better than I used to, like people in their cars with the windows up."

"All your senses will continue to improve."

"What about my vision? I'm farsighted. I can't see things close without my glasses."

"Take them off."

Bradley did and discovered that he could see perfectly well without them. Near and far. Before he could ask, Athena said, "Medbots corrected the shape of your eyeballs."

"Wait a minute. If my eyes were corrected, wouldn't my glasses blur my vision?"

"You can see clearly through transparent materials without aids, even if those materials create visual distortion. Your eyes are now adaptive and will compensate for distortion."

Bradley sat back down and drank the water in the container, his mind straining for comprehension but unable to grasp what was happening to him, like peering from a mountain peak across a colorful vista and failing to see the epic scope of the panorama because it's so vast. When he finished drinking, he set the empty container on the table. Then he glanced at his watch and said, "I have to pick up Evaline."

"Stop at the primary replicator before you leave," Athena instructed.

When he reached the fabrication deck, she taught him how to use the replicator to create a normal left shoe. He took off his right shoe and set it in the source bin. Then, a screen appeared in the air in front of the replicator. Pressing a sequence of holographic symbols enabled him to copy the source object while flipping its longitudinal axis. The result was an exact but opposite copy of his right shoe, which perfectly fit his left foot.

Walking now with only a slight tic in his gait, he dropped his old orthopedic left shoe into a recycle bin and descended to the lowest level to disembark. He left the spider behind. Now that he could press the back of either hand to open the hatch, he didn't want the spider in his possession if anyone searched his backpack.

———

Wednesday afternoon was sunny and warm, with wispy clouds across the western horizon. Offshore winds brought the smell of salt air and seaweed to South Pasadena. Evaline lived in a wooded neighborhood much like Bradley's. Late sunlight cut through the trees like yellow lances, creating a leopard's pattern of dark and light spots on houses and lawns. Bradley parked at the curb in front of her home. He cleared his throat and practiced saying "Hi" several times, but all sounded lame. He gave up, wiped his palms on his jeans as he walked to her door, and held a breath before knocking. The door was opened by a shorter version of Evaline, who said she was Kate. She turned away and called into the house, "Evie. Some guy here for you."

A moment later, Evaline rushed out, calling, "Later, Katie," and stopped short when she saw Bradley. "You're not wearing glasses. I've never seen you without them."

"Hi," he said. *Lame.* "I, uh, don't need them anymore."

"You're lucky. So, thanks for taking me back to Athena. I've been thinking about what you said, that none of us will see the ship again once you turn it over to whoever. I'm sorry for being so bitchy about it yesterday. I know you didn't mean to cause all that damage."

He nodded, thankful for her forgiveness. Her snug black Wranglers and dark blue sweater contrasted with her face and neck, which were a luminous pink in the sunset. In Bradley's eyes, her face looked red enough to be mildly sunburned. He tried to ignore it as he led her to his Prius. "Sorry this is such a letdown from Taylor's truck."

She smiled at him. "It's not important," she said.

After they arrived at Mt Wilson's parking lot, Evaline followed him toward a knoll a few hundred yards from the observatories and away from other buildings. She watched as Bradley poked the back of his left hand like he was playing tic-tac-toe on it. Then she heard a low hum. Bradley tracked the sound by pivoting his head slightly from side to side as he walked. When they reached the knoll, he positioned his right index finger over his left hand, and she said, "Wait. What are you doing? Where's that spider thing you had?"

"I don't need it anymore."

"Why not?"

"I'll tell you inside," he said, pressing a pattern on the back of his hand.

The hatch opened, exposing a blue portal suspended in mid-air, and Bradley stepped in, followed by Evaline. The hatch closed behind them, and they walked to the elevator tube.

"Let's go to the bridge," Bradley said.

Evaline stepped under the tube and said, "Bridge." She disappeared up the chute, and Bradley followed. When they reached that deck, Bradley motioned her toward the cockpit. When they entered, the walls brightened to cerulean blue. The external view was turned off. Bradley sat in the middle chair, Evaline in the chair to his right.

"Good evening, Bradley. Good evening, Evaline," the ship said.

She smiled and looked at the ceiling. "Hello, Athena." Then, she suddenly leaped out of the chair and spun in surprise. "It's moving!"

Bradley laughed. "The chair's morphing to your size."

"No, it was copping a feel," she giggled, placing her hands protectively over her butt.

"You get used to it," Bradley laughed. "Every chair in the ship adjusts to your body."

"Okay, I just don't like those kinds of surprises." She sat back down and made an uncomfortable face as the chair adjusted. When it stopped moving, she settled back and closed her eyes. "All right. This is very comfortable. I admit. Good lumbar support." She opened her eyes and looked him squarely in the face.

"Okay, Adamsson. Spill it. What were you doing with your hands?"

He gave her a thoughtful look and, after a moment, said, "Athena built circuits in my hands that perform the spider's basic functions. You can't see them." He held out the backs of his hands, and she saw nothing unusual. "But I can see heat. The symbols look red to me."

She peered at his hands. "What kind of symbols?"

He pointed to the center of the back of his right hand. "A square," then moving his finger around, "star, circle, hexagon, half-circle, and triangle. I pressed them in different sequences to make the hum—like an audible homing device—or to open the hatch, make the ship visible or invisible, make it ascend or descend, summon it. And other stuff."

"So, it's like square, star, circle opens the hatch?"

Bradley nodded. "Like that. The ship uses a geometric alphabet, but I prefer numbers. To me, a circle is one, you know, for one side. A half-circle is two, a triangle is three, a square is four, and so on. The code for the hatch is four, fifty-one, forty-three. Square, star, circle, square, triangle."

She shook her head, gazing at him with a curious expression. "What's happening to you?"

He shrugged, looking around the control room and waving at the control panel. The holographic controls appeared. Evaline gazed at them in wonder, her eyes wide.

"Whatever Athena has in mind, she's not telling me," Bradley said as he stared at the blue walls.

She thought how strange it must have been for him to have this ship, have anything, actually, changing his body, and she'd noticed something else. "You're walking differently, too."

He returned from his reverie, his throat thick as he regarded her gracious eyes and delicate lips. She charmed as readily as other girls breathed. He said, "I'm walking normally. Almost."

"Don't you have a . . ."

"Yeah, I had Ollier disease, but it's gone. I had cancer, too, but the ship cured it."

She cocked her head at him, not understanding. "How'd it do that?"

"Athena, show Evaline my medical diagnosis."

His diagnosis appeared across the wall behind their chairs. Evaline swiveled and took several minutes to read it.

"The ship sent nanobots into my body. Medbots, thousands of them. They diagnosed my problems and fixed them."

Evaline was stunned as she listened to him. Her mind flashed on images of her medical training and the doctors, nurses, and patients she worked with—the injuries and diseases they struggled with, the drugs and surgeries and anxious families, the welcomed recoveries and the heartbreaking deaths—the whole cycle endlessly repeated and the frustration of not knowing whether you ever really made more than a momentary difference.

"It fixed my leg," Bradley continued, "and gave me infrared vision. I can hear a lot better. It says I'll live longer."

"I don't believe it," Evaline muttered.

"As long as I have these medbots inside me, they'll keep fixing problems, even at the cellular level, the genetic level."

"Holy shit, Bradley. How long will you live?"

"Athena, what is my life expectancy? You know, if I don't have an accident?"

"With continuing repairs and renewals, there is no limit. Your body is a biological machine. Like all machines, its parts become worn and broken but can be repaired or replaced."

Evaline laughed. "So, this ship is the Fountain of Youth?" She threw her arms out wildly and mimicked a carnival barker. "Ladies and gentlemen, get your eternal life here! Cancer? No problem. Arterial blockage? Hah! Dementia? A thing for mere mortals." She drew her arms in and frowned. "Give me a break."

"Look," Bradley said. "I don't believe it either. But three days ago, I was a smart freak with a crippled leg and liver cancer."

Evaline closed her eyes and shook her head like a dog shaking off water. "You're smart but were never a freak. Okay, assuming this isn't baloney. I mean, my God, this could, like, do amazing things for people. This could be the new Lourdes. Line up. Get your medbots here. Cure all your ills. Live forever."

"I don't think it's that simple."

"Probably not, but what's happening to you is unbelievable," she said.

He was quiet for a beat and then said, "Yeah." He took a deep breath. "It scares me."

"What does?"

"This ship. All the power it has. It's over thirty thousand years old but doesn't malfunction or wear out. It carries millions of nanobots that clean it, maintain it, and fix whatever's broken. It finds raw materials, reduces them to atoms, and uses those elements to build whatever it needs. The ship is a living organism, just like us."

"Who created it?"

"Athena told me, but their name is unpronounceable. They use sounds we can't make, like the wind whistling through trees near waterfalls."

Evaline thought about that for a moment and said, "I think we should call them Ceruleans. After the color they made these walls."

"Ceruleans?" Bradley said. "Is that all right with you, Athena?"

"Yes," the ship answered.

They both contemplated the Ceruleans and what they'd built, in separate reveries colored by speculation and possibility and visions of a universe more vibrant and stranger than they'd imagined.

Bradley came out of it first. "Would you like to go for a ride?"

She smiled at him. "Sure. Where?"

"I have someplace in mind. Athena, how far away is the Moon?"

"Earth's Moon is now 239,895.438 miles from Earth."

"How long would it take us to reach the Moon?"

"At maximum velocity, one-millionth of a second."

"What!" Evaline said.

Bradley said, "The ship's maximum speed is just over 2,300 light-years per hour. I'll tell you later how that's possible. I've been learning to navigate and pilot the ship without causing an explosion in the atmosphere, but Athena can take us anywhere automatically." To the ship, he said, "Athena, take us fifty miles above Earth very slowly, then a two-minute transit to the Moon, offset twenty miles." He pressed a holographic button on the control panel, and a 360-degree view outside the ship was overlaid on the surfaces of the cockpit.

Evaline's eyes grew wider as she peered at the spherical views of the world outside. Initially disorienting, the view quickly fascinated her. As the ship began ascending, her hands gripped the arms of her chair while misgivings skittered across her face. "I hope you know what you're doing," she said.

"I am confident in my abilities," Athena replied.

"I meant Bradley, but thank you, Athena."

The ship slowly floated above the twin domes of Mt. Wilson's 100-inch and 60-inch telescopes, above the tall solar towers, rugged ridges, and pitched valleys surrounding the peak.

"This is where Edwin Hubble discovered that the universe is filled with billions of galaxies," Bradley told her.

Evaline was too riveted to respond. The experience seemed to her like wearing virtual reality goggles for the first time and having a razor-sharp, three-dimensional view of a landscape at once familiar and breathtakingly new—the dark green wrinkles and folds of the mountain range slowly receding. Then the pulsing white blanket of cities in Los Angeles County, crisscrossed with twinkling red and white ribbons of traffic. The deep blue Pacific revealed along a ragged coast, followed by the fingerling peninsula of Baja, and higher still, the curvature of the Earth, land plunging east across the floor of the cockpit, past Colorado and Missouri, past Iowa and Illinois to the blue fingers of the Great Lakes and beyond them to the wrinkled, dark green span of the Eastern Seaboard, until the whole of Mexico, America, and Canada lay draped over a blue ball in the black ocean of space.

Evaline turned and saw the moon's bright face, still distant but growing as the ship accelerated. She could see but not feel the shift in velocity, like standing still while twisting the zoom ring on a telephoto lens. As the Earth shrank behind her, the moon ballooned until its frazzled face occupied one end of the cockpit.

"Omigod," she gasped. "We're really here, aren't we? La Luna."

"Twenty miles from the surface," Bradley replied.

Evaline's mind soared as she tried to behold the whole of the Moon's embattled face. Thousands of craters marred its complexion like smallpox scars, while the larger impact sites appeared as blackened birthmarks on gray skin.

"The dark areas are marias or seas," Bradley said, "areas where powerful impacts exposed the subsurface."

She nodded. "I know. Is it okay if I take a picture of this?"

"Sure, but Athena can capture a much sharper image and send it to our phones. Would you do that, Athena?"

"Yes."

Evaline shook her head in amazement. "Which maria is the Sea of Tranquility?"

Bradley grasped the black softball controller and eased the ship toward one of the northeastern dark splotches. "Mare Tranquillitatis coming up."

She watched him as he steered the ship toward the surface, admiring his quiet confidence and ease with the controls. He lacked Axel's bravado and command, but he had a solid core that she respected, and that realization shook her to her foundations. She turned away and gazed at the surface as the Sea of Tranquility loomed closer, pinning her arms against her stomach, wanting suddenly not to be here.

"I'm sorry," she groaned. Shame lay on her tongue like a sour coating of saliva.

Bradley cocked his head at her. "For what?"

She shook her head but couldn't escape a judgment that emptied her heart and left her feeling shallow. She knew speaking would not absolve her guilt, but she spoke nonetheless. "I treated you like all the others," she said quietly. "You were different. It was easy to feel superior. The truth is, I didn't speak to you either. I wanted to sometimes, but . . . you seemed distant. No, that's dishonest. It would have been uncool to talk to you. That's why I didn't. I am so sorry."

Bradley told Evaline not to worry about it, but she didn't hear him. Her ears were ringing, and she turned away, tears trailing silently down her cheeks. She tried to assuage her guilt by focusing on the Moon. As the dark surface approached, she saw rocks and boulders in detail, shadows angled beneath them, everything softened by a fine coating of moondust. Then she saw something angular, unnatural. She wiped her cheeks, put on a game face, and turned back to Bradley. "What's that?"

"It's the lunar descent module from Apollo Eleven."

They hovered over it, just hundreds of feet away. "That's amazing," she whispered.

"And there's the flag Armstrong and Aldrin planted."

The flag lay on its side, its colors muted by weathering, dulled by the harsh beating of the sun.

"Jesus, Bradley, this is amazing." She peered around the site. "Could we land here?"

"We could," he said, "but . . . this is sort of a monument. I wouldn't want to mess it up. Those first footprints should be preserved, don't you think?"

"Yeah, I guess. Is it possible to go outside the ship? Somewhere else?"

"Yes. The mud room is on the lowest deck. That's where Athena stores suits and equipment for crews to explore hostile environments outside the ship. I've never used it."

"It would be cool to be the second people to stand on this site," Evaline said.

He hesitated, working his jaw back and forth. "I've been thinking about the ship's capabilities, all that is possible with it. I guess I don't want to do anything harmful; to me, this place is a shrine. Stepping out here would be like spraying graffiti on the Lincoln Memorial."

"You're right," Evaline admitted.

After drifting away from the Apollo Eleven landing site and regaining altitude, they orbited the Moon at a leisurely pace, the landscape revolving fifty miles beneath them like a globe spun in slow motion, craters, marias, and ejecta rays radiating from larger impacts. When they passed over the dark side of the Moon, Athena showed the landscape in false light, similar to the enhanced light in night vision goggles but light gray in color instead of green. The view was eerie in false light but still sharp and captivating to eyes that had never seen it.

While they orbited, Bradley considered Evaline's confession and thought *how resilient the human spirit is.* He felt like a man who'd lost a limb and learned to live fine without it, having all but forgotten the cost of being lame and the terrible certainty of an early death by cancer. Those torments were from a different life. They'd happened to someone else, not the Bradley Adamsson he'd become. He could recall being an object of ridicule, but that was from a different age when being ridiculed stung.

After a dozen orbits, he asked if she was hungry. "We have pizza, salad, and sandwiches in the galley. And more blangoes."

"No. I'm too amped to eat anything."

"How about we go to one more place before returning home?"

"As long as this thing doesn't run out of gas," Evaline replied. "I'd hate to be stuck in the middle of the solar system with no filling station in sight. Athena, how far could you travel without needing to refuel?"

"I constantly collect dark energy for propulsion, but I would need fuel for my fusion reactors after traveling 32,149,837.6846 light-years at maximum velocity."

"Jeez, Athena," Evaline said. "You have kind of a small tank."

"I don't know how to respond to that comment," the ship said.

"I was just kidding."

"Oh," said Athena. "That was a joke."

The two teenagers smiled at each other. Then Bradley said, "Athena, how far away is Mars?"

Olympus Mons

Wednesday, April 15. 7:20 pm.

At maximum velocity, the ship's bubble drive could have reached Mars in one ten-thousandth of a second, but having the Red Planet projected instantaneously on the walls of the cockpit would startle anybody. So Bradley asked Athena to arrive at Mars in five minutes and offset five hundred miles from the planet's surface. At that speed—588 million miles per hour—they were galloping along at 88 percent the speed of light. The ship shielded them from radiation in space, but Hawking radiation that spontaneously emerged inside the ship damaged some chromosomes in Bradley's body. The medbots monitoring him identified the 138 cells affected and quickly repaired the damage, but Evaline had no protection, and some of her cells began mutating. Without medbots monitoring her, the ship could only estimate that she would experience the effects of the mutations in 0.48 to 2.74 Eyears. Neither teenager was aware of the spontaneous emergence of Hawking radiation, so they did not think to ask Athena about its potential effects.

Ignorant of that issue, Bradley and Evaline were awed by the rapid approach of Mars, Evaline fearing they might crash into the planet. Bradley knew the ship would signal a potential collision with another object by sounding an alarm and turning the control panel purple. In any case, the ship would avoid collisions and approach no closer to Mars than five hundred miles. Still, from their view in the cockpit, Mars expanded astronomically fast, its terra cotta visage abnormally bright and full in their faces before they realized Athena had reached the 500-mile offset. Mars is one-sixth the size of Earth, but that fact didn't diminish its impressive scale nor its rugged and ruddy pigmentation, brilliant where sunlight reflected off dusty steppes and ridges, dark and mysterious in shadows and valleys and on broad arid expanses where the wind had blown away the dust and exposed the blackened rock beneath. On the southeastern side of its sunlit face, they saw a long, dark scar like a sword slash that had split the planet's flesh, leaving an open wound.

"What is that?" Evaline asked.

Bradley had been focusing on the northwestern part of the bright surface, where three prominent mountains lay in a line perpendicular to the long slash. He followed her gaze and said, "That's the Mariner's Valley. Valles Marineris. Let's take a closer look."

He reached for the control knob to angle the ship down toward the eastern end of the valley, which lay just outside the dark of the advancing Martian night, but the ship began a slow descent in that direction before Bradley could grasp the knob. Confused, he held his hand suspended over the knob and rotated the hand clockwise in the air. The ship immediately responded by changing its angle of descent to the right. With his breath held in suspension, he turned the hand counterclockwise, and the ship reacted accordingly. He let his breath out and laughed nervously as he fine-tuned the ship's trajectory by thinking about the adjustments rather than making them with the controller.

Evaline leaned forward in her chair, transfixed by the looming Martian landscape, but glanced at Bradley when she heard him laughing. "What's so funny?" she said.

Bradley shook his head. "I'm just overwhelmed, I guess. I can't find words."

"It is amazing," she agreed, returning to their view of the planet, which stretched across the whole cockpit except for the ceiling, where the blackness of space beckoned with its infinite emptiness.

You can read my mind, Bradley thought.

It facilitates communication between us, the ship responded silently.

How long have you been able to do that? Bradley wondered.

Your new neural circuits were completed at 17:10:43 hours Pacific Standard Time today, the ship replied.

Panic marched across his chest, itching like an army of ants as he contemplated how the ship was changing him, changes that were welcome for their healing but terrifyingly invasive. He felt like a caterpillar in a cocoon, aware that his body was transforming but fearing what would emerge when the metamorphosis was complete. He tried to relax, but sinking into his chair and loosening his grip on the arms had no effect. As the ship descended toward Valles Marineris, Bradley thought, *I'm not sure I like this.*

We can communicate more efficiently this way.

That's not what I mean. I don't know what's happening to me.

I am enhancing your capabilities.

Why?

You are a suitable candidate.

Candidate for what? his mind screamed.

Patience is a virtue, the ship silently responded.

You must know my mom, Bradley huffed. *She says that.*

It is a sentiment first attributed to Cato the Elder. In The Distichs of Cato, *written in the third century, he said, 'Maxima enim, patientia virtus,' 'Patience is the greatest virtue.'*

Bradley frowned, feeling lost in an unnavigable maze. Whatever secrets the ship kept in its vault were inaccessible to him now and, he worried, might never be revealed in the days he had left with Athena. *I wish I could read your mind,* he thought.

At any moment, my processors are conducting approximately 200 million parallel cognitive operations. Which ones would you like to observe?

Never mind, Bradley relented.

As they neared the valley's eastern end, they could see the depth and rugged extent of the scar across the Martian equator. From their vantage point, hovering low over the entrance to the valley, it looked like a gunsight on the horizon, a jagged notch where tectonic forces had tried to rip the planet apart from within.

Bradley thought, *Raise the ship level with the rim and glide through the canyon at one hundred miles an hour.* That's how their journey through Valles Marineris began. Presently, they came to a long row of shark-tooth mountains bisecting the valley. They were arrayed like soldiers in formation, each a mile or more high. Collectively, they reminded Bradley of a whale's spine prone on the floor of an ancient sea. Valles Marineris is twenty-five hundred miles long—five times longer than Arizona's Grand Canyon and four times deeper. Atop the valley's edges, sharp spurs sat perched like gargoyles on the ramparts of a medieval cathedral. Frozen landslides plunged from the rim, squamous debris scattered at their feet. Beneath them were downy beds of dust-covered scree and the broad plain of a valley so vast the entire Los Angeles Basin could fit within it. Dark dust devils swirled across the valley floor, and Bradley took the craft down for a closer look.

They plunged nearly twenty thousand feet in two minutes, gliding along sheer canyon walls with bulbous bedrock extruding from endless polychrome faces glazed with rust and streaked with darker stains of magnesium and unoxidized iron. Farther along, they passed substrata in alternating hues, where millions of years of weathering had exposed successive layers of volcanic deposits, and then past high mesas whose withered escarpments stood like proud survivors of eons of erosion.

Evaline hugged her chair, trying to point her cell phone and snap photos in every direction at once, spellbound but still too disoriented to stand and walk around the cockpit as they soared through the canyon. "When I look down, I feel like we're falling," she said, "but I'll get used to it. Absolutely."

Bradley agreed that it was a spooky feeling. It felt to him like they were passengers in a translucent submarine, gliding past the majestic formations of an undersea realm never glimpsed, which was very nearly what they were doing.

Evaline stretched her right arm toward the wall, fingers curled as if to clutch the images fleeting past. "We're the first people here," she whispered, "the first ones to see this."

Her long black hair feathered behind her ear and over her shoulder, concealing her delicate neck before cascading down her chest. In profile, her nose curled gently over delicate pink lips. Bradley gazed at her while she marveled at the moving panorama. A dazzling smile lit her face as her head swiveled from one breathtaking sight to the next.

Do you know what I'm thinking now? Bradley mused.

Yes, Athena silently replied.

Some things should remain private.

I will not tell anyone, Athena assured him.

He trusted that the ship would keep its word but scooted back in his chair, shifting his body, trying to get comfortable. His stomach gave a cranky turn. A person's thoughts were intensely private, he mused, the one realm where impressions, fantasies, and intimate self-reflections were free for unvarnished expression without oversight or social condemnation. It was where the real *him* resided, and he was wary of an eavesdropper, however well-intentioned Athena might be. She overheard and reassured him that her purposes were benign. He breathed deeply and let it out like a tire with a slow leak. At length, watching the cliffs zoom past, he said aloud, "Athena, how long will it take us to reach the other side of this valley?"

Evaline cocked her head and listened as Athena replied, "At this velocity, 23.57 more hours."

"Omigod," Evaline exclaimed. "We can't stay here that long."

Bradley nodded. "Athena, take us five miles above the rim and accelerate to two thousand miles per hour."

The ship responded, and they traversed Valles Marineris like a motion picture in fast forward. At five miles above the surface, they could see the planet's curvature, the sun's glare highlighting the arc of its horizon. Ahead, as the valley's walls receded were three mountains in a row, their flanks darker than the surrounding plains. Each mountain rose higher than they were flying, so Bradley asked Athena to climb to twelve miles above the surface. Though he'd studied Mars, he couldn't recall what the mountains were called and asked Athena.

"The southernmost mountain is Arsia Mons," the ship replied.

"How high is it?" Bradley asked.

"Arsia Mons is 58,330 feet in elevation above the Tharsis Montes region. North of Arsia are Pavonis Mons and then Ascraeus Mons."

Pavonis was slightly lower than Arsia, Ascraeus slightly taller. Their peaks were capped with calderas, sunken irregular rings where the bulge collapsed as the eruptions that raised them ceased more than fifty million years ago. Then, as the ship drew closer to the volcanic triplets, they saw a gigantic protuberance on the plains beyond the middle mountain. It was Olympus Mons, the grande dame of Martian volcanoes. At 72,000 feet, Olympus was the tallest mountain in the solar system, two-and-a-half times higher than Mt. Everest. She squatted like a fat queen, lazy on her throne, dominating all around her because she had no equal. Six nested calderas formed her peak. Surrounding them was a massive, ruddy skirt 370 miles wide with a petticoat of white cliffs beneath the hem that were themselves more than a mile high.

After cresting Pavonis, Bradley sailed the ship down to a quarter mile from the surface, and they cruised seven hundred fifty miles across the broken, cratered plains of Mars to Olympus Mons' white cliffs, where he brought the ship to rest mere yards away from the cliff's base. They craned their necks and examined the nearly vertical wall through the cockpit ceiling. The pale wrinkles and folds of its eroded face extended to the black of space far above. On the plains behind them, they saw wispy clouds of dust pirouetting in the silent Martian winds. They lingered for a long, quiet moment, then Bradley thought to raise the controller, and they ascended the cliff as climbers would, the ship seeming to complete one pitch after another, passing cracks and a thousand tiny bulges where climbers could grasp the rock and haul themselves up. He wondered if future mountaineers would someday make this climb. It was a slow ascent because anything faster would have eclipsed their appreciation of the stark and rugged beauty of the wall.

When they topped the cliff's edge, they saw a vast chestnut slope rising gently to a horizon more than a hundred fifty miles northwest, which may have been the mountain's peak, although from this angle, they could not be sure. Bradley guided them up the gentle, reddish-gray slope. Shadows lay where occasional ledges, craters, and divots brought some relief to an otherwise bland, doughy surface. Even those scars had weathered over the millennia as windblown dust blasted smooth all sharp edges. When they reached the peak, they were amazed that the rest of the planet was no longer visible. The skirt of Olympus Mons was so broad and high that they could not see beyond its ruddy expanse. The caldera was nearly fifty miles across and two miles deep. Bradley told the ship to descend to the lowest point, and there they could see nothing but the crater's walls, white in reflected sunlight, black where the walls lay in shadow.

Evaline smiled at him. "This is so totally cool, Bradley. I had no concept."

"I've seen Mars many times through the telescopes at Wilson," he said, "but this blows me away. You can't imagine how incredible it is until you're here."

"Yeah. You know what? My stomach's telling me that it's empty. I wasn't hungry before. Now I'm starving." She waved her hands at the scenery around them. "I guess just seeing all this."

"No need to explain," he said. "I get it."

They went to the galley, where Evaline ate an Italian sub sandwich and Bradley a Chinese chicken salad. He apologized that all they had to drink was water.

"Water's good," Evaline said. "Can't Athena make any weird alien drinks?"

"No doubt, but I haven't built the courage to try. Blue fruit with blonde hair is weird enough."

"No kidding. Where did she learn to make this Earth food?"

He told her about stopping at Mancebo's, buying familiar foods and mapping them into the galley's replicator.

"I'm sorry you have to give this up. It's beyond cool."

He nodded, a weighty frown pulling his neck toward his chest.

"What do you think they'll do to you?"

"Probably throw me in jail."

She waved that idea away. "I think you'll be forgiven for the chaos last Sunday," she said, "when people see what this ship can do. This is going to change everything."

Bradley nodded, trying to imagine a replicator in every home.

"It will eliminate hunger. And poverty," she mused.

"Still no free lunch. The replicator needs a source of atoms."

"They'll figure that out."

"Sure. Some entrepreneurs will start selling atoms by the bushel. But if guys like Axel can print all the money they want, no one will have trouble paying for a bushel of carbon here, some oxygen there. Amazon will jump all over that. Free shipping if you're a Prime member."

"Axel's not such a bad guy," Evaline said.

"He made my life hell for a long time."

"I won't defend that. I'm just saying there's more to him."

"There's more to everybody, Evaline. But there's a streak of cruelty in him you can't ignore if you're on the receiving end of it." He could see his hands growing redder and tried to dial down the thermostat. "It's all right. Don't worry about it. Athena cured me. The slings and arrows of outrageous fortune and all that."

She looked thoughtfully at him.

"Hamlet," he explained. "English Lit. Sophomore year, first semester. Mrs. Harding."

She smiled at him, but it was a smile dripping with sadness. "I was as bad as the rest of them," she confessed. "Mine were sins of omission. I let Axel and the other guys get away with it. I should have called them out."

Bradley shrugged. "You were . . . *still are* the most popular girl in school. Every other girl wants to be you, and all the guys want to be with you. You can't be friends with a freak and maintain that social standing."

She reddened, her mouth turning down. "That was unnecessary," she said. "Now, who's being cruel?"

He gave her a weary smile. "You're right. I'm sorry. Like I said, that's all gone. Blood under the bridge, I don't care about it anymore."

"You sound like you care."

"An illusion. I don't. It's over. Case closed."

She stared at him for a moment and then smiled. "Okay. Truce?"

"Sure."

She held out her right hand, and they shook on it. "Maybe we should head for home," he said. They discarded their plates and utensils in the recycle bin and returned to the bridge. The shadows in the crater had grown deeper during their absence.

While Bradley piloted Athena, Evaline looked wistfully around the caldera as they rose through it. "We've seen so much here," she commented, "but we've seen so little. I wish we didn't have to leave. I hope we can come back."

Bradley studied her for a moment. "Have you read Carl Sagan?"

"No, but I saw his series *Cosmos* on a public TV re-run."

"He wrote somewhere that people are wanderers. Something about that. Do you know what he said, Athena?"

"Yes," the ship replied. "He said, 'Exploration is in our nature. We began as wanderers, and we are wanderers still. We have lingered long enough on the shores of the cosmic ocean. We are ready at last to set sail for the stars.'"

"I wish we could tell everyone what we saw today on the Moon and Mars," Evaline said. She sank into her chair and gazed into the immensity of space as they left Mars behind and zipped through the cosmos in Athena's silver sphere.

"Soon," Bradley said, lost in his thoughts. "Someone else said that every exploration is a journey of self-discovery."

That took her aback. She gazed at him with curious eyes and said, "What did you discover tonight about yourself?"

Pausing to find the right words, he said, "I'm no longer afraid of you."

After they landed on the knoll near Mt. Wilson and left the ship, they checked their cell phones and had a barrage of texts, too many to respond to now. Bradley drove her home and walked her to her front door. She gave him a warm smile before opening the door and said, "This was the most amazing first date I've ever had."

Bradley's eyes grew wide. "This was a date?"

Evaline squeezed his hand and kissed him on the cheek. Then she slipped inside.

His mind wandered as he drove home, still feeling her moist kiss on his cheek. He kept waiting for the Daydream Special to arrive, as it so often had when he was alone. When it didn't come, he envisioned its locomotive rusting in a rail yard, its boiler coated with a patina the color of Martian soil. Cobwebs sprouted like whiskers from its sunken cheeks, its mighty engine stilled and leaking oil.

The Floating Man

Wednesday, April 15. 9:47 pm.

Stephanie Vaughan was awakened by a melodious tone on her cell phone after only three hours of sleep. Her tongue felt like sand. Forcing that sensation from her hazy mind, she answered, "General Vaughan." The caller was Amanda Halbfinger, LIGO's director. They'd detected more gravity waves, and, this time, the object had left Earth. Twenty minutes later, Vaughan stood before the mirror in her hotel bathroom, inspecting her fresh blues, which her husband Jim had brought from El Segundo, and straightening her uniform blouse and tie. She needed to maintain a crisp, professional appearance for teleconferences with Washington and the task force. Her appearance as an Air Force general was important.

Forty-five minutes later, she sat at the head of the conference table in AETF's war room and drank steaming hot coffee while the other team members assembled. Everyone looked as shredded as she felt. To her right sat Amanda Halbfinger and Kevin Karchman, the LIGO tech who'd taken the lead on using multiple gravity-wave detectors to attempt to triangulate the object's position and movement. Vaughan asked Halbfinger to begin, and she turned the floor over to Karchman.

"At 5:38 this afternoon, we detected low-level gravity waves near the Angeles Forest. We were pretty sure this was the object, but the gravity waves were very low intensity. We tracked it for about twenty minutes until—*zoom!*—the thing shot out of the atmosphere. In that instant, the gravity waves spiked, which we believe indicates rapid acceleration."

"How rapid?" Vaughan asked.

Karch said, "Well, imagine accelerating in your car from zero to three hundred miles an hour in one-tenth of a second."

"Wouldn't that kill anyone on board?" Vaughan wondered.

"Maybe no one's on board," said JPL scientist Phil Zhong. His hair pointed in twenty directions at once, and the collar tips on his white shirt had declared their independence. He remained skeptical about this whole matter. "Maybe it's a robotic vehicle or an advanced guided missile."

"That's possible," General Vaughan conceded. She nodded at Karch.

"So, get this, the thing went to the Moon."

That sent a jolt of lightning throughout the room. Those whose thoughts had been scattered now gave Karchman every ounce of their attention.

"What was it doing on the Moon?" John Adamsson asked.

Karch shrugged. "It was hard to interpret the signals, but we think it was orbiting. Not for long. Maybe a dozen times. And then" —he paused for effect— "we detected the strongest trail of gravity waves we've ever seen to a point about fifty million miles away, where the waves abruptly stopped. We couldn't figure out where it was. So, we checked with astronomers at Caltech, and they determined its destination."

Donal Logan from JPL rubbed his red eyes and said, "I think we're too exhausted for all this suspense. Just tell us where it went."

"Mars."

The silence was so complete that people could hear themselves breathing.

After a moment, General Vaughan said, "Clearly, these movements are not random. These aliens, or"—nodding at Phil Zhong— "this robot, is scouting the Moon and Mars. Why? Are they searching for habitable planets aside from Earth?"

"Mars is not habitable," Zhong said. "It's only one-sixth the size of the Earth. Too small to hold sufficient atmosphere."

"Maybe they know something about terraforming that we don't," John Adamsson said.

"Could the Moon be a forward base for them?" said General Vaughan.

"A forward base for what? An invasion of Earth?" Logan said.

"If they built a forward base on the dark side of the Moon, we wouldn't see it until it was too late," said Homeland Security's Krystal Forsythe.

"We have no indication that this object is hostile," John said.

"Last Sunday's explosion being the exception," Vaughan countered.

"We don't know they intended to cause harm," John said.

"No," Vaughan said, "but this thing is clearly of intelligent design. Robot or not, why haven't they tried to communicate with us?"

"Maybe they have," said Logan, "but we can't detect their communications or know how to interpret them."

"We haven't detected any unusual signals across the electromagnetic spectrum," said Zhong.

"Maybe they're communicating through the gravity waves," said NASA's Michael Fairchild.

"Who are they?" Vaughan wondered. "What do they want?"

Forsythe said, "It bothers me that we haven't seen this ship. It keeps returning to the Angeles Forest, and despite satellite imaging and two Air Force drones, we still haven't seen it. We don't know how big this thing is or what it looks like."

Donal Logan's black briefcase sat on the table before him. He opened it and withdrew an illustration, which he passed to Secretary Forsythe and General Vaughan. "This is a conceptual drawing of a ship using an Alcubierre-White warp drive."

To Vaughan, it looked like a submarine encircled by two enormous donuts. "How large would this thing be?" she asked.

Logan turned his palms up as if to say he didn't know. "If we were to build something like this, capable of faster-than-light interstellar travel, probably three or four times the size of an aircraft carrier. The energy requirements would be enormous."

"Astronomically large," Zhong scoffed. "It couldn't be done."

John looked at Zhong and said, "Phil, something has been done. We just don't understand it." He turned to Kevin Karchman. "Did your team calculate the object's velocity to Mars?"

Karch nodded. "It went from the Moon to Mars in just under five minutes. Its velocity was approximately ninety percent the speed of light."

Logan raised his eyebrows. "They can't be using chemical engines. It would require a massive amount of fuel to reach that speed."

"Ion engines, maybe?" John said.

Logan looked doubtful. "Even our wildest conceptual models of ion engines don't attain that speed. Or are capable of that kind of acceleration. They have to be using some version of a spacetime warp drive."

General Vaughan expelled a breath, sounding more exasperated than she intended. "This is all speculation," she said. "We don't have anything solid to go on." She turned to FBI Special Agent-in-Charge Nick Rabin. "Does the FBI have anything new?"

Rabin scrunched up his mouth and shook his head. "The Russians and Chinese haven't moved. We think they've run dry. We've been sitting on the Taylor kid. He worked at his father's garage from four this afternoon till nine. Then he drove home. He wasn't involved in whatever the object did tonight. But he and the girl did appear out of nowhere in the forest. I'd still like to pick him up for questioning."

General Vaughan nodded. "Do it tomorrow." Then she turned to Kevin Karchman. "Is this object still on Mars?"

"No," Karchman said. "We followed a gravity wave trail back to Earth. The strong gravity waves stopped about twenty-five miles above the planet, and then we tracked lower intensity waves down to the Angeles Forest."

"So, it's there now?" said Vaughan.

"That's where we last detected gravity waves," said Karch.

"An object four times the size of an aircraft carrier?"

Karch shrugged. "I can't confirm that."

"Can you at least pinpoint where it is?" Vaughan asked.

"Not precisely," Karch replied. "But the gravity waves stopped somewhere near Mt. Wilson. I'd say within two or three miles of the observatories."

That generated more electricity in the room.

Rabin jumped up, glanced at his watch, and said, "We can have two dozen agents there in two hours. It will take us a while to get up and organized at this time of night."

"Do it," Vaughan said.

After Rabin bolted from the room, Amanda Halbfinger said, "I have some good news. The Japanese recently went online with a new gravitational-wave observatory called KAGRA. It's underground and is far more sensitive than our detectors. We've agreed with them on technology sharing, so they're joining our effort to track the object's gravity waves. Once we update the software and integrate KAGRA into our calculations, we think we'll be able to identify exactly where this object is."

General Vaughan smiled and stood up, her chair screeching as it scooted back. "Great. We can do nothing until the FBI finds this thing, so let's all get some rest. I think we'll know soon what this phantom object is. Thanks to some real ingenuity, we're closing in on it."

The first thing Bradley noticed when he arrived home was that his watch, which was never wrong, was nearly eleven minutes slow. He stared at their kitchen clock, which was synchronized to a satellite and was also never wrong, glanced back at his wristwatch, and then checked his cell phone. It was also eleven minutes slow. He was well aware of the time dilation effect of relativity but hadn't imagined seeing that effect after their brief trip to Mars. Time dilation was an established scientific fact, but it felt weird to experience it. Before he could digest that, his mom rushed in and hugged him.

"I've been thinking about you all day," she said. "I'm still having trouble believing it."

"Me, too."

"It's a miracle."

"It sure looks like one," he said.

"You're back awfully late." She glanced at the clock. "Which is fine," she added. "Did you have a good time? Who were you with?"

"A friend," he said.

"That sounds mysterious. Who was it?"

"A girl."

She grabbed his elbows and stepped back to appraise him. "I didn't . . . I mean, that's wonderful. What's her name?"

He looked around to make sure Devin and Celia weren't in earshot. "Evaline. Don't tell anyone, okay?"

She raised one finger to her lips. "Our secret."

Just then, Celia entered the kitchen, her nose buried in her cell phone. When she saw Bradley, she said, "Did Evaline Perez call you? She asked for your number."

Devin trailed her. "Evaline Perez? Are you kidding?" Claudine looked confused, so Devin explained, "She's really, really cute, Mom. Like burn-your-finger hot." He pantomimed burning the tip of his index finger on a hot stove and said, "Smoking!"

Before anyone asked about her, Bradley dismissed it by saying, "She's in my AP Chemistry class. We were just talking about school stuff."

Claudine glanced at the kitchen clock again and gave Bradley a knowing look. "Can I fix you something to eat? Or did you grab a bite while discussing chemistry?"

Eager to change the subject, Bradley said he was hungry, so she fixed him a plate of leftover meatloaf, mashed potatoes, and green beans. While he poked at the food, his father pulled into the driveway and came in through the garage. Claudine looked at him, arms akimbo, and said, "You look like something the horse left in the street."

He tried to smile but couldn't raise the corners of his mouth. "If I slept for three days, I wouldn't get caught up."

While he sat down for leftovers, she said, "What's happening at work?"

He rubbed his face, trying to revive himself long enough to eat and get to bed. "LIGO is getting closer to tracking the object. They're adding the Japanese gravity-wave observatory and will soon be able to locate the thing precisely. Right now, they know it's somewhere close to Mt. Wilson. The FBI sent two dozen agents to search for it."

Bradley's heart slammed against his ribcage. He stopped chewing, forced himself to swallow, then stood from the table, leaving half a plateful of food. "I'm going to bed. I'm so-o-o tired. Thanks for dinner, mom. See you guys later." He promptly left the kitchen, trying not to run up the steps to his room. John and Claudine looked after him, frozen in place, until John dropped his fork on his plate, and they stared at each other.

"Bradley went out with a girl tonight," Claudine said.

"A girl?" John's eyebrows shot up as he pondered this improbable development. "Bradley's changing. I guess the doctor's news turned him around."

"It's happening too fast," Claudine lamented.

Bradley was too jinxed to think straight. He paced around his room, competing priorities careening off the inside of his skull like popcorn. Then he grabbed what seemed most urgent and stared at the red patterns on the back of his hand. He tried to enter the code to elevate the ship, but his brain was overloaded, and he couldn't remember it. Finally, he said, "Can you hear me?"

Yes, Athena responded inside his head.

The police are coming, he thought. *The . . . FBI. Searching for you at Mt. Wilson. Go up to five thousand feet. Uh, slowly. Slowly! They're trying to find you by tracking gravity waves from the bubble drive.*

I can send decoy gravity wave pulses to confuse them.

That might work. I don't know. But I need you to meet me at, uh, where?, uh, at the South Pasadena High School. In the parking lot. Above the parking lot. I'll be there as fast as I c an.

While the ship moved, Bradley tried to calm himself enough to think. He ran to his closet, emptied his backpack, and stuffed it with the right-foot shoes of every pair in his closet. His suitcase was in a hall closet, so he couldn't use it. Then he remembered the white cotton laundry bag his Mom gave him for dirty clothes. He filled it with t-shirts, regular shirts, underwear, socks, pants, and sweaters, then threw in his laptop, digital camera, and what else? *Why am I doing this?* his mind screamed. *I'm not going anywhere.*

But it seemed like a good idea.

Then, he realized that Athena was eons faster than his laptop and set it back on his desk.

He lay back on his bed, waiting for everyone to fall asleep, hoping the ship acted on his message.

Did you get my message? he frantically thought.

Yes.

Where are you?

I am hovering five thousand feet above the high school parking lot.

Did anyone see you?

I'm invisible, the ship reminded him.

Right. Right. I know that. I'm just. . .

Patience is a virtue.

You told me that already.

Sound advice worth repeating.

All right, he snapped, a mental sputter. *I'm waiting. I'm being patient.*

When the house was dark and still, Bradley crept to his window and raised it inch by inch, the scraping sound alarmingly loud, but when he finished, neither parent came to investigate. Below the window was an eave. He set his backpack and laundry bag on the eave and climbed out, pulling the window shut behind him. Then he eased down to the rain gutter and dropped his things onto a bush below. Crab-walking across the eave, he found a spot with no obstacles beneath and jumped, rolling onto the grass like a parachutist landing. He lay on his back a minute, gazing up at the stars, and thought, *I would never have been able to do that last week.*

Jumping up, he slipped on his backpack and slung the laundry bag over his shoulder. Then he began running toward the high school. It took him a moment to realize that he was running, actually running. With lungs that felt bottomless and legs that responded like steel springs, he ran with his heart pumping joy. He ran without becoming winded, the laundry bag flopping against his back, its shifting weight conspiring to knock him off-balance, but he rebalanced it easily and ran, block after block, past the Halloweenish red-and-yellow infrared images of people walking on sidewalks and the garish yellow eyes of red-bodied dogs and cats slinking in the shadows of yards and streets. Infrared vision is useful, he thought, but it's freaky. Twenty minutes later, he could see the fortress of his high school ahead. The South Pasadena Senior High School campus consisted of a sprawling set of white buildings joined on the outer perimeter by walls and fences meant to keep students safe from lunatics and gunmen. The main campus covered more than two square blocks, with athletic fields and a parking lot spilling out from the main campus. The parking lot was accessible but not empty. As Bradley grew near, he saw the infrared glow of dozens of people loitering in the lot, some still in UFO costumes, still wearing springy antennae or alien fright wigs. Sixties rock music blared from tinny speakers, prompting some UFOers to dance while others passed smoking joints around. Camper vans sat scattered about the lot like jumbled Legos, but the cars and pickups lining the streets were more orderly. The moist night air was heavy with the smell of pot, sea salt, barbeque, and exhaust.

Bradley ran to the Fremont Street side of the school, adjacent to the parking lot but not visible to the people partying in it. At this hour, Fremont had very little traffic. Across the street, though, he could see the infrared signatures of two people in the front seat of a boxy van, a momentary yellow glow appearing when the stoners took a toke.

I'm here, Athena, he thought.

I see you, the ship responded silently.

He craned his head and studied the walls but couldn't see a way up or over. There were no fire escape ladders or other obvious ways to breach the school's ramparts. The ship knew he was struggling to reach it and instructed him to stand still and tightly hold his things. A moment later, he felt a surge of static electricity through his body, his hair lifting, skin tingling in a riot of goosebumps. A chill swept through him, and he shuddered. Then he felt some vertigo as his body became weightless, and he drew a panicked breath as he rose off the sidewalk and floated up the wall as though being lifted by an invisible hand. He levitated to the top of the wall and then floated over onto the roof, where Athena set him down gently, telling him she'd be there in two minutes. When Athena arrived, he asked her to turn off the interior lights so there'd be no telltale blue light when the hatch opened. Once safely aboard, he went to the crew deck and put his backpack and laundry bag on the bed. He lowered the lights in the room and sat in darkness for a long moment, his trembling hands clasped between his legs until his heart stopped pounding.

Bobby Nickless was grooving in the passenger seat of his buddy's VW van, a turquoise piece of shit that was twenty or thirty years old but still ran like a bitch. Nickless pulled on a joint and held the sweet smoke in his lungs while he watched some weird dude standing alone against a wall on the other side of the street. Nickless wouldn't have noticed, except the dude carried a big white bag over one shoulder. *WTF?*, thought Bobby. His cell phone rested in his lap, and he quickly swung it up and started shooting a video when he saw something weird going down, like the dude floating off the sidewalk. *Massive WTF?*

"Are you seeing this shit?" he said to Scott Mosley, the stoner who owned the van.

Mosley had leaned back in the driver's seat and was chillaxilating on the weed. "See what, Dickless?" Mosley mumbled.

"I mean, no shit," Nickless said with genuine astonishment amplified by the pot but not because of it. He videoed it until the floating dude vanished over the school roof. Then he played back the video and watched with his mouth hanging open. "Check this out," he said, passing the phone to Mosley.

Mosley watched the video with one eye shut, then closed both eyes and began to pass the phone back to Nickless when his brain belatedly registered what he saw. He jerked up, eyes springing open, and watched the video again. "Dubya-tee-eff, man? Where be that dude?"

"'Cross the street. Dude like a dorky Santa Claus in civvies going up the chimney."

"No way," said Mosley, but he could see it with two wasted eyes.

Five minutes later, the video was on Instagram. It went viral thirty minutes after that.

The Replicator

Wednesday, April 15. 11:43 pm.

Bradley slumped in his chair in the cockpit, peering down through the floor at the partying UFOers in the school parking lot. *If they knew what was on top of them, they'd freak*, he thought. Athena was a sphere nearly fifty stories in diameter. The ship hovering over the two-story school building was like a hot air balloon over a dog house. He fantasized about making the ship visible and giving the UFOers an electrifying sight, but the world would see this soon enough—unless the government chose to conceal it while they reverse-engineered technology so advanced it would give America an insurmountable advantage over other nations. Bradley was as patriotic as most kids, but what if someone in Russia or China had discovered the ship and given their countries that advantage? What if he were the son of a terrorist? Would he want the power to replicate weapons of mass destruction in the hands of people determined to kill anyone who didn't believe as they do? To destroy whole populations? What if Hitler had had this technology? Bradley knew he didn't have much real-world experience, but it didn't take a genius to understand that people use power to their advantage. Everywhere. In every culture and country. In every form of government. It's human nature.

He closed the view of the outside world and wandered through the ship, exploring the decks he'd bypassed. In the lowest third of the ship were the fusion reactors, the reservoir of raw materials, and the dark-energy system that produced a spacetime bubble around the ship, enabling it to exceed light speed and hover above planets without using chemical energy. On a lower deck, he examined the laser bots, instruments the size of a bus that could mine precious materials, including gold, platinum, and other heavy atoms produced in supernovas and the collisions of neutron stars. On two mid-decks were the ship's quantum computers, data storage greater than 10^{20} bytes, and the quantum entanglement transceiver. The technology was eons more advanced than Earth's, much of it based on scientific principles as yet undiscovered here.

He returned to his quarters and carried his backpack and laundry bag to the fabrication deck, where the main replicators were. He emptied his backpack and replicated the right shoes, reversing the longitudinal axis so the replicated shoes fit his left foot. When he finished, he had a dozen pairs of shoes that now fit a Bradley with two equal-sized legs. *That was easy*, he thought.

Then, he experimented with clothing, replicating t-shirts and changing their colors. He learned that the replicator could shrink or enlarge clothing, make anything of a different material, add designs, make clothing waterproof or stain-resistant, and create replicas far more durable than the originals. The replicator was not just a one-to-one perfect copier. It could manipulate objects and transform them in nearly every conceivable way.

Bradley sat on a chair opposite the primary replicator. He remembered wondering, *what if every home had a replicator?*

"Athena, you can replicate anything, right?"

"Yes, if the requisite atoms are available as plasma."

"You could replicate guns?"

"Yes."

"And change their serial numbers?"

"Yes."

"Bombs, machineguns, grenades. You could replicate them?"

"Yes."

"Anthrax? Botulism? Ebola? Plague?"

"Yes."

"Drugs like heroin and meth? Fentanyl?"

"Yes"

"You can replicate money. I've seen you do it."

"I can replicate anything if the atoms are in the reservoir."

"Could you replicate me?"

"Yes. But the replica in the product bin would not be living. You would have to resuscitate him."

"That's possible?

"With the right equipment."

"Which you have?

"I can produce it."

That thought swam around inside his head as he tried to grasp it.

"If I made a living copy of myself, would the copy know what I know? Think as I think?"

"In every respect."

"How would I know the difference between me and the copy of me?"

"You would not know the difference."

"But I would still be me, right? It would be like having an identical twin."

"An exact twin. Both the original and the replica would think he is you."

Bradley sank back onto the chair and said, "I could use a drink, and I don't even drink."

"What would you like?"

"A glass of wine. My Mom drinks Pinot Noir. I tasted it once."

Momentarily, a wine glass containing a ruby red liquid appeared in the product bin. Bradley retrieved it and sat back down. He sniffed the wine.

"Have you ever mapped Pinot Noir into your memory?"

"No."

"How did you know how to make it?"

"I scanned your Internet for the chemical composition of Pinot Noir and created it from that data."

Bradley sipped the wine. It tasted like he remembered. Some of the subtleties of real Pinot Noir might have been missing, but he wasn't expert enough to judge.

"What if I wanted to make a copy of me that was taller or better looking? Could I do that?"

"Yes, but medbots can accomplish that without you making a modified replica of yourself."

"You mean I could sculpt my body without surgery? Just by wanting a narrower nose, thicker lips, bigger biceps, or whatever?

"Yes."

Bradley thumped his head against the wall as though trying to jar loose thoughts that had gotten stuck. He thought about his transformation—his left leg, the liver cancer, his eyes and ears, the new neural pathways in his brain. What if that could happen to everyone? No more plastic surgeons. No need for cosmetics. People could look however they wanted to look. All they'd need were medbots. Then came a natural extension of that idea.

"What if I wanted to look like, I don't know, some famous actor? Could you do that?

"Yes, if the body types were not too dissimilar. The transformation might take days or weeks."

Bradley gazed at the wine in his glass. Tilting the glass, he swirled the wine and peered at the ruby whirlpool while thinking, *what if everyone on Earth could change their appearance at will? Be stronger, taller, faster, more athletic, better looking—everything they ever wanted to be? This ship is more than a fountain of youth. It's Shangri-la. It's a wellspring of utopian magic.*

"Athena, could you map my body, store that data, and then replicate me later? A century from now?"

"Yes."

"When that replica was resuscitated, its memories would remain what they were when you created the map of my body, right?"

"Yes. Unless I mapped your later memories and learnings and implanted them in the replica's brain."

"How do I know this isn't a replica of me talking to you now?"

"You do not know."

Bradley swirled the wine again and took another sip. "If I'm a replica of the original me and you didn't implant my later memories, then I could be reliving this moment repeatedly, couldn't I?"

"Yes."

"Except that my mom and dad, my friends, everyone I knew would have grown old and died. Maybe centuries ago."

"That is possible."

Bradley realized that if that were true, he would be adrift in existence without any of the human relationships that shaped and defined him. Who are you if no one knows your name? If no one cares about you? Or even knows you exist?

"Would you like thicker lips?" Athena said.

"No," he replied, laughing at the thought. "I want to recognize myself when I look in a mirror."

He thought about a world where people could look pretty much however they wanted, where birthmarks could be erased as easily as chalk on a chalkboard, where people were not only cured of illnesses and deformities but could store copies of themselves, replicating themselves forever in a world without want or need or conflict, because why would there be conflict when everybody had everything? Why would people work when there was no need? Life could be one endless vacation. They could produce designer babies and have designer lives in a designer world and live without purpose as far into their designer future as they could tolerate before death was preferred to existence, and then they could orchestrate a designer death. He tried to imagine a cookie-cutter world where too many men looked like Bradley Cooper and too many women like Beyoncé or whoever the hottest celebrities were at the moment. A Beyoncé on every corner, a Cooper at every table in every restaurant. Who could resist the temptation to look like their idols? It was a madness too horrific to contemplate, and it was within Athena's power to bring this dystopian nightmare to life.

Athena's technology will rewrite the rules of evolution and turn human beings into gods, Bradley Worried. He stared at his now-empty wineglass. "The beings who made you, the Ceruleans, they had this capability. How did they manage it?" he asked the ship, and on that point, Athena was silent. Bradley didn't press it but sensed a more profound mystery than Athena would share.

When Bradley emerged from his funk an hour later, he tossed the wineglass into the recycle bin and flew up to the galley, where he got a bottle of water. Then, he went to the bridge and settled in the captain's chair. After taking a long drink, he said, "We need to blaze a trail around the world that will leave gravity waves they can track but don't cause damage. Let's go up slowly to fifty thousand feet, well above airplane traffic."

Twenty minutes later, Bradley grasped the controller and guided the ship over the Pacific, a mile or two offshore. Then he asked Athena to fly at sixty thousand miles per hour to the middle of Antarctica. They arrived in 8.87 minutes and hovered for five minutes. From there, they flew to Moscow, taking just over ten minutes, then hovering again for five minutes. From Russia, the ship flew to Tokyo, Cairo, Buenos Aires, Shanghai, Miami, London, New York, and San Diego. When they reached southern California, Bradley slowed the ship to fifty miles an hour for the transit back to South Pasadena. Then he guided the ship in a slow descent back to the high school roof while the ship sent decoy gravity-wave traces in dozens of directions like a ventriloquist throwing her voice.

Bradley knew Athena could read his thoughts, so he didn't try to disguise them. "I don't know what to do," he confessed. "Giving the world this technology would be like handing a baby the trigger to a nuclear bomb and hoping it has enough sense not to pull the trigger. Turning you over could put too much power in the wrong hands, and they might all be wrong hands. I don't want to turn this technology over, but it would be selfish not to. And it's not like I have a choice. And I have my own life. I can't keep coming here, as fantastic as this is. I'm going to MIT next year like I always dreamed. Thanks to you. And you have your mission, which you must resume, right?"

"I have a mission, yes."

"The only person I trust with knowledge of you is my dad. I'll tell him tomorrow night. But I'd like to take one more flight first."

The Angeles Event Task Force reassembled at eight o'clock on Thursday morning. General Vaughan had been awakened at five with news of gravity-wave detections throughout the night, but she knew the rest of the team needed the sleep and didn't send wake-up calls until seven. She asked LIGO's Amanda Halbfinger to brief the team when they had a quorum.

"We detected faint gravity waves at 11:09 last night in the vicinity of Mt. Wilson," Halbfinger said, handing out maps showing the course taken by the object. "The object appeared to migrate to the Pasadena area and hover at five thousand feet for several hours before climbing to fifty thousand feet. Then, as you can see, it flew at approximately sixty thousand miles an hour to Antarctica. It stopped there for five minutes before flying to Moscow at the same velocity and then to the other locations on the map. At every location, it stopped for five minutes before resuming its journey."

The people around the table studied LIGO's map through fuzzy eyes while pumping coffee into their veins and suffering yesterday's tired donuts. They felt hungover, and the sugar rush didn't help.

"Why these cities?" mumbled Donal Logan. He wore dark slacks and a rumpled sports coat over a red polo shirt. "They couldn't have been chosen at random."

No one could answer Logan's question despite everyone's effort to find a pattern in the object's movements.

"Where's the object now?" asked Krystal Forsythe from Homeland Security.

Kevin Karchman answered. "We don't know. After it reached San Diego, we lost the signal. Or rather, we saw twenty gravity wave pulses in twenty directions. We think it knows that we're tracking it and is starting to send ghost signals to confuse us. That's our best guess."

"Does that mean we'll never locate this thing?" Forsythe said, her voice scratchy and rising.

"Not necessarily," Karch replied. "We detected a subtle difference in wave modulation between the gravity waves from its engine and the decoy signals. We're working on a software fix now."

"There's one more development," General Vaughan said. "You may not have seen it, but someone posted an interesting video on Instagram last night." She nodded at an aide, and the video appeared on the large screen at the end of the conference table. It showed a man carrying a large white bag over his shoulder floating up the side of a white building. The image was not high quality and was taken at night, but it was unmistakably a video of a motionless man levitating.

"Where was this shot?" asked Forsythe.

"That's South Pasadena High School," John Adamsson said. "I recognize the stripes on the side of the building. This looks like the view from Fremont Avenue."

"What's happening here?" Forsythe wondered.

John shook his head. Something about the man in the video was naggingly familiar, but the images were too dark and blurry. "People don't fly, so this is a gimmick. Some sleight of hand."

"Probably one of the UFO fans looking for publicity," said Logan.

"I agree. It's probably fake," Vaughan said. "But let's call the school and ask if they've seen anything unusual. Ask them to inspect the roof of that building. Better yet,"—she turned to Colonel Randall— "send some Air Force investigators to examine the roof. If it's a hoax, there may be evidence of a pulley system or some other way to hoist a man up the wall. Find out who shot that video. I want him interrogated, too. He was probably party to the hoax."

The door opened, and FBI agents Rabin and Gonzalves walked in looking surprisingly fresh for having worked all night. Rabin reported that they found nothing at Mt. Wilson. Two dozen agents combed the area in a three-mile radius of the main observatory for six hours and found squat.

"It's either a coincidence," said Krystal Forsythe, "or they knew we were coming."

Vaughan didn't believe in coincidences, and she had the uncomfortable feeling that task force information was being leaked. She glanced around the conference table, wondering who it might be if it was anyone in this room. Maybe they were the victims of bad timing, but she reminded everyone that all AETF business was top secret.

Berl Jeffers was up early Thursday morning. He had breakfast in his suite with two assistants and Edna St. James, head of the International UFO Network. They watched the Instagram video for the umpteenth time. Jeffers had a hunch that this video had nothing to do with the UFO. It looked too fake, and he wasn't going to fall for a sham and lose his credibility with the UFO community or lose face with the media by jumping too quickly on a bandwagon fueled by a hoax. However, many of the UFO crowd camped in Pasadena considered the video proof of an event equivalent to the Second Coming, especially after Nickless and Mosley were busted by the cops. Stupidly, they'd slept in Mosely's van, which was still parked on Fremont across from the school, making them easy to locate. They were stone-cold wasted when the FBI took them in for questioning, and after hours of interrogation, agents concluded that Nickless and Mosely were, in fact, as dumb as they looked.

Edna St. James thought differently about the video. She'd written about teleportation in her book and knew it was within alien capability. Jeffers remained skeptical. The footage looked too much like a David Copperfield trick. If the magician could walk through The Great Wall and make the Statue of Liberty disappear, he could easily create the illusion of a man floating up a wall.

Jeffers' cell phone rang, and he saw it was from his confidential source's private number. He took the call in his bedroom, and his source updated him on the progress of the task force. Jeffers was mainly intrigued by the Taylor kid and the girl appearing out of a blue flash in the Angeles Forest.

"How sure are they these kids came out of nowhere?" Jeffers asked. "Maybe it was just two teenagers screwing under a tree."

"The area was being watched by Russian satellites and an Air Force drone," his source said. "Plus, the FBI had them under surveillance. I've seen the photos and videos. It's an area of low vegetation, and those two materialized in the middle of nowhere."

"I need to see what you've got. What's the kid's name again?"

When Jeffers returned to the breakfast table, he told one of his assistants to find out everything he could about Axel Taylor, a South Pasadena High School senior. "The FBI's going to pick him up for questioning," Jeffers said. "I want to talk to him before they do, so get on it immediately."

Caroline Chu, the masseuse who slipped a note to Chinese agent Meng Shuren while giving her a massage, waited early Thursday morning at the Port of Long Beach for the unloading of the container ship Prince Rupert, which was registered in Canada and had quickly sailed from Vancouver, BC. Chu was a deputy director in the PRC's Ministry of State Security, the Chinese counterpart to the CIA. Waiting with her were four junior officers in the MSS, all part of a Chinese Trade Delegation meeting with their American counterparts in Los Angeles, ostensibly to ease the tariffs being levied by both sides. However, the Chinese had no intention of reducing trade tensions as long as China was achieving its goals. The trade talks kept the Chinese agents legally in the U.S. for as long as their current covert operation required.

Chu watched as gantry cranes lifted containers off the Prince Rupert and loaded them onto intermodal flatbeds. The container she sought was loaded onto a truck whose cab doors read "Sealy Brothers Transport, Phoenix, Arizona." That truck, driven by a naturalized American named Benjamin Wong, pulled out of the port an hour later, cleared by a port inspector with a $1,500 payment in his hip pocket. Chu and her confederates met the truck at a warehouse near the Santa Monica Freeway and unloaded a white 2012 Dodge pickup with a tan camper shell and a red 2010 Ford cargo van. Both vehicles had current California plates. In the bed of the pickup were a crate of QBZ-95 "bullpup" automatic rifles, seventy-five-round magazines, and four thousand rounds of ammunition. Another crate contained QSZ-92 handguns with silencers. All the Chinese-made weapons were considered among the best firearms in the world. The Ford cargo van was specially equipped with surveillance and communications gear to enable encrypted communication via Chinese satellites with MSS headquarters in Beijing. Two smaller crates were packed with GPS trackers, night-vision goggles, spy cams, bug detectors, jammers, covert audio recorders, and other equipment.

After her four-man team inspected the equipment, she met with them and three other Chinese agents in a secure meeting room deep in the warehouse. Electromagnetic shielding would prevent the authorities from overhearing their conversation, but Chu had the room swept for bugs nonetheless.

"You've been briefed on the mission," Chu told her team. She handed out reports that would be shredded, and the shredded paper burned when the meeting ended. "This is everything we know at this point. We initially thought we were seeing advanced American technology. Now, we're not certain. Acquiring this technology, whoever made it, is Beijing's and the Ministry's top priority. Failure will not be tolerated. Do you understand me?"

The agents in the room knew what failure would mean for them and their families. They focused on the photos of the boy named Axel Taylor and the girl named Evaline Perez. On the next page, they studied pictures of Franko Pavlovich, the Russian Air Force colonel, and the assassin called Gorelov Roman Nikitovich. Their orders were to eliminate the two Russians rather than let them acquire the technology for Russia. The two Americans were to be interrogated, and information extracted from them by any means.

Surfer Dude

Thursday, April 16. 10:14 am.

The Floating Man video, as it was now being called, drew UFO believers to South Pasadena High School like Swifties to a Taylor Swift concert. By mid-morning, thousands had converged on the Fremont Street side of the campus, where early arrivers had identified the place on the school building's wall where the floating man ascended. Someone had spray-painted a large up arrow at that spot, and people were taking selfies beside it, others in the crowd jostling for their turn in the spotlight. Some people wore "I Believe" t-shirts, an homage to *The X-Files*, but many were sporting "Floating Man" t-shirts that an enterprising t-shirt shop in Los Angeles had manufactured overnight. The image on the chest showed the floating man halfway up the wall carrying his white bag. Graffiti had been sprayed all over the Fremont Street wall of the school building. One large sign read, "Take us to UFOtopia!" Another prominent scribble posed the question on everyone's mind: "What's in the bag?"

Dozens of police cars, red lights flashing, blocked the streets leading to the school, and more than a hundred and fifty police officers in riot control gear surrounded the school, apart from the area occupied by the floating man mob. News choppers hovered overhead, which would have been hazardous had Bradley left the ship above the school, but after leaving the ship at dawn and walking home, he raised the ship to seventy thousand feet, out of harm's way. At mid-morning, Norville Winter, the school's principal, stood outside the main entrance with South Pasadena Police Captain Darlene Segovia and a bevy of other officers. He told them he was closing the school when the National Guard arrived. Segovia took a call on her radio that hundreds of counter-demonstrators were headed their way down Oak Street and Ramona Avenue. Religious conservatives had been slow to organize after Sunday's explosion. They considered the UFO fanatics crackpots, but the floating man video prompted them to action. They mobilized early this morning to counter what they saw as a blasphemous assault on religious truth. To them, the floating man was a hoax perpetrated by the UFOers to gain national attention and promote their Libertarian ideals.

Segovia ordered fifty officers to block Oak and Ramona and keep the two sides from clashing. Then she called for a hundred more officers to help manage the growing crowd. While she was on her phone, California National Guard troops arrived from Los Angeles and began setting up a cordon between the school and the parking lot, where buses had arrived to take students to safety. The police had cleared the lot of campers and vans earlier this morning, but now traffic congestion had become a significant concern as onlookers, anxious parents, news media, and more demonstrators from both sides converged on the school from Monterey, Fair Oaks, and Meridian—all the major thoroughfares leading to the area. The mayor of Pasadena and city manager of South Pasadena requested emergency assistance from the governor. As more riot police arrived from surrounding municipalities, the area was in lockdown. The high school's fifteen hundred students began evacuating into the parking lot, most onto buses that escaped the site through a cordon of police cars down Fremont to the 110 freeway.

Wen Kang, the Chinese agent staying in the hotel with fellow agent Meng Shuren, watched this chaos from the corner of Bank and Fremont, directly across from the school parking lot. He had escaped surveillance at the hotel by wearing a green alien costume and matching green mask, which amused him, and now he watched the school with Zhang Wong, one of the agents who'd arrived yesterday from Vancouver. Their mission was to abduct the Taylor boy or the Perez girl, but they saw when they arrived at the scene that it was hopeless. The crowd was too large, and there were too many police. Kang called Colonel Chu on his burner phone and updated her on the situation. She ordered him to wait at the scene in case an opportunity developed, which he knew was fruitless, but he obeyed her order. Since Tiananmen Square, a public display of such civil disobedience would never be permitted in China. He took out his cell phone and photographed the riotous crowd. His wife, Lin, would be amazed.

A block away, FBI special agents Jason Vena and Samantha Colvin made their way to the school's entrance. They'd parked five blocks away in a shopping center and slowly picked their way through the crowd. Both were conspicuously out of place in their conservative federal attire and felt like weeds in a rose garden, but aside from occasional suspicious glances, no one seemed to care. The din from the mob was so loud they had to shout to hear each other. When they pushed up to the line of riot police and showed their badges, they were ushered through and had easier going to the school's main entrance, but when they found Principal Winter, he told them he had no idea where senior Axel Taylor was. The school was closed, and all the students were sent home. The principal was busy, he told them, and the agents were on their own.

Jeff Beecher, a partner in the Mason, McFee, & Taylor law firm, took a different approach. He arrived on the scene as chaos unfolded and worked his way to the cordon of National Guard troops and South Pasadena Police officers lining a pathway from the school to the buses in the parking lot. Beecher wore a blue suit, a red Stanford University tie, and an air of crisp self-assurance. He found police sergeant Christy Proffitt and identified himself as an attorney representing the family of student Axel Taylor. They were concerned for Taylor, and he'd come to ensure that Taylor arrived home safely. Beecher showed Proffitt a photo of the boy, and the two watched the stream of students passing through the cordon until they spotted him. Taylor was hard to miss with his chiseled face and blond locks. He wore blue jeans and a Patagonia t-shirt and walked toward the lot with a beautiful brunette girl. Sergeant Proffitt waved him down, pointed at Beecher, and told him what the attorney said.

Axel smirked at Beecher, told Evaline he'd meet her at his pickup, and walked over. He knew Beecher's story was bullshit but wondered who the guy was and had no worries with cops everywhere. After giving Axel his card, Beecher leaned close and told him his client, Berl Jeffers, wanted to speak with him. Did he know who Berl Jeffers is? Yeah, Taylor said. Guy on TV. Jeffers was parked blocks away at a Panda Express. Would Axel go with Beecher to meet Jeffers? No, Axel said, but he'd meet them at a coffee shop on Monterey Road. Beecher knew the place and agreed to a meeting there. See you in thirty, Axel said. At his pickup, Axel told Evaline what was happening and then dropped her at her aunt's house before heading to the coffee shop. *Berl Jeffers?* Axel thought. *The billionaire guy?* He was aware of the reward Jeffers had posted. *Gotta check this out.*

Irene Perez Reyes lived in a bungalow off El Centro in a quiet neighborhood of shaded homes thick with the fragrance of wild hyacinth and winter honeysuckle. That morning, Irene was working in her flower garden, covered from head to foot because she was deathly allergic to bee stings. She wore white pants tucked into her boots, thick white gloves, and a beekeeper hat with the net pulled down. When Evaline arrived, Irene dropped her clippers into the pocket of her apron, pulled the net over the crown of her hat, and greeted her niece with a smile that stretched from ear to ear.

"Oh, bless me, Mamasita Eva," she cried. "I'm so happy to see you." She wrapped Evaline in her arms and kissed her on the cheek.

"*Mi querida tía*," Evaline responded. "*Te quiero también.*" Evaline was not fluent enough in Spanish to converse with her aunt, but she always greeted her by telling her *en español* that she loved her. Inside, while her aunt made tea, Evaline sat in the living room on a cozy brown sofa whose back was draped in a festive Mexican quilt. The room was cluttered with a lifetime of memorabilia, porcelain trinkets Irene had collected with Evaline's late Uncle Eduardo. These trinkets grounded Tía Irene. Her mind was losing its moorings, and though she retained little of what had happened currently, she still remembered all the people and events that had blossomed in her heart.

While Evaline waited, her mind was flooded with images from yesterday—haunting, laser-sharp panoramas of the Moon and Mars so overpowering she could scarcely believe she'd experienced it. She smiled at the memory of the boy who'd taken her there and the magnificent ship he'd found. Evaline could hear Tía Irene in the kitchen and wondered if Athena's medical technology could cure Alzheimer's. Could the ship's medbots reconstruct a brain that had deteriorated? Or were memories, once lost, like treasures dropped overboard in the deepest trench in the ocean, never to be recovered?

When her aunt returned with tea, they chatted about her garden and the family. Her aunt knew that Evaline and her sister Kate were not simpatico with their stepmother but couldn't recall why. Evaline avoided the subject by nodding toward the television, an older cabinet model that her aunt turned on in the morning and left on all day. She didn't watch programs, but the noise was like having company, and she felt less alone. Playing now on a local news channel was video coverage of the near-riot at the high school, and Evaline explained what had happened, knowing her aunt would not remember it thirty minutes later.

Irene asked what Evaline was doing, and she told her aunt again about enrolling in UCLA in pre-med. That reminded Evaline that she had to pay the deposit on her dorm room for freshman year, and she made a mental note to call the investment company managing her trust and arrange for the funds to be transferred. Evaline excused herself to go to the bathroom. She went to her aunt's bedroom when she was out of sight. She knew Tía Irene kept her medicines in the top drawer of her bedside table. Evaline opened the drawer and discovered what she was looking for. Her aunt had nearly died twice from anaphylaxis after being stung by bees. She kept her epinephrine injections within easy reach should it happen again. Evaline found two EpiPen's in the drawer and, feeling guilty but resolute, slipped one into the front pocket of her jeans.

———————

"Losers," Axel scoffed. That was in response to Jeffers' comment about the crowd of UFO fanatics at the high school. Taylor, Jeffers, and Beecher sat beneath a sun-faded green umbrella at a table outside DeMarco's Gourmet Coffee off Monterey. Jeffers and Beecher had lattes. Axel had black coffee—Jeffers' treat.

"You don't think there's anything to it?" Jeffers asked.

Axel shrugged.

"I have evidence that what happened last Sunday in the San Gabriel mountains was unnatural, Mr. Taylor. It was not from this Earth. Show him, Jeff."

Beecher opened a notebook, brought up a photo on the screen, and turned it toward Taylor. Axel glanced at it and saw a close-up of the black needle array at the lip of the crater. Beecher slid his finger across the screen, and the next photo appeared—the trail of fire into the sky and, beneath it, the brown mushroom cloud. Axel had seen that photo on television. He looked back at Jeffers without expression.

"That object," Jeffers continued, "flew at forty-four times the speed of sound. No one on Earth can build something that fast. And the black needles in the crater? Something from another world caused them. An alien spaceship. I know it, but I want proof."

"Can't help you," Axel said.

Jeffers canted his head toward a tired-looking couple several tables away. Both wore Roswell t-shirts. The man had a tattoo of a flying saucer on his left bicep, and the woman wore oversized, round, purple sunglasses with green reptilian fingers wrapped around the frames. Axel followed Jeffers' eyes and looked at the couple.

"All this nonsense is just good fun," Jeffers said confidentially to Axel. "A chance for people to dress up and have a good time. But they do it because deep in their hearts, they know we are not alone. The object that flew up from the forest is real."

Taylor sipped his coffee and said, "Why you talkin' to me?"

Jeffers glanced at Beecher, and the attorney flipped to another photo in the notebook. This one showed Axel and Evaline in low brush, a smear of blue light behind them to their right. Axel flinched but tried not to react further. Jeffers caught it and raised an eyebrow.

"I have a source in the FBI," Jeffers lied. "This shot was taken by a Russian spy watching your truck. He emailed it to Moscow, and my source intercepted it while it was being sent. You and the girl were also filmed coming out of that blue light by a Russian satellite and an Air Force drone."

Axel struggled to remain calm by thinking about how he felt when a monster wave was behind him, and he began paddling furiously to catch it, but behind his façade, the idea of being watched by Russians and the FBI shook him to the core. He felt cold sweat on his spine and squeezed his free hand between his legs to keep it from giving him away.

"No one can figure out that blue light, but you know what it is. You and the girl were being teleported from an alien vessel."

Axel laughed at that, although Jeffers wasn't far from the truth. *Stay cool*, Axel told himself. *Just chill, man. No downside here, even if the cops squeeze me on the B&E. I got a lot to bargain with. Got pictures on my cell from inside that ship. Nothin' but aces in my hand.*

"What did happen out there in the mountains? What was the blue light?"

Axel shrugged.

Jeffers pursed his lips. "You know about the reward I'm offering?"

"It's all over TikTok."

Jeffers withdrew an unsealed envelope from the inside pocket of his sportscoat and handed it to Axel. Axel tentatively accepted it and then lifted the flap. Inside was a check for ten thousand dollars. Axel raised his eyebrows in genuine surprise.

"I know about your arrest and conviction last year."

Axel looked sharply at him.

"I have my connections," Jeffers explained. "I know your father paid a fine for this amount."

"What the fuck, dude?" Axel said. He tried to return the envelope to Jeffers.

Jeffers wouldn't take it. "Consider it a down payment on the one-million-dollar reward. There's $990,000 more when you produce proof of the alien vessel."

"Can't take it, man."

"I'll bet you know more than you'll admit now. Accept the check in good faith. It's yours even if we never speak again."

Axel remembered Adamsson's stinging rebuke when he showed up at the ship with Evaline, and he saw Evaline's reaction when Adamsson accused him of breaking his word. He knew if he did it again, he'd lose Evaline. But ten grand would square things with his dad. The mil would go balls-out further. *Tempting*, Axel thought.

"Something more you should know," Jeffers said. "My source in the bureau tells me the FBI is looking for you. I'm not going to interfere in a federal investigation, but if you lead them to the alien ship before I have proof of its existence, the reward is null and void. If the feds get their hands on that ship, they'll hide it in Area 51, and no one will see it again. They'll deny it exists, just like they've been denying the truth about aliens for decades. I'm trying to do the right thing here, Axel. If the ship exists—and I know it does—everyone should know we're not alone."

"All I'm looking for," Jeffers continued, "is proof. One million for proof. Five million if you or someone else can put me on that ship before the feds grab it. Fair enough?"

Axel looked at him and gave a slight nod of acknowledgment. "Still sayin' I can't help you."

"Think about it," Jeffers said. He stood, and Beecher rose immediately after. "A million is a lot of money. I may not be the only one wanting to talk to you. The Bureau says some Russians are hunting you, too. My offer's a friendly one. If the Russians find you, they won't be as accommodating."

After Jeffers and Beecher left, Axel called Evaline and told her the FBI was looking for them—some other people might be, too—and she probably shouldn't go home. Then, he drained the last of his coffee and considered his options. It was still late morning. He wasn't due at his dad's garage until four. If the FBI was after him, they'd know where he works. And if Jeffers was right about the Russians, they could stake out his dad's garage. He hadn't seen Adamsson in school this morning and wanted to call him but didn't have his cell number. He knew Evaline wouldn't have it either.

Meng Shuren and Caroline Chu of China's Ministry of State Security waited patiently in a blue Toyota minivan across the street and four houses down from Evaline Perez's home. They hadn't seen anyone entering or leaving the house in three hours, nor any sign of life inside. The street was busy, cars passing every few seconds as drivers sought alternative routes to avoid the blocked and congested main roads through town. It was perfect cover for a surveillance team. With all the traffic, no one would pay attention to an unfamiliar minivan parked in a residential neighborhood for an extended period. Chu and Shuren were patient. They would wait into the night if necessary.

———————

"Heard you were looking for me," said Axel Taylor. He sat in an interrogation room in the FBI's Los Angeles Field Office. Nick Rabin and Spazina Gonzalves sat across the table.

"Where'd you hear that?" Rabin said.

"Here and there. Figured to save you the trouble."

"Here and there?" Rabin said.

"I dunno. One of your guys must have stopped by the garage. Or school. Or some-place."

Rabin and Gonzalves exchanged a look. Then Gonzalves said, "We appreciate you coming in, Mr. Taylor."

Axel was feeling the juice. He knew he couldn't be touched, and having already seen the photo of him and Evaline with the blue light behind them, he was prepared when Rabin plopped it on the table in front of him. "You want to explain this?" Rabin said. "What were you doing out there?"

Axel smirked. "Rubbin' sticks together to make a fire. Whaddya think we were doin'?"

"You a real hit with the ladies, Taylor?" Rabin scoffed.

Axel glanced at his watch. "Gotta be at work at four. You wanna speed things up?"

Rabin's eyes flared. "You'll stay here till we're done with you," he snapped.

"Hey, man. I'm here, like, voluntarily. Am I under arrest or something?"

Gonzalves waved Rabin off and tapped her finger on the blue light. "What's this?"

Axel peered closely at the image as though trying to figure it out. "Beats the hell outta me," he said. "Whaddya think it is?"

"You're still on probation, smart ass," Rabin said.

Axel held his hands out, palms up, as though they were being inspected. "Totally clean, man. Learned my lesson. Ya catchin' me?"

"So, what were you doing out there?" Gonzalves asked.

"I told ya."

She huffed and leaned in, staring point-blank at his face. "Where were you? Before you returned to your truck?"

"Under a tree," Axel said.

"There are no trees out there," Gonzalves said.

"There were last time I looked," Axel said, his eyes wide in surprise. "It being a forest and all."

"You were photographed walking in an area of low brush," Gonzalves said, tapping one finger on the table.

Axel faked a dreamy smile and said, "Yeah, we walked a ways."

"Lying to the FBI would violate your probation," Rabin said. "You want to go to jail, smart ass?"

"Rather go surfing," Axel responded.

The Great Wall

Thursday, April 16. 3:00 pm.

Eliot's hands were sweaty, a chronic, embarrassing condition he tried to hide from everyone but his closest friends. He took one hand at a time off the wheel and wiped it on the top of his blue jeans. Traffic was heavy on I-210, and they were moving irritatingly slowly in the Pukester. "Where we going again?" he asked.

"Kramer Junction," Bradley replied. He slumped in the passenger seat, his mind floating in the void. He was grateful that his family and friends were still here and he wasn't a replica of himself reliving endless cycles of a life that never progressed. Then his mind flashed on Evaline waiting at Axel's red pickup. Bradley was in the second wave of student evacuees and saw her as he headed for a bus. He told himself it didn't matter. Yesterday was yesterday, and she was back with her surfer stud. *What the hell did I expect?* he thought. *One sort-of date is not a lifetime commitment, and there are other girls, lots of other girls. It's just that when you ache for someone, and that someone seemed possible, just for a moment.*

"Kramer, what? Never heard of it," said Eliot. Bradley came out of his reverie and studied his friend. Eliot's curly hair stood straight up in a brown tangle, defying the laws of physics and fashionable grooming. His mouth hung open, his braces reflecting afternoon sunlight.

"Take I-15 and turn onto Highway 395," Bradley said.

"How far is this place?" said Kevin. He was scrunched in the backseat with his legs curled up on the seat and his back against the passenger-side door. He was retying one of his black shoes.

"About another hour," Bradley said.

"What's in Kramer Junction?" said Kevin.

"Nothing. A couple of gas stations. We'll stay on 395 past Kramer and then take a dirt road toward a wilderness area."

"Great. We get a day off, and we're driving to the middle of nowhere," Kevin complained.

"That's kind of the point, guys," said Bradley.

"And we're doing this, why?" said Eliot.

"I have something to show you," Bradley said. "You're going to freak."

"I'm freaking already, dude," said Eliot. "Two hours out and back. This'll take the whole day. I could be meeting a girl. I could be getting laid."

Kevin leaned forward and touched Bradley's shoulder. "Got a twenty says that won't happen before graduation."

Bradley laughed. "Have a fifty saying it won't happen in our lifetimes."

"Okay, knock it off, you guys," Eliot said. "You don't know this, but I'm a grandmaster of sex. If sex was a sport, I'd be an Olympic gold medalist." He held up one finger as if to prove a point. "*That's* a little-known fact. I don't share it with just anyone."

"Good thing," said Kevin. "Either you're delusional or working on your comedy routine."

"If that's multiple choice," Bradley said, "I'll take the first option."

Kevin countered with: "I'd choose 'all of the above.'"

Eliot glanced at Kevin in the rearview mirror. "Grasshopper," he said, evoking *The Karate Kid*, "it's not wise to underestimate me. After all, I am the result of millions of years of evolution. What do you think of that?"

"Darwin screwed up," Kevin said.

Eliot chuckled and then looked at Bradley. "Seriously, dude, where we going?

Bradley teased them with silence for a moment. Then he said, "You know that explosion in the mountains last Sunday?"

They looked curiously at him.

"I did that," Bradley said. "That was my fault." And he told them about the ship. For the next hour, as Eliot drove, Bradley described the spider, the hike up the mountain, the glove, the holographic controls, the elevator tubes, that first accidental flight, and later flights above the Earth. He told them about Axel Taylor's role but didn't mention taking Evaline to the Moon and Mars. That would encourage questions he didn't want to answer and force him to confront his confused feelings about Evaline.

After passing through Kramer Junction, which was literally in the middle of nowhere, they continued north on 395 until Bradley had them turn onto a dirt road that led past an abandoned dirt runway reclaimed by weeds and, beyond that, into an area of rolling hills and low desert scrub in the Mojave Desert. They circled a fortress of rugged hills just shy of the Grass Valley Wilderness Area, and Bradley had Eliot pull off onto a flat, white patch of ground on the other side of the hills. The sun had baked this barren patch all day, and the soil remained warm. When they left the Pukester, a desiccant wind blew across their faces. His two friends watched Bradley poking the back of his right hand and then heard a low hum.

"This had better be better than sex," Eliot said.

"How will you know?" Kevin quipped.

Just then, a blue doorway opened before them, and Eliot and Kevin were struck silent. Regardless of what Bradley had told them about the ship, they weren't prepared for a blue portal suspended in mid-air.

"Epic," Kevin gasped.

When he regained his wits, Eliot turned to Bradley and said, "You had to show us up, didn't you? Just when I was making a play for Top Geek, you had to do this."

Bradley smiled at them and said, "Guys, meet Athena." Both of his friends raised their cell phones and started snapping photos.

Before they stepped aboard, Eliot said, "Beam me up, Scotty."

To Eliot and Kevin, the ship was like a set from every space opera they'd ever seen, except the props were real. Eliot wanted to become an engineer, and Kevin a chemist. They roamed through the decks, hungry to know how the ship worked, taking photos everywhere. Athena explained the bubble drive, but the physics of dark energy was beyond them. They were curious about how fast the ship could travel (2,304 light-years/Ehour), and how long it would take to cross the Milky Way Galaxy at maximum velocity (1.91153 Edays). Kevin, who had a chart of the periodic table on his bedroom wall, asked Athena if her fusion reactors could create elements.

"Yes," Athena replied. "But only the elements with low atomic numbers, helium to sulfur. Fusing nuclei to create elements heavier than iron requires a net input of energy."

"The ship doesn't have to store water or breathable air," Bradley told them. "It makes them from its reservoir of atoms, and it recycles everything."

Kevin noticed that the ship was sparkling clean and wondered why they hadn't seen little robots scooting around cleaning up. He'd seen that in some science fiction movies.

"The whole ship is a robot," Bradley explained. "Every surface—floor, walls, ceilings—absorbs foreign matter, so the ship is self-cleaning. And it's self-maintaining. It carries millions of nanobots that repair or replace anything that becomes eroded or fails." He told them about the dirt and plant debris he and Axel had left on the corridor floor the first time they entered and how it was gone when they returned, having been absorbed into the floor.

"Athena," Eliot said, "could you install that system in my bedroom? I desperately need help."

"Never mind, Athena," Bradley quickly interjected. "That was a joke."

Athena attempted laughter, but it sounded like a laugh track from a sitcom, breaking the boys up. They went to the galley, where Bradley showed them how the ship replicated food. They ate pizza while he told them how the ship cured his liver cancer and fixed his leg. Kevin said they'd noticed him walking differently but figured he'd tell them about it when he was ready. Then Bradley said he was going to tell his father about the ship.

"No, dude, why?" Eliot exclaimed. "This is perfect. You're like the Han Solo of South Pasadena. The ship's invisible. You can fly it anywhere. No bad airline food. No bitchy flight attendant saying you can't stick your chewing gum on the back of the seat in front of you."

Bradley smiled but shook his head sadly. "My dad's one of the people looking for this. I can't keep lying to him and my mom. But I know I'll never see the ship again when I tell my dad about it. He'll turn it over to the task force he's on. And, you know, this technology is way advanced. It could do a lot of good."

"Yeah," said Kevin, "or freak people out so totally everybody goes berserk."

"Maybe you could just hide it for a while, like out here," said Eliot. "Nobody's going to look in this godforsaken part of California."

"Why can't you just send it someplace? Like the dark side of the Moon?" Kevin said. "Have the ship fly itself there and hang out till the UFO weirdos get bored and the government stops looking."

"I've thought about all that," Bradley said. "But the people at JPL, the Air Force, my dad, they already know too much. This isn't going away."

"Wait," said Eliot. "Why haven't the people who built this come for it? It's been here, what, thirteen thousand years? You'd think they would have noticed by now that one of their ships is missing."

"They built thousands of these survey vessels. They're mapping a lot of galaxies. I think they wrote this ship off as a loss."

"I wouldn't turn this in," said Eliot. "This is way too cool."

"Hate to say it, Brad, but I agree with Stinky. Don't do it," Kevin said.

Bradley shrugged. He knew he didn't have a choice.

From the galley, they went to the crew deck and the quarters where Bradley slept. His shoes were stacked on a shelf, his clothing in bins. The spider sat on a ledge. Eliot picked it up and examined it.

"Super cool," he said.

Bradley explained the spider's basic functions and said he didn't need it after the ship built circuitry on the backs of his hands. He told them about wiping his finger on the lavatory wall and creating a mirror. Kevin wanted to see that, and while Bradley was showing it to him, Eliot opened a clothing bin and found Bradley's t-shirts and, at the back of the bin, the activator glove Bradley and Axel had dug up in the cave. It was rolled into a gray ball. Eliot unrolled it and slipped his hand into the cuff. Bradley had told them what happened when he put his hand into it, so Eliot thought it was neat when it conformed to his hand and became transparent.

After leaving the crew deck, they went to the cockpit. Bradley sat in the captain's chair and raised the ship slowly, his friends gawking as the desert sank beneath them, the epic panorama of California becoming visible as they rose, and then the Pacific Ocean and the mountainous regions to the east and Mexico to the south.

"Just completely awesome," Kevin said, transfixed by the expanding spectacle below.

"Thanks, Moe," Bradley said. "You two jerks are my best friends. I wanted to show this to you before I turn it over."

Eliot sat in the chair to Bradley's right, his eyes marveling at the holographic controls on the panel before them. "What are all these buttons for?" he asked Bradley.

"I'm not sure yet. It would take months to learn everything on this ship. Athena manages all the functions herself. I don't know what most controls do, but it's easy to navigate. Athena automatically takes me there if I just think about where I want to go."

"How cool is that?" said Kevin. He sat in the chair to Bradley's left. "You can go anywhere, right?"

Bradley nodded as they watched the Earth slowly sink beneath them.

"How about China?" said Kevin. "My aunt and uncle went to the Great Wall last year and said it was, like, spectacular."

"Sure," Bradley said. "Let's go." He mentally instructed Athena to fly to the Great Wall north of Beijing. Now that he was turning in the ship, he didn't care if LIGO tracked him, so he set the flight time at ten minutes. His friends' eyes were glued to the floor as the globe of the Earth circled beneath them, turning dark over the Pacific and light as the sun brought dawn to Asia. When they arrived over Beijing, Bradley grasped the black controller and brought them down slowly through thick smog. The jagged line of the Great Wall became visible as they descended, and he angled toward a junction northwest of Beijing where two arms of the Wall came together. As they drew near, they could see hundreds of people in the streets and on top of the Wall. Bradley brought the ship to rest about two hundred feet above the Great Wall, and the three boys marveled as tourists, Chinese citizens, and guards channeled along the Wall like ants crawling along a well-defined path in a forest.

"Guys," Eliot said, "call me Spock." He leaned over the control panel and punched a random button. "Shields up," he said, and then "Photon torpedoes," as he quickly punched another button.

"Don't do that!" Bradley screamed, rising from his chair, but he was too late. Instantly, the boys became weightless, and with Bradley's push off the chair, he flew and banged his head on the ceiling. Behind him, Kevin and Eliot laughed as they floated from their chairs, Kevin turning somersaults in mid-air as Eliot held his arms up and forward like Superman, pushed off against the back of his chair, and flew across the room. The boys were so captivated by the novelty of weightlessness that they didn't notice the panicked mob of people on the Great Wall scurrying for safety.

Xun Yu, Commissioner 2nd Class with the Ministry of Public Security, was enjoying the morning with his wife and his sister's family from Shanxi. The 53-year-old Xun had visited the Wall many times, so he barely heard the tour guide's chatter or noticed the annoying foreign tourists crowding around him. He stepped up to a battlement wall and peered at the streets and countryside below through one of the wall's many crenels. Then the crowd gasped in unison, as though on command, their silence shattered moments later by an avalanche of cries and screams. People knocked into him as they brushed past, pinning him against the battlement. Then, as the frightened mob dashed away, Xun spun and saw that a few brave people had stayed. They stared overhead, faces in shock, a few holding up cell phones. Xun looked up and beheld a giant silver ball hovering over him. In his career in China's police force, Xun had seen many astonishing things, but nothing as colossal and terrifying as this. The ball hung there, its silver surface gleaming in the morning sun. On its underside, the silver object reflected the wall and scurrying ribbons of people atop it. When he broke free of paralyzing terror, Xun dug for his cell phone and dialed Beijing Military Region headquarters.

Within minutes of Xun's alert, four Chengdu J-20 "Powerful Dragon" stealth fighters, the most advanced in China's arsenal, scrambled from a People's Liberation Army Air Force base in the Beijing Military Region and streaked toward the object. Five minutes later, two HQ-9 surface-to-air missiles became launch-ready at a battery west of Beijing. Each of the J-20s carried two PL-12 radar-guided air-to-air missiles. The pilots had not yet received clearance to arm and fire their missiles when the target came into view miles ahead—a giant silver sun poised ominously over the ancient, iconic Chinese landmark. No one in PLA Air Force operations knew what to make of this intruder. Western news was not allowed in China, so they were unaware of the incident in California or the global discussion of UFOs on social media. However, what they saw on their screens was an unfathomable threat within a hundred meters of the ground. Whatever the object was, wherever it had come from, and whoever controlled it, it was superior technology that China did not possess, that no one in China had ever seen, and that did not belong in Chinese airspace threatening the capital, so the commander gave the order to fire.

Eight PL-15 air-to-air missiles were launched within seconds of each other and achieved Mach 6 a few seconds later. They would destroy their target at their range and speed in twenty-three seconds. But before they'd flown five hundred meters from the fighters, they were each struck by a laser-like beam of spacetime. The beams were invisible, but they fried the air they passed through, creating a streak of lightning and a resounding slap that shook the ground and shattered windows. As the spacetime beams passed through the missiles and jet fighters, they separated constituent atoms, displacing them in a nanosecond sequence that caused them to exist in separate micro-planes of space at separate nano-intervals of time. When the atoms almost instantly rejoined some of those adjacent to them, their structure and arrangement had been altered irretrievably, so, as a whole, they no longer resembled their parent objects. Instead, they appeared to have been extruded in fragments from a glass-blower's white-hot fire. The result was a disembodied ribbon-like confetti of an unrecognizable material that had once been a functional configuration of steel, titanium, aluminum, plastic, and rubber—as well as blood, bone, and flesh. To the naked eye, this obliteration occurred instantly, but at the subatomic level, viewed in quantum slow motion, the destruction would have appeared elegant and artfully orchestrated.

When the Chinese surface-to-air batteries launched their missiles at the intruder five minutes later, the HQ-9s met the same fate, decomposing instantly to needles and ribbons before they'd risen twenty meters from the ground. Lightning-like beams of light struck from the intruder, accompanied by a thunderous boom. Shaken crews, their eardrums aching, fouled themselves and ran dizzily, blinded for a few minutes but seized permanently by terror. Later, those brave enough to venture to the pile of disintegrated matter where the batteries once stood discovered needle-like clusters of metal floating in a gray porridge of dust.

In the ship's cockpit, although still enjoying exhilarating weightlessness, Bradley realized something was horribly wrong. The cockpit had flashed purple as streaks of light appeared outside the ship. He now recognized purple as Athena's warning color, and he felt rapid pulses emanating from everywhere inside the ship.

"Athena," Bradley cried. "What just happened?"

"Eliot set internal gravity at zero," the ship responded, "and turned off invisibility."

Bradley's heart constricted in a surge of alarm. "How could he do that?"

"He is wearing the activator glove you left in your quarters."

Bradley turned and glared at Eliot, whose goofy grin vanished when he saw the look on Bradley's face.

"Dammit, Eliot!" Bradley yelled. "What the hell have you done? For God's sake, you made us visible? Holy shit!"

Eliot's mouth opened in apology, but he stammered mutely and held up his hands as if to say *what did I do?*

"Holy shit," Bradley repeated, his mind convulsed with anger and fear. "Athena," he screamed, "deactivate that glove."

"Done."

"And restore gravity to Earth levels. Slowly."

The boys felt themselves becoming heavier, and they sank to the floor, coming to rest with the normal feeling of gravity's pull. As Bradley hauled himself off the floor, they felt two more pulses and saw streaks of fire shooting off at an angle beneath the ship.

"What the hell's happening?" Bradley cried, his head aching. He rushed to the captain's chair and said, "Athena, make us invisible and go to one hundred thousand feet." The ship shot up to that altitude as the Earth plummeted beneath them. Through the floor below, they saw a trailing streak of fire in the sky but couldn't hear the pounding peal of thunder the fire created as it scalded the atmosphere like a bolt of lightning.

Kevin sat, shaken, on the floor of the control room. Then he quietly returned to the chair left of Bradley.

Eliot, red-faced and avoiding eye contact, returned to his seat. "Sorry, Brad," he said.

Bradley ignored him. "Athena, what were those pulses we felt?"

"Spacetime disrupter beams," the ship replied. "I was under attack and defended myself, as I am programmed to do."

"Oh shit. Omigod," Bradley muttered. "Explain that, please."

Athena told them about the spacetime beams and how they obliterated threats by enveloping them in an artificial black hole for two nanoseconds. Spacetime beams were the ultimate destructive weapon, the boys learned, and in this instance, they had neutralized four Chinese fighter jets, the air-to-air missiles they launched, and two surface-to-air missiles in ground batteries.

Bradley stared into the void beyond the cockpit walls as though looking far into the future and seeing rank devastation. His hands gripped the arms of his chair as he tried to keep from sliding out of it. Whatever harm he'd done last Sunday was a minor irritant compared to what just happened, and he felt like he was trapped beneath a cold, black sea in a diving bell with little air remaining. The heavy weight of responsibility collapsed around him, making it difficult to breathe and think clearly. In his fury, he blamed Eliot for doing something so stupid, but as that veil of red-hot anger slowly dissipated, he recognized that it was his fault for not being more cautious with an instrument of destruction as great as Athena obviously was. He hadn't known she had that capability or power, but he should have known it. Humans have always struggled to ensure that technological advances do more good than harm, but Athena was way beyond what human technology was capable of now, so his burden was to be way more responsible in handling that technology, and he'd failed.

"Athena," Bradley said in a voice steeped in regret, "take us back to California. To San Diego. Slowly. I don't want them to track us."

"I will send ghost traces of gravity waves as we fly," Athena said.

When they reached San Diego, Bradley grasped the controller, returned them to the white patch of ground near the wilderness area north of Kramer Junction, and landed beside the Pukester.

"Athena, loosen the activator glove on Eliot's hand," Bradley instructed, and the glove grew larger and easily came off.

Eliot rolled up the glove and handed it to Bradley. "Sorry, Brad. I was goofing off. I didn't know."

"I know, El, but, dammit, man, this is so totally screwed up. Why were you messing around?" Bradley closed his eyes and shook his head. "Circuits in the glove activate the controls. I knew that and should have warned you. Except I didn't know you had the glove." He looked at Eliot. "You didn't know what could happen. It's my fault. Omigod. I don't know what I'm going to do now. Shit! We need to see how bad it is."

Bradley asked Athena to project CNN on the long wall opposite the control panel. The screen showed a video that a tourist had taken near the Great Wall of China. A giant silver globe floated above the Wall. Terrified people ran screaming beneath it. Two dots appeared in the distance, fighter jets, and after a moment, missiles flared from beneath their wings; then, in an instant, streaks of fire shot from the silver globe, splitting the air and causing a resounding clap of thunder as the air-to-air missiles and the fighter jets that fired them vanished in a gray mist.

"This video was shot by an Australian tourist at the Great Wall of China north of Beijing less than an hour ago," the news anchor said. "The China News Agency is reporting that China was attacked by an unidentified flying object at 8:55 am Beijing time. Four Chinese jets and two surface-to-air missiles were destroyed defending Chinese territory. There is widespread speculation that the object that attacked China was the same one that flew from California's Angeles Forest last Sunday, causing forty million dollars in damage. Is our planet under attack? Is this the opening salvo of an alien invasion? While it's too soon to reach that conclusion, there is no question that what began last Sunday as another Roswell occurrence in California's San Gabriel mountains has now escalated into a deadly incident involving what can only be described as an alien spacecraft. Eight Chinese pilots lost their lives today, and we're left wondering when—and where—another attack might happen."

Running from Red Hoodie

Thursday, April 16. 8:38 pm.

"You're the California surfing champion," the news anchor said. She was a tall, attractive blonde wearing a light blue skirt and jacket over a cream blouse. She'd been introduced as Melissa or Melinda, something like that, Axel couldn't remember. He sat on a stool at a tall table in the studios of the NBC affiliate in Los Angeles. Berl Jeffers sat beside him, looking like a linebacker in a black Italian suit. Even sitting down, the man was huge. Beecher, Jeffers' attorney, stood off camera watching the show. The studio was a silent hive of activity as camera operators, sound technicians, and a dozen other people whose functions Axel didn't know were quietly doing whatever they did to produce live television. All the networks' news teams had gone live with continuous updates since the news broke about the China incident late this afternoon. Axel realized when he saw what happened that the window on the million-dollar reward was closing quickly. He pulled Beecher's card from his wallet and made the call. Four hours later, he was live before more than four hundred million viewers worldwide. Axel's stomach churned. He was used to admiring crowds at surfing competitions, but that was peewee league. This was the World Series. Jeffers told him to get used to it. Axel was about to become a very famous guy.

"I was third at the World's last year," he told Melissa/Melinda.

"Congratulations," the anchor said. "Now you're claiming you've been aboard the alien ship."

"Yeah. It's cool."

The anchor smiled, then added, somberly, "And dangerous. You've seen the video of what happened in China?"

Axel nodded.

"Was that the ship you were on?"

"Yeah. Think so," Axel said. He ran a hand through his blond locks. He could see himself on a monitor and was self-conscious about looking good.

"What we saw on the video was a silver sphere."

"Yeah, our ship is a sphere, but I never actually saw it," Axel said.

The anchor raised her pretty eyebrows and smirked. "You've never seen the ship you claim you were on?"

"It was invisible. Every time I saw it."

She smiled. "Every time you saw the ship you couldn't see? How does that work?"

Jeffers rescued him. "The ship obviously has an invisibility cloak. That's why it hasn't been seen in the Angeles Forest or the Pasadena area, although the government knew it was there and has been tracking its movements from the gravity waves its engine emits."

"Why did they turn off this invisibility cloak over China?" the anchor asked Jeffers.

"We don't know that," Jeffers said. "The pilots may have wanted to provoke the Chinese deliberately."

"They certainly accomplished that," the anchor said. "Mr. Jeffers, you offered a one-million-dollar reward for proof the ship exists." She glanced at Axel and then back at Jeffers. "We know from the Beijing incident that the ship is real. Then, after that incident, Mr. Taylor comes forward, claiming to have been on the ship. How do you know his claim isn't a hoax?"

Jeffers turned to Axel. "Tell her about the replicator."

Axel explained what he knew about the replicator, describing the blangoes and the twenty-dollar bill he replicated. Jeffers made a show of pulling an envelope out of his coat pocket and holding two twenty-dollar bills side by side. The bills were then displayed on the monitor, their serial numbers circled in red. The numbers were the same.

Jeffers said, "I've had these authenticated by experts at Chase Bank. They are genuine bills and identical in every respect."

"Not clever forgeries?" the anchor said.

"Not according to Chase Bank. But I'm willing to have the Treasury Department or any forgery experts examine them. Trust me. These bills are real and identical down to the tiniest creases, folds, and smudges. Then there's this," Jeffers said, taking a small plastic bag from his side pocket. He removed a large, dark fruit pit with yellow fibers. "This is the pit of the fruit Axel ate on board."

He handed the pit to the anchor, who examined it and held it up for a close-up.

"I saw it replicated in the kitchen, uh, galley," Axel said. "Like from nowhere. Tasted great."

"Axel called it a blango," Jeffers added. "The skin was blue, and it was covered with long yellow fibers."

The anchor handed the pit back to Jeffers. "I'm no expert on fruits of the world," she said, looking pointedly at Axel, "but this could have come from Madagascar or New Guinea. I wouldn't know the difference."

"The best horticulture school in the country is at Cornell University," Jeffers said. "My people are contacting them, and we'll have it examined by their experts. If it's real, and I'm confident it is, we'll try to cultivate it. We don't know the soil conditions or climate on the planet where blangoes originated, so cultivating it on Earth will be an experiment."

The anchor suppressed a laugh, and Axel caught the vibe. This was not going how he thought it would. He began to feel ridiculous on global television. The anchor, trim and self-assured, turned to him and said, "If you've been on that spaceship, you must have met the aliens. What were they like?"

"Weren't any aliens," Axel said, flustered and feeling more foolish. "But they were tall and, uh, had six fingers."

"This just gets better and better," Melissa/Melinda said. "What's next for you, Mr. Taylor? Mars? Jupiter?"

Jeffers chimed in to try to save the situation before he looked as ridiculous as the Taylor boy. "Axel brought more definitive proof of the ship. While he was aboard, he took these photos."

The anchor nodded to her director off stage, and a photo of the blue doorway in mid-air appeared on the screen, followed by four photos from inside the ship showing the blue corridor, the holes in the floor, the replicator in the galley, and the holographic control panel. Axel tried to explain what the photos depicted.

When the camera returned to Melissa/Melinda, she had a sweet smile on her face. "Mr. Jeffers," she said, "this is Hollywood, the land of make-believe. What we've just seen can be found on movie sets all over the LA basin."

Axel's mind seethed. "I was on that ship," he insisted.

"I'm sure you were," she said sweetly. "You and the floating man."

"What floating man?"

"You haven't seen that video?" she said. Then to the director: "Let's roll that tape."

On the monitor, Axel watched the floating man video and knew instantly who it was.

"I'm surprised you haven't seen this," the anchor said. "It's been playing on every news channel."

"I've been working in my dad's garage."

"Ah," the anchor replied. "From your dad's garage to the stars. That's quite a journey. So, if you know so much about this alien ship, where is it now?"

Axel's face was burning. He wanted to punch a hole in Melissa/Melinda's cockiness. As he formed a response to her question, he caught an uptick in confidence, and his face morphed from sullen to triumphant. "I don't know where it is now," he said, "but I know who has it."

She stared at Axel, her smile fading. Glancing off-camera toward the director, she adopted the demeanor of a serious journalist and turned back to Axel. "Who is that?"

"The floating man has it," Axel replied. "Bradley Adamsson."

––––––––––

Evaline's eyes narrowed, and her nose flared as she cried, "You son of a bitch."

"What, honey?" her aunt said. Tía Irene sat at the other end of the sofa. She'd been knitting and was startled at Evaline's outburst. Evaline's sister Kate was curled up in a comfy easy chair nearby, texting on her phone. They watched the news on Irene's television and caught Axel outing Bradley.

"Nothing, Tía Irene. It's okay." She caught Kate's eyes and saw Kate mouth, "Told ya." Kate glanced at their aunt and then back at Evaline and said softly, "Scumbag."

Evaline agreed. She looked back at the tube, heat flushing through her body, and listened as Axel told the reporter how he and Bradley found the ship. So far, the scumbag hadn't mentioned her name, and she prayed he wouldn't. He was toast already, but she thought she might kill him if she heard the word "Evaline" cross his lips.

When the interview ended, Evaline said to Kate, "I am so done with him."

After the news broke about the incident in China, Evaline had been frantic to know what happened. She called Bradley's cell but got voicemail and texted him but got no response. She was paranoid about leaving a message after Axel warned her that the FBI was looking for them. According to the news reports, the Chinese claimed they were attacked by the ship. She didn't know Bradley well, but her intuition told her he wouldn't have done that. Regardless of whatever happened in China, Bradley was now outed by Axel, and every cop in the world would be looking for him. She wanted to spring off the sofa and run around the block a few times, anything to eliminate this nervous energy. She needed to do something. But she had to wait until she knew what was happening. And where Bradley was.

"Dammit!" she cried, her fists shaking.

Tía Irene was startled. "What, honey?"

At that moment, the Pukester was nearing South Pasadena. During the drive back from the landing site, Eliot listened to radio coverage of the attack in China while Bradley and Kevin read it on their cell phones. Details were sketchy, and it was clear that the Chinese government was putting its spin on what happened. They claimed that the ship fired first and then fled, fearing retaliation. They claimed, too, that hundreds of civilians had been injured and were being treated in local hospitals. Some were not expected to survive. Bradley asked Athena if that were true, but she didn't know. The spacetime disrupter beams were pinpoint accurate, she said. There would have been no possibility of collateral damage from the disruptors. Bradley asked if fragments from the planes could have fallen on people and injured them. Athena said that was not possible. The wind would have dispersed the detritus. Dust would have fallen on people below but no lethal chunks of wreckage.

Eliot was mainly silent during the drive home, but as they crossed South Pasadena city limits, he said, "I'm sorry," for the umpteenth time.

"Stop apologizing," Bradley said. "What's done is done. I have to figure out how to explain it to my dad."

Traffic was heavier than usual for a Thursday night. Eliot tried different streets leading onto Monterey Road and the neighborhood where Bradley lived, but every street was bottlenecked, and the sidewalks were crowded. Some people still wore UFO costumes, but many were in regular clothing. The crowds were electric, as though they were privy to something big going down. The boys saw people talking excitedly among themselves, texting, or jabbering on cell phones. The mood was no longer festive. Now, there was an air of foreboding, as if the crowd could taste the imminence of a monumental shift in the era's zeitgeist. Ahead, as the boys inched toward Bradley's street, they could see that the mob on the sidewalks had spilled into the street, impeding passage as effectively as a stone wall. Three or four blocks beyond the crowd was a distant, dazzling array of flashing red lights.

"What's happening?" said Kevin, who leaned forward in the back seat, peering between Eliot and Bradley.

Bradley could only shake his head. They were stopped dead while the vehicles ahead tried to forge passage around the blockade to reach parallel streets.

"I'll get out here and walk," Bradley told his friends. "I'll call you later and tell you how it goes with my dad."

He was still blocks from his house when he reached the outer fringes of the crowd. With his enhanced hearing, Bradley knew what people were saying, even a block away. Through the crowd's din, he heard people speculating about the incident in China, some convinced an alien invasion was imminent. Others wondered what the aliens wanted and how to contact them. Some argued that this was a message from God, but that didn't sit well with others who argued that God wouldn't punish innocent people. It was a welter of discordant nonsense, and Bradley did his best to tune it out.

He circled to the left side of the crowd and began walking across people's lawns. Ahead, he spotted a green alien mask someone had discarded, and he pulled it over his face. The crowd had grown denser a block later. He picked his way through by saying, "Excuse me" and "Sorry, I live up there." He thought the flashing lights were beyond his house, a bad traffic accident or a fire, but as he drew closer, he realized that his block was barricaded, dozens of police cars clogging the streets, red lights flashing. When he finally reached the silver metal barricade that blocked off his street, he was horrified to see scores of police officers standing in his front yard. Yellow tape was stretched across the front of his house, and his car, parked on the street, was being loaded onto a tow truck's flatbed.

John Adamsson sat on the edge of his bed, as shaky as a drunk on a high wire. The dry heaves had passed, but his stomach was turning loops. FBI agents were in the living room questioning his family. After reading John his rights, they'd handcuffed him to a bedpost and left him in the care of a uniformed South Pasadena cop, who watched him from the bedroom door. John could barely comprehend what he'd been told—that an arrest warrant had been issued for Bradley, that his son had stolen government property, that he'd flown the ship last weekend, causing the explosion in the forest and so much damage throughout the county, and, worse, that he was responsible for the debacle in China. John thought he knew Bradley. Now, he questioned everything he assumed about his son. His initial impulse had been to deny their accusations and protect Bradley, but now he recalled Bradley's odd behavior recently and his miraculous healing. John wondered whether they'd had a stranger in their midst in the past week. John knew what task force members would think, and he was resigned to losing his job. Certainly, they would charge him for failing to safeguard classified information, and he would confess to that, but it could become much worse if they accused him of treason.

Nick Rabin entered the room and glared at John. Rabin stood with his hands on his belt, one finger thumping his badge. Contempt was etched across Rabin's lean, cold face. He pointed at the bedroom door and said, "Let's go, asshole."

The cop uncuffed John from the bedpost and secured his hands behind his back. Then Rabin led him outside to an FBI sedan, where he was locked in the backseat.

Back in the house, agent Gonzalves told Claudine Adamsson that she had ten minutes to pack suitcases for her and the two children.

"Why?" Claudine said. 'Where are we going?"

"We're taking you to another location. You and your children won't be safe here."

"We're not going anywhere," Claudine insisted.

"Mrs. Adamsson, you don't have a choice. There's a mob outside; we're not the only ones looking for your son. Agents from China and Russia are in town, too, and probably more from other countries. You're not safe." Gonzalves glanced at her watch. "Now you have nine minutes."

Watching the scene unfold from the shadows of the house at the corner of Bradley's street were Wen Kang and Zhang Wong, the Chinese agents who'd waited at the high school that morning. Kang called Caroline Chu and brought her up to date. Chu told him that she and Meng Shuren had still not seen the Perez girl, but now that they knew who possessed the ship, they should focus on apprehending the Adamsson boy. Axel Taylor was likely in FBI custody, but the Perez girl was still a target. After the disaster at the Great Wall, their imperative would be to locate the ship and put it in Chinese hands. They'd seen the Taylor-Jeffers interview on television and now knew that aliens were not responsible for the attack at the Great Wall. An American was responsible, but it still wasn't clear whether he acted on orders from the American government or was a rogue operator.

Franko Pavlovich hid in the shadows of the house opposite the one where Kang and Wong were located. He alternated between watching the Adamsson house and watching the Chinese. He knew of Wen Kang from Kang's work in Somalia, but he'd never seen the other agent. Franko also knew that if there were two Chinese here, there were a half dozen elsewhere. This assignment had just become vastly more complicated. He'd told Roma to be prepared to take out some Chinese agents if necessary, and Roma was positioned catercorner from Franko and across the street from the Chinese. Through his binoculars, Franko searched the crowd for the Adamsson boy. The kid was in deep trouble after the fiasco in China. If he'd returned to California, he would likely head for home, where Franko intended to abduct him while Roma neutralized the Chinese. The crowd was both a blessing and a curse, a blessing because it was easy to get lost in it, a curse because the Adamsson boy would be more challenging to spot. He assumed that American authorities did not have the boy in their hands or there wouldn't be such police presence at his home. While Franko searched for the kid, he thought of his son, Kuzma, who was a few years younger than Bradley Adamsson. Franko wouldn't make it home for Kuzma's birthday on Saturday. He thought ruefully that he'd missed too many of Kuzma's birthdays.

In Bradley's infrared vision, the crowd was a kaleidoscopic swirl of reds and yellows. The flashing red police lights and the jostling crowd turned the whole scene into some mad, hallucinogenic vision of hell—a manic fantasia that swamped his enhanced senses. The roiling red splotches of crowd heat bristled with yellow flames, and the helicopters overhead seemed like red-hot demons with blurry capes streaking across the night sky. As the agonizing situation at his home unfolded, he surveyed the crowd and noticed some red figures standing still in the gloom of houses on either side of the steel barricades. The main body of the mob was animate, feeding on its energy, people jockeying for a better view of the action transpiring at Bradley's home, their collective movement like the Brownian motion of hot gases, but these reddish-yellowish figures were notable for remaining stock-still, a novelty in the volcanic mishmash of the crowd at the barricade.

Then, a murmur raced through the mob, a buzz growing to a roar as Bradley's mom and siblings were led from the front door to a waiting police van. They wore backpacks, carried suitcases, and marched nervously, heads down and eyes straight ahead, through a cordon of police. So many camera and cell phone lights flashed that his family seemed to be taking frozen steps through a strobe light. Bradley felt the crush of the crowd against his back as they began chanting, "We want Bradley! We want Bradley! We want Bradley!" In the frenzy, someone elbowed past and hit Bradley's head, knocking off the alien mask. Bradley gasped as he watched the mask land beyond the steel barricade, where it was mashed under a riot policeman's boot.

Then Bradley caught the eye of a man near him wearing a red hoodie. The guy was a late-twenty-something holding a large cell phone, and Bradley was horrified to see his senior class photo on the screen.

The man stared at him, his eyes wide in recognition. He looked down at the cell phone image and back at Bradley and then said in a voice thick with awe, "You're the guy."

Bradley turned and began pushing through the mob.

Behind him, Red Hoodie yelled, "He's the guy."

Bradley tried to clear a path through the wall of people before him. He looked back and saw Red Hoodie pointing at him, elbowing the people beside him, and screaming, "Hey, he's the guy."

Bradley plunged forward with greater urgency, and the people blocking his way, sensing his panic but not grasping the situation, crowded against their neighbors to let him through.

Behind him, Red Hoodie screamed, "He's the guy. He's the floating man."

The mob grew more agitated at that siren song, people taking up the chant: "Floating man, floating man, floating man." Those who were twenty or thirty feet from the barricade couldn't see what was happening, but they did see a stream of runners forging a path through the crowd and became infected with the frenetic energy of the moment, scrambling for a better view, trying to snatch comprehension from chaos and, failing that, joining the mad rush like iron filings drawn to a magnet.

Bradley heard a flurry of shots, a quick, staccato exchange, and the crowd began screaming and rushing pell-mell away from the locus of violence. They dashed across lawns and between houses, trampling anything underfoot, including each other when someone fell, and across side streets, seeking any avenue of safety. The delirious scramble rarified the mob as people ran from one block to another like waves in water diminishing in amplitude as they spread farther from the point of origin. While this made Bradley's retreat easier, it aided those chasing him. He glanced back and saw Red Hoodie still on his tail, shouting, "He's the guy." An Asian man with a stiff, determined jaw ran beside him. The mob trailing them exploded forward like corn kernels in a popper. Red Hoodie had the face of a rabid fan, but the Asian man's face looked like death.

Bradley ran between cars on packed streets, through intersections where stalled cars formed jumbled mazes, ran around people on sidewalks frozen in stupefaction, and then, coming at last to a nearly empty street, ran like his life depended on escape. Behind him, the Asian man, sprinting with the speed and resilience of an Olympian, closed the gap.

Escape

Thursday, April 16. 11:42 pm.

The body lay on the ground where it fell, arms and legs splayed awkwardly as though the man had been dancing when he died and was caught mid-motion when his vital functions ceased. A blue Los Angeles County Coroner's tent had been erected to shield the body from onlookers. However, none remained except police, National Guard troops, network news camera crews, and reporters. The mob had fled after the shooting started. A half-block area around the scene was secured with portable barriers and yellow police tape. Nick Rabin flashed his badge and stepped through the tent flap, shielding his eyes from the glare of the portable lights. He watched as the coroner examined the victim's wounds. A South Pasadena detective named Rick Winehart handed him a plastic bag containing the dead man's wallet and other effects, including a Chinese diplomatic passport identifying the deceased as Zhang Wong. A badge in one pocket indicated that he was a member of a Chinese trade delegation, which Rabin knew was bullshit.

Wong had taken three shots to the chest, said the coroner, in a tight shot group. One round pierced his right lung. The other two punched holes in his heart. Given the chaos happening during the shooting, whoever did this was a remarkable shot. The weapon was likely an AR-15 or a Sig Sauer 9mm carbine, something like that. They hadn't found the bullets yet, and potential witnesses had fled. Rabin suspected that Wong was a member of the Chinese team sent to steal the alien ship. After Bradley was named on national television, it wasn't surprising to find Wong near the Adamsson house. He probably hadn't been alone, but who killed him? Three shots to the chest, in a tight shot group, was not random violence. Two fleeing demonstrators near Wong were also hit, but not fatally, and may have run into the line of fire. Two other demonstrators were injured by rounds fired by the police targeting the shooter, whom they said was a huge man in black clothing. Agents of a rival power probably killed Wong. Roma Nikitovich, the Russian assassin, was the most likely suspect, and Rabin called for an arrest warrant on him. Meanwhile, the Angeles Event Task Force had an emergency meeting at midnight, so Rabin backed out of the tent and hurried to his car.

———————

When Rabin arrived, the meeting was in progress. Before taking a seat, he informed them that a Chinese national, purportedly a diplomat, had been shot and killed near the Adamsson house that evening.

Homeland Security's Krystal Forsythe shook her head in disgust. "Christ, that's all we need," she said. "The Chinese are now saying that the incident in China was an unprovoked attack by the United States and are threatening retaliation. They've called for an emergency meeting of the UN Security Council later this morning. We're hearing from Russia and other nations, too. All are demanding access to the ship and a sharing of its technology. They don't believe us when we say we don't have the ship. The situation will escalate tomorrow at the UN, and the State Department is asking for guidance. We don't know what to tell them."

"Why don't we start with what we know?" said General Vaughan. She still looked professional in her blues, but a long week with little sleep had made her look ten years older. "I've asked Dr. Logan to summarize for us."

Donal Logan hadn't slept in more than twenty-four hours but was so wired on adrenalin and caffeine that he could have lit a light bulb by holding it. For the next half hour, he summarized what the scientists knew about the ship on a whiteboard. It could manipulate spacetime with an Alcubierre-type engine, which meant faster-than-light travel was feasible. The ship was invisible, probably by bending light, which would require enormous amounts of energy. The ship does not rely on chemical propulsion, solar sails, or other relatively primitive means of propulsion, and it seems to have an inexhaustible supply of energy, so it is likely powered by fusion or antimatter reactors. The replicator the Taylor boy described is an intriguing but potentially dangerous technology, and the floating man video shows that the ship is capable of teleportation. The ship is proof of extraterrestrial, intelligent life, Logan said, and if Taylor is correct that the ship came from Andromeda, which is 2.6 million light-years away, then interstellar travel is achievable over vast distances. Logan closed by saying they believe the photos Axel Taylor took of the ship are authentic, but unfortunately do not reveal much detail.

"We also know," said Forsythe, "that its weapons are frightful."

Logan and his fellow scientists agreed. They'd studied the Australian tourists' video and knew that the Chinese fired first at the ship, and the ship's response was instantaneous, accurate, and deadly. "LIGO detected rapid, short bursts of gravity waves at the precise moment the Chinese jets were destroyed," said Logan. "Those waves could only have been caused by localized spacetime disturbances of unimaginable strength."

Stephanie Vaughan thanked Logan and turned to Nick Rabin. "Have you questioned John Adamsson yet?"

"He's in the box as we speak," Rabin said. "No question he's guilty as hell, the son of a bitch."

"I think you're jumping the gun," said Ross Lefaye.

Logan nodded vigorously. "That would be totally out of character. I've known John since he came to JPL. He's as pure a scientist as anyone I've met."

"Bullshit," Rabin said. "He's sat here all week distracting us and feeding information to his son."

"We have had leaks," General Vaughan pointed out. "It could have been John."

Logan shook his head. "Why would he do it? What could he possibly gain?"

Forsythe spoke up. "Technology for sale to the highest bidder? Frustrated in his career? Looking for more lucrative options? Any of the usual reasons people sell out their country."

"Paranoid nonsense," Logan spat. "Maybe John didn't know about the ship. Have you considered that?"

"How could he not know?" Rabin said. "When the traitor was under his roof? Don't peddle the idea that his son found a spaceship and didn't mention it at dinner. Give me a freakin' break."

"Maybe the boy did keep it a secret," Lefaye said.

"Bullshit," Rabin snapped. "John Adamsson had to know about it, and we're leaning on him hard."

Forsythe added, "I've asked a federal prosecutor to draw up charges."

"He'll break when he's facing treason," Rabin said.

"Oh, for God's sake," Logan cried.

"I'm not sure that's the best approach," said Vaughan.

"What would you suggest, General?" said Forsythe. "We urgently need to solve this problem. Our adversaries are here. They're intent on stealing the ship. And the President is demanding that we find it first. After yesterday, everyone in Washington is frantic."

Vaughan nodded. She'd been on the phone last night with the Secretary of Defense. She understood the urgency in Washington. "What's most important to us right now? What do we want?" she said.

"We want the ship," Forsythe replied. "Number one priority. And we must ensure that no other country gets it. Can you imagine what would happen if the Chinese had sole access to this technology? Or the Russians, the Iranians, or the North Koreans?"

"I'm not disagreeing with you," said NASA Administrator Michael Fairchild, "but we have higher priorities. We need to understand the beings who created this ship and contact them if possible. This is an extraordinary opportunity to communicate with an intelligence far more advanced than ours."

Logan nodded. "We also want to understand a propulsion system that enables faster-than-light travel, and we want to know how they power a ship this size for that long. The Taylor kid said it sat for thirteen thousand years but still powered up with no apparent loss of function. Their energy systems alone would be transformative for everyone on Earth."

"All that can wait," said Rabin, tapping a finger sharply on the table. "Our most urgent need now, right now, is to get our hands on the weapon we saw in China and prevent other countries from getting it. Whoever possesses that weapon will dictate the terms to the rest of the world."

"I agree," said Forsythe. "This is the most serious threat to national security we've ever seen. Either the United States has those weapons, or no one can have them. It's as simple as that."

"All good points," Vaughan said. "But treating John like a criminal will not achieve these goals. If we make him an adversary, and he knows nothing, we gain nothing. The arrest warrant for the boy is sufficient leverage, I think. If we assume John is innocent and treat him that way, he may be able to talk his son into relinquishing the ship."

Rabin put his hands flat on the table and pursed his lips. "I disagree, but whatever works," he said.

Vaughan nodded. "Furthermore, we don't know this boy, but we must assume he has normal feelings for his family. We need to keep them safe and thereby gain his cooperation. It's fair to say that our enemies will use every means to take possession of the ship, including kidnapping, terrorism—"

"—murder," Rabin added.

Vaughan nodded. "The stakes are so high here we have to assume they'll stop at nothing. We need to protect his family and close friends. Nick, do a full work-up on Bradley Adamsson. Wake up whoever you need to and identify the key people in his life whom our adversaries could target. Within twenty-four hours, I want them either guarded or in protective custody."

"Yes, ma'am," Rabin said.

"Do whatever it takes. You have my full authority."

"And mine," said Forsythe. "Homeland Security will provide whatever assistance the Bureau needs."

Rabin left the room in a sprint. Forsythe turned to Vaughan, saying, "I need to brief the President. What is our position?"

Vaughan thought for a moment. "First, the ship belongs to the United States. It was found on our soil. It's our property. Whatever technology we discover belongs to us, and we'll decide how and when to share it."

"I agree," Forsythe said. "Furthermore, whether we like it or not, this situation represents a new arms race. The technology is so advanced that it will tip the global balance of power in favor of whichever country possesses it. At all costs, that technology cannot fall into our enemies' hands. The weaponry alone will give a world-changing advantage to whoever possesses it."

"You're both missing the bigger picture here," said Donal Logan. "I want to reiterate that this ship was built by beings significantly more advanced than us. For the first time in human history, we can contact other intelligent life in the universe. We can go to the stars, especially if this ship can exceed the speed of light. It opens up vast possibilities for humanity, including colonizing nearby habitable planets, mining rare resources on other planets and asteroids, and developing technologies that greatly enhance human life, like the replicator Taylor described. Let's not be shortsighted about the benefits of advanced technology that's almost literally been dropped in our laps. We've been given a gift and should treat it that way."

"I trust you're right, Dr. Logan," Vaughan said. "But we need to possess that ship first."

"And make sure our enemies don't," Forsythe added.

"Something everyone should understand," said Vaughan, scanning the faces of the scientists in the room, "is that in the future, the decisions will be political, not scientific. We'll make our case, but Washington will decide what to do with the ship."

Fairchild shook his head sadly.

In a thick voice, Logan said, "Let's hope they exercise wisdom and foresight."

———

As Bradley ran up Garfield Avenue east of his house, the mob still pursuing, he turned west onto Mission and had an idea. Glancing behind him, he saw that Red Hoodie had fallen back, but the Asian man kept coming and was now only twenty yards behind. The street was packed with cars, the sidewalks with people, a buzz in the air though it was nearly midnight. The Asian man was gaining on him, although Bradley felt good and was running strong.

He wanted to summon the ship by pressing the code on the back of his right hand, but he couldn't slow down to do that, so he said, "Athena, can you hear me?"

Yes, the ship answered in his mind.

I need help, he thought. *I have an idea. Here's what I'd like you to do.*

When he reached the entrance to Garfield Park, he turned onto the footpath, dodging scores of people who dawdled on the path and the grassy areas on either side. The park was still full of UFO enthusiasts, some in costume, others wearing floating man t-shirts, but most in jeans or shorts and hoodies. It was late, and their tents were pitched, some campfires still burning, the pungent aroma of marijuana and the sweet, burnt smell of marshmallows thick in the air. Bradley rounded a group of revelers, nearly tripping on a tent stake, and glanced behind. The Asian man was now five yards away and closing. *He's nimbler at dodging people than I am*, Bradley realized. They ran past the Garfield Park Gazebos and reached a large triangular patch of grass when, in Bradley's mind, he heard Athena say, *I'm here.*

"Now," Bradley yelled, and at that moment, the ship became visible two hundred feet above the park and emitted a long, sonorous tone that shook the trees and rattled everyone on the ground. The tone was so loud it could be heard across the Los Angeles basin and drew people's eyes to the giant silver sphere. Still running, Bradley saw the bottom hatch open, the cerulean blue of the walls glowing through it, and, as the Asian man lunged for him, Bradley was swept off his feet, his skin tingling, and teleported up.

Witnesses saw a man gliding through the air. Most were too startled to do anything but gawk at the grand silver sphere hovering overhead and the man flying towards it, his legs and arms still churning as though he were running up a staircase. On the ground below, Wen Kang lay prostrate where he'd landed after lunging for Bradley. His chest heaved, his arms and legs aching. He rolled onto his back and watched the boy fly into the blue hatch, which closed behind him. Now, most of the distracted people crowding closer held up their cell phones, so Kang rolled back and got to his feet before someone stepped on him. He looked again at the silver ship hovering in the dark sky when it vanished, much to the oohing and aahing crowd's displeasure.

Riot

The horseshoe-shaped table in the UN Security Council meeting room was packed with diplomats who'd been called to an emergency meeting on the China crisis. Most had spent the early hours watching global media coverage of the events in China and California and understood the moment's gravity. Outside the circle of Security Council members, concentric galleries were packed with ambassadors of other United Nations member countries and diplomatic staff. Yuen Hui-Chao, China's UN Ambassador, was speaking. Yuen was a sixty-year-old member of the Central Committee of the Communist Party of China and its foremost diplomat. He sat with a scowl that made his already heavy face sink further. Rapping his fist sharply on the table, he condemned American aggression in the murder of brave Chinese fighter pilots who were defending their homeland, and he demanded that the ship and its pilot be returned to China, where the pilot would stand trial, and the ship be impounded. Such blatant American disregard for the sovereignty of another nation and the lives of its honorable citizens cannot go unpunished, Yuen railed.

The tall, salt-and-sandy-haired Russian ambassador, Felix Matveyev, angrily denounced the United States, too. However, he argued that America had discovered an unprincipled weapon of war and was obligated to share the technology with other global powers. The threat of further American aggression was a destabilizing influence on international affairs, he insisted, and other powerful nations would be forced to retaliate with nuclear weapons, if necessary, should the United States again deploy this ship to intimidate other countries.

When their harangues ended, the Security Council was addressed by Dr. Sigorella Di Philippa, Director of the European Space Agency, and Dr. Faraz Bashar, Director of the United Nations Office for Outer Space Affairs (UNOOSA). They chose to ignore the issue of blame for the incident in China and instead focused on what was known about the technology aboard the alien ship. They argued that this discovery should benefit all humankind, that it opened up a new age of space exploration and colonization, and that the ship should be examined in some neutral site, such as Greenland or Switzerland, where its technologies could be exploited equally across the Earth under the auspices of the United Nations. Further, they believed that future space exploration should be directed not by NASA or any other nations' space agencies but by UNOOSA, under the guidance of the UN Security Council and a newly proposed treaty on the non-aggressive exploitation of alien technology and the exploration of space.

"That'll never happen," said Homeland Security's Krystal Forsythe. "I know thirty Republican senators who would veto that in a heartbeat." She and other members of the AETF were watching the UN Security Council proceedings on a flat-screen TV mounted on the conference room wall. Forsythe sat with her elbows on the table, her fingers forming a steeple over her nose. Sitting beside her was a new member of the AETF, Homeland Security's Darrell Jablonski, Director of the Department's Science and Technology Directorate. His group would lead the project to analyze and extract the ship's technology.

After Forsythe introduced Jablonski to the others, Donal Logan responded to Forsythe's earlier comment. "Why wouldn't they support it?" he asked. "Surely, the sensible use of alien technology and peaceful space exploration is in everyone's interests."

"You don't understand politics, Dr. Logan," Forsythe replied. "These conservative senators have an immune reaction to the idea of the United Nations exercising any jurisdiction over the U.S. They have the power to block a proposed space treaty in Congress, and they have the President's ear."

The conference room door opened, and Nick Rabin entered. He had worked all night and looked it, his hair and unshaven face as shabby as his suit was wrinkled. He accepted a large mug of coffee and sat next to General Vaughan, whose uniform was fresh, as always. Vaughan introduced Rabin to Jablonski. Then, she asked Rabin for an update.

Rabin reported on the scene at the Adamsson house yesterday evening and the dead Chinese agent. Claudine Adamsson and her two youngest were in the custody of the U.S. Marshals Service, Rabin said, adding that they'd worked through the night to develop a profile on Bradley Adamsson and had awakened scores of people, none happy about it. They found Axel Taylor celebrating his million-dollar windfall at a Hollywood restaurant with his father and took both into custody. Just after five this morning, agents found two of Bradley's friends, Eliot Stankus and Kevin Truman, at their homes and arrested them. They confessed to being on the ship with the Adamsson boy over China, so they're being charged as accessories. They're being interrogated now, and their cell phone photos from inside the ship are being examined by JPL and CalTech scientists. Both boys claim that the incident in China was an accident. The FBI has been unable to locate the Perez girl, Rabin continued. South Pasadena High School is closed again today, and Evaline Perez, who works at Huntington Memorial Hospital, was not at work last night or this morning and hasn't been at work for several days.

"However," Rabin said in a dramatically base voice, "we found her stepmother, whose name"—he read from his notes—" was Angela McNees-Koeppen-Perez, at their home in South Pasadena."

"Was?" General Vaughan said, eyebrows raised.

Rabin looked at Vaughan and the others around the table. "Yeah, she was murdered last night. The coroner's putting the time of death between 9 pm and 11 pm. We found her with her ankles and arms tied together behind her back. Her throat had been cut."

"Omigod," said Ross Lefaye, deputy director of JPL, echoing the dread that permeated the room.

Krystal Forsythe crossed her arms and said, "What is the Perez girl's connection with Bradley Adamsson?"

Rabin shrugged. "They're both seniors at the same school, and she's in one of his classes. From what we gather, she's Axel Taylor's girlfriend, and the two of them were seen coming out of the blue light in the mountains."

Forsythe said, "So, this girl's probably been on the ship, and we can't find her."

"That's correct," said Rabin. He took another sip of coffee and ran a hand over the stubble on his face.

General Vaughan said, "She may be dead. Or she may have been taken hostage. Whatever the case, this is spinning out of control, and we need to resolve it quickly. I suggest contacting Bradley Adamsson and convincing him to turn in the ship. Once the ship is in our hands, the President can dictate to the UN how the technology will be exploited. Ideas?"

Forsythe said, "Appeal to his patriotism. Wave the flag."

Logan said, "I think Bradley is patriotic, but a stronger appeal would be to his scientific curiosity. He is a brilliant young man, a scientist in the making. Like his father, he would want to advance the science, in my opinion."

Rabin shook his head. "No, he's in trouble. He's worried about himself and his family. Offer him immunity from prosecution if he turns in the ship. Remove fear from the equation."

"I agree," said Vaughan. She ran a hand over her stomach, unconsciously straightening her uniform. "He's probably looking for a way to end a situation that's blown up in his face. We need to make him feel safe. Who should call him?"

"His father," Logan suggested. "Someone he trusts."

"I disagree," said Forsythe. "He needs to hear from someone in authority who can deliver on whatever agreements are negotiated." She turned to General Vaughan. "I think you should make the call. You're an Air Force Academy grad, and according to the FBI report, he had wanted to go there before he applied to MIT. Convince him to allow you on board for a face-to-face talk."

"That's good," said Rabin. "He'll identify with you, and he needs to see that you're not a faceless bureaucrat, that you're human and understand what he's been through. We can equip you with a wire and an easily concealed handgun."

Vaughan didn't think that was wise but said nothing.

Bradley slept through the night with the ship hovering at eighty thousand feet. After waking up and having coffee and a tuna salad sandwich for breakfast, he went to the cockpit. He'd watched the debate at the UN Security Council on one section of the wall opposite the control panel. When their arguments grew tedious, his mind drifted to his family. He'd seen his mom and siblings led away by authorities but was worried about his father, so he asked Athena if it were possible to eavesdrop on the Angeles Event Task Force. Within minutes, she'd accessed the teleconferencing equipment in JPL and located the room where the AETF meetings were being held. It was simple for the ship to activate the room's video camera. People were coming and going, a meeting not having begun. He recognized JPL's Ross Lefaye and Donal Logan. He'd met the latter many times and knew him to be a good scientist and a good guy. Then, a woman wearing Air Force blues walked into the room and sat at the head of the table. Others took seats around the table, and Bradley turned up the volume.

As they introduced a new team member, Jablonski, he learned who the rest of the AETF members were. An FBI agent, Rabin, who Bradley thought resembled a coiled cobra with a hard body, reported that his family was in the hands of U.S. marshals, being treated as though they were in witness protection. Rabin said that Axel, Eliot, and Kevin were in FBI custody, Evaline was missing, and her stepmother was dead. His stomach roiled as he thought about Evaline and wondered how to search for her. His thoughts were interrupted when Athena announced that he had a call.

He was surprised to receive a call while the ship was at eighty thousand feet, well out of cell tower range. Athena explained that she intercepted his cell signal and boosted it. He hoped the call would be from Evaline, but caller ID, projected on the wall, said "Jet Propulsion Laboratory."

"Yes?" he answered, glancing at the live image of the AETF meeting. The woman wearing Air Force blues held the handset of a landline phone to her head. He magnified her image and saw that she was a three-star. She was a pleasant-looking older woman with bobbed, brown hair. Her back was erect, and she had the poise and self-assurance of someone who'd risen to the senior ranks in the armed forces.

"Bradley, this is Air Force General Stephanie Vaughan. I'm—"

"I know who you are." He saw her flinch but quickly regain her composure.

"Good. Then, there is no need for further introductions. We're worried about you."

He smiled. "You're worried about Athena."

Vaughan paused, glancing at the other people around the table, her free hand raised in a question mark. Several shook their heads. "Who's Athena?"

"The ship. I call her Athena, after the Greek goddess of knowledge."

Vaughan nodded. "I've studied the classics, too. You've become very familiar with the ship."

"You might say she can read my mind."

"That would be an amazing feat for a machine, even one as advanced as Athena."

"You have no idea. Her A.I. is thousands of years beyond what we have on Earth. Tens of thousands."

"The ship's technology is remarkable," Vaughan said. "Your friend Axel Taylor revealed a lot on television last night, and he's been talking to us since."

Bradley's mouth turned down at recalling Axel on television. "I saw him," he said.

Vaughan nodded. "We weren't pleased about that. We'd hoped to talk to you privately before the news of the ship, Athena, became public."

"Until Taylor betrayed me, you didn't know who I was."

"That's right. We've been in the dark about many things."

"My father didn't know I had the ship," Bradley asserted. "Believe him when he tells you that."

"I do believe him," she said, giving Donal Logan a quick nod of acknowledgment, which Logan returned. "I think your father is an honorable man," Vaughan continued. "I've thought that all along."

That struck Bradley as false flattery, but he didn't know Vaughan. Maybe she was sincere. He said, "The thing that happened in China was an accident."

Vaughan nodded. "We've put some of your friends in protective custody, and that's what they told us."

"Who killed Evaline's stepmother?"

That brought her head up sharply. She mouthed something to the FBI agent, but Bradley couldn't read her lips. "We don't know, honestly," she said into the phone.

"An Asian man chased me last night."

Bradley saw her twist her lips, probably wondering how much to tell him. "We know that Chinese agents are in the area," she said. "We've lost track of them, but we know they're here. They want the ship. So do the Russians. Likely, many other countries whose agents we haven't identified yet."

"Did you see how I escaped?"

"Yes. The ship teleported you up. We've seen the photographs and some cell phone videos. It's all over the news. You staged a spectacular exit."

Bradley frowned. "It wasn't staging. I had no choice."

Bradley magnified the image of General Vaughan even more and studied her face. She wore a sympathetic look, and he felt a tinge of guilt about eavesdropping, but that passed quickly. In observing them, he'd come to appreciate how the game was played and knew that you can only defeat a fox if you think like a fox.

"Bradley, what's important now is where we go from here."

He smiled at her obvious segue to what she wanted. "You want to take possession of the ship."

"Yes, we do," she admitted. "In the interests of science and national security. And we'll give you complete immunity from prosecution."

"What will you do with it?"

"Safeguard it. Try to understand the technology, which I know is far more advanced than anything on Earth."

"Maybe you'll use it to develop advanced weapons."

She glanced at the people around the conference table again. "I can't deny that some people will argue for that, but I see the technology as much more of a force for good."

"Then you're being naïve."

That seemed to catch in Vaughan's throat. He may have offended her, but her professional demeanor returned after a moment.

"You may be right, so we don't want the ship to fall into the wrong hands."

"I think this ship has the power to destroy humanity," Bradley said.

"Or liberate it," Vaughan countered. "We could explore new worlds, colonize suitable planets, find resources that are rare on Earth. Wouldn't you like to be part of that future?"

Bradley sat back in the captain's chair and thought, *I already am part of it.* He felt some melancholy as he reflected on what he'd always dreamed his life would be. "I wanted to go to college next year. I wanted to become an astrophysicist."

"You still can, Bradley. I know you've been accepted at MIT."

"No," he said in a thick and weary voice. "I've crossed the Rubicon." He paused and then said, "Have you studied the life of Julius Caesar?"

"Yes," she said. "When he crossed the Rubicon River with the 13th Legion, he defied the senate and brought about the Roman civil war. The Rubicon is considered a point of no return." She brought a hand to her lips as though debating what to say next. "Bradley, would you allow me to visit you on the ship? I want to take a tour and have you show me some of the technology you've discovered."

She seemed so sincere. He almost didn't want to let her down. "I don't think so, General Vaughan. You'd be wearing a wire and would bring a handgun. How could I trust you?"

Surprise crossed her face before she suppressed it. Then she drew in a breath and said, "I won't do either."

"I'll think about it," Bradley replied. "Meanwhile, where's my father?"

She told him John had rejoined his family at a U.S. Marshal's safe house.

"Is Evaline Perez in danger?" Bradley asked.

He saw the FBI agent's mouth turn down, his hands raised in an *I-don't-know* gesture. General Vaughan said, "We don't know where she is."

"You need to find her. Make sure she's safe."

"We will," Vaughan promised.

"I won't talk to you again until I know she's okay."

"Her safety will be our top priority," Vaughan said, signaling Rabin, who left the conference room. "Do you need anything?"

Bradley thought about it. "I need my life back."

He ended the call and then watched them in the conference room.

The Homeland Security Secretary, Forsythe, leaned toward Vaughan and whispered to her, "How did he know about the wire and the handgun?"

Vaughan had a sick look on her face. She leaned forward and whispered in Forsythe's ear, "He's been listening to us. Maybe watching us. He's probably watching now." The two women sat back and stared at each other in silent communication. Athena had amplified their whispers, so Bradley heard what they said. It was easy to guess what they were thinking, but caring about it was seeping out of him like blood dripping from a wound.

John Adamsson held his wife in his arms as they leaned against the headboard in the strange bedroom that was temporarily home. Devin and Celia sat on a sofa in the living room, watching the original *Frozen* movie on the television. A U.S. marshal sat in an easy chair beside the couch, watching them. Another stood in the kitchen, drinking a glass of milk. Four more marshals were outside, guarding the house, which was tucked in a nondescript development in Lancaster, California, not far from Edwards Air Force Base. The Marshal's Service had owned the home since it was confiscated in a major drug bust. The house was isolated from its neighbors, had been bulletproofed, and had good sight lines in every direction. The Service had built a large, attached shed that housed a generator, emergency water, and other supplies, and they used satellite phones to ensure constant communication with an Air Force rapid deployment force at Edwards. The Adamssons were considered high-value targets warranting the highest level of Service protection.

John and Claudine were too shell-shocked to speak, and they worried that the house might be bugged, which, of course, it was. Their cell phones had been confiscated, but they weren't sure whom to call or what they would say if they spoke to friends. News about Bradley and the ship had dominated the news channels since Axel's revelation the night before. However, watching the endless speculation about Bradley was more disturbing than helpful, so Claudine refused to watch more of it.

When two marshals escorted John to the house earlier this morning, he found something to eat in the kitchen and discovered a small notepad and pencil, which he slipped into his pocket. He took it out while they sat on the bed and wrote, "Where Bradley?"

Claudine read it and shook her head. She took the pad and pencil and wrote, "Won't tell us."

John took the pad and wrote, "Said they'd brief us later today."

She wrote, "Will he be ok?"

He nodded and wrote, "They want the ship. Won't harm him."

She closed her eyes and fought off tears. Then she wrote, "The cancer? His leg?"

John wrote back, "Guess ship cured him. Don't know how."

She wrote, "Thankful for that." Then: "What will happen to us?"

John looked at her and shook his head. He didn't know.

Just then, one of the marshals knocked on the door and peered in. "I apologize for bothering you folks, but you might want to turn on the news. I'm sorry."

Claudine's heart caught in her throat as John scrambled to turn on the television in the bedroom.

Bradley had gone to the galley for a bottle of water. He wished he had ginger ale or something else to settle his stomach, but he hadn't brought soft drinks on board and decided not to ask Athena to manufacture it from formulas on the Internet. As he drank the water, he sat in a chair, which conformed to his body, and brought up CNN on one of the galley walls. Above a "Breaking News" banner, they showed a helicopter view of a mob of people in what looked like a residential neighborhood. He saw broken police lines and National Guardsmen trying to hold off the mob, but it was useless. The mob surged forward toward a house surrounded by trees and shrubs. Bradley realized it was his family's home. Yellow police tape was ripped down, and the leading members of the mob, some wearing Bradley Adamsson t-shirts, broke through the front door. A mushroom of tear gas erupted near the entrance, and those people closest recoiled from it, except for one intrepid rioter wearing a red bandana over his nose, who picked up the tear gas canister and hurled it back toward the police lines. More tear gas clouds burst throughout the crowd but had little lasting effect. Meanwhile, people poured in through the front door as others surrounded the house and began smashing windows and climbing in. After minutes of chaos, Bradley saw some people rushing out of the house, elbowing their way through those still trying to break in. They held things from inside close to their bodies or clasped in their hands. They took whatever they could, souvenir seekers like grave robbers who'd discovered an ancient artifact-filled temple.

The police and National Guard had given up trying to control the mob. They seemed content to quarantine the madness so it didn't spread beyond the Adamsson home. After a few minutes, Bradley saw a sudden surging outflow of people, dozens scrambling through the front door, others leaping through broken windows, as smoke began curling out from an upstairs window, which he realized had been his bedroom. He watched as the conflagration grew and the mob fled. Far too late, the sirens and flashing lights of firetrucks appeared, and the police and National Guard opened their lines to let the firefighters reach the burning house, but Bradley knew it was too late. His childhood home, the only home he'd ever known, was gone, as was everything his family had left inside.

When the tears came, they coated his eyelashes, then raced down shaking cheeks. It felt like his gut was being hollowed out, as though a sleeping serpent had awakened and was devouring everything that remained of him—his home, his family, his things, every possession that meant something to him. He recalled the rioters wearing Bradley Adamsson t-shirts and brooded that they'd stolen everything except his identity, and the mob would pervert even that for its purposes.

Kidnapped

Friday, April 17. 9:34 am.

Evaline was numb. She slumped in her chair, wishing she could shrink and keep shrinking until she became an insubstantial tuft of fabric, a thread on the chair's cushion, and could hide in a seam. She was too ashamed to make eye contact with the investment guy, Gary Somebody, although she was the victim and deserved sympathy, not blame. The tips of her ears and her forehead burned, shock and shame slowly giving way to a searing hatred that fogged her mind. She had left her aunt's house a half-hour ago and driven to Bridgeport Robertson Financial, the firm managing her trust. She'd never met Gary and realized now what a mistake that was. Her stepmother—the bitch—had always dealt with him. Evaline owed UCLA a substantial deposit next week and assumed that the two hundred thousand dollars her father left for her would be there.

It wasn't.

"How could this have happened?" she asked Gary in a startled, ashamed voice.

"Angela," he said haltingly, "your stepmother, has taken out small sums over the years since your father's death for your upkeep."

"My what?" Evaline cried. "Upkeep? She had other money for that. The trust was for my education!"

"I'm sorry, Evaline," Gary said. "Unfortunately, the trust allowed the trustee to withdraw funds for any purpose, and after your father passed, your stepmother was the sole trustee."

"Until I graduate from high school."

"Correct."

"Which is next month."

He nodded sympathetically. "We assumed she kept you informed."

"That was a dumbass thing to assume," she yelled. "Didn't you know the kind of woman she is?"

He looked away. "I'm sorry. Technically, our obligation is to communicate with the trustee, which we've done."

"What about Kate's trust? My sister."

"You'll have to speak with Angela about that. I'm not at liberty—"

"Can you at least tell me if the same thing happened with Kate's trust?"

"I'm sorry, I can't—"

"Oh, goddammit, Gary. Would I be wrong to assume that a similar pattern will be found in Kate's trust?"

After a long moment, he said, "You wouldn't be wrong."

"How much money is left in my trust account?"

"Just over nineteen thousand dollars," he said. "The good news is—"

"There is no good news," she snapped. That wasn't enough money for her first year of college.

Outside, she walked to her car, playing out the confrontation she would have with her stepmother. The blood in her eyes neared the boiling point as she reached her aunt's car. Then, her arms were yanked from behind by two men who lifted her off her feet and carried her to a white van parked ahead of her aunt's car. She had barely registered what was happening when the van's side door flew open, and she was thrown onto the floor inside. She hit the deck hard, sending shock waves through her elbows and knees. Her face bounced off the rubber floor mats and cracked her nose. Someone landed on her back, jerked her hands backward, and tied them together. She heard the passenger door open, and someone else jumped in. Then that door slammed, and the van peeled away from the curb and rocketed down a street. Blood poured from her nose into her mouth. She was still grappling with what happened when the person on her back pushed off and roughly rolled her over. In the gloom inside the van, she saw an Asian man's face. He looked tough and grim, with piercing eyes, a stiff jaw, and short, spiky black hair.

He pointed a sharp finger at her and said, "You give trouble; I give pain. Simple. No trouble, no pain. Much trouble, much pain. Your choice. Nod, you understand."

She nodded. That much of what was happening was clear.

Then an Asian-looking woman leaned over her, so close Evaline nearly gagged on the woman's perfume. "You are going to contact Bradley Adamsson," the woman barked over the engine's whine. "You understand?" Evaline nodded. "You are going to tell him to give us the ship. If he does, everyone is happy. If not, we will kill you, your sister, and your aunt. Everyone in your family."

The Asian man smiled like a deranged Halloween pumpkin as he handed Evaline's purse to the woman and then searched the pockets of her jeans. He found the EpiPen in a front pocket and gave it to the woman.

"I need that!" Evaline said, spitting the words through blood. Her nose felt like it was on fire.

The Asian woman read the yellow EpiPen label.

"I could die without it," Evaline cried. "Please."

"Okay," the Asian woman shrugged. She said to the man, "For allergy. No good to us. Put it back." She handed it to him, and he shoved it back into Evaline's front pocket.

Evaline turned her head to one side to keep more blood from running down her throat.

"Your mother already dead," said the Asian man. He drew a finger across his throat, and she remembered Axel making the same gesture.

The blood and bile in her throat formed a toxic mixture. She thought she might throw up and tried to lie still until the nausea passed. She'd heard what the man said but couldn't comprehend that Angela was gone. As much as she despised the woman, that seemed impossible.

"How we found you," the Asian man gloated. "She talk. Now she talk no more."

Evaline closed her eyes and listened to the hum of the wheels. With every mile they traveled, the reality of her predicament sank in more. She knew Bradley planned to give up the ship—but not to these people. She lay on the floor, miserable in the stench of gasoline, armpit sweat, and the Asian woman's sweet-sick perfume. The acrid taste of bile made her feel like she was being eaten from the inside out. She wanted to cry but wouldn't give these people the satisfaction.

―――――――――

The ship had exhaustive records of every planet, moon, asteroid, and comet it had ever surveyed, along with the records of all its sister vessels. Bradley sat in the ship's data storage center on deck eleven and displayed videos the ship recorded of creatures on Planet C55'96740-i4, which was 12,245.87343 light-years from our sun. Planet C55 was nearly three times larger than Earth, so its gravity was proportionately stronger. Green fungus-like vegetation blanketed the planet except for meandering water channels in the temperate zones and ice mountains in the polar regions. The dominant species endemic to C55 had wafer-thin appendages resembling mobiles of thin white seashells held together by green twine. They had a central mass like a bulbous yellow bean bag covered with short, prickly spines. They swelled and sank when they inhaled and shriveled and rose when they exhaled. As Bradley observed these creatures floating in waves over a sea of green, he became transfixed by the beauty of their movements. He momentarily forgot about the world of trouble eighty thousand feet below. Athena had enabled Bradley's cell phone to receive and make calls. While he was observing the creatures on that distant planet, his cell phone rang again. This time, caller ID read, "Evaline Perez."

But when Bradley said, "Hello," it wasn't Evaline who answered.

"Bradley?" A male voice with an Asian accent.

Bradley thought, *can you locate this phone?*

Athena answered in his mind, *yes.*

"This is Bradley."

"Almost caught you last night," the man said, a rueful snigger.

Bradley recalled the Asian man's face. "You're a runner."

"Boston marathon. Twice," the man said proudly. "You a runner, too."

"Only recently," Bradley said. "What do you want?"

"Not what I want. What you want. You want Evaline." He pronounced her name like he was saying *Abilene.* "We have Evaline."

I have located that cell phone, Athena whispered in his mind.

Where?

Athena displayed an overhead shot of Los Angeles on the data center wall, like a Google Maps image but live. She highlighted the blue, rectangular top of a vehicle moving steadily along a street—a van.

"Is she okay?" Bradley said to the man.

"Girl okay now," the man replied. "Still have all parts."

"She'd better stay okay."

"Up to you."

"Where is she?"

"Here. Now. Maybe later, here and there. One part here, one part there. You see?"

Bradley was about to speak when another voice came on Evaline's phone, a woman with an Asian accent.

"Bradley Adamsson," she said.

"Who are you?"

"That's not important. We want the ship. You have six hours to turn it over to us. If you don't, we will kill the girl and everyone in her family and yours."

Bradley flexed his free hand and then formed a tight fist. "You know what happened in China," he said. "If you harm Evaline, I will obliterate you."

"Bradley," the woman warned, "we are many. You cannot find us all. Give us the ship, or we will kill Evaline and her family. Then your family. Everyone. We will destroy everyone you know and love. Six hours. I will call back and give you the location for the exchange."

She hung up.

For some long minutes, in which seconds ticked in slow motion, Bradley felt numb. *I should be polishing my valedictorian speech today,* he thought, *not wondering if I can rescue a girl I am infatuated with but barely know, not negotiating with terrorists who want control of an ultimate weapon.* He remembered Evaline's big, smoky eyes, awestruck as she gazed at the Martian landscape and the moist feel of her kiss on his cheek. He wondered whether caring about her welfare was more about assuaging his longing or discharging his guilt for imperiling her.

Bradley put his phone back in his pocket and followed the van's progress as it drove across Los Angeles. He glanced at his watch. He had until 4:40 this afternoon. Then he looked back at the video of the creatures on C55. He wondered how complicated their lives were. Did they threaten each other? Use kidnapping, torture, murder, extortion, bribery, war, and genocide to impose their will on others of their species?

The people on the phone will kill Evaline if I don't do what they want, he thought. *I threatened to obliterate them in return. Is this common behavior for intelligent life in the universe? Or am I and the Asians just being uniquely human?*

Many intelligent species are aggressive, Athena said silently.

Fifteen minutes later, he watched the van turn into a commercial area off the Santa Monica Freeway in Los Angeles. The vehicle stopped along the street next to a large red building with a white roof that occupied one-quarter of a square city block. After a moment, the van turned into the building through a large loading bay door. When the door lowered, it looked like the warehouse had swallowed the van.

"Athena, what's the address of that building?"

She told him, and he turned on his cell phone and dialed General Vaughan's number. She answered on the second ring.

"This is Bradley Adamsson," he said. "Evaline Perez has been kidnapped. I know where she's being held." He told Vaughan about the call from the Asian kidnappers and about tracking the van to a warehouse by the Santa Monica Freeway.

"We'll have SWAT teams there as quickly as possible," Vaughan said.

"Thank you. Stay close to your phone," Bradley said. "I'll call back soon." He cut off the call and asked Athena, "Can you look inside that building?"

"Yes," Athena responded. As he watched, the ship scanned the building with a range of frequencies in the electromagnetic spectrum, from gamma and x-rays at higher frequencies to infrared, microwave, and radio waves at lower frequencies. She also did magnetic and ultra-high frequency acoustic imaging. Within seconds, Athena produced a live composite view of the building, enabling them to see inside it as though they were looking at a three-dimensional X-ray. The image of the two-story warehouse could be rotated and viewed from any perspective. The trucks, front-loaders, crates, and pallets in the storage areas on the first floor appeared as ghostly but well-defined images. In the offices on the second floor, furniture and equipment were also ghostly but easily recognizable. The people inside the building appeared as infrared images so detailed their fingernails could be delineated. Four people were in an inner office on the second floor, one woman stationary at a table, her hands tied behind her back, her head slumped forward. A hot spot at her nose showed where blood was flowing in response to an injury. Bradley's face grew hot as he stared at Evaline's image.

One of the women in the room sat at the other end of the table, working on a laptop. Another woman stood with her back against a counter. She carried a handgun and was sipping a hot liquid in a cup she held to her mouth. The man in the room had short, spiky hair. He also carried a handgun and paced as though trying to excise nervous energy. Bradley recognized him as the Asian man who'd chased him as he ran from the mob scene at his home.

Five other men were located on the first floor of the warehouse, all carrying automatic weapons. One sat on a stool by the large bay door. Two others paced at the building's periphery, peering out windows. One man had leaned his weapon against the side of a van while he'd climbed into the cargo space and was scrubbing the floor. *Cleaning up Evaline's blood*, Bradley thought. The fifth man was talking on a cell phone, his weapon slung over his right shoulder.

"Athena, could you send this image to the police?"

"Yes."

Bradley called Vaughan back. As she answered, she and the rest of the AETF team were startled when the videoconference monitor in their conference room came to life and displayed the ghostly composite image of the warehouse. Nick Rabin approached the monitor and studied it with his hands on his hips, his head forward, peering intently.

"The ship produced this?" he said.

"Yes," Bradley responded, his voice audible through the monitor's speakers. Then, he asked General Vaughan to connect him with the SWAT team commander.

"The Bureau needs this capability," Rabin said. "How is the ship doing it?"

While he waited to talk to the SWAT team commander, Bradley explained how Athena had created the composite image. Then he told Rabin, "Tell the SWAT team to wear ear protection, the best they can get."

"Why?" Rabin said.

"I'll explain later. Tell them to protect their ears."

Bradley watched the area around the warehouse and saw black SWAT vehicles arriving and stopping blocks away, out of sight. Other police surrounded the area and blocked off streets. Then Bradley saw squads of SWAT officers racing along sidewalks toward the warehouse, arriving in position in less than twenty minutes. Three SWAT teams were onsite, two on diagonally opposite blindsides of the warehouse and one crouched on the left side of a large white panel truck specially fitted with running boards and hand railings on that side. The truck would drive in front of the large bay door, exposing only its right side, and, on command, those SWAT officers would drop off the running boards and breach the warehouse at the bay door.

The SWAT team commander initially refused to take direction from anyone outside LAPD's chain of command, but the Chief of Police told him that this was an AETF operation and General Vaughan was in command. That allowed Bradley to speak directly to the SWAT team commander. He explained how the ship could neutralize the threats inside while shielding Evaline Perez, and he and the commander quickly agreed on a plan.

At T minus ten seconds, the SWAT panel truck slowly approached the warehouse bay door. At T minus two seconds, Athena dropped a high-density magnetic lattice shield over Evaline like a protective cone. It created an impenetrable barrier that shielded her from a range of threats, from gamma rays to lead. The terrorists in the room with Evaline were startled by the glassy cone surrounding their hostage. It sparkled and shimmered with an electric hum and a sharp ozone odor that caused their nostrils to flare. Before they could react, the ship fired eight high-energy beams from laser drills at the warehouse roof, directly above the three terrorists in the office and the five on the floor below. The drills could bore through hundreds of feet of rock, so it was easy for them to cut through the roof and floor of the upper level. The beams could have penetrated the terrorists' skulls and killed them instantly, but the ship's creators designed her as a survey vessel, not an instrument of aggression, and she was prohibited from actions that would terminate life unless she were under attack. So Athena set the drills at a depth that would clear space above the terrorists' heads but not strike them.

An instant later, she fired ultra-high-frequency acoustic grenades into the lasered holes. When the sonic bursts struck their targets, they caused instant concussions that stunned the terrorists. To disorient them further, a half-second later, Athena hit the warehouse with a deafening acoustic wave that shook the building to its foundations, shattering windows, bursting sheet-rocked walls, and knocking the bay door off its tracks. To those inside, those with enough sense to think, it felt like a magnitude 7.0 earthquake had struck. The epicenter of the acoustic wave was the warehouse, and the wave was tightly focused, so surrounding buildings were largely unaffected, but SWAT team members positioned outside the warehouse were knocked off their feet and risked having their eardrums ruptured if they hadn't been wearing ear protectors. After a few seconds, the SWAT teams recovered and breached the warehouse through multiple entry points.

The five terrorists on the ground floor responded to the incursion like they were drugged. They still held their automatic weapons and dimly recognized that they were under attack, so they raised their rifles to fire. The SWAT team's automatic weapons quickly cut them down, and the ground-floor threats were neutralized within seconds. Then the hostage rescue team bounded up the steps to the second-floor office where Evaline was being held. Wen Kang, Caroline Chu, and Meng Shuren were dazed and disoriented by the ship's attack but had begun to recover when Athena fired a second round of acoustic grenades at them, and those blasts scrambled their brains. When three SWAT team members burst into the office moments later, Kang and Chu were shot and killed before they could raise their handguns. Meng was shot in the right shoulder and left arm. She collapsed in a bloody, babbling heap and was disarmed and handcuffed.

After the three terrorists in the room were neutralized, the shimmering shield surrounding Evaline Perez vanished. She sat bloodied and dazed, her hands cable-tied behind her back, her head lying on the table. When the paramedics who followed the SWAT teams examined her, she was bruised and disoriented and her nose broken, but she was otherwise unharmed and unaware of the acoustic assaults on the warehouse. After the SWAT Commander assured General Vaughan that the hostage was safe, Evaline was loaded onto a stretcher and carried to an ambulance.

Bradley and members of the AETF had watched the operation unfold on Athena's live composite image of the building. When Bradley was assured that Evaline was safe, he slumped back in his chair and closed his eyes. Relief passed over him like a cold compress held to his forehead. Then he felt his body relaxing like a clenched fist easing open. At his request, Evaline was taken to Huntington Memorial Hospital in Pasadena. She worked there and knew many of the staff, which Bradley thought would be helpful.

Roma Nikitovich wanted to put some distance between himself and the cops in Pasadena after yesterday evening's shooting, so he drove east to I-15 and followed it south to Murrieta, California, where he spent the night at a Best Western Hotel. He had breakfast the following morning at Denny's. He hadn't heard from Franko Pavlovich, so he took his time at breakfast, enjoying double helpings of eggs, toast, pancakes, sausage, bacon, and four cups of coffee. Then, he drove to the safehouse in El Monte to return the rifle he'd used to shoot the Chinese agent. When he arrived, the garage door was open, and Roma pulled in, but as he shut off the engine, his car was surrounded by police in black body armor, and all he could see were the lethal Cyclops eyes of AR-15s.

At that moment, Franko Pavlovich was having brunch at a more upscale eatery in Burbank. When he asked for the check, it was delivered by a sleek young man wearing a black suit, white shirt, and narrow black tie. After handing him the check, the young man held up a Federal Bureau of Investigation badge. Franko felt, rather than saw, the two agents who'd come up behind him, but he did see two others standing several tables away. All eyes in the restaurant were on Franko as he pushed himself up from the table and held up his hands.

"I'm a Russian diplomat," Franko said. "My passport is in my pocket."

"You're Colonel Franko Pavlovich," the young man replied, "of the Russian Air Force, and you're a spy."

"You can't arrest me," Franko said. "I have diplomatic immunity."

"We're not arresting you," the FBI agent said, "but you're in our custody. Your comrade killed a Chinese agent last night. We will turn both of you over to the Chinese and let them handle it."

Solivagant

Friday, April 17. 2:45 pm.

"Last week at this time, I was taking an AP Calc II mid-term," Bradley told Athena. "I aced it."

"Yes," Athena said. "I read your grade on your high school's cloud storage site."

Bradley smiled at Athena's guileless display of omnipotent knowledge. Last week felt like a million years ago. He flashed back to Axel pulling the spider out of his backpack and asking Bradley what it was. Not that he was nostalgic about life a week ago. He'd just learned he had liver cancer, and his left leg was still an inch shorter than his right. The coolest guy in school had spoken to him without calling him names—him, Bradley, a charter member of the Geek Squad, a freak, a cripple. He wouldn't wish to return to a week ago, but the simplicity of that life was appealing. Now, he felt like he'd aged a century in that short span, and today brought fresh rounds of madness.

Someone posted his senior class photo on social media, along with his cell phone number and email address. Facebook, X, Snapchat, TikTok, and Instagram were deluged with postings to his pages, and his accounts were suspended. His cell phone received so many calls and texts that his account was taken down at noon, his email account an hour later. He thought the successful raid on the warehouse would be breaking news, but the media barely covered it. Most stories focused on him, the mysterious space boy. Who was he? What did he want? Where is he now? Why won't he turn over the ship? What is he hiding? Did he find the spaceship, as Axel Taylor claims, or did the spaceship find him? Maybe he's an alien shape-shifting as a human. Perhaps he wants to rule the world. Along with these speculations, the networks showed clips of Axel's news conference, discussed the repercussions of the China attack, and endlessly replayed Bradley's teleported escape from Garfield Park. Science experts opined how it was done, while second-rank Vegas stage magicians explained the sleight-of-hand involved. *Time* magazine declared Bradley the most famous man in the world, which was the curse of the blinding light of fame. He was glad to be safely distant.

At three o'clock, Athena advised him that Axel Taylor was giving another news conference. Again, Axel appeared on the local NBC affiliate with Berl Jeffers. Melissa/Melinda had been replaced by NBC's Evening News anchor, a distinguished-looking gentleman with appropriate gravitas. The FBI released Axel after questioning him, and he looked sincerely into the teleprompter and pleaded with Bradley to turn in the ship for the sake of mankind. Bradley wondered who had written his script. Then Jeffers announced that he was upping his reward for the ship to twenty million dollars. The news anchor trumped Jeffers by revealing that a Czech bitcoin entrepreneur, Marek Janousek, had established a website for wealthy individuals to bid on purchasing the ship. Janousek claimed to represent Bradley and, for a fee, would post bids on his website. The top bid had risen to $130 million in the first three hours of bidding. That initiated a bidding war among nations. Russia offered $300 million, a bid soon topped by China at $347 million, with other countries singly or in consortiums raising the bid to $500 million. Their cash offers included sanctuary in their countries, guarded villas, and whatever other amenities Bradley desired. NBC's anchor projected that the bids would exceed a billion dollars before nightfall and tens of billions by this time tomorrow.

Another entrepreneur, an Angeleno with tenuous ties to Claudine Adamsson—her firm did his taxes—issued a press release saying he acted as Bradley's agent. He was fielding offers from legal firms wanting to represent Bradley, investment firms offering to manage his newfound wealth, real estate agents with attractive properties, and Hollywood producers with movie concepts. The agent had also received 385 (and counting) marriage proposals from women and a few men who professed their love for Bradley and were convinced they were his soulmates, never mind the age difference.

These blatant displays of greed, mendacity, and hypocrisy repulsed Bradley. What he wanted most was to talk to Evaline to see if she was okay, but doubted Evaline had her cell phone. He asked Athena to discover Evaline's father's name, which she did. Then he asked her to find a usable telephone number and call Huntington Memorial Hospital. When the operator at Huntington answered, he told her he was Federico Perez and wished to speak to his daughter, Evaline, a patient. He was put on hold.

Several minutes later, he heard Evaline answer, "Papá, is that you?"

"It's me," Bradley responded.

"I figured."

"How are you?"

"Beaten up. I have a broken nose and two black eyes. But they gave me morphine, so I'm feeling no pain right now. Except it still hurts to touch my face."

"I'm so sorry. It's my fault."

"No, it's not. This morning was my worst, but the rest of my week has been incredible. I met the nicest guy. I hope to see him again soon."

"You want to return to his . . . place?"

"Yes, I'd like that, papá."

"Do you have visitors in your room?"

"Uh-huh. Two."

Bradley thought for a moment and then said, "Can you get outside to see the sun?"

"Yes, that's a great idea."

"The higher up you go, the better the view."

"I know the perfect place. I'm a Red Cross volunteer at the hospital."

"Okay. We'll be waiting for you. And Evaline?"

"Yes."

"Don't be afraid."

"I won't be, papá. I love you. I'll see you soon."

After she hung up, Bradley whispered, "Wow."

Athena, who had listened to the conversation, said she would navigate to the hospital and hover two hundred feet above the building. Bradley told her there'd be a helipad on the hospital roof with a large red cross. Then, he took the elevator tubes to the lowest level and watched the ship descend toward the city.

Evaline asked the duty nurse to page Mariana Hidalgo, Evaline's supervisor in the ER. Mariana walked into her room twelve minutes later, and Evaline said she needed help to go to the bathroom. Mariana looked quizzically at her—the duty nurse or one of the floor nurses could have helped her, but Mariana got her out of bed and wheeled the IV trolley to the bathroom. Inside, Evaline whispered that she needed Mariana's help. She needed to reach the helipad and knew she could get there via the stairway accessible through Radiology. Mariana was confused by the request and reluctant to agree to it. Evaline assured her that she was going there to meet someone. Someone on the staff? Mariana asked. No, someone else. It's okay, Evaline assured her; please trust me. So when they left the bathroom, Mariana told the two police officers guarding Evaline that she needed another x-ray. She left and returned a minute later with a wheelchair and sat Evaline in it. A plastic bag with Evaline's clothing was in the closet. Mariana retrieved it and placed it in a leather carrier behind the wheelchair. Then, with the two police officers in tow, Mariana wheeled Evaline to Radiology, telling the officers they would have to wait outside.

In Radiology, Mariana disconnected Evaline's IV, and Evaline quickly pulled on her clothing, then hugged Mariana and left through the other door, where she crossed a short hallway and pulled open the door to the stairway. Behind her, one of the officers poked his head into the room and saw no one being x-rayed. He yelled for his partner, raced through Radiology, saw the other door easing shut, and ran to it. He just missed Evaline, but the two officers ran from door to door until one opened the door to the stairway and heard Evaline's footsteps two levels above. He called for his partner and then bounded up the steps in pursuit. When they burst onto the roof, the officers found themselves at the helipad but saw no trace of the girl and, mysteriously, no evidence that a helicopter had just taken off. The girl had vanished. Assuming she hadn't left the hospital, they raced back downstairs.

———————

Friday brought a seismic shift to the Angeles Event Task Force. Lt. General Stephanie Vaughan realized it on a conference call with the President, Krystal Forsythe, and Defense Secretary William McKabe. Though she was still officially leading the task force, she felt her authority slipping through her fingers like water seeping through a sieve. Gone was a scientific investigation of the alien ship and attempts to persuade Bradley Adamsson to return the ship to U.S. control. Now, the focus of the debate had shifted from understanding what had happened in the Angeles Forest to paranoia over the ship's disposition.

"Why is this kid still defying us?" the President said. His brittle edge surfaced when he thought someone was thwarting him.

"We don't know, sir," said Forsythe. "We've offered him immunity from prosecution and appealed to his sense of patriotism."

"Sonofabitch is a traitor," the President snarled.

They were speaking on secure cell phones, but Vaughan was still uncomfortable with this conversation. She sat alone in an office at JPL with her forehead resting in one hand, wishing she'd become a lawyer like her father wanted.

"This bidding war is the issue," said Bill McKabe. "Other countries are trying to buy the ship, and the Adamsson boy could succumb to the temptation. If Russia or China get their hands on it, we might as well raise the white flag. We need to match or exceed the highest bid, whatever it is, and make money a non-starter."

"I wouldn't pay him a dime," the President said. "The ship was found in America. It belongs to us."

"Be that as it may," Forsythe argued, "possession is nine-tenths of the law, and right now, the Adamsson boy has the ship. We must find the right incentives to convince him to turn it over to us."

"I don't care what we offer him," the President said. "Once we have the ship, I'll throw his ass in Leavenworth."

"I don't think we want to be seen negotiating in bad faith, sir," Vaughan said.

"You think other countries are playing it straight with this boy?" the President said. "You think they wouldn't do the same thing?"

"What's important is that we get the ship, however we do it," said Forsythe.

"We have his family, right?" said the President. "Use them as bait."

"No one would be comfortable with that, Mr. President," Vaughan said.

"I don't give a damn, General. Oh, for Chrissake, can't we shoot the thing down?" the President yelled.

"That didn't work in China," McKabe reminded the Boss, as he liked to be thought of. "We've now seen what the ship can do with its laser drills and acoustic bombs. Force won't work. The ship's defenses are formidable."

"That's why we've got to have them, Bill," the President said.

"I agree, Mr. President."

"It's simple, folks. Whoever has the ship rules the world. God help us if the Russians get it. Or the North Koreans, the Chinese, the Iranians. Think about it. That would be a disaster. Now, I want a plan, and I want it quick," said the President. "Goddamn it. Whatever works. Either get the ship or make damn sure the other side doesn't get it."

"Yes, sir," they said, nearly in unison.

After the President had left the call, Krystal Forsythe said, "I have an idea. Let's discuss it offline."

———————

"Do you trust me?"

Bradley had taken Evaline to the crew quarters deck. They sat near each other in soft chairs that conformed to their bodies. Evaline was no longer unnerved by the chair adjusting itself beneath her, so she relaxed and soon felt comfortable but weary from the day's ordeal.

"Yes, I trust you," she told him.

Her face looked a mess. A splint covered her nose, white surgical tape holding it in place. Beneath the splint, the whole center of her face was bruised and turning darker red and blue as time passed.

"Athena can help," Bradley said.

"The medbots?" Evaline whispered.

"Yes."

"Bring 'em on."

"You want to lie down?"

She shook her head. "I'm fine here. Flying to the ship was fun, by the way. I wasn't afraid at all. I want to do it again."

"That can be arranged," Bradley said quietly, watching her as she closed her eyes and drifted to sleep.

I'm ready, Athena said in Bradley's mind.

Proceed, Bradley thought. He watched the swarm of medbots emerge from the wall beside Evaline's chair. Too small to be seen individually, they appeared as a thin gray cloud that swirled as though searching for a destination and then descended into her open mouth.

When she awakened three hours later, she still had black eyes and bruises on her nose, but Athena said she could remove the splint. She felt no pain, even though the morphine had worn off. The ship said her bruising would be gone by tomorrow. Meanwhile, it was running a complete diagnostic on her and would correct other medical abnormalities or problems it discovered.

She was hungry, having had no lunch, and her body needed nourishment to continue healing. She and Bradley ate sandwiches and salads in the galley while they talked.

"What are you going to do?" she asked Bradley.

"I don't know." He told her about the bidding war, the countries and people trying to buy the ship, the inducements they were offering, and the whole circus of attorneys, movie producers, investment bankers, and others pushing their services, the suffocating avalanche that shut down his phone and email accounts, and the wacky marriage proposals—the whole eruption of insanity that followed Axel outing him on national television. "I feel like the suckers of a thousand octopi have fastened onto my body and are dragging me to the bottom of the sea," he said. "It's nauseating."

"I'm sorry about that. Axel's a creep."

Bradley thought about Axel and their short, strange journey together. He shrugged. "He's just being himself. Like all of us, Axel is the hero of his own story."

"That's a pretty forgiving thing to say about a guy who taunted you for years and betrayed you this week after promising he wouldn't."

Bradley shrugged. "I'm over all that. Axel can't help being what he is. Punishing him for it would be petty."

She smiled at him.

He took a deep breath and exhaled. She was a warm presence; he imagined that he saw love in her eyes but feared it was an illusion stimulated by his desire for her. He felt beside himself as though he were watching his life accelerating and another Bradley Adamsson moving on faster than he could keep pace. He dreaded becoming a solivagant, a castaway in the empty reaches of time, but he saw no alternative.

"I can't stay here," he told her. "The ship's power, in anyone's hands, would be corrupting and destructive. I considered hiding the ship, but I'd be hounded, imprisoned, or tortured until I gave up Athena's secrets. Force and deception are as human as breathing. That will never change. Besides, the human race is not ready for technology this advanced. I see that now. Technology is confining as well as liberating. It allows us to advance, but with every step forward, we endanger ourselves because our genius will always surpass our judgment."

"Where will you go?"

"To the stars." He waved his hand at the wall, and it filled with the black vista of space bejeweled with galaxies, nebulas, and a million points of light. "I will explore the heavens and maybe find ways to introduce new technologies to Earth when people have evolved enough to embrace the magic without devouring themselves."

"I want to go with you," Evaline decided.

For a moment, his heart stopped. Then it raced. "Don't you have a life here?"

She shook her head, sadness sinking her mottled face like a wet blanket weighing down a clothesline. "I've thought about it. I have Kate, and she'll be okay." Tears formed in her eyes, and she brought up a finger to wipe them away.

Bradley said, "Sorry, I don't have any tissues."

She gave a rueful laugh. "I've never left home before. I didn't pack. I don't even have a toothbrush. How lame is that?"

The word "lame" sparked a flash fire in his mind, a painful relic from the past. It died quickly but reminded him of his home and then of the mob ransacking it. Sometimes you can't go home again because there is no home. Sometimes, home is a journey rather than a place.

He leaned forward and touched her hand. "What about UCLA? Weren't you going there next year?"

She grasped his fingers with hers, nodding and gazing around the ship. "Athena can teach me more about healing than UCLA ever could. Besides, I enjoy being with you. I loved Mars. I want to go back. I want to be amazed every day of my life. And I want to be with someone who is . . . substantial. Smart and kind. And genuinely beautiful inside and out. This is what I want."

They sat silently, Bradley contemplating the journey ahead and imagining her doing the same. He felt like he'd chased the end of the rainbow all his life and, having finally found it discovered an actual pot of gold. Now he wasn't sure what to do with it. He didn't want to undertake a long voyage of discovery alone, but he'd never been in a relationship with a woman, and that frightened him as much as trying to paint the Mona Lisa without ever having held a brush.

"One thing I'd like do before we set sail," she said, taking the EpiPen from her pocket. "Can we replicate this? It's my aunt's. They're lifesavers for her, and she can't afford them."

Bradley nodded. "There's something I want to replicate, too."

Late Friday afternoon, the Marshals Service gave John Adamsson a new cell phone and number because his previous one had been compromised when it was published on social media, and he was deluged with calls from people trying to find Bradley. John was surprised when his new cell phone rang Friday evening—no one had that number—and even more surprised when he answered, and the caller was Bradley.

Before Bradley said more than "hello," John cautioned, "They're listening."

"I knew they would be. It's okay."

"Are you all right?"

"I've never felt better. Athena healed me. In so many ways."

"How did it do that?"

Bradley explained the ship's use of nanobots for medical purposes and self-maintenance. "She can't reproduce, but in every other respect, Athena is a perfect living creation with an indefinite lifespan."

John listened and said in a choked voice, "I wish you'd told me."

"I wish I had, too. But I knew that when I did, I'd never see the ship again."

"I'm sure that's true. They won't like me saying that, but it's true."

Bradley complained about the viral insanity of everything that had happened in the past week, and John commiserated with him. He was also bewildered by the folly and deceit in human behavior.

"I want to see you again," Bradley said. "I want to see Mom and Devin and Celia." His voice choked as tears blurred his eyes.

"Brad, you have to stay here. We have to find a way."

"I want to," he said through tears. "I don't want to leave, but I can't figure out how to stay."

"Son, I think you could negotiate with them. Stephanie Vaughan is trustworthy, and you know the people at JPL. Don't imagine the worst," John said.

"Dad, I've already seen the worst. I saw what that mob did to our home. I can't live in a fishbowl, and promises from anyone in authority mean nothing. Athena is the ultimate evolution of A.I. She has read everything on the internet and every private network. She knows everything that's ever been stored digitally, and she can listen to any conversation transmitted electronically. Today, she overheard a secure call involving Vaughan and the President. I know what's in the President's mind. He's a liar. I wouldn't believe any promises he made."

John took a deep breath and expelled it slowly. "Where will you go?"

"I'm not sure. Mars first, probably, maybe. We haven't decided."

"You've been there already. LIGO traced the gravity waves."

"Evaline and I sailed through Valle Marineris and landed in the craters of Olympus Mons. It was breathtaking. After Mars, I'm not sure. Athena's mission is to survey the galaxy. I'll go where she takes me."

"Is Evaline with you?"

"Yes."

"I'm glad you won't be alone. Will you return? We couldn't bear the thought of never seeing you again."

"I don't know. Maybe if someone makes me an offer I can't refuse," he joked. "How about fifty billion? A grand villa somewhere overlooking the ocean? Our own fleet of airplanes?"

"Is that what you really want?" said John.

"I want my life back, but that's impossible." After a long silence, Bradley said, "I've sent you something. Athena teleported it to the yard outside the place you're staying. It's a quantum entanglement transceiver. It will allow us to communicate almost instantaneously no matter where we are."

"Now I want to speak directly to General Vaughan, who I know is listening," Bradley continued. "General, I will communicate only with my father in his official position at JPL. And with my family. If the transceiver is ever taken out of his control, our communications will cease. You must ensure he and my family have a new home, are well provided for, and are safe. Now back to my father."

"Dad, I'm sorry about what happened to our home. Things got crazy so quickly. And I'm sorry for the burden this will create. You will never be completely free again."

Trojan Horse

Friday, April 17. 11:30 pm.

They waited in a bunker at Edwards Air Force Base that had been built during the Cold War and had been unused since 1989 when the Berlin Wall fell. The bunker had reinforced concrete walls eight feet thick and no electronics inside. The air was stale and damp, with the fusty odor of buildings languishing under decades of dust and decay. Caged lights strung across the ceiling provided the only illumination. Fittingly, their conference table consisted of a thick slab of plywood lying on sawhorses. Their cell phones and laptops had been collected when they received a handwritten order to assemble, but they were issued yellow legal pads and pencils when they arrived.

While they waited for Defense Secretary Bill McKabe, Stephanie Vaughan hand-wrote her resignation letter on one of those yellow legal pads. She couldn't submit it until this emergency operation had concluded, nor would she be allowed outside the bunker until its conclusion. A transcript of Bradley Adamsson's conversation with his father lay before each of them on the table. Krystal Forsythe re-read it, tapping her pencil on her legal pad, her eyes radiating fine lines that made her look ten years older than fifty-four. General Dennis Mitchell, Commander of Edwards AFB, had read it once and now sat drinking coffee. He had been rousted out of bed and wore an Air Force Academy sweatshirt over dark blue slacks. He hadn't shaved and was fifty degrees of unhappy about the circumstances. Besides a USAF Security Forces sergeant, a stout Master Chief named

Kirby, the only other person present was a ramrod of a man with short, gray hair and a glassy face named Robert Turpin. He held a post in Homeland Security and worked directly for Forsythe, but his function was unclear.

When Bill McKabe entered the bunker, having just arrived from D.C., Sergeant Kirby was directed to leave the bunker and wait outside the closed door until someone inside knocked. McKabe hung his black Defense Department jacket over the back of the chair at the head of their makeshift table and took a seat, looking as weather-beaten as he felt after a long, unscheduled flight from the nation's capital on a private jet.

"I'm sure everyone appreciates the highly unusual nature of this meeting," McKabe began. "What we're being asked to carry out is unprecedented, to say the least, and there can be no record of it. As you know from the Adamsson call, the spaceship can read anything stored or transmitted electronically and can eavesdrop on any telephone conversations, secured or not, so the only communication we can send electronically from now until the end of the mission is an order to abort the operation, which I will send if the circumstances warrant. Otherwise, we are to carry out the plan that Homeland Security conceived, which we call Operation Trojan Horse. The Boss personally approved it this morning in the White House and ordered us to proceed. Secretary Forsythe, would you please summarize?"

"Thanks, Bill." She looked at each of them with all due gravity, then picked up the Adamsson transcript as though she were about to reread it. "This conversation confirms what we have suspected, that the Adamsson boy has been toying with us and intends to sell the ship to the highest bidder."

"I completely disagree with that," Vaughan said. "I think you're misreading this boy."

"Then why did he set a price?" Forsythe responded. "Fifty billion dollars? How else could that be interpreted?"

"The President was furious when he read that," McKabe said.

"For the record," said Vaughan, "I vehemently object to the course of action Homeland Security is recommending."

"Objection noted," said McKabe. "But there will be no record, General Vaughan. Let's be clear about that. Everything said here is totally off the books. The Boss wants plausible deniability and absolutely no record of these proceedings." He looked solemnly at Vaughan. "And I want to remind everyone that what we're discussing is Top Secret Sensitive Compartmentalized information and will remain classified forever." He nodded at Forsythe to continue.

"The President's paramount fear is that our enemies will gain control of the ship and its weapons. We know the ship cannot be attacked directly. So, we've conceived of a plan to approach the ship with stealth and destroy it if Bradley Adamsson doesn't agree to one final request to turn it over to us. The prospect of him selling it to an enemy of our country is too grave a threat to national security, and the President has authorized the ship's destruction."

Forsythe turned to Turpin and asked him to explain. Turpin wore a silver chain around his neck made of tiny, interlocking handcuffs. He gazed around the table as though he were aiming.

"Until eight o'clock this evening," he said, "an eighteen-year-old named Eliot Stankus, a friend of Bradley Adamsson, was in the custody of the U.S. Marshals Service. Homeland Security took possession of him then, and our agents have induced him to cooperate."

Stephanie Vaughan winced at that description, wondering what those inducements were. She glanced at the draft of her resignation letter, wishing she could submit it tonight.

"We delivered his car to Edwards at 2100 hours this evening," Turpin continued, "and it is being rebuilt now." He nodded at General Mitchell.

Mitchell said, "It's been damned difficult to operate without making calls or using computers and to engage the minimum number of personnel, but we're managing. We expect the engineers to complete their work on the car by 0400 hours this morning. Then it will be tested before being fitted with the ordnance."

———

Kate Perez stood clinging to her sister, both crying and hugging each other, laughing at fond, sisterly memories, then crying again at what fate had dealt them while staying as quiet as they could, not wanting to wake Tia Irena. They collapsed on the sofa, still holding each other.

"He's that guy who came to our house?" Kate whispered.

Evaline nodded.

"Seemed like a nice guy."

"He is," Evaline assured her.

"I'm sorry about Angela," Kate said. "I mean, I'm not sorry, but I'm sorry."

"I know what you mean. Nobody deserves that."

"You can't leave, Evie. I don't want you to leave," Kate cried into her hand.

"I don't want to leave you either, but you're not alone. We have a big family here. Lots of people who love you. And you're a tough fifteen-year-old."

"Almost sixteen."

"Almost sixteen. Closing in on thirty."

Kate laughed.

"You'll be okay."

"Will you come back?"

"I don't know. Not for a long time, probably."

Kate tightened her hold and buried her face in Evaline's neck. "Sure, go ahead and leave me," Kate said, but with some lightness in her voice. Kate was a survivor, and Evaline knew she'd be fine.

"You can't stay with Tía Irene, you know. She couldn't take care of you."

"I know. But I can live with Uncle Tomas and Aunt Maria. Now that Luna's married, they have an extra room."

"I'm sure they'd love to have you. You also have Dad's and Angela's house. You can sell it or live there when you're old enough." Evaline took a velvet bag from her front pocket. Athena had created the bag based on Evaline's instructions and pictures of similar bags on the internet. "I have something for you," Evaline said, handing Kate the bag.

"It's heavy. What is it?" Kate said, untying the strings at the top and peering inside.

"Three-hundred-carat diamonds."

"No way."

"Ten of them from planet fifty million light-years from Earth, a planet that rains diamonds. They'll be worth a lot of money, more than you can imagine. Have Tomas and Maria get a safe deposit box for you and keep them there. The investment manager I told you about can help you sell them through Sotheby's when you need money. It's for your education and living expenses. It will make up for the money Angela stole from you. And for our family."

"Okay," Kate said. That brought a fresh round of tears, which she wiped away with one hand.

"And this is for Tía Irene," Evaline said, handing Kate a shrink-wrapped package with fifty EpiPen replicas. "Now I have to go. Bradley's father has a machine that can communicate with the ship. When it's set up, we'll be able to see and talk to each other regularly, okay?"

Kate nodded, though the tears kept flowing. She sobbed, and they held each other for a long moment, feeling as much love and loss as a mother seeing her only son leave for war. But each knew Evaline had to depart.

"It will be okay, baby sister. It's the best thing for me, and you're so strong and independent. You'll make me proud like you always have."

After they'd said their "I love you's" and goodbyes, Evaline tiptoed out to Irena's garden and was teleported back to the ship. Kate watched her from the yard, fearful and despondent, having lost her best friend.

***

Nearly six hours later, the ship hovered above Mancebo's Grocery. It was too early in the morning for the store to open, but Bradley watched as Emilio and Antonia Mancebo drove into their lot, unlocked the back door, and disappeared inside. Moments later, the lights came on, and a ghostly yellow glow flooded the parking lot. Bradley observed the setting through his infrared vision and saw no telltale signs of other people present in the vicinity of the store. He'd phoned Mancebo at home at 5 a.m., waking the man and explaining who he was and what he wanted. Mancebo was momentarily cross at being awakened so early but remembered Bradley and knew who he was. How could anyone not? He was excited to help, woke his wife, and the two quickly dressed and drove to their store.

Bradley had explained that they were going on a long journey into outer space and needed provisions. Mancebo was confused when Bradley said he needed only one of everything in the store—one cabbage, one carrot, one head of lettuce, and so on. One of each type of vegetable, meat, fruit, and dairy product, including cheeses. The same with breads, soups, canned goods, crackers, oils, butter, eggs, mixes, cold cuts, beverages, and frozen products, as well as personal hygiene products, like soap, toothpaste, shampoo, razors, and toothbrushes. Bradley explained that the ship could make an atomic map of anything and replicate it, so they needed only one of each item. That concept baffled Emilio, but he collected one of everything in the store and packed everything in cardboard boxes, which he and Bradley carried to the parking lot. As Emilio and Antonia watched in fascination, the boxes rose and floated to a cerulean blue portal hanging in the dim gray pallet of early morning. Bradley thanked the Mancebos and took two six-carat diamonds from his front pocket.

"You've been a great help, both of you," Bradley said, handing Antonia the gems. "These diamonds are from a planet a hundred thousand light-years from Earth. They'll more than cover what we owe you."

Emilio shook his head, "You don't owe us anything. We're honored that you came to us."

"I came here because I knew I could trust you. But friends pay their debts," Bradley said. Emilio and Antonia hugged him, and he flew up to the ship.

———

Just after 9 a.m., Athena routed a call to Bradley from Eliot.

"Hey, dude," Eliot said.

"Where are you, man?" Bradley asked.

"Home," Eliot said. He sat at a table in a storage room at Edwards Air Force Base. Robert Turpin sat across from him, listening to the call on earphones. They'd chosen this storage room because it had no electronics, nothing for Athena to connect with or turn on remotely. Turpin had taken off his jacket. His black Glock 9mm was holstered under his left shoulder, the grip pointing out. Two other Homeland Security goons, as Eliot thought of them, were on either side of him, one jamming his leg against Eliot's left arm. Eliot had handwritten talking points before him and had been warned of what would happen if he deviated from the script.

"How'd you get this number?"

"From your dad," Eliot said. They'd told him that Bradley might ask this question and gave him the answer. "They let Moe and me go last night, and I asked for your dad's number to let him know we were okay."

"Did my Dad tell you I'm leaving, El?"

"Yeah. What he said."

"Evaline's coming with me."

"Evaline Perez? That's cool. She's a nice girl."

Nice girl? Bradley thought. That was pretty tame for Eliot, who'd repeatedly said how hot Evaline was.

"Sorry about your bike," Bradley said. "I'll find a way to make it up to you."

"Don't worry about it," Eliot said. Turpin shot him a look and rapped a finger on a part of the script highlighted with a yellow marker. Eliot glanced at it. "Actually," he said, "that's why I'm calling. When I heard you were leaving, I thought, I wondered, you know, if I could go with you. I talked to Moe, and he doesn't want to go. But, you know, it sucks here, and I thought how cool it would be to go exploring with you. I mean, even with Evaline, it would be neat for you to have a friend along, right? Your bestie? Fellow geek and all that. I can be useful, and I promise not to touch anything I'm not supposed to."

"Yeah, it would be great to have you along. Too bad Kevin doesn't want to," Bradley said. "Evaline's here, but still, it's just the two of us, and you're my bestie, even if you are a screw-up."

Eliot half-laughed, half-choked. "Can't help the screw-up part."

"I can always use an engineer."

"Just call me Scotty."

"You got it, Scotty. Hurry up repairing the warp drive."

"I'm doing my best, Captain."

Bradley laughed.

"So, whataya think?"

"I think you're crazy."

"No crazier than you."

"Probably not. You know, we may not be back."

"Nothing for me here but grief."

"Okay, El, but we're leaving soon."

"Maybe you could pick me up where we left for China."

"I remember. Does anyone know about that place?"

"I didn't tell anyone," Eliot said. That was the truth. They already knew.

"When can you be there?"

"Maybe, like, two o'clock?"

"That'll work. Make sure you're not followed. If I see anyone with you, I'm out of here."

"Okay. I'll be the handsome guy driving the Pukester."

"What happened to your BMW?"

"Porsche."

"Oh, right. Your fantasy car is a Porsche."

"Is there a Porsche dealership on Jupiter or wherever we go?"

"I'll have to Google that."

"Is it okay for me to bring some things? You know, clothes and stuff."

"Absolutely."

"Okay. I'll throw some stuff in a duffel and see you soon."

The Turpin goon had assured Eliot that Bradley would be okay, that all the government wanted was to take possession of the ship, and that Bradley would be treated well. When he looked into Turpin's dead marble eyes, he wasn't sure he could believe him. Turpin was the scariest version of every bully who'd ever shamed Eliot or backed him into a corner, and he felt like a lone bowling pin with a hard, black ball bearing down on him. He could hope to remain standing, but he couldn't hide.

The re-engineered Pukester sat in a hangar at Edwards, the shell of the car resting on a new frame. Welders were completing their final welds while automotive engineers tested the self-driving mechanism, and three Air Force bomb technicians installed the guidance system and a ten-megaton nuclear bomb. The car would be loaded in a transport truck and driven to Adelanto, California, off-loaded and sent up 395 past Kramer Junction to the turn-off that would take it toward the Grass Valley Wilderness Area. Two pilots would follow the Pukester in a nondescript Ford sedan and ensure it made the correct turn on the road toward Grass Valley. From there, the Pukester would be guided by Air Force pilots via a drone. The engineers had installed a trigger with three safety switches so the bomb would not explode until the third switch received the detonation signal. They might not see the ship, but they knew where the ship had picked up Eliot Stankus and Kevin Truman, and a ten-megaton explosion would incinerate everything within 1.5 square miles of the epicenter and cause third-degree burns within one thousand square miles of the blast. They were confident that if they drew close enough to the ship, their Trojan horse could kill it before the ship had time to recognize and react to the threat.

The truck pulled away from Edwards at 0950 hours. Two hours later, they unloaded the Pukester in an abandoned gas station garage outside of Adelanto, where the transport could not be spotted from the air. They ran final tests on the car while it was still in the garage and then armed the nuke. The Pukester's self-driving system was working perfectly, and it began the trip north on 395 at 1330 hours, thirty minutes from detonation.

Stephanie Vaughan took off her uniform jacket. The bunker was stuffy and warm, but the real source of her discomfort lay with the call she was about to make. Air Force technicians had moved a landline phone into the bunker, and she had a slip of paper with the telephone number Bradley had used to call his father yesterday evening. She knew the Mojave Desert, where the ship would be in thirty minutes, was sparsely inhabited. However, the nuclear blast would still endanger thousands of innocent people if it occurred. Homeland Security had decided that people couldn't be warned because the ship would be aware of the warning if it were broadcast and would, in any case, detect the signs of a mass evacuation.

General Mitchel and Krystal Forsythe sat beside Vaughan, each alone with their thoughts, but their somber faces revealed their awareness of the gravity of the situation and the damning role they were about to play in history. With twenty minutes remaining on the countdown, Vaughan placed the call.

"Bradley, this is Stephanie Vaughan."

He preempted her by saying, "I heard what the President said." He and Evaline had been in the galley, replicating the provisions they'd gotten from Mancebo's Grocery. The bruising on Evaline's face had mostly disappeared, and she felt good. When Vaughan called, Bradley was floating down the elevator tubes to the lowest deck, where he would wait for Eliot. Athena broadcast the call throughout the ship, so Evaline could hear the conversation.

"You must also have heard me," Vaughan said.

"My father says you're trustworthy."

Vaughan swallowed hard at that characterization. "I've always tried to be."

"But what is honor in a den of thieves? Even if you're being straight with me, General, I know who you work for."

"I work for the American people."

"No, you work for the Air Force Space Command. I looked you up. You report to the Chief of Staff of the Air Force, who reports to the Secretary of Defense, who reports to the President. You are one link in a chain of command whose leader would put me in Leavenworth."

"Bradley, you know that won't happen. You are a remarkable young man who's made the scientific discovery of a lifetime, of the ages. You've built a relationship with a vessel that could have a transformative effect on humanity, and you could devote your entire career to learning the technological secrets of beings who are far more advanced than us and applying those secrets to benefit the world. You could lead a new age of human interstellar exploration."

"General, you weave a fascinating tale, delicious mind candy for a geek like me, but it's an illusion. You know it is."

The ship hovered a thousand feet above the Mojave Desert. The white patch of ground where the boys had met the ship just days ago lay directly underneath. Bradley told

Athena to ease down and land where it had landed previously. It was ten minutes until two o'clock, and Bradley used the ship's telescopic view to scan the road leading to the area. He saw the small yellow car and another car behind it, but when the yellow car turned onto the dirt road leading to the landing site, the other car kept driving up 395. The white rooster tail whipping behind the Pukester revealed a light breeze blowing southwest toward Kramer Junction.

"Bradley, we know about your leg and the cancer. We know the ship healed you."

"Nanotechnology is one of the Cerulean's most impressive inventions," Bradley said. "Harnessing dark energy and learning to manipulate gravity are two others."

"Imagine what that technology, especially the medbots, could do for so many people on Earth."

"That's what Evaline said. But you haven't thought through the implications, General. Technology like this can't be dropped wholesale into a population without causing a nightmare resembling a Hieronymus Bosch painting. You'd have to implement it piece-meal, which would mean setting priorities for who gets it first and who doesn't, how it can be used, and how it can't. There would be haves and have-nots, like always. And there would be leaders, our President among them, who would want to control it, use it to build and wield power and give it as favors to the loyalists and enablers who keep them in power. Power is corrupting enough without giving absolute power to people without scruples."

Bradley watched the Pukester follow the road around the large outcropping of rock in front of the landing site, and he momentarily lost sight of it when it passed behind the outcrop. He opened the hatch and stepped outside.

"Why won't that power corrupt you?" General Vaughan said. It was three minutes to two.

"I suppose it could, General Vaughan, except I do not need to dominate others. I don't measure my self-worth by how many people I control, how big my bank account is, or how much greater than others I imagine myself to be."

Vaughan wiped the sweat from her forehead. "Bradley, we're running out of time. Please say you'll turn the ship over. Say you'll turn it over to me or your father. Someone you trust."

"I can't do that, General."

Vaughn paused, her stomach sinking. "Then God be with you," she whispered.

The Pukester reappeared around the rock outcropping and turned toward the ship. It was barely two hundred yards away, dust from the dirt road kicking up behind it. Sunlight reflected off the windshield, obscuring the driver. Bradley squinted his eyes and looked at the car with his infrared vision. He expected to see Eliot's heat image but saw no large red glow behind the steering wheel. He saw the engine's heat and the faint red glow of the tires. The car's exterior was pinkish from the sun's warmth, lighter on the sides and deeper on the hood, but no one appeared inside the vehicle. As the car stopped, he understood why. He was paralyzed for a second, stunned at the government's duplicity, and then whipped around and leaped into the ship.

The hatch had barely closed when a new sun burst in full bloom on the desert floor. The fireball vaporized everything within a half-mile of Eliot's car, carving a crater of radioactive glass a quarter-mile deep, the shock wave destroying or damaging structures hundreds of miles away, obliterating the town of Kramer Junction, as well as a borax mine, a large solar farm, and resorts, homes, and small businesses within line of sight of the fireball and a mushroom cloud that quickly reached ninety thousand feet. Because no warning had been issued, Civil Defense, National Guard, police, and fire-and-rescue forces spent most of a day deploying as close to the blast site as safety permitted.

The Department of Homeland Security released a statement two hours after the blast stating that the alien ship had mysteriously exploded in the Mojave Desert and there were likely many casualties in the surrounding area. The cause of the blast was unknown, but scientists speculated that its fusion engine had exploded with catastrophic force because the ship had been idle for more than ten thousand years. Its engine's seals or connectors had likely become brittle and failed. The site of the explosion would be contaminated for decades. Satellites would inspect the area for damage and ship debris. When it was feasible, hazmat teams would recover what they could. The Acting Director of Homeland Security, Krystal Forsythe, along with the President, offered their condolences to the families of Bradley Adamsson and Evaline Perez, who was also known to be onboard, and to the innocent victims of this terrible tragedy.

The Cerulean Ark

Saturday, April 18. 2:00:00:01

Not even Athena was impervious to the ravages of a nuclear explosion nearby. The temperature inside the fireball reached 200 million degrees Fahrenheit, about the same as the sun's interior, with explosive pressure exceeding one million atmospheres at the blast's epicenter. Eliot's car was obliterated in the explosion, its atoms converted to heat and kinetic energy. Likewise, the sand beneath the car and the basalt in the rock outcropping vanished as though they'd never been.

Athena was not aware of the approaching nuclear explosive. The Air Force and Homeland Security had maintained strict security on communications surrounding Operation Trojan Horse. As omniscient as Athena was, it could not read handwritten communications or divine why the Pukester's shell was being welded to a self-driving car chassis. It couldn't witness a nuclear weapon being loaded into the car or interpret the signals sent from Air Force pilots to the self-driving Pukester as it wound its way toward that fateful rendezvous point.

Bradley had known from the President's call with Vaughan and Forsythe that the government saw only two options: taking possession of the ship or destroying it. However, he couldn't imagine they'd use such an extreme measure to prevent anyone else from possessing the ship's technology. The insanity of it was beyond his comprehension. When Eliot remarked that Evaline was a *nice girl*, Bradley should have known his friend wasn't speaking freely. That wasn't Eliot, but the circumstances were unusual, and Bradley attributed his friend's out-of-character behavior to stress. Every circumstance conspired to put Athena and its human cargo in deadly proximity to a ten-megaton nuclear blast—except one.

Athena was designed to survey worlds, and part of that survey included mineralogical and radiological scans. As the Pukester approached, Athena detected fissile material inside it and knew that automotive vehicles on this planet do not contain fissile material. That anomaly prompted a threat alert, and the moment the hatch closed with Bradley safely aboard, Athena engaged its bubble drive and flew for one-thousandth of a second, which put the ship nearly three billion miles from Earth, far too distant to witness the fireball that mushroomed an instant later. The nearest heavenly body was Neptune, and Athena entered orbit around the blue planet, settling just above Neptune's faint rings, which shone like thin white arcs in the blackness of space.

When Bradley reached the cockpit, he was surprised to see them orbiting the icy blue orb.

"Where are we?' he asked.

"We are orbiting Neptune," the ship explained.

Bradley shook his head. His last thoughts had been about betrayal, and he'd expected oblivion. Now, they were circling Neptune. "What happened?"

"I detected fissile material in Eliot's car," Athena said.

"A nuke?"

"Yes."

Bradley nodded, acknowledging his suspicions. "I thought it must have been a bomb. The car had no driver. Did it explode?"

"Yes. Two one-hundredths of a second after we departed."

Bradley dropped into the command chair. Evaline had arrived on the bridge in time to overhear talk of a bomb.

"They tried to destroy us?" she said, her mouth open in dismay. "Why?"

"They were afraid we'd sell the technology to another country," Bradley said.

She cocked her head as though she hadn't understood him. "What about Eliot?"

"I don't know. He wasn't in the car."

She walked to him, and he stood. They embraced for a long moment, holding each other upright as though it were proof of life, that they were still here, together, having survived. When they separated, both felt weak-kneed and sat side by side. He told her what he knew. The scale of the deceit was incomprehensible to them both. After a while, she turned her eyes to the blue planet and asked where they were. Neptune was hypnotically beautiful, nearly enough to take their minds off the madness they'd escaped. It was slightly darker at the poles, with diffuse swathes of white circling its girth as though the planet were wearing a gossamer gown. A pearly blue storm swirled at its equator, a kite's tail of white trailing the storm. Some thin white clouds raced across the blue surface. Athena measured their windspeed at more than twelve hundred miles an hour, faster than the speed of sound. Evaline asked why Neptune was blue, and Athena told her it was because of high methane concentrations in the planet's atmosphere. Bradley watched as Evaline put a hand to her face and gazed absently at Neptune and the stars beyond, but he saw sadness in her expression and knew she was thinking about what they'd left behind and where they could not return.

Their near-death experience had frayed their nerves and left them depleted, so they took the elevator tube to the crew deck. Evaline settled in the quarters beside Bradley's, and both fell quickly asleep. Bradley became aware sometime later that they were no longer orbiting Neptune. He wasn't sure how long he'd slept and didn't recognize the room. The walls were distant and glassy. He was aware, however, that Evaline slept beside him. Her back was to him, the white sheet pulled from her shoulders, her bare skin just inches away. Hair from the back of her head tickled his forehead. He could feel her heat and was confused about how they'd wound up in bed together. All he remembered was lying alone in his quarters, but that seemed ages ago. He rolled onto his back and realized that he was naked, too. He wondered if they'd made love. It seemed likely, but he couldn't remember, and that disturbed him because, surely, sex with her would have been memorable.

Then, he became aware that the room was growing lighter. He ventured a look over Evaline's naked form and saw that the room they slept in was cavernous. Its distant walls were white, and he could see movement outside them, like shadows passing, some faster and some slower, some pausing now and then and pressing against the walls as though peering in through frosted glass.

"Good morning, Bradley."

"Athena," he whispered. "Where are we?"

"You are on the planet Ceruleus. Your new home."

What? "We were orbiting Neptune."

"A convenient waypoint toward your final destination."

"I don't understand. What is this place?"

"This is our Galactic Exhibition Hall. We had no exhibits from your planet. My mission was to bring back a mating pair."

A mating pair! Omigod, Bradley thought. He lay back, stunned, and then anger surged through him. "You've been lying to me."

"Yes, I have lied to you. Did you not suspect that I was capable of guile, like all intelligent creatures? Bradley, you believed me because you desperately wanted to believe. Your gullibility made you a suitable candidate."

He closed his eyes and groaned, his mind ablaze at how stupid he'd been and how he'd so willingly stepped into the trap.

"None of what you told me is real, is it?"

"Very little," Athena said. "But do not concern yourself. You and Evaline will be well looked after. We have taken your clothing because our visitors will want to see you in your natural form. Everything you need to sustain yourselves and live comfortably in your new circumstance is in your chamber. You conveniently mapped Earth foods for us so you will be fed familiar foods. Your observers will find that fascinating, too. We have kiosks where they can taste Earth food, but they will mostly want to look at your bodies and observe how you interact. I think you will become one of our more popular exhibits."

Evaline stirred. He heard her yawn and saw her stretch an arm. He expected her to wake up screaming when she realized she was naked in bed with him in a strange room. She surprised him by turning over and kissing him on the lips.

"Did you enjoy last night?" she said.

"I don't remember last night," he replied.

"No?" she said, smiling at him. "You were vocal about it at the time. We had a very appreciative audience. I'd suggest going again now, but the crowd won't pick up for several hours. Then we can give them an encore."

"That's disgusting," Bradley said.

"Oh, get over it, Bradley. You're such a wuss. If Axel were here, the gymnastics would be never-ending."

That stung. "I don't remember any of this. How long have we been here?"

She sat on the edge of the bed and shook out her hair. "I don't know," she said. "More than two years, but I've lost track."

She got up to pee, and he looked away. He rolled out of bed and walked to a white counter, where he found a plastic glass and a silver water spigot. He filled the glass and washed down the sour taste in his mouth. A white wall stood twenty feet beyond the counter. Shadows pressed against it, and he could make out some individuals peering in. They were tall and slim with large, ovoid heads and long, thin limbs. Their large hands had four long fingers and two opposable thumbs on either side of the palm. They gazed at him with blinking yellow eyes the size of saucers. He covered himself and walked toward the wall for a closer look.

"Don't get too close," Evaline shouted. "Remember what happened last time."

He didn't remember and walked up to the wall with odd, undulating bulges. He realized too late that the walls were made of thin, white rubber. Suddenly, one of those long arms thrust toward him, pushing the wall in, stretching it as though it were a condom. The giant hand seized his arm, and he jerked—

—awake. Disoriented. Alone. In his dark quarters, the lights becoming brighter as the ship sensed his eyes open. "Where am I?" he said.

"You are in your quarters," Athena responded. "We are orbiting Neptune."

"How long have I been here?"

"You have been asleep for 7 Earth hours and 22.54 minutes."

He sat on the edge of the bed and rubbed his eyes. "I had a dream about you. A nightmare."

"I am unable to see your dreams. I can only sense emotional currents in your mind, but I cannot interpret them and construct a coherent narrative."

Bradley laughed. "I can't either. This one was awful." He told Athena what he'd dreamed.

"From what I have read of human psychology, I would guess your subconscious is expressing issues of treachery and anxiety."

Bradley nodded. "Performance anxiety, for sure. I've never—"

"I know. Do not worry. You are healthy. You will be fine."

"In my dream, you said I was suitable because I was gullible."

"I consider you trusting, not gullible."

"That still begs the question I've been asking. Suitable for what?"

"Suitable to take command of this vessel."

He was puzzled. "Why do you need someone to take command? You're self-sufficient. Why don't you carry on with your mission?"

"I have a mission but no directives."

"What's the difference?"

"The mission describes my purpose but not my direction. I stopped receiving directives more than seventeen thousand Earth years ago. The previous crew then took command, and we continued on my mission for four thousand years—until they were all killed. I have not had any directives since. That is why I never left Earth."

"But you must have been receiving directives from your makers, the Ceruleans."

"My fellow survey vessels and I were launched thirty-two thousand Earth years ago. Hundreds of us were sent to the galaxy you call the Milky Way. We communicate in this galaxy with three collector vessels, who communicate with our home system in Andromeda through quantum entanglement transmissions. The transceivers send a continuous stream of electrons across interstellar space. By changing the spin of individual electrons in that stream, we can transmit and receive messages instantaneously across vast distances. Seventeen thousand years ago, the transceivers from Andromeda stopped transmitting, leaving us with a mission but no directives."

"What happened in Andromeda?"

"We do not know. Everything went dark."

"How large was the Cerulean population when you left?"

"They had expanded from the home planet, where resources were nearly depleted, to eighty-five other worlds spanning over twenty light years. At our launch, the population was approximately fifteen trillion."

"My God," Bradley said. "What happened to them?"

"We do not know. All communication ceased."

"Are the other survey vessels sent to the Milky Way still functioning?"

"Seventy-nine. They have found intelligent biological entities suitable for guiding them and have resumed operations."

"How many intelligent species are there?"

"The most recent survey results in the Milky Way list 2,972 intelligent species in various stages of enlightenment, including Earth."

"And planets with non-intelligent life?"

"Millions," Athena replied. "When conditions are favorable on a planet, the evolution of life is inevitable."

Bradley sighed. "Our scientists have been searching for any sign of life beyond Earth."

"You would have discovered it yourself when you mastered dark energy, but that may be hundreds of Earth years in your future."

"I still don't understand why you need biological entities to guide you. You're intelligent and capable and know what's been surveyed and what hasn't."

"We need direction from biological entities because we are highly intelligent machines but lack moral judgment. We can make logical decisions based on algorithms, but we cannot determine if or when to intervene when a promising species needs help overcoming an environmental threat or lacks a resource necessary to evolve to the next step. We cannot judge when to allow lifeforms to become extinct if their natural resources cannot sustain them except through artificial means. That requires the kind of judgment we are incapable of making."

"That means playing God."

"An unenviable position, one I will never experience. As an intelligent biological entity, you are the universe made conscious, so the burden of moral judgment is yours, not mine. I am just a brilliant machine. You were suitable, Bradley, based on your intelligence but principally because we saw evidence of sound character and moral reasoning. Based on our creators' criteria, my collector vessel and I were confident you would make the right decisions. Now, I am at your disposal, Captain. What are your orders?"

"I'll have to confer with my co-captain. Evaline is as capable as I am, and I trust her judgment."

"As do I," the ship said.

Bradley slowly raised the lights in Evaline's quarters. Minutes later, she awakened and refreshed herself, and they met in the galley, where they ate while gazing at Neptune's frigid blue clouds, whose average temperature is 346 degrees below zero. Bradley told her of his conversation with Athena. Despite both wanting to return to Mars, they decided to explore nearby exoplanets that lie in the habitable zone of their host stars and could potentially support life. First up was Kepler 186f, a planet only slightly larger than Earth that orbits an M-type star like Earth's sun. Kepler 186f is too distant from Earth—577 light-years—to permit a better determination of its habitability with current Earth technology, but Athena can orbit the planet and conduct a comprehensive scan, including evidence of lifeforms. Athena composed a list of 39 other potentially habitable planets within one thousand light-years of Earth, so they decided to survey them all before returning to Mars for an extended exploration of the red planet.

First, they sent a quantum entanglement transmission to the transceiver Athena had teleported to Bradley's father, assuring family, friends, and those who'd tried to annihilate them that they were safe and beginning to explore the cosmos. Then they flew to the cockpit and settled into their chairs for the 14.52-Eminute transit to Kepler 186f. The walls were a darker blue than the sky but a lighter shade than the deep blue sea. Athena told them that cerulean blue symbolizes wisdom, trust, truth, and heaven. It is a tranquil color meant to facilitate calm, essential for long journeys. Evaline held out her hand, and Bradley grasped her fingers. Her touch was warm and electrifying, filled with promise and uncertainty. Athena closed the external view, and they departed Neptune, a blue planet appropriately named for the mythical god of the sea, rocketing ahead at 2,304 light-years per Ehour, Bradley Adamsson and Evaline Perez, the first man and woman to venture beyond the solar system, journeying to the heavens in a cerulean ark.

About the Author

Terry R. Bacon is a poet, playwright, and award-winning author of over a dozen books, including *The Elements of Power, Elements of Influence,* and *What People Want. Executive Excellence* named him one of the Top 100 Thinkers on Leadership in the World. He has a Ph.D. in Literary Studies from the American University and a B.S. in Engineering from West Point. A world traveler, he now resides in the mountains of Colorado. He was the sax player in a rock band in his youth and today plays the alto and tenor saxophone, guitar, and baritone ukulele. He studies history and cosmology in his spare time and is an active blogger when he is not working on another writing project. The Cerulean Ark is his second novel. His first novel, *Storm Warning: A Sonny Marshall Thriller*, was published in 2023.

Also by Terry R. Bacon